Praise for *Nine Perfect Strangers*

"If three characters were good in *Big Little Lies*, nine are even better in *Nine Perfect Strangers*. . . . Satisfying . . . The novel raises fascinating questions about our relentless quest for self-improvement, why we seek out others to transform us, and whether external change causes internal change, or vice versa."

—*The New York Times Book Review*

"Witty and poignant, Moriarty's storytelling is worth every penny." —*People* (Book of the Week)

"Moriarty's latest . . . has no shortage of secrets, lies, and social intrigue. But at its core, it's also just good old-fashioned storytelling, full of feeling and well-wrought lines." —*Entertainment Weekly*

"As she did in *Big Little Lies*, Liane Moriarty writes compelling, realistic characters. Readers will devour *Nine Perfect Strangers*." —*Real Simple*

"An entrancing read . . . *Nine Perfect Strangers* is a darkly comical novel that defies classification. It manages to be wildly funny and richly emotional at the same time, proving that the *Big Little Lies* author still has a lot to offer her readers." —*Bustle*

Liane Moriarty

Nine Perfect Strangers

FLATIRON BOOKS
NEW YORK

NOTE: If you purchased this book without a cover you should be aware that this book is stolen property. It was reported as "unsold and destroyed" to the publisher, and neither the author nor the publisher has received any payment for this "stripped book."

Grateful acknowledgment is made for permission to reproduce from the following:

Extract from "The High Mark" reprinted with the permission of Bruce Dawe AO.

This is a work of fiction. All of the characters, organizations, and events portrayed in this novel are either products of the author's imagination or are used fictitiously.

NINE PERFECT STRANGERS. Copyright © 2018 by Liane Moriarty. All rights reserved. Printed in the United States of America. For information, address Flatiron Books, 120 Broadway, New York, NY 10271.

www.flatironbooks.com

Designed by Anna Gorovoy

The Library of Congress Cataloging-in-Publication Data is available upon request.

ISBN 978-1-250-75583-4

Our books may be purchased in bulk for promotional, educational, or business use. Please contact your local bookseller or the Macmillan Corporate and Premium Sales Department at 1-800-221-7945, extension 5442, or by email at MacmillanSpecialMarkets@macmillan.com.

Originally published in 2018 by Pan Macmillan Australia Pty Ltd

10 9 8 7 6 5 4 3 2 1

For Kati
And for Dad
With lots of love from me

You suppose you are the trouble
But you are the cure
You suppose that you are the lock on the door
But you are the key that opens it

Rumi

Just when I discovered the meaning of life, they changed it.

George Carlin

1

Yao

"I'm fine," said the woman. "There's nothing wrong with me."

She didn't look fine to Yao.

It was his first day as a trainee paramedic. His third call-out. Yao wasn't nervous, but he was in a hyper-vigilant state because he couldn't bear to make even an inconsequential mistake. When he was a child, mistakes had made him wail inconsolably, and they still made his stomach cramp.

A single bead of perspiration rolled down the woman's face, leaving a snail's trail through her makeup. Yao wondered why women painted their faces orange, but that was not relevant.

"I'm fine. Maybe just twenty-four-hour virus," she said, with the hint of an Eastern European accent.

"Observe everything about your patient and their environment," Yao's supervisor, Finn, had told him. "Think of yourself as a secret agent looking for diagnostic clues."

Yao observed a middle-aged, overweight woman with pronounced pink shadows under distinctive sea-green eyes and wispy brown hair pulled into a sad little knot at the back of her neck. She was pale and clammy, her breathing ragged. A heavy smoker, judging by her ashtray scent. She sat in a high-backed leather chair behind a gigantic desk. It seemed like she was something of a bigwig, if the size of this plush corner office and its floor-to-ceiling harbor views were any indication of corporate status. They were on the seventeenth floor and the sails of the Opera House were so close you could see the diamond-shaped cream and white tiles.

The woman had one hand on her mouse. She scrolled through emails on her oversized computer screen, as if the two paramedics checking her over were a minor inconvenience, repairmen there to fix a PowerPoint. She wore a tailored navy business suit like a punishment, the jacket pulled uncomfortably tight across her shoulders.

Yao took the woman's free hand and clipped a pulse oximeter onto her finger. He noted a shiny, scaly patch of reddish skin on her forearm. Pre-diabetic?

Finn asked, "Are you on any medication, Masha?" He had a chatty, loose manner with patients, as if he were making small talk at a barbecue, beer in hand.

Yao noticed that Finn always used the names of patients, whereas Yao felt shy talking to them as though they were old friends, but if it enhanced patient outcomes, he would learn to overcome his shyness.

"I am on no medication at all," said Masha, her gaze fixed on the computer. She clicked on something decisively, then looked away from her monitor and back up at Finn. Her eyes looked like they'd been borrowed from someone beautiful. Yao assumed they were colored contact lenses. "I am in good health. I apologize for taking up your time. I certainly didn't ask for an ambulance."

"I called the ambulance," said a very pretty, dark-haired young woman in high heels and a tight checked skirt with interlocking diamond shapes similar to the Opera House tiles. The skirt looked excellent on her but that was obviously of no relevance right now, even though she was, technically, part of the surrounding environment Yao was meant to be observing. The girl chewed on the fingernail of her little finger. "I'm her PA. She . . . ah . . ." She lowered her voice as if she were about to reveal something shameful. "Her face went dead white and then she fell off her chair."

"I did not fall off my chair!" snapped Masha.

"She kind of slid off it," amended the girl.

"I momentarily felt dizzy, that is all," said Masha to Finn. "And then I got straight back to work. Could we cut this short? I'm happy to pay your full, you know, cost or *rate*, or however it is you charge for your services. I have private health insurance, of course. I just really don't have time for this right now." She turned her attention back to her assistant. "Don't I have an eleven o'clock with Ryan?"

"I'll cancel him."

"Did I hear my name?" said a man from the doorway. "What's going on?" A guy in a too-tight purple shirt swaggered in carrying a bundle of manila folders.

He spoke with a plummy British accent, like he was a member of the royal family.

"Nothing," said Masha. "Take a seat."

"Masha is clearly not available right now!" said the poor PA.

Yao sympathized. He didn't appreciate flippancy about matters of health, and he thought his profession deserved more respect. He also had a strong aversion to spiky-haired guys with posh accents who wore purple shirts a size too small to show off their overly developed pecs.

"No, no, just sit down, Ryan! This won't take long. I'm fine." Masha beckoned impatiently.

"Can I check your blood pressure, please, ah, Masha?" said Yao, bravely mumbling her name as he went to strap the cuff around her upper arm.

"Let's take that jacket off first." Finn sounded amused. "You're a busy lady, Masha."

"I actually really do need her sign-off on these," said the young guy to the PA in a low voice.

Yao thought, *I actually really do need to check your boss's vital signs right now, motherfucker.*

Finn helped Masha out of her jacket and put it over the back of her chair in a courtly way.

"Let's see those documents, Ryan." Masha adjusted the buttons on her cream silk shirt.

"I just need signatures on the top two pages." The guy held out the folder.

"Are you kidding me?" The PA lifted both hands incredulously.

"Mate, you need to come back another time," said Finn, with a definite edge to his barbecue voice.

The guy stepped back, but Masha clicked her fingers at him for the folder, and he instantly jumped forward and handed it over. He obviously considered Masha scarier than Finn, which was saying something, because Finn was a big, strong guy.

"This will take fourteen seconds at the most," she said to Finn. Her voice thickened on the word "most" so that it sounded like "mosht."

Yao, the blood-pressure cuff still in his hand, made eye contact with Finn.

Masha's head lolled to one side, as though she'd just nodded off. The manila folder slipped from her fingers.

"Masha?" Finn spoke in a loud, commanding voice.

She slumped forward, arms akimbo, like a puppet.

"Just like that!" screeched the PA with satisfaction. "That's exactly what she did before!"

"Jesus!" The purple-shirt guy retreated. "*Jesus*. Sorry! I'll just . . ."

"Okay, Masha, let's get you onto the floor," said Finn.

Finn lifted her under the armpits and Yao took her legs, grunting with the effort. She was a very tall woman, Yao realized; much taller than him. At least six feet and a dead weight. Together he and Finn laid her on her side on the gray carpet. Finn folded her jacket into a pillow and put it behind her head.

Masha's left arm rose stiff and zombielike above her

head. Her hands curled into spastic fists. She continued to breathe in jerky gasps as her body postured.

She was having a seizure.

Seizures were disquieting to watch but Yao knew you just had to wait them out. There was nothing around Masha's neck that Yao could loosen. He scanned the space around her, and saw nowhere she could bang her head.

"Is this what happened earlier?" Finn looked up at the assistant.

"*No.* No, before she just sort of fainted." The wide-eyed PA watched with appalled fascination.

"Does she have a history of seizures?" asked Finn.

"I don't think so. I don't know." As she spoke, the PA was shuffling back toward the door of the office, where a crowd of other corporate types had now gathered. Someone held up a mobile phone, filming, as if their boss's seizure were a rock concert.

"Start compressions." Finn's eyes were flat and smooth like stones.

There was a moment—no more than a second, but still a moment—in which Yao did nothing as his brain scrambled to process what had just happened. He would remember that moment of frozen incomprehension forever. He *knew* that a cardiac arrest could present with seizure-like symptoms and yet he'd still missed it because his brain had been so utterly, erroneously convinced of one reality: *This patient is having a seizure.* If Finn hadn't been there, Yao may have sat back on his haunches and observed a woman in cardiac arrest *without acting*, like an airline pilot flying a jet into the ground because he is overly reliant on his faulty instruments. Yao's finest instrument was his brain, and on this day it was faulty.

They shocked her twice but were unable to establish a consistent heart rhythm. Masha Dmitrichenko was in full cardiac arrest as they carried her out of the corner office to which she would never return.

2

Ten years later

Frances

On a hot, cloudless January day, Frances Welty, the formerly bestselling romantic novelist, drove alone through scrubby bushland six hours northwest of her Sydney home.

The black ribbon of highway unrolled hypnotically ahead of her as the air-conditioning vents roared arctic air full blast at her face. The sky was a giant deep blue dome surrounding her tiny solitary car. There was far too *much* sky for her liking.

She smiled because she reminded herself of one of those peevish TripAdvisor reviewers: *So I called reception and asked for a lower, cloudier, more comfortable sky. A woman with a strong foreign accent said there were no other skies available! She was very rude about it too! NEVER AGAIN. DON'T WASTE YOUR MONEY.*

It occurred to Frances that she was possibly quite close to losing her mind.

No, she wasn't. She was fine. Perfectly sane. Really and truly.

She flexed her hands around the steering wheel, blinked dry eyes behind her sunglasses, and yawned so hugely her jaw clicked.

"Ow," she said, although it didn't hurt.

She sighed, looking out the window for something to break the monotony of the landscape. It would be so harsh and unforgiving out there. She could just imagine it: the drone of blowflies, the mournful cry of crows, and all that glaring white-hot light. Wide brown land indeed.

Come on. Give me a cow, a crop, a shed. I spy with my little eye something beginning with . . .

N. Nothing.

She shifted in her seat, and her lower back rewarded her with a jolt of pain so violent and personal it brought tears to her eyes.

"For God's *sake*," she said pitifully.

The back pain had begun two weeks ago, on the day she finally accepted that Paul Drabble had disappeared. She was dialing the number for the police and trying to work out how to refer to Paul—her partner, boyfriend, lover, her "special friend"?—when she felt the first twinge. It was the most obvious example of psychosomatic pain ever, except knowing it was psychosomatic didn't make it hurt any less.

It was strange to look in the mirror each night and see the reflection of her lower back looking as soft, white, and gently plump as it always had. She expected to see something dreadful, like a gnarled mass of tree roots.

She checked the time on the dashboard: 2:57 P.M. The turn-off should be coming up any minute. She'd told the reservations people at Tranquillum House that she'd be there around 3:30 to 4 P.M. and she hadn't made any unscheduled stops.

Tranquillum House was a "boutique health and wellness resort." Her friend Ellen had suggested it. "You need to *heal*," she'd told Frances after their third cocktail (an excellent white-peach Bellini) at lunch last week. "You look like *shit*."

Ellen had done a "cleanse" at Tranquillum House three years ago when she, too, had been "burnt out" and "run-down" and "out of condition" and—"Yes, yes, I get it," Frances had said.

"It's quite . . . unusual, this place," Ellen had told Frances. "Their approach is kind of unconventional. Life-changing."

"How exactly did your life change?" Frances had asked, reasonably, but she'd never got a clear answer to that question. In the end, it all seemed to come down to the whites of Ellen's eyes, which had become really white, like, freakily white! Also, she lost three kilos! Although Tranquillum House wasn't about weight loss—Ellen was at great pains to point that out. It was about *wellness*, but, you know, what woman complains about losing three kilos? Not Ellen, that's for sure. Not Frances either.

Frances had gone home and looked up the website. She'd never been a fan of self-denial, never been on a diet, rarely said no if she felt like saying yes or yes if she felt like saying no. According to her mother, Frances's first greedy word was "more." She always wanted more.

Yet the photos of Tranquillum House had filled her with a strange, unexpected yearning. They were golden-hued, all taken at sunset or sunrise, or else filtered to make it look that way. Pleasantly middle-aged people did warrior poses in a garden of white roses next to a beautiful country house. A couple sat in one of the "natural hot springs" that surrounded the property. Their eyes were closed, heads tipped back, smiling ecstatically as water bubbled around them. Another photo showed a woman enjoying a "hot stone massage" on a deck chair next to an aquamarine swimming pool. Frances had imagined those hot stones placed with delightful symmetry down her own spine, their magical heat melting away her pain.

As she dreamed of hot springs and gentle yoga, a message flashed urgently on her screen: *Only one place remaining for the exclusive Ten-Day Mind and Body Total Transformation Retreat!* It had made her feel stupidly competitive and she clicked *Book now*, even though she didn't *really* believe there was only one place remaining. Still, she keyed in her credit card details pretty damned fast, just in case.

It seemed that in a mere ten days she would be "transformed" in ways she "never thought possible." There would be fasting, meditation, yoga, creative "emotional-release exercises." There would be no alcohol, sugar, caffeine, gluten, or dairy—but as she'd just had the degustation menu at the Four Seasons, she was stuffed full of alcohol, sugar, caffeine, gluten, and dairy, and the thought of giving them up didn't seem that big a deal. Meals would be "personalized" to her "unique needs."

Before her booking was "accepted," she had to answer a very long, rather invasive online questionnaire about her relationship status, diet, medical history, alcohol consumption in the previous week, and so on. She cheerfully lied her way through it. It was really none of their business. She even had to upload a photo taken in the last two weeks. She sent one of herself from her lunch with Ellen at the Four Seasons, holding up a Bellini.

There were boxes to tick for what she hoped to achieve during her ten days: everything from "intensive couples counseling" to "significant weight loss." Frances ticked only the nice-sounding boxes, like "spiritual nourishment."

Like so many things in life, it had seemed like an excellent idea at the time.

The TripAdvisor reviews for Tranquillum House, which she'd looked at *after* she'd paid her nonrefundable fee, had been noticeably mixed. It was either the best, most incredible experience people had ever had, they wished they could give it more than five stars, they were evangelical about the food, the hot springs, the staff, or it was the worst experience of their entire lives, there was talk of legal action, posttraumatic stress, and dire warnings of "enter at your own peril."

Frances looked again at the dashboard, hoping to catch the clock tick over to three.

Stop it. Focus. Eyes on the road, Frances. You're the one in charge of this car.

Something flickered in her peripheral vision and she flinched, ready for the massive thud of a kangaroo smashing her windshield.

It was nothing. These imaginary wildlife collisions were all in her head. If it happened, it happened. There probably wouldn't be time to react.

She remembered a long-ago road trip with a boyfriend. They'd come across a dying emu that had been hit by a car in the middle of a highway. Frances had stayed in the passenger seat, a passive princess, while her boyfriend got out and killed the poor emu with a rock. One sharp blow to the head. When he returned to the driver's seat he was sweaty and exhilarated, a city boy thrilled with his own humane pragmatism. Frances never quite forgave him for the sweaty exhilaration. He'd *liked* killing the emu.

Frances wasn't sure if she could kill a dying animal, even now when she was fifty-two years old, financially secure, and too old to be a princess.

"You could kill the emu," she said out loud. "Certainly you could."

Goodness. She'd just remembered that the boyfriend was dead. Wait, was he? Yes, definitely dead. She'd heard it through the grapevine a few years back. Complications from pneumonia, supposedly. Gary always did suffer terribly from colds. Frances had never been especially sympathetic.

At that very moment her nose dripped like a tap. Perfect timing. She held the steering wheel with one hand and wiped her nose with the back of her other hand. Disgusting. It was probably Gary vindictively making her nose drip from the afterlife. Fair enough too. They'd once been on road trips and professed their love and now she couldn't even be bothered to remember he was dead.

She apologized to Gary, although, really, if he was able to access her thoughts, then he should know that it wasn't her fault; if he'd made it to this age he'd know how extraordinarily vague and forgetful one became. Not all the time. Just sometimes.

Sometimes I'm as sharp as a tack, Gary.

She sniffed again. It seemed like she'd had this truly horrendous head cold even longer than the back pain. Wasn't she sniffling the day she delivered her manuscript? Three weeks ago. Her nineteenth novel. She was still waiting to hear what her publisher thought. Once upon a time, back in the late nineties, her "heyday," her editor would have sent champagne and flowers within two days of delivery, together with a handwritten note. *Another masterpiece!*

She understood she was no longer in her heyday, but she was still a solid, mid-level performer. An effusive email would be nice.

Or just a friendly one.

Even a brisk one-liner: *Sorry, haven't got to it yet but can't wait!* That would have been polite.

A fear she refused to acknowledge tried to worm its way up from her subconscious. No. No. Absolutely not.

She clutched the steering wheel and tried to calm her breathing. She'd been throwing back cold and flu tablets to try to clear her nose and the pseudoephedrine was making her heart race, as if something wonderful or terrible was about to happen. It reminded her of the feeling of walking down the aisle on both her wedding days.

She was probably addicted to the cold and flu tablets. She was easily addicted. Men. Food. Wine. In fact, she felt like a glass of wine right now and the sun was still high in the sky. Lately, she'd been drinking, maybe not excessively, but certainly more enthusiastically than usual. She was on that slippery slope, hurtling toward drug and alcohol addiction! Exciting to know she could still change in significant ways. Back home there was a half-empty bottle of pinot noir sitting brazenly on her writing desk for anyone (only the cleaning lady) to see. She was Ernest frigging Hemingway. Didn't he have a bad back too? They had so much in common.

Except that Frances had a weakness for adjectives and adverbs. Apparently she scattered them about her novels like throw cushions. What was that Mark Twain quote Sol used to murmur to himself, just loud enough for her to hear, while reading her manuscripts? *When you catch an adjective, kill it.*

Sol was a real man who didn't like adjectives or throw cushions. She had an image of Sol, in bed, on top of her, swearing comically as he pulled out yet another cushion from behind her head, chucking it across the room while she giggled. She shook her head as if to shake off the memory. Fond sexual memories felt like a point for her first husband.

When everything was good in Frances's life she wished both her ex-husbands nothing but happiness and excellent erectile function. Right now, she wished plagues of locusts to rain down upon their silvery heads.

She sucked on the tiny vicious paper cut on the tip of her right thumb. Every now and then it throbbed to remind her that it might be the smallest of her ailments but it could still ruin her day.

Her car veered to the bumpy side of the road and she removed her thumb from her mouth and clung to the steering wheel. "Whoops-a-daisy."

She had quite short legs, so she had to move the driver's seat close to the steering wheel. Henry used to say she looked like she was driving a bumper car. He said it was cute. But after five years or so he stopped finding it cute and swore every time he got in the car and had to slide the seat back.

She found his sleep-talking charming for about five years or so too.

Focus!

The countryside flew by. At last a sign: *Welcome to the town of Jarribong. We're proud to be a TIDY TOWN.*

She slowed down to the speed limit of fifty kph, which felt almost absurdly slow.

Her head swiveled from side to side as she studied the town. A Chinese restaurant with a faded red and gold dragon on the door. A service station that looked closed. A red-brick post office. A drive-through bottle shop that looked open. A police station that seemed entirely unnecessary. Not a person in sight. It might have been tidy but it felt postapocalyptic.

She thought of her latest manuscript. It was set in a small town. *This* was the gritty, bleak reality of small towns! Not the charming village she'd created, nestled in the mountains, with a warm bustling café that smelled of cinnamon and, most fanciful of all, a *bookstore* supposedly making a profit. The reviewers would rightly call it "twee," but it probably wouldn't get reviewed and she never read her reviews anyway.

So that was it for poor old Jarribong. Goodbye, sad little tidy town.

She put her foot on the accelerator and watched her speed slide back up to one hundred. The website had said that the turnoff was twenty minutes outside of Jarribong.

There was a sign ahead. She narrowed her eyes, hunched over the wheel to read it: *Tranquillum House next turn on the left.*

Her heart lifted. She'd done it. She'd driven six hours without quite losing her mind. Then her heart sank, because now she was going to have to go through with this thing.

"Turn left in one kilometer," ordered her GPS.

"I don't want to turn left in one kilometer," said Frances dolefully.

She wasn't even meant to be here, in this season or hemisphere. She was meant to be with her "special friend" Paul Drabble in Santa Barbara, the Californian winter sun warm upon their faces as they visited wineries, restaurants, and museums. She was meant to be spending long lingering afternoons getting to know Paul's twelve-year-old son, Ari, hearing his dry little chuckle as he taught her how to play some violent Play-Station game he loved. Frances's friends with kids had laughed and scoffed over that, but she'd been looking *forward* to learning the game; the story lines sounded really quite rich and complex.

An image came to her of that detective's earnest young face. He had freckles left over from childhood and he wrote down everything she said in laborious longhand using a scratchy blue ballpoint. His spelling was atrocious. He spelled "tomorrow" with two m's. He couldn't meet her eye.

A sudden rush of intense heat enveloped her body at the memory.

Humiliation?

Probably.

Her head swam. She shivered and shook. Her hands were instantly slippery on the steering wheel.

Pull over, she told herself. *You need to pull over right now.*

She signaled, even though there was no one behind her, and came to a stop on the side of the road. She had the sense to switch on her hazard lights. Sweat poured from her face. Within seconds her shirt was drenched. She pulled at the fabric and smeared back strands of wet hair from her forehead. A cold chill made her shake.

She sneezed, and the act of sneezing caused her back to spasm. The pain was of such truly biblical proportions that she began to laugh as tears streamed down her face. Oh yes, she *was* losing her mind. She certainly was.

A great wave of unfocused primal rage swept over her. She banged her fist against her car horn over and over, closed her eyes, threw back her head, and screamed in unison with the horn, because she had this cold and this back pain and this broken bloody heart and—

"Hey!"

She opened her eyes and jumped back in her seat.

A man crouched next to her car window, rapping hard on the glass. She saw what must be his car pulled up on the opposite side of the road, with its hazard lights also on.

"You okay?" he shouted. "Do you need help?"

For God's sake. This was meant to be a private moment of despair. How deeply embarrassing. She pressed the button to lower the window.

A very large, unpleasant, unkempt, unshaven man peered in at her. He wore a T-shirt with the faded emblem of some ancient band over a proud solid beer belly and low-slung blue jeans. He was probably one of those outback serial killers. Even though this wasn't technically the outback. He was probably on holiday from the outback.

"Got car trouble?" he asked.

"No," said Frances. She sat up straighter and tried to smile. She ran a hand through her damp hair. "Thank you. I'm fine. The car is fine. Everything is fine."

"Are you *sick*?" said the man. He looked faintly disgusted.

"No," said Frances. "Not really. Just a bad cold."

"Maybe you've got the proper flu. You look *really* sick," said the man. He frowned, and his eyes moved to the back of her car. "And you were screaming and sounding your horn like you . . . were in trouble."

"Yes," said Frances. "Well. I thought I was alone in the middle of nowhere. I was just . . . having a bad moment." She tried to keep the resentment from her voice. He was a good citizen who had done the right thing. He'd done what anyone would do.

"Thank you for stopping but I'm fine," she said nicely, with her sweetest, most placatory smile. One must placate large strange men in the middle of nowhere.

"Okay then." The man straightened with a groan of effort, his hands on his thighs to give himself leverage, but then he rapped the top of her car with his knuckles and bent down again, suddenly decisive. *I'm a man, I know what's what.* "Look, are you too sick to drive? Because if you're not safe to drive, if you're a danger to other drivers on the road, I really can't in good conscience let you—"

Frances sat up straight. For heaven's sake. "I just had a hot flash," she snapped.

The man blanched. "Oh!" He studied her. Paused. "I always thought it was a hot *flush*," he said.

"I believe both terms are used," said Frances. This was her third one. She'd done a lot of reading, spoken to every woman she knew over the age of forty-five, and had a double appointment with her GP, where she had cried, "But no one ever said it was like this!" For now they were monitoring things. She was taking supplements, cutting back on alcohol and spicy foods. Ha ha.

"So you're okay," said the man. He looked up and down the highway as if for help.

"I really am perfectly fine," said Frances. Her back gave a friendly little spasm and she tried not to flinch.

"I didn't realize that hot flashes—flushes—were so . . ."

"Dramatic? Well, they're not for everyone. Just a lucky few."

"Isn't there . . . what's it called? Hormone-replacement therapy?"

Oh my Lord.

"Can you prescribe me something?" asked Frances brightly.

The man took a little step back from the car, hands up in surrender. "Sorry. It's just, I think that was what my wife . . . Anyway, none of my business. If everything is okay, I'll just be on my way."

"Great," said Frances. "Thank you for stopping."

"No worries."

He lifted a hand, went to say something else, evidently changed his mind, and walked back toward his car. There were sweat marks on the back of his T-shirt. A mountain of a man. Lucky he decided she wasn't worth killing and raping. He probably preferred his victims less sweaty.

She watched him start his car and pull out onto the highway. He tipped one finger to his forehead as he drove off.

She waited until his car was a tiny speck in her

rearview mirror and then she reached over for the change of clothes she had waiting on the passenger seat ready for this exact situation.

"Menopause?" her eighty-year-old mother had said vaguely, on the phone from the other side of the world, where she now lived blissfully in the South of France. "Oh, I don't think it gave me too much trouble, darling. I got it all over and done with in a weekend, as I recall. I'm sure you'll be the same. I never had those hot flushes. I think they're a myth, to be honest."

Hmmph, thought Frances as she used a towel to wipe away her mythical sweat.

She thought of texting a photo of her tomato-red face to her group of school friends, some of whom she'd known since kindergarten. Now when they went out to dinner they discussed menopause symptoms with the same avid horror with which they'd once discussed their first periods. Nobody else was getting these over-the-top hot flushes like Frances, so she was taking it for the team. Like everything in life, their reactions to menopause were driven by their personalities: Di said she was in a permanent state of rage and if her gynecologist didn't agree to a hysterectomy soon she was going to grab the littler fucker by the collar and slam him up against the wall, Monica was embracing the "beautiful intensity" of her emotions, and Natalie was wondering anxiously if it was contributing to her anxiety. They all agreed it was totally typical of their friend Gillian to die so she could get out of menopause and then they cried into their Prosecco.

No, she wouldn't text her school friends, because

she suddenly remembered how at that last dinner she'd looked up from her menu to catch an exchange of glances that most definitely meant: "Poor Frances." She could not bear pity. That particular group of solidly married friends was meant to *envy* her, or they'd pretended to envy her anyway, for all these years, but it seemed that being childless and single in your thirties was very different from being childless and single in your fifties. No longer glamorous. Now kind of tragic.

I'm only temporarily tragic, she told herself as she pulled on a clean blouse that showed a lot of cleavage. She tossed the sweaty shirt onto the back seat, restarted the car, looked over her shoulder, and pulled out onto the highway. *Temporarily Tragic*. It could be the name of a band.

There was a sign. She squinted. *Tranquillum House*, it said.

"Left turn ahead," said her GPS.

"Yes, I *know*, I see it."

She met her own eyes in the rearview mirror and tried to give herself a wry "isn't life interesting!" look.

Frances had always enjoyed the idea of parallel universes in which multiple versions of herself tried out different lives—one where she was a CEO instead of an author; one where she was a mother of two or four or six kids instead of none; one where she hadn't divorced Sol and one where she hadn't divorced Henry—but for the most part she'd always felt satisfied or at least accepting of the universe in which she found herself . . . except for right now, because right now it felt like there had been some sort of cataclysmic quantum-physics administrative error. She'd slipped universes. She was meant to be high on lust and love in America, not pain-ridden and grief-stricken in Australia. It was just wrong. Unacceptable.

And yet here she was. There was nothing else to do, nowhere else to turn.

"Goddamn it," she said, and turned left.

3

Lars

"This one is my wife's favorite." The vineyard manager, a chunky, cheery guy in his sixties with a retro mustache, held up a bottle of white wine. "She says it makes her think of silk sheets. It has a creamy, velvety finish I think you'll enjoy."

Lars swirled the tasting glass and breathed in the scent: apples and sunshine and wood smoke. An instant memory of an autumnal day. The comfort of a large warm hand holding his. It felt like a childhood memory but probably wasn't; more likely a memory he'd borrowed from a book or movie. He sipped the wine, let it roll around his mouth, and was transported to a bar on the Amalfi Coast. Vine leaves over the light fixture and the smell of garlic and the sea. That was a bona fide happy memory from real life with photos to prove it. He remembered the spaghetti. Just parsley, olive oil, and almonds. There might even be a photo of the spaghetti somewhere.

"What do you think?" The vineyard manager grinned.

It was like his mustache had been perfectly preserved from 1975.

"It's excellent." Lars took another sip, trying to get the full picture. Wine could fool you: all sunshine and apples and spaghetti and then nothing but sour disappointment and empty promises.

"I also have a pinot grigio that might appeal . . ."

Lars held up his hand and looked at his watch. "I'd better stop there."

"Have you got far to travel today?"

Anyone who stopped here would be on their way to somewhere else. Lars had nearly missed the small wooden *Tasting Cellar* sign. He'd slammed on the brakes because that's the sort of man he was: spontaneous. When he remembered to be.

"I'm due to check in at a health resort in an hour's time." Lars held the wineglass up to the light and admired the golden color. "So no alcohol for me for the next ten days."

"Ah. Tranquillum House, right?" said the manager. "Doing the—what do they call it?—ten-day cleanse or some such thing?"

"For my sins," said Lars.

"We normally get guests stopping in here on their way home. We're the first vineyard they drive by on the road back to Sydney."

"What do they have to say about the place?" asked Lars. He pulled out his wallet. He was going to order some wine to be delivered as a welcome-home treat.

"Some of them seem a bit shell-shocked, to be

honest. They mostly just need a drink and some potato chips and they get the color back in their cheeks." The manager placed his hand around the neck of the bottle, as if for comfort. "Actually, my sister just got a job working in the spa there. She says her new boss is a bit . . ." He squinted hard as if trying to see the word he wanted. Finally, he said, "Different."

"I'm forewarned," said Lars. He wasn't concerned. He was a health-retreat junkie. The people who ran these places tended to be "different."

"She says the house itself is amazing. It's got a fascinating history."

"Built by convicts, I believe." Lars tapped the corner of his gold Amex against the bar.

"Yeah. Poor buggers. No spa treatments for them."

A woman appeared from a door behind him, muttering, "Bloody internet is down *again*." She stopped when she saw Lars and did a double take. He was used to it. He'd had a lifetime of double takes. She looked away fast, flustered.

"This is my wife," said the vineyard manager with pride. "We were just talking about your favorite Sémillon, love—the silk-sheets Sémillon."

The color rose up her neck. "I wish you wouldn't tell people that."

Her husband looked confused. "I *always* tell people that."

"I'm going to get a case," said Lars.

He watched the wife pat her husband's back as she moved past him.

"Make it two cases," Lars said, because he spent his days dealing with the shattered remnants of broken marriages and he was a sucker for a good one.

He smiled at the woman. Her hands fluttered to her hair while her oblivious husband pulled out a battered old order book with a pen attached by a string, leaned heavily on the counter, and peered at the form in a way that indicated this was going to take some time. "Name?"

"Lars Lee," said Lars, as his phone beeped with a text message. He tapped the screen.

Can you at least think about it? Xx

His heart lurched as if at the sudden scuttle of a black furry spider. For fuck's sake. He'd thought they were done with this. His thumb hovered over the message, considering. The passive-aggressiveness of the "at least." The saccharine double kiss. Also, he didn't like the fact that the first kiss was uppercase and the second was lowercase and he didn't like the fact that he didn't like this. It was mildly OCD-ish.

He tapped in a rude, boorish uppercase reply: *NO. I WILL NOT.*

But then he deleted it, and shoved his phone back into the pocket of his jeans.

"Let me try that pinot grigio."

4

Frances

Frances drove twenty minutes down a bumpy dirt road that jolted the car so hard her bones rattled and her lower back screamed.

At last she came to a stop in front of what appeared to be an extremely locked gate with an intercom. It was like arriving at a minimum-security jail. An ugly barbed-wire fence stretched endlessly in either direction.

She had envisaged driving up a stately tree-lined drive to the "historic" house and having someone greet her with a green smoothie. This didn't feel very *healing*, to be frank.

Stop it, she told herself. If she got into that *I'm a dissatisfied consumer* mode everything would start to dissatisfy her, and she was going to be here for ten days. She needed to be open and flexible. Going to a health resort was like traveling to a new country. One must embrace different cultures and be patient with minor inconveniences.

She lowered her car window. Hot thick air filled her

throat like smoke as she leaned out and pressed the green button on the intercom with her thumb. The button burned from the sun and it hurt her paper cut.

She sucked on her thumb and waited for a disembodied voice to welcome her, or for the wrought-iron gate to magically open.

Nothing.

She looked again at the intercom and saw a handwritten note sticky-taped next to the button. The writing was so small she could only make out the important word "instructions" but nothing else.

For goodness' sake, she thought, as she went through her handbag for her reading glasses. Surely a good proportion of visitors were over forty.

She found her glasses, put them on, peered at the sign, and *still* couldn't make it out. Tut-tutting and muttering, she got out of the car. The heat grabbed her in a heavy embrace and beads of sweat sprang up all over her scalp.

She ducked down next to the intercom and read the note, written in neat, tiny block letters as if by the tooth fairy.

NAMASTE AND WELCOME TO TRANQUILLUM
HOUSE WHERE A NEW YOU AWAITS.
PLEASE PRESS THE SECURITY CODE 564–312
FOLLOWED IMMEDIATELY BY THE GREEN
BUTTON.

She pressed the security code numbers then the green button and waited. Sweat rolled down her back.

She would need to change her clothes *again*. A blowfly buzzed near her mouth. Her nose dripped.

"Oh come *on*!" she said to the intercom with a sudden spurt of rage, and she wondered if her agitated sweaty face was appearing on some screen inside, while an expert dispassionately analyzed her symptoms, her misaligned chakras. *This one needs work. Look at how she responds to one of life's simplest stresses: waiting.*

Had she got the damned code wrong?

Once again she carefully punched in the security code, saying each number out loud, in a sarcastic tone, to prove a point to God knows who, and gave the hot green button a slow, deliberate push, holding it for five seconds just to be sure.

There. Now let me in.

She took off her reading glasses and let them dangle in her hand.

The baking heat seemed to be melting her scalp like chocolate in the sun. Silence again. She gave the intercom a fierce, hard look as if that would shame it into acting.

At least this would make a funny story for Paul. She wondered if he'd ever been to a health resort. She thought he'd most likely be a skeptic. She herself was—

Her chest constricted. This wouldn't make a good story for Paul. Paul was gone. How humiliating for him to have slipped into her thoughts like that. She wished she felt a surge of white-hot anger instead of this utter sadness, this pretend grief for what was never real in the first place.

Stop it. Don't think about it. Focus on the problem at hand.

The solution was obvious. She would *ring* Tranquillum House! They would be mortified to hear that their intercom had broken and Frances would be calm and understanding and brush away their apologies. "These things happen," she'd say. "Namaste."

She got back in the car, cranked up the air conditioner. She found the paperwork with her booking details, and rang the number listed. All her other communications had been by email, so it was the first time she'd heard the recorded message that immediately began to play.

"Thank you for calling the historic Tranquillum House Health and Wellness Hot Springs Resort, where a new you awaits. Your call is so important and special to us, as is your health and well-being, but we are experiencing an unusually high volume of calls at the moment. We know your time is precious, so please do leave a message after the chimes and we will call you back just as soon as we can. We so appreciate your patience. Namaste."

Frances cleared her throat as wind chimes made their annoying twinkly dinging sounds.

"Oh yes, my name is—"

The wind chimes kept going. She stopped, waited, went to speak, and stopped again. It was a wind-chime *symphony*.

At last there was silence.

"Hello, this is Frances Welty." She sniffed. "Excuse

me. Bit of a cold. Anyway, as I said, I'm Frances Welty. I'm a guest."

Guest? Was that the right word? Patient? Inmate?

"I'm trying to check in and I'm stuck outside the gate. It's, ah, twenty past three, twenty-five past three, and I'm . . . here! The intercom doesn't seem to be working even though I've followed all the instructions. The teeny-tiny instructions. I'd appreciate it if you could just open the gate? Let me in?" Her message finished on a rising note of hysteria, which she regretted. She put the phone down on the seat next to her and studied the gate.

Nothing. She would give it twenty minutes and then she was throwing in the towel.

Her phone rang and she snatched it up without looking at the screen.

"Hi there!" she said cheerfully, to show how understanding and patient she really was and to make up for the sarcastic "teeny-tiny" comment.

"Frances?" It was Alain, her literary agent. "You don't sound like you."

Frances sighed. "I was expecting someone else. I'm doing that health retreat I told you about, but I can't even get through the front gate. Their intercom isn't working."

"How incompetent! How *unsatisfactory*!" Alain was easily and often enraged by poor service. "You should turn around and come back home. It's not *alternative*, is it? Remember those poor people who died in that sweat lodge? They all thought they were becoming enlightened when in reality they were being cooked."

"This place is pretty mainstream. Hot springs and massages and art therapy. Maybe some gentle fasting."

"Gentle fasting." Alain snorted. "Eat when you're hungry. That's a *privilege*, you know, to eat when you're hungry, when there are people starving in this world."

"Well, that's the point—we're *not* starving in this part of the world," said Frances. She looked at the wrapper for the Kit Kat bar sitting in the console of her car. "We're eating too much processed food. So that's why us privileged people need to detox—"

"Oh my Lord, she's falling for it. She's drunk the Kool-Aid! Detoxing is a *myth*, darling, it's been debunked! Your liver does it for you. Or maybe it's your kidneys. It's all taken care of somehow."

"*Anyway*," said Frances. She had a feeling he was procrastinating.

"Anyway," said Alain. "You sound like you've got a cold, Frances." He seemed quite anguished about her cold.

"I do have a very bad, persistent, possibly permanent cold," said Frances. She coughed to demonstrate. "You'd be proud of me. I've been taking a *lot* of very powerful drugs. My heart is going at a million miles per hour."

"That's the ticket," said Alain.

There was a pause.

"Alain?" she prompted, but she knew, she already knew exactly what he was going to say.

"I'm afraid I am not the bearer of good news," said Alain.

"I see."

She sucked in her stomach, ready to take it like a man, or at least like a romance novelist capable of reading her own royalty statements.

"Well, as you know, darling," began Alain.

But Frances couldn't bear to hear him hedging, trying to soften the blow with compliments.

"They don't want the new book, do they?" she said.

"They don't want the new book," said Alain sadly. "I'm so sorry. I think it's a beautiful book, I really do, it's just the current environment, and romance has taken the worst hit, it won't be forever, romance always comes back, it's a *blip*, but—"

"So you'll sell it to someone else," interrupted Frances. "Sell it to Timmy."

There was another pause.

"The thing is," said Alain, "I didn't tell you this, but I slipped the manuscript to Timmy a few weeks back, because I did have a tiny fear this might happen and obviously an offer from Timmy before we had anything on the table would have given me leverage, so I—"

"Timmy *passed*?" Frances couldn't believe it. Hanging in her wardrobe was a designer dress that she'd never be able to wear again because of the stain from a piña colada Timmy had spilled on her while he had her cornered in a room at the Melbourne Writers Festival, his voice hasty and hot in her ear, looking back over his shoulder like a spy, telling her how much he wanted to publish her, how it was his *destiny* to publish her, how no one else in the publishing industry knew how to publish her the way he did, how her loyalty to Jo was admirable but misplaced because Jo thought she understood romance but she *didn't*, only Timmy did, and only Timmy could and *would* take Frances "to the next level," and so on and so forth until Jo turned up and rescued her. "Oi, leave my author alone."

How long ago was that? Not that long surely. Maybe nine, ten years ago. A decade. Time went by so fast these days. There was some sort of malfunction going on with how fast the earth was spinning. Decades went by as quick as years once did.

"Timmy loved the book," said Alain. "Adored it. He was nearly in tears. He couldn't get it past Acquisitions. They're all shaking in their boots over there. It was a hell of a year. The decree from above is psychological thrillers."

"I can't write a thriller," said Frances. She never liked to kill characters. Sometimes she let them break a limb but she felt bad enough about that.

"Of course you can't!" said Alain too quickly, and Frances felt mildly insulted.

"Look, I have to admit I was worried when Jo left and you were out of contract," said Alain. "But Ashlee seemed to really be a fan of yours."

Frances's concentration drifted as Alain continued to talk. She watched the closed gate and pushed the knuckles of her left hand into her lower back.

What would Jo say when she heard Frances had been rejected? Or would she have had to do the same thing? Frances had always assumed that Jo would be her editor forever. She had fondly imagined them finishing their working lives simultaneously, perhaps with a lavish joint retirement lunch, but late last year Jo had announced her intention to retire. *Retire!* Like she was some sort of old grandma! Jo actually was a grandmother, but for goodness' sake that wasn't a reason to *stop*. Frances felt like she was only just getting into the swing of things, and all of a sudden people in her circle were doing old-people things: having grandchildren, retiring, downsizing, dying—not in car accidents or plane crashes, no, dying *peacefully* in their sleep. She would never forgive Gillian for that. Gillian always slipped out of parties without saying goodbye.

It shouldn't have come as a surprise when Jo's replacement turned out to be a child, because children were taking over the world. Everywhere Frances looked there were children: children sitting gravely behind news desks, controlling traffic, running writers' festivals, taking her blood pressure, managing her taxes, and fitting her bras. When Frances first met Ashlee she had genuinely thought she was an intern. She'd been about to say, "A cappuccino would be lovely, darling," when the child had walked around to the other side of Jo's old desk.

"Frances," she'd said, "this is such a *fan girl* moment for me! I used to read your books when I was, like, *eleven*! I stole them from my mum's handbag. I'd be like, Mum, you've got to let me read *Nathaniel's Kiss*, and she'd be like, No way, Ashlee, there's too much sex in it!"

Then Ashlee had proceeded to tell Frances that her next book needed more sex, a lot more sex, but she knew Frances could totally pull it off! As Ashlee was sure Frances knew, the market was changing, and "If you just look at this chart here, Frances—no, *here*; that's it—you'll see that your sales have been on kind of a, well, sorry to say this, but you kind of have to call this a *downward trend*, and we, like, really need to reverse that, like, super fast. Oh, and one other thing . . ."

Ashlee looked pained, as if she were about to bring up an embarrassing medical issue. "Your social media presence? I hear you're not so keen on social media. Neither is my mum! But it's kind of essential in today's market. Your fans really do need to see you on Twitter and Instagram and Facebook—that's just the bare minimum. Also, we'd love you to start a blog and a newsletter and perhaps do some regular vlogs? That would be so much fun! They're like little films!"

"I have a website," replied Frances.

"Yes," said Ashlee kindly. "Yes, you do, Frances. But nobody cares about websites."

And then she'd angled her computer monitor toward Frances so she could show her some examples of other, better-behaved authors with "active" social media presences, and Frances had stopped listening and waited for it to be over, like a dental appointment. (She couldn't see the screen anyway. She didn't have her glasses with her.) But she wasn't worried, because she was falling in love with Paul Drabble at the time, and when she was falling in love she always wrote her best books. And besides, she had the sweetest, most loyal readers in the world. Her sales might drop but she would always be *published*.

"I will find the right home for this book," said Alain now. "It might just take a little while. Romance isn't dead!"

"Isn't it?" said Frances.

"Not even close," said Alain.

She picked up the empty Kit Kat wrapper and licked it, hoping for fragments of chocolate. How was she going to get through this setback without sugar?

"Frances?" said Alain.

"My back hurts a great deal," said Frances. She blew her nose hard. "Also, I had to stop the car in the middle of the road to have a hot flush."

"That sounds truly awful," said Alain with feeling. "I can't even imagine."

"No you can't. A man stopped to see if I was all right because I was screaming."

"You were *screaming*?" said Alain.

"I felt like screaming," said Frances.

"Of course, of course," said Alain hurriedly. "I understand. I often feel like screaming."

This was rock bottom. She'd just *licked a Kit Kat wrapper*.

"Oh dear, Frances, I'm so sorry about this, especially after what happened with that horrendous man. Have the police had anything new to say?"

"No," said Frances. "No news."

"Darling, I'm just *bleeding* for you here."

"That's not necessary," sniffed Frances.

"You've just had such a bad trot lately, darling—speaking of which, I want you to know that review had absolutely no impact on their decision."

"What review?" said Frances.

There was silence. She knew Alain was smacking his forehead.

"Alain?"

"Oh God," he said. "Oh God, oh God, oh God."

"I haven't read a review since 1998," said Frances. "Not a single review. You know that."

"I absolutely know that," said Alain. "I'm an idiot. I'm a fool."

"Why would there be a review when I don't have a new book out?" Frances wriggled upright in her seat. Her back hurt so much she thought she might be sick.

"Some bitch picked up a copy of *What the Heart Wants* at the airport and did an opinion piece about, ah, your books in general, a mad diatribe. She kind of linked it to the Me Too movement, which gave it some clickbait traction. It was just ridiculous—as if romance books are to blame for sexual predators!"

"*What?*"

"Nobody even read the review. I don't know why I mentioned it. I must have early-onset dementia."

"You just said it got traction!"

Everyone had read the review. Everyone.

"Send me the link," said Frances.

"It's not even that bad," said Alain. "It's just this prejudice against your genre—"

"Send it!"

"No," said Alain. "I won't. You've gone all these years without reading reviews. Don't fall off the wagon!"

"Right now," said Frances in her dangerous voice.

She used it rarely. When she was getting divorced, for example.

"I'll send it," said Alain meekly. "I'm so sorry, Frances. I'm so sorry about this entire phone call."

He hung up, and Frances immediately went to her email. There wasn't much time. As soon as she arrived at Tranquillum House she would need to "hand in" her "device." It would be a digital detox, along with everything else. She was going "off the grid."

SO SORRY! said Alain's email.

She clicked on the review.

It was written by someone called Helen Ihnat. Frances didn't know the name and there was no picture. She read it fast, with a wry, dignified smile, as if the author was saying these things to her face. It was a terrible review: vicious, sarcastic, and superior, but, interestingly, it didn't hurt. The words—*Formulaic. Trash. Drivel. Trite*—slid right off her.

She was fine! Can't please everyone. Comes with the territory.

And then she felt it.

It was like when you burn yourself on a hot plate and at first you think, *Huh, that should have hurt more*, and then it does hurt more, and then all of a sudden it hurts like hell.

A quite extraordinary pain in her chest radiated throughout her entire body. Another fun symptom of menopause? Maybe it was a heart attack. Women had heart attacks. Surely this was more than hurt feelings. This, of course, was why she'd given up reading reviews in the first place. Her skin was too thin. "It was the best decision I ever made," she'd told the audience at the Romance Writers of Australia Conference when she gave the keynote address last year. They'd probably all been thinking: *Yeah, maybe you should read a review or two, Frances, you old has-been.*

Why did she think it was a good idea to read a bad review directly after she'd just received her first rejection in thirty years?

And now something else was happening. It appeared and, gosh, this was just so fascinating, but it seemed she was losing her entire sense of self.

Come on now, Frances, get a grip, you're too old for an existential crisis.

But apparently she wasn't.

She scrabbled hopelessly after her self-identity, but it was like trying to catch water rushing down a drain. If she was no longer a published writer, who was she? What was the actual point of her? She wasn't a mother or a wife or a girlfriend. She was a twice-divorced, middle-aged, hot-flushing/-flashing menopausal woman. A punch line. A cliché. Invisible to most—except, of course, to men like Paul Drabble.

She looked at the gate in front of her that *still would not open* and her vision blurred with tears and she told herself not to panic, you are not *disappearing*, Frances, don't be so melodramatic, this is just a rough trot, a bad patch, and it's the cold and flu tablets making your heart race, but it felt like she was hovering on a precipice, and on the other side of the precipice was a howling abyss of despair unlike anything she'd ever experienced, even during those times of true grief—and this is *not* true grief, she reminded herself, this is a career setback combined with the loss of a relationship, a bad back, a cold, and a paper cut; this is not like when Dad died, or Gillian died—but actually it wasn't that helpful to start remembering the deaths of loved ones, not helpful at all.

She looked around wildly for distraction—her phone, her book, *food*—and then she saw movement in her rearview mirror.

What was it? An animal? A trick of the light? No, it was something.

It was too slow for a car.

Wait. It *was* a car. It was just driving so slowly it was barely moving.

She sat up straight and ran her fingers under her eyes where her mascara had run.

A canary-yellow sports car drove down the dirt drive slower than she would have thought possible.

Frances had no interest in cars, but as it got closer even she could tell this was a spectacularly expensive piece of machinery. Low to the ground and shimmery-shiny with futuristic headlights.

It came to a stop behind hers and the doors on either side opened simultaneously. A young man and woman emerged. Frances adjusted her mirror to see them more clearly. The man looked like a suburban plumber off to a Sunday barbecue: baseball cap on backward, sunglasses, T-shirt, shorts, and boat shoes with no socks. The woman had amazing long curly auburn hair, skin-tight capri pants, an impossibly tiny waist, and even more unlikely breasts. She teetered on stilettos.

Why in the world would a young couple like that come to a health retreat? Wasn't this sort of place for the overweight and burnt out, for those grappling with bad backs and pathetic midlife identity crises? As Frances watched, the man turned his baseball cap around the right way and tipped his head back, arching his back as if he, too, found the sky overwhelming. The woman said something to him. Frances could tell by the way her mouth moved that it was sharp.

They were arguing.

How delightfully distracting. Frances lowered her window. These people would pull her back from the precipice, bring her back into existence. She would regain her self-identity by existing in their eyes. They would see her as old and eccentric and maybe even annoying, but it didn't matter how they saw her, as long as they saw her.

She leaned clumsily out the car window, waggled her fingers, and called out, "Helloooo!"

The girl tottered over the grass toward her.

5

Ben

Ben watched Jessica walk like a baby giraffe toward the Peugeot 308—overpriced piece of crap—parked at the gate, engine running. One of the Peugeot's brake lights was gone and the muffler looked like it was bent, no doubt from that dirt road. The lady behind the wheel was leaning halfway out her window, practically falling out, waving wildly at Jessica as if she couldn't be more pleased to see her. Why didn't she just open her car door and get out?

It looked like the health resort was closed. A burst water main? A mutiny? He could only hope.

Jessica could hardly walk in those stupid shoes. It was like she was on stilts. The heels were as skinny as toothpicks. She would twist an ankle any minute.

Ben squatted down next to his car and ran his fingers over the paintwork, searching for stone chips. He glanced back at the road they'd just come down and winced. How could a place that charged eye-watering rates have a road like that? There should have been a warning on the website. He'd thought for sure they were going to bottom out on some of those potholes.

No scratches that he could see, which was a miracle, but who knew what damage there was to the undercarriage? He'd have to wait till he could get it back up in the workshop, take a look. He wanted to do it right now, but he was going to have to wait ten days.

Maybe he should get the car towed back to Melbourne. He could call Pete's guys. It wasn't the craziest of ideas, except that he'd never hear the end of it if any of his former workmates saw that he'd driven *this* car down *that* road. He suspected his ex-boss would cry, literally cry, if he saw what Ben had done.

Pete's eyes had gotten suspiciously shiny after the scratch incident last month. "Scratchgate," they all called it.

"Jealous fuck," Pete said when Ben showed him the long deliberate scratch left by some evil person's key on the passenger door. Ben couldn't work out where and when it had happened. He never left the car in public car parks. It felt like it had to be someone they knew. Ben could name multiple people who might resent him and Jessica enough to have done it. Once he would have found it hard to name a single enemy in his life. Now it seemed they had a nice little collection. He knew Jessica thought it was Ben's sister who had done it, although she never accused Lucy out loud. He could read her mind by the thin fold of her lips. Maybe she was right. It could have been Lucy.

Pete fixed the scratch with the same care as if he were restoring a priceless painting, and Ben had been vigilant until right now, when he'd put the car at huge, unforgivable risk by driving down that hellish road.

Ben should never have given in to Jessica. He'd tried. He stopped the car and told her, calmly and without swearing, that driving a car like this down an unpaved road was *negligent* and that the consequences could be catastrophic. They could, for example, rip out the exhaust system.

It was almost like she seriously didn't care about the exhaust system.

They'd yelled at each other for ten minutes straight. Proper yelling. Spitballs flying. Their faces red and ugly and contorted. The head-exploding frustration he'd felt during that argument was like something half-remembered from childhood, when you couldn't express yourself properly and you had no control over your life because you were a kid, so when your mum or dad said you couldn't have the new *Star Wars* action figure you wanted with all your heart you totally lost your shit.

There had been a moment there when he'd clenched his fists; when he had to tell himself, *Don't hit her.* He hadn't known he was capable of feeling the desire to hit a woman. He folded right then. He said, "Fine. I'll ruin the car. Whatever."

Most guys he knew wouldn't have even stopped for the yelling. They would have just done a U-turn.

Most guys would never have agreed to this crazy idea in the first place.

A *health resort*. Yoga and hot springs. He didn't get it. But Jessica said they needed to do something dramatic and this would fix things. She said they needed to detox their minds and their bodies to save their marriage. They were going to eat organic lettuce and get "couples counseling." It was going to be ten days of pure torture.

Some celebrity couple had come to this place and saved their marriage. They had "achieved inner peace" and got back in touch with their "true selves." What a load of crap. They may as well have handed over their money to Nigerian email scammers. Ben had a horrible feeling the celebrity couple might have got together on *The Bachelorette*. Jessica loved celebrities. He used to think it was sweet, a dumb interest for a smart girl. But now she was making too many life decisions based on what celebrities did, or what it was reported they did; it was probably all crap anyway, they were probably getting paid to support products on their Instagram accounts. And there was Jessica, his poor innocent, hopeful Jessica, soaking it all up.

Now it was like she thought she was one of those people. She was imagining *herself* at those trashy red-carpet events. Every time she got her photo taken these days she put her hand on her hip, like she was doing the actions for "I'm a Little Teapot," then turned side on and thrust out her jaw with this maniacal smile. It was the weirdest thing. And the time she took setting up these photographs. The other day she spent forty-two minutes (he'd timed it) taking a photo of *her feet*.

One of their biggest fights recently had been about one of her Instagram posts. It was a photo of her in a bikini top, leaning over, pushing her arms together so her new boobs looked even bigger and pouting her puffy new lips at the camera. She'd asked what he thought of the photo, her face all hopeful, and because of her hopeful face he hadn't said what he really thought— that it looked like she was advertising a cheap escort service. He'd just shrugged and said, "It's okay."

Her hopeful face fell. You'd think he'd called her a name. Next thing he knew she was screaming at him (these days she could go from zero to a hundred in a second) and he felt sucker-punched, unable to understand what had just happened. So he'd walked away while she was in the middle of yelling and went upstairs to play the Xbox. He thought walking away was a *good* thing to do. A mature, manly thing to do. To disengage and give her time to calm down. He kept getting these things wrong. She ran up the stairs after him and grabbed the back of his T-shirt before he reached the top.

"Look at me!" she screamed. "You don't even look at me anymore!"

And it killed him to hear her say that, because it was true. He avoided looking at her. He was trying *really* hard to get over that. There were men who stayed married to women who were disfigured by accidents, burns or scars or whatever. It shouldn't make a difference that Jessica was disfigured by her own hand. Not literally her own hand. Her own credit card. Willful disfigurement.

And then all her stupid friends encouraged her, "Oh my God, Jessica, you look incredible."

He wanted to yell at them, "Are you blind? She looks like a chipmunk!"

The thought of separating from Jessica was like having his guts ripped out, but these days being married to Jessica was like having his guts ripped out. Whatever way you looked at it: guts ripped out.

If this retreat worked, if they got back to the way they used to be, it was even worth the damage to the car. Obviously it was worth it. Jessica was meant to be the mother of his children—his future children.

He thought of the day of the robbery, two years ago now. He remembered the way her face—it was still her own beautiful face back then—had crumpled like a little kid's, and the rage he'd felt. He'd wanted to find those fuckwits and smash their faces.

If not for the robbery, if not for the fuckwits, they wouldn't be at this place. He wouldn't have the car, but at least he wouldn't be stuck here for the next ten days.

On balance, he still wanted to smash their faces.

"Ben!"

Jessica beckoned him over. She was all social and smiley, like they hadn't just been yelling at each other. She was so good at that. They could drive to a party and fight all the way, not say a word to each other as they walked up someone's stairs, and then the door of the apartment opens and—bang—different person. Laughing, joking, teasing him, touching him, taking selfies, like they were so having sex tonight, when they were so not having sex tonight.

Then, back in the car on the way home, she'd *restart* the fight. It was like flicking a switch on and off. It freaked him out. "It's just good manners," she told him. "You don't take your fight to a party. It's no one else's business."

He straightened up, adjusted his cap, and went over to stand beside Jessica to perform like her monkey.

"This is my husband, Ben," said Jessica. "Ben, this is Frances. She's doing the same retreat as us. Well, probably not exactly the same . . ."

The lady smiled up at him from the driver's seat. "That's a very fancy car, Ben," she said. She spoke as if she already knew him. Her voice was snuffly and hoarse, the tip of her nose bright red. "It's like something from a movie." He could see straight down the huge chasm of her cleavage; he couldn't help it, there was literally nowhere else to look. It wasn't *bad*, but she was old, so it wasn't good either. She wore red lipstick and had a lot of curly gold-colored hair pulled back in a ponytail. She reminded him of one of his mum's tennis friends. He liked his mum's tennis friends—they were uncomplicated and didn't expect him to say much—but he preferred them not to have cleavage.

"Thanks," he said, trying to focus on her very shiny, friendly eyes. "Nice to meet you."

"What sort of car is it?" asked Frances.

"It's a Lamborghini."

"Ooh la la—a Lamborghini!" She grinned up at him. "This here is a Peugeot."

"Uh, yeah, I know," he said, pained.

"Don't think much of the Peugeot?" She tilted her head to one side.

"It's a heap of shit," said Ben.

"*Ben!*" said Jessica, but Frances laughed delightedly.

"I love my little Peugeot," purred Frances as she caressed her steering wheel.

"Well," said Ben. "Each to their own."

"Frances says nobody is answering the intercom," said Jessica. "She's been sitting out here waiting for twenty minutes."

Jessica was using her posh new voice, where she made each word sound as fat and round as an apple. She was using it almost exclusively now, except when she really lost her temper or got upset, like last night, when she forgot to be posh and yelled at him, "Why can't you just be happy? Why are you *ruining* this?"

"Have you phoned them?" he said now to the cleavage lady. "Maybe there's something wrong with the intercom."

"I've left a message," said Frances.

"I wonder if this is like a test," said Jessica. "Maybe it's part of our treatment plan." She lifted her hair up to cool her neck. Sometimes, when she spoke normally, when she was just being herself, he could forget the frozen forehead, the blowfish lips, the puffy cheeks, the camel eyelashes ("eyelash extensions"), the fake hair ("hair extensions") and fake boobs, and there, for just a moment, was his sweet Jessica, the Jessica he'd known since high school.

"I thought that too!" said Frances.

Ben turned to look at the intercom.

"I could hardly read the instructions," said Frances. "They were so tiny."

Ben could read them perfectly well. He punched in the code and pressed the green button.

"I will be absolutely furious if it works for you," said Frances.

A tinny voice sprang from the intercom. "Namaste and welcome to Tranquillum House. How may I help you?"

"What the hell?" Frances mouthed in comical disbelief.

Ben shrugged. "Just needed a man's touch."

"Oh *you*," she said. She reached out of the car and flicked his arm with her hand.

Jessica bent down next to the intercom and spoke too loudly. "We're here to check in." It was cute, like Ben's grandma on the phone. "The name is Chandler, Jessica and Ben—"

There was a burst of static from the intercom and the gate began to creak open. Jessica straightened, tucked her hair behind her ear, worried as always about her dignity. She never used to take herself so seriously.

"I promise you I pressed that code correctly, or I thought I did!" said Frances, as she buckled her seatbelt and revved her tappety little engine. She gave them a little wave. "I'll see you in there! Don't try to race me with your fancy-schmancy Ferrari."

"It's a *Lamborghini*!" protested Ben.

Frances winked at him, as if she knew that perfectly well, and drove off, faster than he would have expected, or recommended, on this road.

As they walked back toward the car, Jessica said,

"We're not telling anybody, right? That's the deal. If anyone asks, just say the car isn't even yours. Say it belongs to a friend."

"Yeah, but I'm not as good a liar as you," he said. He meant it as a joke or even a compliment, but he was leaving the interpretation up to her.

"Fuck you," she said, though without much heat.

So maybe they were okay. But sometimes the embers of a dying argument sparked without warning. You never knew. He would stay alert.

"She seemed nice," said Ben. "The lady. Frances." That was safe. Frances was old. There could be no possibility of jealousy. The jealousy was a fun new development in their relationship. The more Jessica changed her face and body, the less secure she got.

"I think I recognized her," said Jessica.

"Really?"

"I'm pretty sure she's Frances Welty, the writer. I used to be crazy about her books."

"What sort of books?" asked Ben. He opened his car door.

She said something he didn't catch. "Sorry, what?"

"*Romance.*" Jessica slammed the passenger door so hard he winced.

6

Frances

That's more like it, thought Frances when she got her first look at the Victorian mansion emerging majestically in the distance. The road was paved now, thankfully, and the bushland became progressively greener and softer. Tranquillum House was sandstone, three storys, with a red corrugated-iron roof and a princess tower. Frances had the delightful sensation of time-traveling to the late nineteenth century, although the sensation was somewhat spoiled by the yellow Lamborghini purring along behind her.

How could those kids afford that car? Drug dealers? Trust-fund kids? Drug dealing seemed more likely than trust fund; neither of them had that creamy entitled look of old money.

She glanced in the rearview mirror again. From here, with her hair blowing in the wind, Jessica looked like the pretty girl she was meant to be. You couldn't see all the procedures she'd had done to her young face. The thick layer of makeup was bad enough, but oh goodness me, the blinding white teeth, the enormous puffy lips, and the work, it was such *bad* work. Frances was not opposed to cosmetic procedures—in fact she was very fond of them—but there was something so sad and garish about this sweet child's plumped-up, smoothed-out face.

Surely all that jewelry she was wearing couldn't be real, could it? Those massive sapphires in her ears would be worth . . . what? Frances had no idea. A lot. The car was obviously real, though, so maybe the jewelry was real too.

Up-and-coming mobsters? YouTube stars?

The boy, Jessica's "husband" (they seemed too young for such grown-up terms), was cute as a button. Frances would try not to flirt with him. The joke might wear thin after ten days. Possibly even bordering on . . . sleazy? *Possibly bordering on pedophilia, darling*, Alain would say. It was awful to think of lovely Ben shuddering over Frances the way Frances had once shuddered over the behavior of older male authors at publishing parties.

They used to be particularly hideous if they'd recently won a literary prize. Their dialogue was so powerful and impenetrable it didn't require punctuation! So naturally they didn't require permission to slip-slide their hairy hands over the body of a young writer of *genre* fiction. In their minds, Frances virtually owed them sex in return for her unseemly mass-market sales of "airport trash."

Stop it. Don't think about the review, Frances.

She'd marched in the Women's March! She was not

"a blight on feminism" just because she described the color of her hero's eyes. How could you fall in love with someone if you didn't know the color of his eyes? And she was *obliged* to tie everything up at the end with a "giant bow." Those were the rules. If Frances left her endings ambiguous, her readers would come after her with pitchforks.

Do not think about the review. Do not think about the review.

She dragged her mind back to Ben and Jessica. So, yes, she would remember to be age-appropriate with Ben. She would pretend they were related. She'd behave like his aunt. She certainly wouldn't *touch* him. My God, she hadn't touched him already, had she? The review was making her doubt everything about herself. Her hands tightened around the steering wheel. She had a habit of touching people on the arm to make a point, or when they said something that made her laugh, or when she felt in any way fondly toward them.

At least talking with Ben and Jessica had calmed her down. She'd scared herself for a moment there. Loss of self, indeed. What a drama queen.

The road circled up toward the house. Ben politely kept his powerful car at a respectable distance behind Frances even though he probably longed to floor it on the curves.

She drove up a stately driveway lined with towering pine trees.

"Not too shabby," she murmured.

She'd prepared herself for a seedier reality than the website pictures, but up close Tranquillum House was

beautiful. The lacy white balconies glowed in the sunlight. The garden was lush and green in the summer
heat, with a sign helpfully proclaiming THIS PROPERTY
USES RAINWATER so no one could criticize the lushness.

Two white-uniformed staff members, with the
floaty, straight-backed postures of the spiritually ad-
vanced, emerged unhurriedly from the house onto the
wide veranda to greet them. Perhaps they'd been off
meditating while she was stuck outside the gate trying
to ring them. Frances had barely come to a complete
stop when her car door was opened by the man. He was
young, of course, like everyone, Asian, with a hipster
beard and a man bun, bright-eyed and smooth-skinned.
A delightful man-kid.

"Namaste." The man-kid pressed his palms together
and bowed. "A very warm welcome to Tranquillum
House."

He spoke with a tiny . . . measured . . . pause between
each word.

"I'm Yao," he said. "Your personal wellness consultant."

"Hello, Yao. I'm Frances Welty. Your new victim."

She undid her seatbelt and smiled up at him. She
told herself she would not laugh, or attempt to imitate
his yogic voice, or let it drive her mad.

"We'll take care of everything from here," said Yao.
"How many bags do you have?"

"Just the one," said Frances. She indicated the back
seat. "I can carry it. It's quite light." She didn't want
to let the bag out of her sight because she'd packed a
few banned items, like coffee, tea, chocolate (dark

chocolate—antioxidants!), and just *one* bottle of a good red (also antioxidants!).

"Leave your bag right there, Frances, and your keys in the ignition," said Yao firmly.

Damn it. Oh well. Her slight embarrassment over her contraband, even though there was no way he could tell just by looking at the bag (she was normally such a good girl when it came to rules), caused her to hop out of the car awkwardly and too fast, forgetting her new fragility.

"Ooof," she said. She straightened slowly and met Yao's eyes. "Back pain."

"I'm sorry to hear that," said Yao. "I'm going to arrange an urgent massage at the spa for you." He took a small notepad and pencil out of his pocket and made a note.

"I also have a paper cut," said Frances solemnly. She held up her thumb.

Yao took hold of her thumb and peered at it. "Nasty," he said. "We'll need to get some aloe vera on that."

Oh God, he was gorgeous with his little notebook, taking her paper cut so seriously. She caught herself studying his shoulders and looked away fast. *For God's sake, Frances.* Nobody had warned her that this would happen during middle age: these sudden, wildly inappropriate waves of desire for young men, with no biological imperative whatsoever. Maybe this was what men felt like all their lives? No wonder the poor things had to pay out all that money in lawsuits.

"And you're here for the ten-day cleanse," said Yao.

"That's right," said Frances.

"Awesome," said Yao, causing Frances to fortunately lose all desire in an instant. She could never sleep with someone who said "awesome."

"So . . . may I go inside?" asked Frances snappily. Now she felt quite ill at the thought of sex with the man-kid, or sex with anyone for that matter; she was far too hot.

She saw that Yao was distracted by the sight of Ben and Jessica's car, or possibly by Jessica, who was standing with one hip cocked, slowly curling a long strand of hair around her finger while Ben talked to another white-uniformed wellness consultant, a young woman with skin so beautiful it looked like it was lit from within.

"That's a Lamborghini," said Frances.

"I know it is," said Yao, forgetting to put the tiny pauses between his words. He gestured toward the house, stepping aside to let Frances cross the threshold first.

She walked into a large entrance hall and waited for her eyes to adjust to the dim light. The soft hush unique to old houses washed over her like cool water. There were beautiful details wherever she looked: honey-colored parquetry floors, antique chandeliers, ornately carved ceiling cornices, and leadlight windows.

"This is so beautiful," she said. "Oh—and look at that. It's like the staircase from the *Titanic*!"

She walked over to touch the lustrous mahogany wood. Flecks of light streamed from a stained-glass window on the landing.

"As you may know, Tranquillum House was built in 1840 and this is the original red-cedar and rosewood staircase," said Yao. "Other people have commented on the resemblance to the *Titanic*'s staircase. So far we've had much better luck than the *Titanic*. We won't sink, Frances!"

He'd clearly made this joke many times before. Frances gave him a more generous laugh than it deserved.

"The house was built of locally quarried sandstone by a wealthy solicitor from England." Yao continued to recite facts like a nerdy museum guide. "He wanted a house that would be 'the best in the colony.'"

"Built with the help of convicts, I understand," said Frances, who had read the website.

"That's right," said Yao. "The solicitor was granted five hundred acres of good farming land and assigned ten convicts. He got lucky because they included two former stonemason brothers from York."

"We have a convict in our family tree," said Frances. "She was transported from Dublin for stealing a silk gown. We're tremendously proud of her."

Yao gestured away from the staircase to make it clear she wasn't to go up there just yet. "I know you'll want to rest after that long drive, but first I'd like to give you a quick tour of your new home for the next ten days."

"Unless I don't last the distance," said Frances. Ten days suddenly seemed like a very long time. "I might go home early."

"No one goes home early," said Yao serenely.

"Well, yes, but they *can*," said Frances. "If they *choose*."

"No one goes home early," repeated Yao. "It just doesn't happen. No one *wants* to go home at all! You're about to embark on a truly transformative experience, Frances."

He led her to a large room at the side of the house with bay windows overlooking the valley and one long monastery-like table. "This is the dining room where you'll come for your meals. All the guests eat together, of course."

"Of course," said Frances hoarsely. She cleared her throat. "Great."

"Breakfast is served at seven A.M., lunch at noon, and dinner at six P.M."

"Breakfast at *seven A.M.*?" Frances blanched. She could manage the communal meals for lunch and dinner, but she couldn't eat and talk with strangers in the morning. "I'm a night owl," she told Yao. "I'm normally comatose at seven A.M."

"Ah, but that's the old Frances—the new Frances will have already done a sunrise tai chi class and guided meditation by seven," said Yao.

"I seriously doubt that," said Frances.

Yao smiled, as if he knew better.

"There will be a five-minute warning bell before meals are served—or smoothies, during the fast periods. We do ask that you come promptly to the dining room as soon as you hear the warning bell."

"Certainly," said Frances, with a rising sense of horror. She'd quite forgotten about the "fast periods." "Is there . . . ah, room service?"

"I'm afraid not, although your morning and late-evening smoothies will be brought to your room," said Yao.

"But no club sandwiches at midnight, hey?"

Yao shuddered. "God no."

He led her past the dining room to a cozy living room lined with bookshelves. A number of couches surrounded a marble fireplace.

"The Lavender Room," said Yao. "You're welcome to come here any time to relax, read, or enjoy an herbal tea."

He said "herbal" the American way: *erbal*.

"Lovely," said Frances, mollified by the sight of the books. They walked by a closed door with the word PRIVATE stenciled on it in gold letters which Frances, being Frances, felt strongly compelled to open. She couldn't abide member-only lounges to which she didn't have membership.

"This leads to our director's office at the top of the house." Yao touched the door gently. "We do ask that you only open this door if you have an appointment."

"By all means," said Frances resentfully.

"You will meet the director later today," said Yao, as if this were a special treat she'd been long anticipating. "At your first guided meditation."

"Awesome," said Frances through her teeth.

"Now you'll want to see the gym," said Yao.

"Oh, not especially," said Frances, but he was already leading her back across the reception area to the opposite side of the house.

"This was originally the drawing room," said Yao. "It's been refurbished as a state-of-the-art gym."

"Well *that* is a *tragedy*," Frances proclaimed when Yao opened a glass door to reveal a light-filled room

crowded with what appeared to be elaborate torture devices.

Yao's smile faltered. "We kept all the original plas-
terwork." He pointed at the ceiling.

Frances gave a disdainful sniff. *Marvelous. You can
lie back and admire the ceiling rose while you're being
drawn and quartered.*

Yao looked at her face and hurriedly closed the gym
door. "Let me show you the yoga and meditation studio." He continued past the gym to a door at the far
corner of the house. "Watch your head."

She ducked unnecessarily beneath the doorjamb
and followed Yao down a flight of narrow stone stairs.

"I smell wine," she said.

"Don't get your hopes up," said Yao. "It's the ghost
of old wine."

He pushed back a heavy oak door with some effort
and ushered her into a surprisingly large cavelike room
with an arched wood-beamed ceiling, brick walls lined
with a few chairs, and a series of soft blue rectangular
mats laid out at intervals on the hardwood floor.

"This is where you will come for yoga classes and
all your guided sitting meditations," said Yao. "You'll
be spending a lot of time down here."

It was quiet and cool, and the ghostly smell of wine
was overlaid by the scent of incense. The studio did
have a lovely, peaceful feel to it, and Frances thought
she would enjoy being here, even though she wasn't
that keen on yoga or meditation. She had done a transcendental meditation course years ago, hoping for
enlightenment, and every time, without fail, she'd nod

off within two minutes of focusing on her breathing, waking up at the end to discover that everyone else had experienced flashes of light, memories of past lives, and *rapture* or whatever, while she'd snoozed and drooled. Basically, she'd paid to have a forty-minute nap at the local high school once a week. No doubt she would be spending a lot of time *napping* down here, dreaming of wine.

"At one point, when the property operated a vineyard, this cellar could hold up to twenty thousand bottles of wine." Yao gestured at the walls, although there were no longer any facilities for keeping wine. "But when the house was originally built, it was used for storage, or as somewhere to secure misbehaving convict workers, or even to hide from bushrangers."

"If these walls could talk," said Frances.

Her eye was caught by a large flat-screen television hanging from one of the beams at the end of the room. "What's that screen for?" It seemed especially incongruous after Yao's talk of the house's early colonial history. "I thought this was a screen-free environment."

"Tranquillum House is absolutely a screen-free environment," agreed Yao. He glanced at the television screen with a slight frown. "But we recently installed a security and intercom system so we can all communicate with each other from different parts of the resort when necessary. It's quite a large property and the safety of our guests is paramount."

He changed the subject abruptly. "I'm sure you'll be interested in *this*, Frances." He ushered her over to a corner of the room and pointed to a brick almost concealed by the joinery of one of the arched beams. Frances put on her reading glasses and read out loud the small, beautifully inscribed words: *Adam and Roy Webster, stonemasons, 1840.*

"The stonemason brothers," said Yao. "The assumption is that they did this secretly."

"Good for them," said Frances. "They were proud of their work. As they should have been."

They silently contemplated the inscription for a few moments before Yao clapped his hands together. "Let's head back up."

He led her up the stairs into the house and to another glass door featuring just one beautiful word: SPA.

"Last but not least, the spa where you will come for your massages and any other wellness treatments scheduled for you." Yao opened the door and Frances sniffed like Pavlov's dog at the scent of essential oils.

"This was another drawing room that was remodeled," said Yao carefully.

"Ah well, I'm sure you did a good job retaining the original features." Frances patted his arm as she peered inside the dimly lit room. She could hear the trickling sound of a water feature and one of those ridiculous but divine "relaxation" soundtracks—the kind with crashing waves, harp music, and the occasional frog— piped through the walls.

"All spa treatments are complimentary, part of the package—you won't receive a scary bill at the end of your stay!" said Yao as he closed the door.

"I did read that on the website but I wasn't sure if it could be true!" said Frances disingenuously, because if it wasn't true she would be making a complaint to the Department of Fair Trading quick-smart. She made her eyes wide and grateful, as Yao seemed to take personal pride in the wonders of Tranquillum House.

"Well, it *is* true, Frances," said Yao lovingly, like a parent telling her that tomorrow really *was* Christmas Day. "Now we'll just pop in here and get your blood tests and so on out of the way."

"I'm sorry—what?" said Frances, as she was shepherded into a room that looked like a doctor's office. She felt discombobulated. Weren't they just talking about spa treatments?

"Just sit right here," said Yao. "We'll do your blood pressure first."

Frances found herself seated as Yao wrapped a cuff around her arm and pumped it enthusiastically.

"It might be higher than usual," he said. "People feel a little stressed and nervous when they arrive. They're tired after their journey. It's natural. But let me tell you, I've never had a guest finish their retreat without a significant drop in their blood pressure!"

"Mmm," said Frances.

She watched Yao write down her blood pressure. She didn't ask if it was high or low. It was often low. She had been checked out for hypotension before because of her tendency to faint. If she got dehydrated or tired, or saw blood, her vision tunneled and the world tipped.

Yao snapped on a pair of green plastic gloves. Frances looked away and focused on a point on the wall. He buckled a tourniquet around her arm and tapped her forearm.

"Great veins," he said. Nurses often said that about Frances's veins. She always felt momentarily proud and then kind of depressed, because what a waste of a positive attribute.

"I didn't actually realize there would be a blood test," said Frances.

"Daily blood tests," said Yao cheerfully. "Very important because it means we can tweak your treatment plans accordingly."

"Mmm, I might actually opt out of the—"

"Tiny ouch," said Yao.

Frances looked back to her arm, and then quickly away again as she caught sight of a test tube filling with her blood. She hadn't even registered the prick of a needle. She felt all at once as powerless as a child, and was reminded of the few times in her life she'd had to go into hospital for minor surgeries, and how much she disliked the lack of control over her body. Nurses and doctors had the right to prod at her as they pleased, with no love or desire or affection, just expertise. It always took a few days to fully reinhabit her body again.

Did this young man currently helping himself to her blood even have medical expertise? Had she really done her due diligence on this place?

"Are you trained as a . . . ?" She was trying to say, "Do you know what the hell you're doing?"

"I used to be a paramedic in a previous life," replied Yao.

She met his eyes. Was he possibly a little mad? Did he mean he was a reincarnated paramedic? You never knew with these alternative types. "You don't mean, literally, a previous life?"

Yao laughed out loud. A very normal-sounding laugh. "It was about ten years ago now."

"Do you miss it?"

"Absolutely not. I'm passionate about the work we do here." His eyes blazed. Maybe just slightly mad.

"Right, that's that," said Yao, removing the needle and handing her a cottonwool ball. "Press firmly." He labeled her test tube and smiled at her. "Excellent. Now, we'll just check your weight."

"Oh, is that really necessary? I'm not here for weight loss; I'm here for, you know . . . personal transformation."

"Just for our files," said Yao. He removed the cotton-wool ball, pressed a circular Band-Aid onto the tiny red pinprick, and indicated a scale. "On you hop."

Frances averted her eyes from the number. She had no idea of her weight and no interest in learning it. She knew she could be thinner, and of course when she was younger she was indeed much thinner, but she was generally happy with her body as long as it wasn't giving her pain, and bored by all the different ways women droned on about the subject of weight, as if it were one of the great mysteries of life. The recent weight-losers, evangelical about whatever method had worked for them, the thin women who called themselves fat, the average women who called themselves obese, the ones desperate for her to join in their lavish self-loathing. "Oh, Frances, isn't it just so *depressing* when you see

young, thin girls like that!" "Not especially," Frances
would say, adding extra butter to her bread roll.

Yao wrote something on a form in a cream-colored
file marked in black marker block letters with her
name, FRANCES WELTY.

This was starting to feel too much like a visit to the
doctor. Frances felt exposed and vulnerable and regret-
ful. She wanted to go home. She wanted a muffin.

"I'd really like to get to my room now," she said. "It
was a long drive."

"Absolutely. I'm going to book you into the spa for
an urgent massage for that back pain," said Yao. "Shall
I give you half an hour to settle into your room, enjoy your welcome smoothie, and read your welcome
pack?"

"That sounds like heaven," said Frances.

They walked back past the dining room, where her
darling drug dealers, Jessica and Ben, stood with their
own white-uniformed wellness consultant, a dark-
haired young woman who, according to her name
badge, was called Delilah. Delilah was delivering the
same spiel as Yao about the warning bells.

Jessica's plastic face was filled with worry, so much
so that she was almost, but not quite, pulling off a
frown. "But what if you don't hear the bell?"

"Then off with your head!" said Frances.

Everyone turned to look at her. Ben, whose cap was
now the wrong way around again, raised a single eyebrow.

"Joke," said Frances weakly.

Frances saw the two wellness consultants exchange

looks she couldn't quite read. She wondered if they were sleeping together. They'd have such aerobic, flexible sex with all that wellness pumping through their young bodies. It would be just so *awesome*.

Yao led her back toward the *Titanic* stairs. As Frances hurried to keep pace, they passed a man and two women coming down the staircase together, all three in olive-green robes featuring the Tranquillum House emblem.

The man lagged behind to put on glasses so he could closely examine the wall on the landing. He was so tall the dressing gown was more like a miniskirt, revealing knobbly knees and very white, very hairy legs. They were the sort of male legs that made you feel uncomfortable, as if you were looking at a private part of the body.

"Well, my point is that you just don't see craftsmanship like this anymore!" he said, as he peered at the wall. "That's what I just love about houses like this: the attention to detail. I mean, think of those tiles I was showing you earlier. What's extraordinary is that somebody took the time to *individually*—hello again, Yao! Another guest, is it? How are you?"

He took off his glasses, beamed at Frances, and thrust out his hand. "Napoleon!" he cried.

It took her a terrifying second to realize he was introducing himself, not just yelling out a random historical figure's name.

"Frances," she said in the nick of time.

"Nice to meet you! Here for the ten-day retreat, I assume?"

He was on the stair above her, so his height was even more pronounced. It was like tipping her head back to look at a monument.

"I am." Frances made a tremendous effort not to comment on his height, as she knew from her six-foot friend Jen that tall people were well aware they were tall. "I most certainly am."

Napoleon indicated the two women farther down the stairs. "Us too! These are my beautiful girls, my wife, Heather, and daughter, Zoe."

The two women were also notably tall. They were a basketball team. They gave her the restrained, polite smiles of a celebrity's family members who are used to having to wait while he is accosted by fans, except that in this case it was Napoleon doing the accosting. The wife, *Heather*, bounced on the balls of her feet. She was wiry, with extremely wrinkled, tanned skin, as if she'd been scrunched up and then spread smooth. *Heather skin like leather*, thought Frances. That was a really mean mnemonic but Heather would never know. Heather had gray hair pulled back in a tight ponytail and bloodshot eyes. She seemed very intense, which was fine. Frances had some intense friends; she knew how to cope with intensity. (Never try to match it.)

The daughter, *Zoe*, had her dad's height and the casual grace of an athletic, outdoorsy girl. Showy Zoe? But she wasn't showy at all. *Not-showy Zoe*. Zoe certainly didn't look like she was in need of a health resort. How much more rejuvenated could you get?

Frances thought about the young couple, Ben and Jessica, who also seemed in sparkling good health.

Were health resorts only attended by the already healthy? Was she going to be the least healthy-looking person here? She'd never been bottom of the class, except for that one time in Transcendental Meditation for Beginners.

"We thought we'd explore the hot springs, maybe have a quick soak," said Napoleon to Yao and Frances, as if they'd asked. "Then we'll do a few laps of the pool."

Clearly, they were one of those active families who threw their bags down on the floor and left their hotel room the moment they checked in.

"I'm planning a quick nap before an urgent massage," said Frances.

"Excellent idea!" cried Napoleon. "A nap and a massage! Sounds perfect! Isn't this place *amazing*? And I hear the hot springs are incredible." He was an extremely enthusiastic man.

"Make sure you rehydrate after the hot springs," Yao said to him. "There are water bottles at reception."

"Will do, Yao! And then we'll be back in time for the noble silence!"

"Noble silence?" said Frances.

"It will all become clear, Frances," said Yao.

"It's in your information pack, Frances!" said Napoleon. "Bit of a surprise; I wasn't expecting the 'silence' aspect. I've heard of silent retreats, of course, but must admit they didn't appeal—I'm a talker myself, as my girls here will tell you. But we'll roll with the punches, go with the flow!"

As he talked on in the comforting way of the

chronically loquacious, Frances watched his wife and daughter farther down the stairs. The daughter, who wore black flip-flops, put one heel on the step above her and leaned forward as if she were discreetly stretching her hamstring. The mother watched her daughter, and Frances saw the ghost of a smile, followed almost immediately by an expression of pure despair that dragged all her features down, as if she were clawing at her cheeks. Then in the next instant it was gone and she smiled benignly up at Frances, and Frances felt as though she had seen something she shouldn't have.

Napoleon said, "It wasn't you who arrived in that Lamborghini, was it, Frances? I saw it from our room. That's one hell of a car."

"Not me—I'm the Peugeot," said Frances.

"Nothing wrong with the Peugeot! Although I hear those jackals charge like wounded bulls when it comes to servicing, right?"

He mixed his metaphors most delightfully. Frances was keen to talk more with him. He was someone who would answer any question with candor and vigor. She loved those sorts of people.

"Dad," said his daughter. Not-showy Zoe. "Let the lady pass. She's only just got here. She probably wants to get to her room."

"Sorry, sorry, I'll see you at dinner! Although we won't be chatting then, will we?" He tapped the side of his nose and grinned, but there was a trapped, panicky look in his eyes. "Lovely to meet you!" He clapped Yao on the shoulder. "See you later, Yao, mate!"

Frances followed Yao up the stairs. At the top, he turned right and led her down a carpeted hallway lined with historical photos that she planned to study later.

"This wing of the house was added in 1895," said Yao. "You'll find all the rooms have original fireplaces with marble mantelpieces of Georgian design. Not that you'll be lighting any fires in this heat."

"I didn't expect to see families doing this retreat," commented Frances. "I must admit I thought there'd be more . . . people like me."

Fatter people than me, Yao. Much fatter.

"We get people from all walks of life here at Tranquillum House," said Yao as he unlocked her room with a large old-fashioned metal key.

"Probably not *all* walks of life," mused Frances, because come on now, the place wasn't cheap, but she stopped talking as Yao held open the door for her.

"Here we are."

It was a large, airy, plush-carpeted room filled with period furniture, including an enormous four-poster bed. Open French doors led to a balcony with a view that stretched to the horizon: a rolling patchwork quilt of vineyards and farmhouses and green-and-gold countryside. Flocks of birds wheeled across the sky. Her bag sat like an old familiar friend in a corner of the room. There was a fruit basket on the coffee table, along with a glass of green sludgelike smoothie with a strawberry on the side. Everything except the smoothie looked extremely appealing.

"That's your welcome smoothie there," said Yao.

"There are six organic smoothies a day, prepared specifically for your changing individual needs."

"They're not wheatgrass, are they? I once had a wheatgrass shot and it scarred me for life."

Yao picked up the glass and handed it to her. "Trust me, it's tasty!"

Frances looked at it doubtfully.

"The smoothies *are* mandatory," said Yao kindly. It was confusing because you'd think from his tone that he'd said, "They *are* optional."

She took a sip. "Oh!" she said, surprised. She could taste mango, coconut, and berries. It was like drinking a tropical holiday. "It's quite good. Very good."

"Yes, Frances," said Yao. He used her name as often as a desperate real estate agent. "And the good news is it's not only delicious but brimming with natural goodness! Please make sure you drink the entire glass."

"I will," said Frances agreeably.

There was an awkward pause.

"Oh," said Frances. "You mean now?" She took another, larger sip. "Yum!"

Yao smiled. "The daily smoothies are crucial for your wellness journey."

"Gosh, well, I want to keep my wellness journey on track."

"Absolutely you do," said Yao.

She met his eyes. There was no irony as far back as she could see. He was going to shame that snark right out of her.

"I'm going to leave you to relax," said Yao. "Your

welcome pack is right here. Please take the time to read it because there are important instructions for the next twenty-four hours. The noble silence that Napoleon mentioned will be beginning shortly, and I know you're going to find that so beneficial. Oh, now, speaking of silence, Frances, I'm sure you can guess what I need next from you!" He looked at her expectantly.

"No idea. Not more blood, I hope?"

"It's time to hand over all your electronic devices," said Yao. "Mobile phone, tablets, everything."

"No problem." Frances retrieved her phone from her handbag, switched it off, and handed it to Yao. A not unpleasant feeling of subservience crept over her. It was like being on an airplane once the seatbelt sign was turned on and the flight attendants were now in charge of your entire existence.

"Great. Thanks. You're officially 'off the grid!'" Yao held up her phone. "We'll keep it safe. Some guests say the digital detox is one of the most enjoyable elements of their time with us. When it's time to leave, you'll be saying, 'Don't give it back! I don't want it back!'" He held up his hands to indicate someone waving him away.

Frances tried to imagine herself in ten days and found it strangely difficult, as if it wasn't ten days but ten years she was imagining. Would she really be transformed? Thinner, lighter, pain-free, able to leap from her bed at sunrise without caffeine?

"Don't forget your massage at the spa," said Yao. "Oh—and that nasty paper cut!"

He walked to a sideboard, selected a tube from an array of Tranquillum House–branded cosmetics, and said, "Let's see that thumb."

Frances presented it to him and he placed a dab of soothing cool gel on her paper cut with tender care.

"Your wellness journey has begun, Frances," he said, still holding her hand, and instead of smirking Frances found herself close to tears.

"I've actually been feeling *very* unwell lately, Yao," she said pitifully.

"I know you have." Yao put both his hands on her shoulders and it didn't feel silly or sexual; it felt healing. "We're going to get you well, Frances. We're going to get you feeling as well as you've ever felt in your life." He closed the door gently behind him as he left.

Frances turned in a slow circle and waited for that inevitable moment of solitary traveler gloom, but instead her spirits lifted. She wasn't alone. She had Yao to take care of her. She was on a wellness *journey*.

She walked out onto her balcony to admire the view and gasped. A man on the balcony next to hers was leaning so far over it he looked in danger of falling.

"Careful!" she warned, but only under her breath so as not to startle him.

The man turned in her direction, lifted his hand, and smiled. It was Ben. She recognized the baseball cap. She waved back.

If they raised their voices they could probably hear each other perfectly well, but it was better to pretend they were too far away to chat, otherwise they'd feel obligated to talk every time they happened to see each other on their balconies, and there was going to be enough obligatory chatting at every meal.

She looked in the other direction and saw a row of identical balconies stretching to the end of the house. All the guest rooms shared this same view. The other balconies were empty, although as Frances watched, the figure of a woman emerged from the room at the farthest end of the house. She was too far away to distinguish her features, but Frances, keen to be friendly, gave her a wave. The woman instantly spun around and went back inside her room.

Oh, well, perhaps she hadn't seen Frances. Or perhaps she suffered from tremendous social anxiety. Frances could handle the dreadfully shy. You just needed to approach slowly, as if they were little woodland creatures.

Frances turned back to Ben, and saw that he'd also gone back inside. She wondered if he and Jessica were still arguing. Their rooms were adjoining, so if things got heated Frances might overhear. Once, on a book tour, she'd stayed in a thin-walled hotel where she had the pleasure of overhearing a couple argue passionately and descriptively about their sex life. That had been great.

"I don't get the obsession with strangers," her first husband, Sol, once said to her, and Frances had struggled to explain that strangers were by definition interesting. It was their *strangeness*. The not-knowing. Once you knew everything there was to know about someone, you were generally ready to divorce them.

She went back inside her room to unpack. It might be

nice to have a cup of tea and a few squares of chocolate while she read her information pack. She was sure it was going to have rules she would prefer not to follow; the noble silence that was beginning shortly sounded foreboding and she would need sugar to cope. Also, she hadn't exactly followed the suggestion about reducing her sugar and caffeine intake in the days leading up to the retreat so as to avoid withdrawal symptoms. Frances couldn't be dealing with a headache right now.

She went to pull out her contraband from where she'd carefully hidden it right at the bottom of her bag, underneath her underwear, wrapped in her nightie. She'd laughed at herself for hiding it; it wasn't like they were going to be checking her bag. This wasn't rehab or boarding school.

"You've got to be kidding," she said out loud.

It wasn't there.

She emptied all her clothes onto her bed with a growing sense of fury. They wouldn't, would they? It was unconscionable. Illegal, surely.

It was *very* bad manners!

She turned the bag upside down and shook it. The nightie was still there, neatly folded by invisible hands, but the coffee, tea, chocolate, and wine were most definitely gone. Who had been through her bag? It couldn't be Yao; he'd been with her the whole time from when she arrived. Someone else had rifled through her underwear and confiscated her treats.

What could she do? She couldn't ring reception and say, "Somebody took my chocolate and wine!" Well, she could, but she didn't have the requisite chutzpah.

The website made it clear that snacks and coffee and alcohol were all banned. She'd broken the rules and she'd been caught.

She would say nothing and they would say nothing and on the last day they would hand it all back to her with a knowing smirk as she checked out, like returning a prisoner's personal effects.

This was *deeply* embarrassing.

She sat on the end of her bed and looked dolefully at the lovely fruit bowl. She laughed a little, trying to turn it into a funny story her friends would enjoy, and selected a mandarin from the bowl. As she plunged her thumb into its fleshy center, she heard something. A voice? It didn't come from Ben and Jessica's room. It was the other room adjoining hers. There was a thud, followed immediately by the unmistakable sound of something breaking.

A male voice swore, loudly and forcefully. "Fuck it!"

Indeed, thought Frances, as the malevolent beginnings of a headache crept slowly across her forehead.

7

Jessica

Jessica sat on the four-poster bed and tested the mattress with the palm of her hand while Ben stood on the balcony, one hand shielding his eyes. He wasn't enjoying the beautiful view.

"I'm sure they haven't stolen it," she said. She meant to sound funny and lighthearted but she couldn't seem to get the tone of her voice to come out right these days. A hardness kept creeping in.

"Yeah, but *where* have they parked it?" said Ben. "That's what I don't get. I'd just like to know where it is. Have they got an underground bunker somewhere? Did you notice that when I asked if it was parked under cover, she sort of avoided answering the question?"

"Mmm," said Jessica noncommittally.

She couldn't bear another fight about the car, or about anything. Her stomach was still recovering from the last screaming match. Whenever they fought she got instant indigestion, and that meant that these days she nearly always had indigestion. Their arguments were like submerged rocks they kept crashing up against. They couldn't be avoided. *Wham. Wham. Wham.*

She lay back on the bed and looked at the light fixture. Was that a spiderweb near the globe? This house was so old and dark and depressing. She'd been aware it was going to be a "historic" house, but she thought they might have, you know, *renovated*. There were cracks all over the walls, and a kind of damp smell.

She turned on her side and looked at Ben. Now he was leaning dangerously over the balcony railing, trying to see the other side of the house. He cared about that car more than he cared about her. Once, she saw him running his hand along the hood and for just a moment she'd felt *envious of the car*, of the way Ben was touching it so gently and sensuously, the same way he used to touch her. She was going to tell their counselor that. She'd written it down so she wouldn't forget. She felt like it was a really profound, powerful thing to mention, quite significant and *telling*. It made her eyes prickle with tears when she thought of it. If the counselor ever wrote a book about her experience as a marriage counselor she would probably mention it: *I once had a patient who treated his car more tenderly than he treated his wife.* (No need to mention the car was a Lamborghini, otherwise all the male readers would say, "Oh, well, then.")

She wished the "intensive couples counseling" part of this retreat would hurry up and start, but "Delilah," their "wellness consultant," had been annoyingly vague about when it would begin. She wondered if the counselor would ask them about their sex life, and if she (Jessica assumed she would be a *she*) would be able to hide her surprise when she heard they were down to having sex, like, *once a week*, which meant their marriage was officially in dire trouble.

Jessica didn't know if she could talk about sex in front of the counselor anyway. The counselor might automatically assume that she was sexually unskilled or that there was something wrong with her, in a very personal, gynecological kind of way. Jessica was beginning to wonder that herself.

She was obviously prepared to get more surgery (even down there) or do a course. Read a book. Improve her skills. She'd always been prepared to improve, to listen to the advice of experts. She read a lot of self-help books. She Googled. Ben had never read a self-help book in his life.

Ben came back inside from the balcony, lifting up his T-shirt to scratch his stomach. He didn't bother with crunches or planks and his stomach still looked that good.

"That author we met is in the room next to us," he said. He picked up an apple from the fruit bowl and tossed it from hand to hand like a baseball. "Frances. Why do you reckon she's here?"

"I expect she wants to lose weight," said Jessica. Like, duh. She thought it was kind of obvious. Frances had that *padded* look middle-aged women got. Jessica herself would never allow that to happen. She'd rather be dead.

"You reckon?" said Ben. "What does it matter at

her age?" He didn't wait for an answer. "What are her books like?"

"I used to love them," said Jessica. "I read them all. There was one called *Nathaniel's Kiss*. I read it in high school and it was just really . . . romantic, I guess."

"Romantic" was too ineffectual a word to describe the feelings *Nathaniel's Kiss* had provoked in her. She remembered how she'd cried big heaving shuddering sobs, and then she'd kept rereading that last chapter for the pleasure of more crying. In some ways, it felt like Nathaniel was the first man she ever loved.

She couldn't tell Ben that. He never read fiction. He wouldn't understand.

But was that one of the problems in their marriage? That she didn't even bother to try to communicate how she felt about things that were important to her? Or did it not matter? She didn't need to hear him talk about his passion for his car. He could talk about his car with his mates. She could talk about her memories of *Nathaniel's Kiss* with her girlfriends.

Ben took a giant bite of the apple. Jessica couldn't do that anymore, not with her new capped teeth. The dentist wanted her to wear some sort of a mouth guard at night to keep her expensive crowns all safe. It was annoying that the better stuff you got, the less relaxed you could be about it. It was like the new rug in their hallway. Neither of them could bear to walk on something so astoundingly expensive. They shuffled down the sides and winced when their guests marched straight down the middle in dirty sneakers.

"That smoothie was pretty good," said Ben, his mouth full of apple. "But I'm starved. I don't know if my body can cope without pizza for ten days. I don't see why we even have to do that part! What's that got to do with marriage counseling?"

"I *told* you," said Jessica. "It's, like, a holistic approach. We have to work on everything: our minds, bodies, and spirits."

"Sounds like a load of—" He cut himself off and walked over to the row of light switches by the wall and started playing with the one that made the ceiling fan work.

He put the fan on to cyclonic speed.

Jessica put a pillow over her face and tried to go for as long as she could without saying, "Turn it off." Once, she wouldn't have thought about this. She would have just yelled, "Oh my God, turn it off, you idiot!" and he would have laughed and kept it on, and she would have tried to turn it off, and he wouldn't have let her, and they would have pretend-wrestled.

Did they laugh more before?

Back when she was working in admin and he was an auto-body mechanic working for Pete, back when Ben drove a V8 Commodore that didn't make anyone look twice, and she had B-cup boobs that didn't make anyone look twice either, back when they thought going to a movie and the local Thai restaurant on the same night was *splurging* and when the arrival of the credit card statement each month was, like, really stressful and even once made her cry?

She didn't want to believe it was better before. If it

was, then her mother was right, and she couldn't stand it if her mother was right.

Ben turned the fan down to a gentler breeze. Jessica removed the pillow from her face, closed her eyes, and felt her heart race with fear of something unnamed and unknown.

It made her think of the vertiginous fear she'd felt the day of the robbery. It was two years ago now that she'd come home from work to discover their ground-floor apartment had been robbed, their possessions strewn everywhere with aggressive, malicious abandon, every drawer open, a black footprint across her white T-shirt, the glint of broken glass.

Ben arrived home just moments later. "What the hell?"

She didn't know if he immediately thought of his sister, but she did.

Ben's sister, Lucy, had "mental health issues." That was the euphemism Ben's lovely, long-suffering mother used. The truth was that Ben's sister was an addict.

Lucy's life was an endless roller coaster and they all had to take the same ride, over and over, without getting off. Lucy was missing. No one had heard from her. Lucy had turned up in the middle of the night and trashed the house. Ben's mum had to call the police. They were planning an intervention! But they were going to handle this intervention differently from the last intervention; this time it would work. Lucy was doing well! Lucy was talking about rehab. Lucy was *in* rehab! Lucy was out of rehab. Lucy had been in another car accident. Lucy was pregnant again. Lucy was fucked up and there would never be an end to it, and because Jessica had never known the Lucy of before, the Lucy who was supposedly funny and smart and kind, it was hard not to hate her.

Lucy was the reason for the underlying tension at every event with Ben's family. Would she turn up demanding money or screaming insults or crying crocodile tears because "she just wanted to be a mum" to the two children she was incapable of bringing up?

Everyone knew Lucy stole. You went to a barbecue at Ben's place and you hid your cash. So it was perfectly natural that Jessica's first thought when she walked into the apartment that day was: *Lucy.*

She'd tried so hard not to say it but she couldn't help it. Just that one word. She wished she could take it back. She hadn't made it sound enough like a question. She'd made it sound like a statement. She wished she'd at least said, "Lucy?"

She remembered how Ben shook his head. His face was drawn tight with shame.

She had thought, *How do you know it wasn't her?*

But it turned out he was right. The robbery had nothing to do with Lucy. She was on the other side of the country at the time.

So it was just an ordinary happens-to-lots-of-people house robbery. They hadn't lost much because they didn't have much to lose: an old iPad with a cracked screen, a necklace that Ben had given Jessica for her twenty-first. It had a tiny diamond pendant and it had cost Ben something like two months' salary. She'd loved that necklace and still mourned it, even though it had just been a crappy little necklace with a smidge of a diamond, like a *quarter* carat. The thieves had rejected the rest of Jessica's jewelry box, which she found humiliating. Jessica and Ben had both hated the feeling of knowing that someone had walked through their home, sneering, as if browsing through an unsatisfactory shop.

The insurance company paid out without much fuss, but that wasn't the point.

It was just an ordinary robbery, except that it ended up changing their lives forever.

"Why are you staring at me like that?" asked Ben. He stood at the end of the bed, looking down at her.

Jessica's gaze came back into focus. "Like what?"

"Like you're planning to cut off my balls with a cheese knife."

"What? I wasn't even looking at you. I was *thinking*."

He kept chewing the remains of his apple and raised an eyebrow. The very first time they ever made eye contact in Mr. Munro's maths class he did that: a cool, laconic lift of his left eyebrow. It was *literally* the *hottest* thing she'd seen in her entire life and maybe if he'd raised two eyebrows, instead of one, she wouldn't have fallen in love with him.

"I don't even have a cheese knife," said Jessica.

He smiled as he threw the apple core into the bin from across the room and picked up their welcome pack.

"We'd better read this, hey?" He ripped open the envelope and papers went flying. Jessica managed to

stop herself from grabbing at it and putting it all back
in order. She was the one in charge of paperwork. If it
were up to Ben they would never file a tax return.

He opened what looked like a cover letter. "Okay, so
this is a 'guide map' for our 'wellness journey.'"

"Ben," said Jessica, "this isn't going to work if we
don't—"

"I know, I know, I am taking it seriously. I drove
down that road, didn't I? Didn't that show my commitment?"

"Oh, *please* don't start on the car again." She felt
like crying.

"I only meant—" His mouth twisted. "Forget it."

He scanned the letter and read out loud. "*Welcome
to your wellness journey*, yada, yada. *The retreat will
begin with a period of silence lasting five days, during
which there will be no talking, apart from counseling
sessions, no touching, no reading, no writing, no eye
contact with other guests or your own companions—*
what the?"

"This wasn't mentioned on the website," said Jessica.

Ben continued to read out loud, "*You may be familiar with the term 'monkey brain.'*"

He looked up at Jessica. She shrugged, so he kept
reading. "*Monkey brain refers to the way your mind
swings from thought to thought like a monkey swinging from branch to branch.*" Ben made a sound like a
monkey and scratched under his arm to demonstrate.

"Thanks for that." Jessica felt the tug of a smile.
Sometimes they were fine.

Ben read on. "*It takes at least twenty-four hours to*

silence monkey brain. A period of nourishing silence and reflection settles the mind, body, and soul. Our aim will be to discover a beautiful state that Buddhism calls 'noble silence.'"

"So we're just going to spend the next five days avoiding eye contact and not talking?" said Jessica. "Even when we're alone in our room?"

"It's not like we don't have any experience with that," said Ben.

"Very funny," said Jessica. "Give me that."

She took the letter and read. *"During the silence we request that you walk slowly and mindfully, with intention, heel-to-toe, about the property, while avoiding eye contact and conversation. If you must communicate with a staff member, please come to reception and follow the instructions on the laminated blue card. There will be guided meditation sessions—both walking and sitting—throughout each day. Please listen for the bells."*

She put the letter down. "This is going to be so freaky. We'll have to eat with strangers in total silence."

"Better than boring small talk, I guess," said Ben. He looked at her. "Do you want to do it properly? We could talk here in our room and nobody would ever know."

Jessica thought about it.

"I think we should do it properly," she said. "Don't you? Even if it sounds stupid, we should just follow the rules and do whatever they say."

"Fine with me," said Ben. "As long as they don't tell me to jump off a cliff." He scratched his neck. "I don't get what we're going to *do* here."

"I told you," said Jessica. "Meditate. Yoga. Exercise classes."

"Yeah," said Ben. "But in between all that. If we can't talk or watch TV, what will we do?"

"It will be hard without screens," said Jessica. She thought she was going to miss social media more than coffee.

She looked again at the letter. "*The silence begins when the bell rings three times.*" She looked at the clock in the room. "We've got half an hour left where we're allowed to talk."

Or *touch*, she thought.

They looked at each other.

Neither spoke.

"So the silence shouldn't be too hard for us then," said Ben.

Jessica laughed, but Ben didn't smile.

Why weren't they having sex right now? Wasn't that what they once would have done? Without even talking about it?

She should say something. Do something. He was her husband. She could touch him.

But a tiny fear had trickled into her head late last year and now she couldn't get rid of it. It was something about the way he looked at her, or didn't look at her; a clenching of his jaw.

The thought was this: *He doesn't love me anymore.*

It seemed so ironic that he could fall out of love with her now, when she had never looked so good. Over the last year she had invested a lot of time and money, and a fair amount of pain, in her body. She had done *everything* there was to do: her teeth, her hair, her skin, her lips, her boobs. Everyone said the results were amazing. Her Instagram account was filled with comments like: *You look so HOT, Jessica!* and *You look better and better every time I see you.* The only person without anything positive to say was her own husband, and if he didn't find her attractive now, when she was her very best self, then he must never have found her attractive. He must have been faking it all along. Why did he even marry her?

Touch me, she thought, and in her head it was an anguished wail. *Please, please touch me.*

But all he did was stand up and walk back over to the fruit bowl. "The mandarins look good."

8

Frances

"When did the pain start?"

Frances lay naked on a massage table, a soft white towel draped over her back.

"Everything off and then under this towel," the massage therapist had barked when Frances arrived at the spa. She was a large woman with a gray buzz cut and the intimidating manner of a prison guard or a hockey coach, not quite the soft-voiced, gentle masseuse Frances had been anticipating. Frances hadn't quite caught her name but she'd been too distracted following instructions to ask her to repeat it.

"About three weeks ago," said Frances.

The therapist placed warm hands which seemed to be the size of ping-pong paddles on her back. Was that possible? Frances lifted her head to see them but the therapist pressed against Frances's shoulder blades so her head fell forward again.

"Did anything in particular set it off?"

"Not anything physical," said Frances. "But I did

have kind of an emotional shock. I was in this relationship—"

"So no physical injury of any sort," said the therapist
tersely. Clearly she hadn't got the Tranquillum House
memo about speaking in a slow, hypnotic voice. In fact,
she was the opposite: it was like she wanted to get any
speaking over and done with as quickly as possible.

"No," said Frances. "But I feel like it was definitely
connected. I had a shock, you see, because this man I
was dating, well, he disappeared and—I remember this
very clearly—I was actually phoning the police when
I felt this kind of sensation, like I'd been *slammed*—"

"It's probably better if you don't talk," said the therapist.

"Oh. Is it?" said Frances. *I was about to tell you a
very interesting story, scary lady.* She'd told the story
a few times now, and she felt that she told it quite well.
She was improving it with each telling.

Also, she didn't have long before she had to stop
talking for *five days*, and she wasn't sure how she was
going to cope with so much silence. She'd only just
avoided that terrifying abyss of despair in the car. Silence might tip her over again.

The therapist pressed her giant thumbs on either side
of Frances's spine.

"*Ow!*"

"Focus on your breathing."

Frances breathed in the citrus-scented essential oils
and thought about Paul. How it began. How it ended.

Paul Drabble was an American civil engineer she met
online. A friend of a friend of a friend. A friendship that

turned into something more. Over a six-month period, he sent her flowers and gift baskets and handwritten notes. They talked for hours on the phone. He'd FaceTimed with her and said he'd read three of her books and loved them, and he talked expertly about the characters and even quoted his favorite excerpts, and they were all excerpts that made Frances feel secretly proud. (Sometimes people quoted their favorite lines to her and Frances thought, *Really? I thought that wasn't my best.* And then she felt weirdly annoyed with them.)

He sent her photos of his son, Ari. Frances, who'd never wanted children of her own, fell hard for Ari. He was tall for his age. He loved basketball and wanted to play it professionally. She was going to be Ari's stepmother. She'd read the book *Raising Boys* in preparation and had a number of brief but pleasurable chats with Ari on the phone. He didn't say much, understandably—he was a twelve-year-old boy, after all—but sometimes she made him laugh when they Skyped, and he had a dry little chuckle that melted her heart. Ari's mother—Paul's wife—had died of cancer when Ari was in preschool. So sad, so poignant, so . . . "convenient?" suggested one of Frances's friends, and Frances had slapped her wrist.

Frances was planning to move from Sydney to Santa Barbara. She had her flights booked. They would need to get married to secure her green card, but she wasn't going to rush into things. If and when it happened, she planned to wear amethyst. Appropriate for a third wedding. Paul had sent her photos of the room in his house that he'd already set up as her writing room. There were empty bookshelves waiting for her books.

When that terrible phone call came in the middle of the night, Paul so distraught he could barely get the words out, crying as he told her that Ari had been in a terrible car accident and there was a problem with the health insurance company and that Ari needed immediate surgery, Frances didn't hesitate. She sent him money. A vast amount of money.

"Sorry, *how* much?" said the young detective who carefully wrote down everything Frances said, his professionalism slipping for just a moment.

That was Paul's only misstep: he underplayed his hand. She would have sent double, triple, quadruple—anything to save Ari.

And then: terrifying silence. She was frantic. She thought Ari must have died. Then she thought Paul had died. No answers to her texts, her voicemail messages, her emails. It was her friend Di who made the first tentative suggestion. "Don't take this the wrong way, Frances, but is it possible that . . . ?" Di didn't even need to finish the sentence. It was as if the knowledge had been lurking away in Frances's subconscious all along, even while she booked nonrefundable airfares.

It felt personal but it wasn't personal. It was just business. "These people are getting so smart," the detective had said. "They're professional and polished and they target women of your age and circumstances." The sympathy on his handsome young face was excruciating. He saw a desperate old lady.

She wanted to say, "No, no, I'm not a woman of age

and circumstance! I'm me! You're not seeing *me*!" She
wanted to tell him that she had never had any trouble meeting men, she had been *pursued* by men all
her life, men who truly loved her and men who only
wanted to have sex with her, but they were all real men,
who wanted her for herself, not con artists who wanted
her money. She wanted to tell him that she'd been told
on multiple occasions by multiple sources that she was
really very good in bed, and her second serve caused
consternation on the tennis court, and, although she
never cooked, she could bake an excellent lemon me-
ringue pie. She wanted to tell him she was *real*.

The shame she experienced was extraordinary. She
had revealed so much of herself to this scammer. How he
must have sniggered, even as he somehow responded
with sensitivity, humor, and perfect spelling. He was a
mirage, a narcissistic reflection of herself, saying exactly what she so obviously wanted to hear. She realized weeks after that even his name, "Paul Drabble,"
was probably designed to begin the act of seduction by
subconsciously reminding her of Margaret Drabble,
one of her favorite authors, as she had posted for all to
see on social media.

It turned out many other women had been planning
lives as Ari's stepmother too.

"There are multiple ladies in the same situation as
you," the detective said.

Ladies. Oh my God, ladies. She couldn't believe she
was a lady. That sexless, gentrified word made Frances
shudder.

The details of each scam were different but the

boy's name was always "Ari" and he always had a "car accident" and the distraught phone call always came in the middle of the night. "Paul Drabble" had multiple names, each with a carefully curated online presence, so that when the *ladies* Googled their suitors—as they always did—they saw exactly what they wanted to see. Of course, he was not the friend of a friend of a friend. Or not in the real-world way. He'd played a long game, setting up a fake Facebook page and pretending an interest in antique restoration furniture, which had gotten him accepted into a Facebook group run by a university friend's husband. By the time he sent Frances a friend request, she'd seen enough of his (intelligent, witty, concise) comments on her friend's posts to believe him to be a real person in her extended circle.

Frances met up with one of the other women for coffee. The woman showed Frances pictures on her phone of the bedroom she'd created for Ari, complete with *Star Wars* posters on the wall. The posters were actually a little young for Ari—he wasn't into *Star Wars*—but Frances kept that to herself.

The woman was in a far worse state than Frances. Frances ended up writing her a check to help her get back on her feet. Frances's friends spluttered when they heard this. Yes, she gave more cash to yet another stranger, but for Frances it was a way of restoring her pride, taking back control, and fixing some of the trail of destruction left by that man. (She did think a thank you card from her fellow scam victim might have been nice, but one mustn't give only in expectation of thank you cards.)

After it was all over, Frances packed away the evidence of her stupidity in a file. All the printouts of emails where she'd spilled her foolish heart. The cards that accompanied real flowers with fake sentiments. The handwritten letters. She went to shove the folder into her filing cabinet and a sheet of paper sliced open her thumb like the edge of a razor blade. Such a tiny trite injury and yet it hurt so much.

The therapist's thumbs moved in small hard circles. A liquid warmth radiated across Frances's lower back. She looked through the hole in the massage table at the floor. She could see the therapist's sneakered feet. Someone had used a Sharpie to doodle flowers all over the white plastic toes of her shoes.

"I fell for an internet romance scam," said Frances. She needed to talk. The therapist would just have to listen. "I lost a lot of money."

The therapist said nothing, but at least she didn't order Frances to stop talking again. Her hands kept moving.

"I didn't care so much about the money—well, I *did*, I'd worked hard for that money—but some people lose everything in these kinds of scams whereas I just lost . . . my self-respect, I guess, and . . . my innocence."

She was babbling now, but she couldn't seem to stop. All she could hear was the therapist's steady breathing.

"I guess I've always just assumed that people are who they say they are, and that ninety-nine percent of people are good people. I've lived in a bubble. Never been robbed. Never been mugged. Nobody has ever laid a hand on me."

That wasn't strictly true. Her second husband hit her once. He cried. She didn't. They both knew the marriage was over in that moment. Poor Henry. He was a good man, but they brought out something terrible in each other, like allergic reactions.

Her mind wandered off down the road of her long and complicated relationship history. She'd shared her relationship history with "Paul Drabble" and he'd shared his. His had sounded so real. It must have had some truth to it? So says the novelist who makes up relationships for a living. *Of course he could have fabricated his relationship history, you idiot.*

She kept talking. Better to talk than to think.

"I honestly thought I was more in love with this man than any other man I'd met in the real world. I was quite deluded. But then again, love is just a trick of the mind, isn't it?"

Just shut up, Frances, she's not interested.

"Anyway, it was all very . . ." Her voice trailed off. "Embarrassing."

The therapist was completely silent now. Frances couldn't even hear her breathing. It was like being massaged by a giant-handed ghost. Frances wondered if she was thinking, *I'd never fall for something like that.*

The sharpest knifepoint of her humiliation was this: before, if Frances had been asked to pick the sort of person likely to fall for an internet scam, she would have picked someone like *this* woman, with her bulky body, buzz cut, and questionable social skills. Not Frances.

Frances said, "I'm sorry, I missed your name before."

"Jan."

"Do you mind me asking, Jan, are you married . . . in a relationship?"

"Divorced."

"Me too," said Frances. "Twice."

"But I've just started seeing someone," offered Jan, as if she couldn't help herself.

"Oh. Great!" Frances's mood lifted. Was there anything better than a new relationship? Her whole career was based on the wonder of new relationships. "How did you meet?" she asked.

"He breath-tested me," said Jan, with a laugh in her voice.

The laugh told Frances everything she needed to know. *Jan was newly in love.* Frances's eyes filled with happy tears for her. Romance would never be dead for Frances. Never.

"So . . . he's a policeman?"

"He's a new cop in Jarribong," said Jan. "He was bored sitting on the side of the road doing random breathalyzers, and we got chatting while he waited for another car to come along. It took two hours."

Frances tried to imagine Jan chatting for two hours.

"What's his name?" asked Frances.

"Gus," said Jan.

Frances waited, giving Jan the opportunity to wax lyrical about her new boyfriend. She tried to imagine him for herself. Gus. A local country cop. Broad-shouldered, with a heart of gold. Gus probably owned a dog. A lovable dog. Gus probably whittled. He probably had a tuneful whistle. He probably *whistled* while he *whittled*. Frances was already half in love with Gus herself.

But Jan had gone silent on the subject of Gus.

After a while, Frances continued talking, as if Jan had actually shown interest.

"You know, sometimes I think it was almost worth it, the money I paid, for the companionship over those six months. For the hope. I should email him, and say, *Look, I know you're a scammer, but I'll pay you to keep pretending to be Paul Drabble*." She paused. "I would never really do that."

Silence.

"It's funny, because I'm a romance writer. I create fictional characters for a living, and then I fell for one."

Still nothing. Jan mustn't be a reader. Maybe she was just embarrassed for Frances. *Wait till I get home and tell Gus about this loser.*

Gus would give a long low (tuneful) whistle of surprise and sympathy. "That's what happens in the big smoke, Jan."

Frances managed to stay silent for a few moments as Jan kneaded her knuckle into a spot on her lower back. It hurt in a glorious, necessary-feeling way.

"Do you work full-time here, Jan?"

"Just casual. When they need me."

"You like it?"

"It's a job."

"You're very good at it."

"Yup."

"*Extraordinarily* good."

Jan said nothing and Frances closed her eyes. "How long have you worked here?" she asked sleepily.

"Only a few months," said Jan. "So I'm still a newbie."

Frances opened her eyes. There was something in Jan's voice. Just a shadow. Was it possible she wasn't quite sold on the Tranquillum House philosophy? Frances considered asking her about the missing contraband, but how would the conversation progress?

"I think someone went through my bags, Jan."

"Why do you think that, Frances?"

"Well, some things were missing."

"What sort of things?"

She was too ashamed and too vulnerable without her clothes to confess.

"What is the director like?" asked Frances, thinking of the reverence with which Yao had looked at that closed door.

Silence.

Frances watched Jan's feet in their chunky sneakers. They didn't move.

Finally, Jan spoke. "She's very passionate about her work."

Yao had also said he was *passionate* about his work. It was the theatrical language of movie stars and motivational speakers. Frances would never say she was "passionate" about her work, although she *was* in fact passionate about her work. If she went too long without writing she lost her mind.

What if she was never published again?

Why would anyone publish her again? She didn't deserve to be published.

Don't think about the review.

"Passion is good," she said.

"Yup," said Jan. She chose another spot for knuckle-digging.

"Is she possibly too passionate at times?" asked Frances, trying to understand the point, if any, that Jan was trying to make.

"She cares a lot about the guests here and she's prepared to do . . . whatever it takes . . . to help them."

"Whatever it takes?" said Frances. "That sounds—"

Jan's hands moved to Frances's shoulders. "I need to remind you that the noble silence will begin in just a few moments. Once we hear the third bell we're not allowed to talk."

Frances felt panicky. She wanted more information before this creepy silence began.

"When you say 'whatever it takes'—"

"I only have positive things to say about the staff here," interrupted Jan. She sounded a little robotic now. "They have your best interests at heart."

"This is sounding kind of ominous," said Frances.

"People achieve great results here," said Jan.

"Well that's good."

"Yup," said Jan.

"So are you saying that some of their methods are possibly a little . . ." Frances tried to find the right word. She was remembering some of those angry on-line reviews.

A bell rang once. It reverberated with the melodic authority of a church bell, clear and pure.

Damn it.

"Unorthodox?" continued Frances hurriedly. "I guess I'm just cautious now, after my experience with that man, that scammer. Once bitten—"

The second bell, even louder than the first, sliced through the middle of her cliché so that it hung foolishly in the air.

"Twice shy," whispered Frances.

Jan pressed her palms down hard on Frances's shoulder blades as if she were performing CPR and leaned forward so that her breath was warm against Frances's ear.

"Just don't do anything you're not comfortable with. That's all I can say."

The third bell rang.

9

Masha

The director of Tranquillum House, Maria Dmitri-chenko—Masha to everyone except the tax office—sat alone in her locked office at the top of the house as the third bell rang. Even from all the way up here she could sense the silence fall. It felt like she'd walked into a cave or a cathedral: that feeling of release. She bowed her head toward her favorite fingerprint-shaped whorl in the surface of her white oak desk.

She was on her third day of a water-only fast, and fasting always heightened her senses. The window of her office was open and she breathed in great gusts of clean country air. She closed her eyes and remembered how she'd once breathed in all the strange, thrilling scents of this new country: eucalyptus, fresh-cut grass, and petrol fumes.

Why was she thinking about this?

It was because her ex-husband had emailed yes-terday, for the first time in years. She'd deleted his email, but just seeing his name for even an instant had infiltrated her consciousness, so that now the merest scent of eucalyptus on a breeze was enough to transport her back thirty years to the person she'd once been, someone she could barely remember. And yet she *did* remember everything about that first day, after those endless flights (Moscow, Delhi, Singapore, Melbourne); how she and her husband had looked at each other in the back of that little van, marveling at all the lights, even in the middle of the street. They'd whispered to each other about the way strangers kept *smiling* at them. It was bizarre the way they did this! So friendly! But then—it was Masha who first noticed this—when they turned their heads, *their smiles shrank to nothing.* Smile, gone. Smile, gone. In Russia, people didn't smile like that. If they smiled at all, they smiled from the heart. That was Masha's first-ever experience of the "polite smile." You could see the polite smile as a wonderful or terrible thing. Her ex-husband smiled back. Masha did not.

Nu naher! She did not have time for the past right now. She had a health resort to run! People were depending on her. This was the first time she'd begun a retreat with a period of silence, but she knew already that it was right. The silence would give her guests clarity. It would frighten some of them, they would resist, and people would break the silence, accidentally or deliberately. Couples might whisper in their beds, but that was fine. The silence would set the right tone going forward. Some guests treated this place like summer camp. Middle-aged women got overexcited at not having to cook dinner each night. All that high-pitched chatter. If two men became "mates," you could be sure rules would be broken.

In the early days, when Masha first opened Tranquillum House to the public, she'd been shocked to discover an order for a family-sized Meatlovers pizza being delivered at the back fence. *"Nu shto takoye!"* she'd shouted, scaring the life out of both the poor delivery boy and the guest. *What's going on here?*

She had learned the funny ways of her guests. Now she took precautions. Security cameras around the property. Regular monitoring. Bags checked. All for their own good.

She turned sideways in her chair and lifted one leg, pressing her forehead to her shinbone. She occupied her body with the ease of a ten-year-old boy and she liked to say that she *was* only ten years old, because it was coming up to the tenth anniversary of the day it happened. Her cardiac arrest. The day she died and was born again.

If not for that day, she would still be in the corporate world, and she would still be fat and stressed. She had been global operations director for a multinational producer of dairy products. She had been taking Australia's most trusted cheese to the world! (She no longer ate cheese.) She remembered her office, with its views of the Sydney Opera House, and the pleasure she once took in ticking off tasks, formulating policies to streamline procedures, bringing a room full of men to heel. Her life then had been spiritually void, but intellectually stimulating. She especially loved new-product development and seeing the company's entire product line laid out on the boardroom table: the lushness of choice, the brightly colored packaging. In a strange way, it fulfilled the yearning she'd felt as a child when she'd flicked through illicit shopping catalogues from the West.

But the pleasure she took in her corporate life had been like a polite smile. There was no substance to it. Her mind, body, and soul had operated like different divisions of a corporation without a good flow of communication. This nostalgia she felt for her old job was as fraudulent as fond thoughts of her ex-husband. The memories her mind kept throwing up were nothing but computer glitches. She must focus. Nine people were depending on her. Nine perfect strangers who would soon become like family.

She ran her finger down a printout of their names:

Frances Welty
Jessica Chandler
Ben Chandler
Heather Marconi
Napoleon Marconi
Zoe Marconi
Tony Hogburn
Carmel Schneider
Lars Lee

Nine strangers who, right now, were settling into their rooms, exploring the property, nervously reading their information packs, drinking their smoothies, perhaps enjoying their first spa treatments, worrying about what lay ahead.

She loved them already. Their self-consciousness and self-loathing, their manifest lies, their defensive jokes to hide their pain as they cracked and crumbled before her. They were hers for the next ten days, hers to teach and nurture, to shape into the people they could be, should be.

She found the file for the first name on her list.

Frances Welty. Aged fifty-two. The photo she'd submitted showed a woman wearing red lipstick holding a cocktail.

Masha had treated a hundred women like Frances. It was simply a matter of peeling back their layers to reveal the heartache beneath. They longed to be peeled, for someone to be interested enough to peel them. It wasn't hard. They'd been hurt: by husbands and lovers, by children who no longer needed them, by disappointing careers, by life, by death.

They nearly all loathed their bodies. Women and their bodies! The most abusive and toxic of relationships. Masha had seen women pinch at the flesh of their stomachs with such brutal self-loathing they left bruises. Meanwhile their husbands fondly patted their own much larger stomachs with rueful pride.

These women came to Masha overfed and yet malnourished, addicted to various substances and chemicals, exhausted and stressed and experiencing migraines or muscular pain or digestive issues. They were easy to heal with rest and fresh air, nutritious food and attention. Their eyes brightened. They became expansive and exhilarated as their cheekbones reemerged. They wouldn't shut up. They left Masha with hugs and tears in their eyes and bright toot-toots of their car horns. They sent heartfelt cards, often with photos enclosed showing how their journeys had continued as they applied Masha's lessons to their day-to-day lives.

But then, two, three, four years later, a good proportion *came back to Tranquillum House*, looking as unhealthy as they'd been at their first visits—or even unhealthier. "I stopped my morning meditation," they would say, all wide-eyed and apologetic, but not *that* apologetic; they seemed to think their lapses were natural, cute, to be expected. "And next thing I was back drinking every day." "I lost my job." "I got divorced." "I had a car accident." Masha had only reset them temporarily! In times of crisis they returned to their default settings.

That was not good enough. Not for Masha.

This was why the new protocol was essential. There was no need for the strange anxiety that was waking her up in the dark of the night. The reason Masha had been so successful in her corporate career was because she had always been the one prepared to take risks, to think laterally. It was the same here. She tapped her fingertip against the bleary, bloated face of Frances Welty and checked to see which boxes she had selected for what she wanted to achieve over the next ten days: "stress relief," "spiritual nourishment," and "relaxation." It was interesting that she hadn't ticked "weight loss." It must be an oversight. She seemed like the careless sort. No attention to detail. One thing was clear: this woman was *crying out* for a spiritually transformative experience, and Masha would give it to her.

She opened the next file. Ben and Jessica Chandler.

Their photo showed an attractive young couple sitting on a yacht. They were smiling with their teeth but Masha couldn't see their eyes because of their dark sunglasses. They had ticked the box for couples counseling and she was confident she could help. Their problems would be fresh, not calcified after years of arguments and bitterness. The new protocol would be perfect for them.

Next up, Lars Lee. Forty. The photo he'd attached was a glossy corporate headshot. She knew this type of guest very well. He saw attendance at health resorts as a part of his grooming regime, like a haircut or a manicure. He would not try to smuggle in contraband but he would feel that inconvenient rules did not apply to him. His reaction to the new protocol would be interesting.

Carmel Schneider. Thirty-nine. Mother of young children. Divorced. Masha looked at her photo and clucked. She heard her mother's voice: *If a woman doesn't look after herself, her man looks after another woman.* Poor little bunny. Low self-esteem. Carmel had ticked every single box on the list except for "couples counseling." Masha felt lovingly toward her for this. No problem, my *lapochka*. You will be one of my easy ones.

Tony Hogburn. Fifty-six. Also divorced. Also here for weight loss. That was the only box he ticked. He would become grumpy and possibly aggressive when his body reacted to the changes in his self-medicating lifestyle. One to monitor.

The next file made her frown.

Could this be her wild card?

The Marconi family. Napoleon and Heather. Both aged forty-eight. Their daughter, Zoe. Aged twenty.

This was the first time a family group had booked a Tranquillum House retreat. She'd had many couples, mothers and daughters, siblings and friends, but never a family, and the daughter was the youngest guest ever to come to Tranquillum House.

Why would a perfectly healthy-looking twenty-year-old choose to do a ten-day health retreat with her parents? Eating disorder? That could be it. They all looked underfed to Masha's practiced eye. Some sort of strange family dysfunction going on?

Whoever filled in the questionnaire for the family's group booking had ticked only one box: "stress relief."

The photo the Marconi family had submitted showed the three of them in front of a Christmas tree. It was clearly a selfie, because they had their heads at funny angles trying to get into the camera frame. They were all smiling but their eyes were flat and empty.

"What happened to you, my *lapochki*?"

10

Heather

As soon as the third bell rang, Heather Marconi felt the silence fall, as though a blanket had been gently dropped over Tranquillum House. It was remarkable how palpable it was. She hadn't been especially aware of any ambient noise beforehand.

She had just come out of the bathroom when the bells began to ring, much louder and more commanding than she had anticipated. She had been of two minds as to whether she'd bother to go along with this absurd "silence"—if they'd wanted a silent retreat they would have booked a silent retreat, thank you very much—but the religious sound of the bells froze her on the spot. Ignoring the silence now felt disrespectful, even in the privacy of their own room.

Her husband sat on an antique sofa in the corner of their room, his finger to his lips like a schoolteacher, because Napoleon *was* a schoolteacher, a beloved schoolteacher in a disadvantaged area, and you couldn't spend twenty-five years teaching geography to recalcitrant boys without bringing home some teacher-like habits.

Heather thought, *Don't shhhh me, darling. I'm not one of your students. I'll talk if I want to talk.* She met his eyes to give him a wink and Napoleon's gaze skittered away as if he had something to hide, but he was always the one with nothing to hide, he was the open bloody book, and the reason he was avoiding her eyes was because the paperwork had specified "no eye contact" for the next five days and Napoleon would never forget a rule or regulation, even one as pointless and arbitrary as this. What possible good could come of avoiding eye contact between husband and wife? But Napoleon was deeply respectful of road signs and tiny clauses on bureaucratic forms. For him, rules were about politeness and respect and ensuring the survival of a civilized society.

She studied him as he sat in his too-short dressing gown, his long hairy legs entwined. He had a feminine way of crossing his legs, like a supermodel being interviewed on a talk show. His two shorter, chunkier older brothers gave him hell about the girly way he crossed his legs, but he just grinned and gave them the finger.

His hair was still wet from their visit to the hot springs and swim in the pool.

The hot springs were an easy walk from the back of the house, down a generously signposted walking track. There had been nobody else around. They had found the Secret Grotto, a rocky shaded pool just big enough for the three of them to sit in a semicircle and enjoy the views of the valley. Heather and Zoe had listened as Napoleon talked on and on about how the minerals in the water would help their circulation and reduce their stress levels and so on and so forth; she couldn't really remember what he'd said. Napoleon's conversation was like background noise in her life, a radio permanently on talk-back, only random phrases making their way into her subconscious. He had obviously been panicked at the thought of five days of silence and had been speaking even faster than usual, without pause, his voice bubbling endlessly, like the frothy warm sulfuric-smelling water that bubbled about their bodies.

"Sweetheart, of course I can cope without speaking for five days!" he'd reassured Zoe, who had looked at her father with genuine concern on her beautiful young face. "If you can cope without your phone and your mother can cope without caffeine, I can cope without conversation!"

Afterward, the three of them had cooled off in the pool; the relief of the cold blue chlorinated water had been magical after the hot springs. Heather watched Zoe try to race her dad: he swam butterfly, she swam freestyle with a five-second head start. He still won, even though he didn't want to win, but he couldn't get away with pretending to lose like when she was a kid. Then they sat by the pool and Zoe told them a funny story about one of her university tutors that Heather didn't quite get, but she could tell by Zoe's face that it was meant to be funny, so it was easy to laugh. It had been a rare and special moment of happiness. Heather knew they would all three have noted it, and hoped it was a sign of something good.

And now they had to spend the next five days not talking.

Heather felt a burst of powerful irritation—or perhaps it was simply her body demanding a macchiato—because this so-called "holiday" was not meant to be about suffering. There were undoubtedly multiple other health resorts that offered the same peaceful environment without these draconian deprivations. None of the three of them needed to lose weight. Weight was just not an issue for Heather! She weighed herself every morning at six on the dot and if she ever saw the needle move in the wrong direction she adjusted her diet. Her BMI was in the "underweight" category but only by a kilo. She'd always been lean. Zoe sometimes accused Heather of having an eating disorder, just because she was kind of picky about when and what she ate. She didn't put just anything in her mouth—unlike Napoleon, who ate like a vacuum cleaner, hoovering up whatever was around him.

Napoleon stood. He lifted his suitcase onto the bed, unzipped it, and removed a beautifully folded T-shirt, a pair of shorts, and some underpants. He packed like a soldier whose kit bag would be inspected. He took off his dressing gown and stood in all his skinny white hairy naked magnificence.

His uncharacteristic silence made him suddenly a stranger.

The muscles on his back moved in unison like an

exquisitely engineered machine as he pulled on his T-shirt. Napoleon's height and nerdy demeanor disguised his sexiness.

The first time they had sex, all those years ago, Heather kept thinking to herself, "Well, *this* is a surprise," because who knew that a guy like *Napoleon* would have the moves? She'd *liked* him well enough, he was sweet and funny and attentive, but she'd kind of thought sleeping with him would be like doing community service. It was meant to be polite, friendly "thanks so much for dinner and the Kevin Costner movie" sex, not mind-blowing sex. She knew Napoleon's memory of their first date was different from hers. His memory was wholesome and sweet and correct, the way the memory of a first date between a future husband and wife should be.

Napoleon zipped up his shorts and buckled his belt. He slid the brown leather through the silver metal clasp with irritatingly quick, efficient moves. He must have felt her eyes upon him, but he didn't look at her; he was so determined to follow these silly rules, no matter what. He was such a good man, so fucking perfect in every fucking way.

The rage hit her with the power and momentum of a contraction during active labor. There was no escaping it. She saw herself punching his face with a closed fist, crunching his cheekbone, the diamond cluster of her engagement ring breaking his skin, over and over and over and over, blood dripping. The rage wrapped itself around her body, almost lifted her off her feet. She had to grip her toes to the floor to stop herself lunging at

Napoleon as he zipped the bag back up and placed it on the floor in the corner of the room where nobody could trip over it.

She focused on a point on the wall where there was a small island-shaped scratch in the wallpaper and used the variable breathing method she taught mothers to use during the transition phase of labor: pant, pant, *blow*, hee-hee-*hoo*, pant, pant, *blow*.

Napoleon walked across the room and stepped out onto the balcony. He stood with his legs apart and his hands clenching the railing as if he were on the deck of a lurching ship.

The rage eased, receded, vanished.

Done. She'd got through it again. The oblivious object of her rage bowed his head, exposing his defenseless white neck. He would never know. He'd be horrified and so deeply wounded if he ever knew the violence of her secret thoughts.

Heather felt shaky. Her mouth tasted of bile. It was as though she'd just vomited.

She opened her own suitcase and found shorts and a tank top. Later this afternoon, after the "meditation," she would need to run. She wouldn't be relaxed after sitting and focusing on her breathing for an hour; she'd be on the verge of madness.

Coming here was a mistake. An expensive mistake. They should have gone to a big anonymous hotel.

She tied the laces on her sneakers with vicious tugs and opened her mouth to speak. She was definitely going to speak. This silence was *unnecessary*. They wouldn't speak in the presence of the other guests, but there was no need to maintain this awkward, weird, and unhealthy silence in the privacy of their own room.

And what about poor Zoe, alone and silent in the room next door? Heather and Napoleon both panicked if she was alone in her bedroom at home for too long, which was hard because she was twenty years old and needed to study. If there had been no sound for a while one of them would make an excuse to go and check on her. She never complained and she never closed her door. But there were no family suites at Tranquillum House. They'd had no choice but to book her a single room.

She said she was fine, she constantly reassured them she was fine, she was happy; she understood their need to be reassured. But she'd worked so hard this year, much too hard, tapping away grimly on her computer as if a "media studies" degree was a matter of life and death, and she deserved a break.

Heather looked at the wall above their bed that separated their room from Zoe's and wished she could see straight through it. What was she doing right now? She didn't have her phone. Twenty-year-olds *needed* their phones by their sides at all times. Zoe found it stressful if her battery power dropped below eighty percent.

They shouldn't be risking their daughter's mental health like this. Zoe didn't sleep alone in a bed until she was ten years old.

Had Zoe *ever* stayed in a hotel room on her own before?

Never. Zoe had been away on holidays with her girl-friends but they would have always shared a room, or so Heather would have thought.

She just broke up with her boyfriend and now she is alone in her room with nothing but her thoughts.

My God. Her heart raced. She knew she was cata-strophizing. *She is an adult. She's fine.*

Napoleon turned from the balcony, caught her eye, and once again dropped his gaze. Heather felt her molars grind. He'd be so disappointed in her if she spoke only five minutes into "the noble silence."

Jesus. This was unexpectedly hard. The silence made her thoughts scream. She hadn't realized how much distraction Napoleon provided with his incessant chatter. How ironic if *she* was the one who couldn't handle silence, not him.

They didn't need silence or fasting or detoxifica-tion. They just needed a refuge from January. Last January they'd stayed home and that had been a disas-ter. It was even worse than the year before. It seemed that January was a cruel-eyed, clawed vulture that would terrorize Heather's tiny family forever.

"Maybe we should go away this time," Napoleon had suggested a few months ago. "Somewhere peaceful and quiet."

"Like a monastery," Zoe had said. Then her eyes brightened. "Or, I know, a health resort! We'll get Dad's cholesterol down."

Napoleon's school had offered all the teaching staff free health assessments back in June and Napoleon had been told his cholesterol was high, and his blood pressure was becoming worrisome, and it was great that he exercised, but he needed to make dramatic changes to his diet.

So Heather had Googled "health resorts."

Are you in need of significant healing?

That was the opening line on the home page for the Tranquillum House website.

"Yes," Heather had said quietly to her computer screen. "Yes, we are."

It seemed likely that Tranquillum House targeted people of a socioeconomic status a few income levels higher than those of a high school teacher and a mid-wife, but their last proper holiday had been years ago, and Napoleon's inheritance from his grandfather had been sitting there in the bank. They could afford it. There was nothing else they needed or wanted.

"Are you sure you want to be stuck with your parents at a health resort for ten days?" she'd asked Zoe.

Zoe shrugged, smiled. "I just want to spend this holiday sleeping. I'm so tired."

Normal twenty-year-old girls shouldn't be spending that much of their summer break with their parents, but then Zoe wasn't a normal twenty-year-old girl.

Heather had clicked *Book now* and instantly regretted it. It was strange how something could appear so attractive and then, the very moment you committed to it, become wildly unattractive. But it was too late. She'd agreed to the terms and conditions. They could change the time they went, but they couldn't get their money back. The three of them were doing a ten-day "cleanse" whether they liked it or not.

She'd spent days kicking herself. They didn't need to be "transformed." There was nothing wrong with their bodies. Everyone always said the three of them were exercise fanatics! This wasn't the place for the Marconis; it was the place for people like that woman Napoleon had accosted on the stairs. What was her name? *Frances.* You could tell just by looking at her that she filled her life with lunches and facials and her husband's work functions.

She looked vaguely familiar to Heather—probably because Heather knew so many women just like her: wealthy middle-aged women who hadn't worked since before their children were born. There was nothing wrong with those women. Heather *liked* them. She just couldn't be with them for too long without succumbing to rage. They were utterly unscathed by life. The only thing they had to worry about was their bodies, because all that lunching didn't help their figures, so they needed to come to places like this to "recharge" and to hear the experts tell them the amazing news that if you eat less and move more, you will weigh less and feel better.

Once the silence was over and they were allowed to talk again, Napoleon and Frances would get on like a house on fire. Napoleon would listen with genuine interest as Frances humble-bragged about how her children were studying at Harvard or Oxford or taking a gap year in Europe, where they seemed to be visiting more nightclubs than museums.

Heather wondered idly if she should suggest to

Napoleon that he take the opportunity to have an affair while they were here. Perhaps the poor man craved sex, and Frances would be a fine buxom choice.

Heather knew the exact date she'd last had sex with her husband. It was three years ago. If she'd known it was going to be the last time she'd have sex for the rest of her life, she might have bothered to remember the details. She was sure it was good; it generally was good. It just wasn't possible anymore, not for Heather.

She sat on the end of the bed, and Napoleon came and sat down next to her. She could feel the warmth of his body along hers, but their bodies didn't touch, as per the rules.

They waited for Zoe, who was going to knock on their door once she was showered. That was the plan. Then the three of them would wait, *silently*, for the bell and go downstairs together for the first "guided sitting meditation."

Zoe was fine. Of course she was fine. She was a good girl. She would do what she said she would do. She always did. She tried so hard to be everything for them while they tried so hard to pretend that she wasn't their only reason for living.

Heather felt the pierce of grief as sharp as a samurai sword.

She could always hide the rage, but never the grief. It was too visceral. She put her hand to the base of her throat and a tiny mouselike sound escaped.

"Just ride it out, sweetheart," murmured Napoleon. He spoke so quietly it was almost a whisper. Without looking at her, he took her hand, enfolding it in the warmth of his palms, breaking his beloved rules for her.

She clutched at him, her fingers locked into the grooves between his knuckles, like a woman in labor holds her partner's hand as the pain tries to drag her away.

11

Frances

The bell rang for the first "guided sitting meditation" and Frances opened the door of her room at the same time as Ben and Jessica next door. Nobody said anything, which Frances found almost unendurable, and they all avoided eye contact as they walked down the corridor toward the stairs.

Ben wore the same clothes as earlier, while Jessica had changed into skintight yoga gear, revealing a figure so magnificent Frances wanted to compliment her on her efforts. It took a lot of commitment and silicone to look that good, and yet the poor kid didn't sashay as she deserved; rather she *scurried*, her shoulders hunched as though she were somewhere out of bounds and trying to escape notice.

Ben, on the other hand, had the stiff, stoic walk of a man being taken off to prison for a crime to which he'd pled guilty. Frances wanted to take them both out to a bar and listen to their life stories while they all ate peanuts and drank sangria.

Why was she even thinking about *sangria*, for heaven's sake? She hadn't drunk sangria in years. It was like her brain kept tossing out random suggestions for every type of food or drink she was going to be denied for the next ten days.

Just ahead of them on the stairs was the chatty giant Napoleon together with his family. The mother was Heather. *Heather Like Leather.* The daughter was *Not-showy Zoe. Well done, Frances, you're a genius.* Although what was the point of her excellent name-remembering skills? She wasn't at a cocktail party. She wasn't even allowed to look at them.

Napoleon walked in a very odd way, head bowed like a monk, each leg lifted and dropped with agonizing slowness, as though he were pretending to be a spacewalker. Frances was nonplussed for a moment and then remembered the instructions about mindful walking during the silence. She slowed her pace and saw Jessica flick Ben on the arm to tell him to do the same.

All six of them walked down the stairs in mindful heel-to-toe slow motion, and Frances tried not to notice the absurdity of it. If she started laughing she would become hysterical. She was already quite light-headed from hunger. It had been hours since she licked the Kit Kat wrapper.

Everyone yielded to Napoleon as the most enthusiastically mindful walker and they all followed him mindfully through the house and then down the stairs to the cool and dark yoga and meditation studio.

Frances took her place on one of the blue mats toward the back of the room and attempted to imitate the posture of the two wellness consultants who sat in the front corners of the room, like exam supervisors, except that their legs were folded like origami, their hands resting on their knees, thumbs and fingers touching, irritating half smiles on their smooth, tranquil faces.

She noted once again the big television screen and wondered if desperate guests ever crept down in their pajamas and tried to get a late-night TV fix, although there didn't seem to be a remote anywhere.

As she tried to make herself comfortable she registered a slight but noticeable improvement in her back after her massage. The pain was still there, but it was like one of multiple bolts had been fractionally loosened.

She sniffed. She understood from her long-ago course that meditation was mostly about breathing correctly, but right now she couldn't breathe. People would think of her as the aggravating sniffling lady at the back of the room, and when she inevitably fell asleep she'd suddenly jerk awake after doing one of those loud snorty snores.

Why hadn't she gone on a *cruise*?

She sighed, and looked around the room for guests she hadn't yet met. To the right of her was a man of about her own age, with a pallid, unhappy face. He sat stolidly on his mat with his legs stuck straight out in front of him, cradling his big solid belly on his lap as if it were a baby that had been handed to him without his consent. Frances smiled kindly at him. It was nice to see someone here who truly *needed* a health resort.

His eyes met hers.

Wait. No. Please, no. Her stomach lurched. It was the man who had stopped on the side of the road and witnessed her screaming and banging on her horn like a lunatic. It was the man with whom she had freely discussed her menopausal symptoms. *The serial killer on vacation.*

She had not cared what the serial killer thought of her because she was never going to see him again. She had never considered that he might also be checking in to Tranquillum House, because he was driving in the opposite direction, *away* from Tranquillum House, *deliberately* misleading her.

This was fine. This was highly embarrassing, but fine. She smiled again, her mouth pulled down in a self-deprecating way to show that she was mildly mortified that she was going to spend the next ten days with him after he'd witnessed her roadside meltdown, but she was a grown-up, he was a grown-up, what the heck.

He sneered at her. He absolutely, most definitely, sneered at her. And then he looked away. Fast.

Frances loathed him. He had been so arrogant on the side of the road, telling her he couldn't let her drive. Was he the police? No. (She felt like they were generally better groomed.) Of course, she would absolutely give the serial killer the *chance* to redeem himself—first impressions could be wrong, she'd read *Pride and Prejudice*—but she rather hoped he would continue to be loathsome for the next ten days. It was invigorating. Probably speeded up the metabolism.

Two more guests came into the room and Frances gave them her full attention. She would befriend them the moment she was allowed to speak. She was excellent at making friends. She felt quite sure that the serial killer was *not* excellent at making friends and she would therefore win.

The first was a woman, whom Frances guessed to be in her mid- to late thirties, wearing an oversized brand-new-looking white T-shirt that hung almost to her knees over black leggings, the standard outfit for an average-sized woman who starts a new exercise program and thinks her perfectly normal body should be hidden. Her thick black woolly hair was tied back in a long braid with glinting gray strands and she wore red-rimmed cat's-eye glasses: statement glasses favored by those who want to appear quirky and intellectual. (Frances had a pair.) The woman had a flustered look about her, as if she'd only just made her bus and she had lots of other places to be today, and might need to leave early.

The flustered lady was followed by an *astonishingly* handsome man with high cheekbones and flashing eyes who paused at the front of the room as if he were a movie star walking out onto the set of a chat show to rapturous applause. He was perfectly stubbled, perfectly proportioned, and deeply, deservedly, in love with himself.

Frances wanted to laugh out loud at the sight of him. He was too good-looking even to be the tall, dark, and handsome hero in one of her books. The only way it would work would be if she put him in a wheelchair. He'd look great in a wheelchair. Honestly, she could probably get away with removing both his legs and he could still play the lead.

He sat himself down on a yoga mat in the easy manner of someone with a daily yoga "practice."

The tendons of Frances's neck began to ache from the strain of trying to hold her body so she didn't see the serial killer in her peripheral vision. She rolled her shoulders. Sometimes she exhausted herself.

She turned her head and looked directly at him.

He sat slumped, poking his finger into a hole near the hem of his T-shirt.

She sighed, looked away. He wasn't even worth loathing.

Now what?

Now . . . nothing. They were all just sitting here. Waiting. What were they meant to be *doing*?

The desire to interact was an irresistible itch.

Jessica, who sat directly in front of Frances, cleared her throat as if she were about to speak.

Someone else coughed discreetly at the back of the room.

Frances threw in a cough too. Her cough sounded quite bad, actually. She probably had a chest infection. Would they have antibiotics here? Or would they try to cure her with natural supplements? In which case she'd get sicker and sicker and eventually die.

All this coughing and clearing of throats reminded her of being in church. When was she last in a church?

It must have been for a wedding. Some of her friends' children were starting to get married. Girls who wore fuck-me boots in the eighties were now wearing mother-of-the-bride outfits with pretty bolero jackets to conceal their upper arms.

At least at a wedding you could quietly chat to the other guests while you waited for the bride. Compliment your friend on her pretty bolero jacket. This was more like a funeral, although even funerals weren't this silent as people murmured their soft condolences. She was *paying* to be here and it was worse than a *funeral*.

She looked dolefully around the room. There were no nice stained-glass windows to enjoy like in a church. There were no windows or natural light at all. It was almost dungeonlike. She was in a *dungeon* on an isolated property with a group of strangers, at least one of whom was a serial killer. She shivered violently. The air-conditioning was on too high. She thought of the inscription Yao had showed her from the convict stonemasons and wondered if the place might be haunted by their tortured spirits. She'd set a couple of her books in haunted houses. It was helpful for when you wanted your characters to leap into each other's arms.

Napoleon sneezed. A high-pitched shriek of a sneeze, like a dog's yelp.

"Ge*sun*dheit!" cried the handsome man.

Frances gasped. He'd broken the noble silence already!

The handsome man clapped his hand to his mouth. His eyes danced. A wave of laughter ballooned in her chest. Oh God, it was like trying not to laugh in class.

She saw the handsome man's shoulders shake. He
chuckled. She giggled. In a moment she'd be *crying*
with laughter and someone would order her to leave the
room "until she could control herself."

"Namaste. Good afternoon."

The atmosphere changed instantly as a figure strode
into the room, altering the particles of air around her,
drawing every eye, bringing the coughs and sneezes
and throat-clearing to an instant halt.

The laughter trapped in Frances's chest vanished.
The handsome man went still.

"A very warm welcome to Tranquillum House. My
name is Masha."

Masha was an extraordinary-looking woman. A supermodel. An Olympic athlete. At least six feet tall,
with corpse-white skin and green eyes so striking
and huge they were almost alienlike.

In fact, Masha did seem like a different species, a *superior* species, to every other person in the room, even
the handsome man. Her voice was low and deep for a
woman, with an attractive accent that made certain syl-
lables shift sideways. Namaste became *nem*aste. The
cadence of her speech rolled back and forth between
broad Australian and what Frances picked as exotic
Russian. Indeed, the woman could easily be a Russian
spy. A Russian assassin. Like all the staff, she wore
white, except on her it looked less like a uniform and
more like a choice: the perfect choice, the only choice.

The muscles on her arms and legs were sculpted in
clean, sleek lines. Her hair was bleached platinum and
cut so short she'd be able to shake her head, doglike,

when she got out of the shower and be ready to face the day.

As Frances's eyes ran over Masha's exquisitely toned body and she compared it to her own, she sank into herself. She was Jabba the Hutt, all pillowy bosom and hips and soft oozing flesh.

Stop it, she told herself. It wasn't like her to indulge in self-loathing.

Yet it would be disingenuous to deny the aesthetic pleasure of Masha's body. Frances had never bought into "everyone is beautiful," a platitude only women had to be sold, as men could be beautiful or not without feeling as though they weren't really men. This woman, like the handsome man, had a dramatic, almost shocking, physical presence. Frances had to talk or write or flirt or joke or in some way *act* before she could make an impact on people around her, otherwise, as she knew from experience, she could stand at a counter in a shop and be ignored forever. No one could ignore Masha. All she had to do for attention was exist.

For a long agonizing moment Masha surveyed the room, turning her head in a slow arc that took in their cross-legged, silent subservience.

There's something demeaning about this, thought Frances. *We're sitting at her feet like kindergarten kids. We're silent, she speaks.* Also, the rule was no eye contact, and yet Masha appeared to be inviting it. She set the rules so she could break them. *I'm paying for this*, thought Frances. *You work for me, lady.*

Masha met Frances's gaze with warmth and humor. It was as if she and Frances were old friends and she knew exactly what Frances was thinking and found her adorable for it.

At long last, she spoke again. "I thank you for your willingness to take part in the noble silence." I *thenk* you.

She paused.

"I understand that some of you may find this period of silence particularly challenging. I understand, too, that the silence was unexpected. Some of you may be experiencing feelings of frustration and anger right now. You may be thinking: But I didn't sign up for this! I understand, and to you I say this: Those of you who find the silence the most challenging will also find it the most rewarding."

Mmm, thought Frances. *We'll see about that.*

"Right now you're at the foot of a mountain," Masha continued, "and the summit seems impossibly far away, but *I am here to help you reach that summit*. In ten days, you will not be the person you are now. Let me be clear on this, because it's important."

She paused again. She looked slowly around the room, as if she were satirizing a politician. The drama of her delivery was so deliberately hyperbolic it wasn't even funny. It *should* have been funny, yet it wasn't.

Masha repeated, "In ten days, you will not be the person you are now."

No one moved.

Frances felt hope rise in the room like a delicate mist. Oh, to be transformed, to be someone else, to be someone *better.*

"You will leave Tranquillum House feeling happier, healthier, lighter, freer," said Masha.

Each word felt like a benediction. Happier. Healthier. Lighter. Freer.

"On the last day of your stay with us, you will come to me and you will say this: Masha, you were right! I am not the same person I was. I am healed. I am free of all the negative habits and chemicals and toxins and thoughts that were holding me back. My body and mind are clear. I am changed in ways I could never have imagined."

What a load of crap, thought Frances, while simultaneously thinking, *Please let it be true.*

She imagined driving home in ten days: pain-free, energized, her head cold cured, her back as flexible as an elastic band, the hurt and humiliation of her romance scam long gone, washed clean! She would walk tall, stand tall. She would be ready for whatever happened with the new book. The review would have faded to nothing.

(She could actually feel the review right now, like a sharp-edged corn chip stuck in her throat, making it hard to breathe and swallow.)

She might even—and here she felt a burst of child-like anticipation, as if for Christmas Day—be able to zip that amazing Zimmermann dress all the way up again, the one that used to guarantee her compliments (often from other people's husbands, which was always so pleasing).

Perhaps her transformed self would go home and

write a thriller or an old-fashioned murder mystery featuring a cast of colorful characters with secrets and a delightfully improbable villain. It might be fun to murder someone with a candlestick or a cup of poisoned tea. She could set it at a *health resort*! The murder weapon could be one of those stretchy green elastic bands she'd seen in the gym. Or she could make it more of a historical health resort where everyone wafted about looking pale and interesting as they recovered from tuberculosis. She could surely throw in a romantic subplot. Who didn't like a romantic subplot?

"There *will* be surprises on this journey," said Masha. "Each morning at dawn you will receive your daily schedule, but there will be unexpected detours and plans that change. I know this will be difficult for some of you who hold your lives with tight fists."

She held up her fists to demonstrate her point and smiled. It was a stunning smile: warm and radiant and sensual. Frances found herself smiling back and looked around the room to see if everyone else was similarly affected. Yes, indeed. Even the serial killer smiled at Masha, although it seemed as if his lips had been forced up only temporarily without his consent and the moment he got control back he was once again slack-jawed and sullen, pulling at a piece of thread on the fraying edge of his T-shirt.

"Imagine you are a leaf in a stream," said Masha. "Relax and enjoy the journey. The stream will carry you this way and that, but will carry you forward to where you need to go."

Napoleon nodded thoughtfully.

Frances studied the still, straight backs of Ben and Jessica in front of her, somehow vulnerable in their slim youthfulness, which didn't make sense because they probably didn't say "oof" each time they stood up from a chair.

Ben turned toward Jessica and opened his mouth as if he were about to break the silence, but he didn't. Jessica moved her hand and the light bounced off an enormous diamond on her finger. Good Lord. How many carats was that thing?

"Before we begin our first guided meditation, I have a story to share," said Masha. "Ten years ago I died."

Well, that was unexpected. Frances sat a little straighter.

Masha's face became oddly jovial. "If you don't believe me, ask Yao!"

Frances looked across at Yao, who seemed to be trying not to smile.

"I went into cardiac arrest and I was clinically dead." Masha's green eyes shone with crazy joy, as if she were describing the best day of her life.

Frances frowned. Wait, why did you mention Yao? Was he there? Keep your narrative on track, Masha.

"They call my experience a 'near-death experience,'" said Masha. "But I feel that is the wrong terminology because I wasn't just near death, I *was* dead. I experienced death, a privilege for which I am eternally grateful. My experience, my so-called 'near-death experience,' was ultimately life-changing."

There were no coughs, no movement in the room. Were people rigid with embarrassment or still with awe?

Here comes the tunnel of light, thought Frances. Hadn't they proved there was a scientific reason for that phenomenon? Yet even as she scoffed, she felt a tingle of goose bumps.

"That day, ten years ago, I temporarily left my body," said Masha. She said this with casual conviction, as if she didn't expect to be doubted.

Her eyes swept the room. "There may be doubters among you. You may be thinking, Did she really die? Let me tell you, Yao was one of the paramedics who took care of me that day."

She nodded at Yao, who nodded back.

"Yao can confirm that my heart did indeed stop. We later developed a friendship and a mutual interest in wellness."

Yao nodded even more vigorously. Did Frances imagine it, or did the other wellness consultant roll her eyes at that? Professional jealousy? What was her name again? *Delilah*.

What happened to Delilah after she cut off Samson's hair? Frances longed to Google it. How was she going to cope for ten days without instant answers to idle questions?

Masha continued to speak. "I wish I could tell you much more about my near-death experience, but it is so hard to find the right words, and I'll tell you why—it is simply beyond human comprehension. I don't have the vocabulary for it."

At least give it a shot. Frances scratched irritably

at her forearm, which she understood from a click-bait article to be a symptom of Alzheimer's, although she couldn't be one hundred percent sure because she couldn't goddamn Google it.

"I can tell you this," said Masha. "There is another reality that sits alongside the physical reality. I now know that death is not to be feared."

Although still best avoided, thought Frances. The more earnest people got, the more flippant she became. It was a flaw.

"Death is simply a matter of leaving behind our earthly bodies." Masha moved her own earthly body with unearthly grace. She seemed to be demonstrating how one shrugged off a body. "It is a natural progression, like walking into another room, like leaving the womb."

She stopped. There was movement at the back of the studio.

Frances turned and saw the youngest person there, Zoe, stand from her cross-legged position in one fluid movement.

"Sorry," she said in a low mumble.

Frances noticed Zoe's ears were studded with a multitude of earrings in unusual spots Frances didn't even know it was possible to pierce. Her face was pale. She was so exquisite and heartbreaking, just because she was young, or maybe just because Frances was old.

"Excuse me."

Both her parents looked up at her in alarm, their hands outstretched as if to grab her. Zoe shook her head violently at them.

"Bathrooms are just over there," said Masha.

"I just need a little . . . air," said Zoe.

Heather got to her feet. "I'll come with you."

"Mum, no, I'm fine," said Zoe. "*Please*, just let me . . ." She indicated the door.

Everyone watched to see who would prevail.

"I'm sure she is fine," said Masha decisively. "Come back when you are ready, Zoe. You are tired after your long journey, that's all."

Heather surrendered with obvious reluctance and sat back down.

Everyone watched Zoe leave.

The room felt unsettled now, as if Zoe's departure had put things out of balance. Masha breathed in deeply through her nostrils and out through her mouth.

Someone spoke.

"Listen, now this, ah . . . *noble silence* . . . has been broken, could I ask a question?"

It was the serial killer. He spoke belligerently, just like a serial killer, his mouth barely open, so that his words came out in pellets. He was clearly very upset.

Frances saw Masha's eyes widen ever so slightly at this infraction. "If you feel it's important right now."

He jutted his chin. "Did someone go through our bags?"

12

Zoe

Zoe stood at the bottom of the stairs outside the heavy oak door of the meditation room, bent double, her hands on her thighs, trying to catch her breath.

Lately she'd been having the occasional mini panic attack. Not proper panic attacks, which she understood to be awful and had people calling for ambulances, just these mini episodes where suddenly out of nowhere she felt like she'd spiked her heart rate in a spin class. It was fine to be puffing and panting when she was doing a spin class, but not when she was sitting cross-legged on the floor doing nothing except listening to a madwoman talk about death.

She wondered if this was how it was for Zach. He used to say that asthma felt like someone had placed ten bricks on his chest.

Zoe put a hand to her chest. No bricks. It wasn't asthma. Just run-of-the-mill panic.

She could always trace back the causes. This time it

was hearing Masha's mad thoughts on the wonderful-
ness of her near-death experience. It had made Zoe remember the poem her uncle Alessandro had read at her
brother's funeral, "Death Is Nothing At All." Zoe had
started thinking about how much she hated that poem,
because it was all lies: her brother had not just gone
into another room, he was *gone*, so *gone*, so silent, not
a text not a post not a tweet not a word, and next thing
she was struggling for breath and all she could think
was, *Get out*.

She felt bad about breaking the noble silence, especially after her dad's sneezing created havoc in the
room. The people at this retreat had no idea that those
were her dad's most *subdued* sneezes. One of his students had once made a three-minute film called *Mr.
Marconi Sneezes* which was just a montage of her dad
sneezing at different times with a soundtrack. It had
gone a bit viral.

"Did someone go through our bags?" said a man's
voice from behind the door.

She'd put money on it being the seedy-looking guy
who was nearly as tall as her dad and twice as wide.
Zoe couldn't hear the response.

She climbed the narrow stone staircase and shoved
hard to open the second heavy door that led back into
the main part of the house.

She couldn't disappear for too long because her
parents would worry, which wasn't at all suffocating.
Ever since Zach died it was as if Zoe's life was in
permanent jeopardy and only her parents' secret, ongo-
ing vigilance would save her. Her mum and dad truly

believed that if Zoe didn't get the flu shot, if her car brakes weren't checked every six months, if she didn't have a plan for getting home, she would die. It was as simple as that. And when they so casually asked a question like, "Are you getting an Uber?," their faces averted, their hands busy doing something else, they couldn't disguise the dread beneath their words, and so she didn't brush them off, she didn't walk away when her mother stood next to her and tried to secretly listen to her breathing, even though, unlike Zach, who'd had asthma from when he was a child, Zoe had never had asthma in her life. She clamped down hard on her irritation and let them listen to her breathe and gave the answers and constant reassurances they needed.

She wouldn't disappear on them now. She'd just take ten minutes for herself and then she'd sneak back in and hopefully Mad Masha would have gotten everyone under control by then and they'd all be silently meditating.

There were no staff about as she wandered into the Lavender Room. It was lavishly lavender. There were multiple tall vases stuffed with sprigs of lavender, the soft furnishings and cushions were all in various shades of lavender, and just in case you'd missed the point, *pictures* of lavender adorned the lavender-colored walls.

Zoe went over to the window which looked straight out onto the rose garden, a rectangle of lush green grass bordered by high hedges, with garden beds of abundant white roses. This was where they would do tai chi at dawn tomorrow morning.

This place was all very nice, if dull—but it was kind

of shocking if they really had searched the bags! Luck-
ily Zoe had taken precautions just in case. She knew
how to get alcohol into alcohol-free parties. She'd
wrapped up her contraband like a present, using bubble wrap to disguise the wine-bottle shape, complete
with a gift tag that said: *Happy Anniversary, Mum and
Dad!* She'd checked when she got to the room and the
present was untouched in her bag.

On Zach's twenty-first birthday Zoe was going to
toast him at midnight with a glass of wine. When she
and Zach were born the maths teacher at her dad's
school had given them each a bottle of Grange, strange
presents for babies. The bottles were probably meant
to be in a temperature-controlled cellar but Zoe's family wasn't big on alcohol. The bottles had been sitting
in the back of the linen cupboard, behind the bath towels, all these years, waiting for their twenty-first birthday. According to the internet, this particular vintage
had a *beautiful limp aspect with a melange of dried
fruits and spices and then a long, imperious finish.*

Zach would have found that description funny: *A
long, imperious finish.*

Her eyes followed the softly curved silhouette of the
blue-green hills along the horizon and she thought of her
ex-boyfriend and how hard he'd tried to convince her to
join him on a surfing trip to Bali with a group of friends.
He couldn't believe it when she insisted it was impossible. "I have to be with my parents," she'd told him. "Any
other time, just not January." In the end he got angry,
and then all of a sudden they were taking a break and

next thing they were broken up. She'd kind of thought she had loved him.

She banged her forehead gently against the glass of the window. Did he think she *wanted* to be here with her parents? Did he think she wouldn't prefer to be in Bali?

Last January had been terrible, like her parents were burning to death from the inside, their internal organs being liquefied while they pretended that everything was just fine.

"Hello there. It's Zoe, isn't it? We met earlier. I'm Frances."

Zoe turned from the window. It was the blond lady with the bright red lipstick whom her dad had accosted on the stairs. She was adjusting an old-fashioned giant tortoiseshell clip in her hair and she looked flushed in the face.

"Hi," said Zoe.

"I know we're not meant to be speaking, but I feel like this has turned out to be an unplanned interlude in Masha's noble silence."

"What's going on down there?"

"It's all got very awkward," said Frances. She sat down on one of the lavender couches. "Oh dear, this is one of those swallow-you-up couches." She shoved two cushions behind her back. "Ow. My back. Ow." She wriggled about. "No. I'm okay. That's better. Well. You know the man, the grumpy-looking one with the hacking cough? Not that I can talk. Don't come too close to me, I don't want to infect you, although I feel like my germs are nicer than his germs. Anyway, he's getting very worked up because apparently he smuggled in a whole *minibar*, by the sound of it, and, well, this is embarrassing, but they took some things from my bag too, and I kind of felt like I should have been supporting the grumpy man. You know, like, that *is* a breach of privacy, you can't do that, we have rights!" She punched a fist in the air.

Zoe sat on the couch opposite her and smiled at the fist punch.

"But I got embarrassed because I didn't want everyone to know I also brought in contraband that was confiscated, and I know this isn't an episode of *Survivor*, but I didn't want to form an alliance with that man, because he seems so . . . well . . . so I said I needed some air too, which I feel like was one of the bravest things I've ever done."

"I brought in contraband too," said Zoe.

"*Did* you?" Frances brightened. "Did they find it?"

"No, if they searched my bag they missed it. I wrapped it up like a present for my parents."

"That's genius. What is it?"

"It's a bottle of wine," said Zoe. "Really expensive wine. Oh, and a bag of Reese's Peanut Butter Cups. I'm addicted."

"Yum." Frances sighed. "Congratulations. I like your ingenuity."

"Thank you," said Zoe.

Frances picked up a cushion and hugged it. "I'm perfectly capable of going for ten days without a glass of wine, I just . . . well, I don't know, I was being wicked."

"I don't even like wine," said Zoe.

"Oh. Did you just want to prove you could beat the system?"

"I brought the wine to toast my brother's twenty-first birthday. It's in a few days. He died three years ago."

She saw Frances's inevitably stricken face.

"It's okay," she told her quickly. "We weren't close."

People usually looked relieved when she told them that, but Frances's face didn't change at all.

"I'm so sorry," she said.

"It's fine. Like I said, we really . . . didn't get on." Zoe tried to clarify it for her. *Don't stress! You're off the hook*.

She remembered her friend Cara, the day after Zach's funeral, saying, "At least you weren't close." Cara was really close to her sister.

"What was your brother's name?" asked Frances, as if this was somehow important.

"Zach," said Zoe, and the name sounded odd and painful in her mouth. She heard a roaring sound in her ears and felt for a moment as if she might faint. "Zoe and Zach. We were twins. Very cutesy names."

"I think they're lovely names," said Frances. "But if you're twins that means it's your birthday in a few days too."

Zoe took a sprig of lavender out of a vase and began to shred it. "Technically. But I don't celebrate on that day anymore. I kind of changed my birthday."

She'd officially moved her birthday to the eighteenth of March. It was a nicer date. A cooler, less tempestuous time of year. The eighteenth of March was Grandma Maria's birthday, and Grandma Maria used to say it had never once rained on her birthday and maybe that was true; everyone said they should check the weather records in case it was some sort of phenomenon only Grandma Maria had noticed, but nobody ever got around to it.

Grandma Maria had always said she'd live to one hundred like her own mother, but she died one month after Zach of a broken heart. Even the doctor said it was a broken heart.

"Zach died the day before our eighteenth birthday," said Zoe. "We were meant to be having a 'Z' party. I was going as Zoe. Which seemed really funny at the time."

"Oh, Zoe." Frances leaned forward. Zoe could tell she wanted to touch her but was stopping herself.

"So that's why I changed it," said Zoe. "It's, like, not fair to Mum and Dad to have to celebrate my birthday the day after when they're still totally wrecked from the anniversary. January is really hard for my parents."

"Of course it would be," said Frances. Her eyes were bright with sympathy. "Hard for all of you, I imagine. So you thought it would be good to . . . get away?"

"We just wanted somewhere quiet, and a health re-sort seemed like a good idea because we're all *really* unhealthy."

"Are you? You don't look at all unhealthy to me."

"Well, for a start, I have way too much sugar in my diet," said Zoe.

"Sugar is the new villain," said Frances. "It used to be fat. Then it was carbs. It's hard to keep up."

"No, but sugar is seriously bad," said Zoe. It wasn't hard to keep up at all! Everyone knew sugar was terrible for you. "They've done all this research. I need to withdraw from my sugar addiction."

"Mmm," said Frances.

"I eat too much chocolate and I'm addicted to Diet Coke, that's why my skin is so bad." Zoe put a fingertip to a blind pimple near her lip. She couldn't stop touching it.

"Your skin is *gorgeous*!" Frances gesticulated wildly, probably because she was trying not to look at Zoe's pimple.

Zoe sighed. People should be honest.

"My parents are exercise fanatics, but my dad has a junk-food addiction and Mum basically has an eating disorder." She reflected. Her mother would not like any aspect of this conversation. "Please don't tell her I said that. She doesn't really have an eating disorder. She's just kind of weird about food."

Even before Zach died Zoe's mother had been like that. She couldn't bear to see lavish displays of food, which was a problem, seeing as she'd married a man with a big extended Italian family. Heather suffered from heartburn and stomach cramps and other "digestive issues" she referred to only obliquely. She never saw food as just food. She always had some fierce emotional response to it. She was *starving* or *bloated* or *craving* something specific and unattainable.

"Anyway, what about you?" she asked Frances. She wanted to shift the focus; she'd revealed far too much about herself and her family to this stranger. "Why did you decide to do this?"

"Oh, you know: I'm run-down, I've done something to my back, I have a cold I can't seem to shake, I suppose I could do with losing a few kilos . . . just the normal middle-aged stuff."

"How old are your kids?" asked Zoe.

Frances smiled. "No kids."

"Oh." Zoe was taken aback, worried that she might have made some kind of sexist faux pas. "Sorry."

"Don't be sorry," Frances said. "It was my choice not to have children. I just never saw myself as a mother. Ever. Even when I was a kid."

But you're so motherly, thought Zoe.

"No husband either," said Frances. "Just two ex-husbands. No boyfriend. I'm very single."

It was cute the way she said *boy*friend.

"I'm very single too," said Zoe, and Frances smiled, as if *Zoe* had said something cute.

"I thought I was in love with someone recently but he wasn't who he said he was," said Frances. "It turned out to be an internet 'romance scam.'" She made quote marks with her fingers.

Oh my God, thought Zoe. *How stupid would you have to be?*

"What do you do for a living?" She changed the subject because she was literally going bright red with embarrassment for the woman.

"I write romance novels," said Frances. "Or I did. I might be in need of a career change."

"Romance novels," repeated Zoe. It was getting

worse. She tried to keep her face neutral. *Please, God, don't let it be erotica.*

"Are you a reader?" asked Frances.

"Sometimes," said Zoe. Never, ever romance. "What made you become a romance writer?"

"Well, when I was about fifteen I read *Jane Eyre* and it was a strange, sad time in my life—my dad had just died, and I was hormonal and grieving and just very impressionable. And when I got to that famous line— you know the one: *Reader, I married him*—it just had this profound effect on me. I'd sit in the bath and mur- mur to myself, 'Reader, I married him,' and then I'd just sob. It had remarkable staying power. Reader, I married—ooohhh!" She demonstrated herself sobbing dramatically like a teenage girl, hand to her forehead.

Zoe laughed.

Frances said, "You've read *Jane Eyre*, right?"

"I think I saw the movie once," said Zoe.

"Ah well," said Frances sympathetically. "Anyway, I know that *Reader, I married him* line has become virtu- ally a cliché now, it's referenced so often: *Reader, I di- vorced him. Reader, I murdered him.* But for me, at that time of my life, it was . . . well, profound. I remember being amazed that *four words* could affect me in that way. So I guess I just developed an interest in the power of words. The first romance story I ever wrote was heav- ily influenced by Charlotte Brontë, except without the madwoman in the attic. My leading man was a heady mix of Mr. Rochester and Rob Lowe."

"Rob Lowe!" said Zoe.

"I had his poster on my wall," said Frances. "I can

still taste his lips. Very smooth and papery. Matte gloss."

Zoe giggled. "I felt the same way about Justin Bieber."

"There might even be one of my books here," said Frances. "There often is in places like this." She scanned the shelves of paperbacks then smiled, a hint of pride. "Bingo."

She stood up, clutching her back, went to one of the shelves, and squatted down to pull out a battered-looking chunky paperback. "There you go." She handed it to Zoe and sat back down on the couch with a grunt.

"Awesome," said Zoe. The book looked *terrible*.

It was called *Nathaniel's Kiss* and the picture on the front showed a girl with long curly fair hair staring wistfully out to sea. At least it didn't look erotic.

"Anyway, my last book got rejected," said Frances. "So I might be looking for a new career soon."

"Oh," said Zoe. "I'm sorry."

"Well," said Frances, and she shrugged, gave her a half smile, her palm up, and Zoe knew what she was trying to say. Zoe's friend Erin thought she wasn't allowed to complain about her life anymore without first prefacing it, "I know this is nothing compared to what you've been through," with this solemn wide-eyed look, and Zoe always said, "Erin, it's been three years, you're allowed to complain about your life!" And then she nodded along sympathetically while thinking: *You're right, your car needing three new tires is nothing to complain about.*

"I guess I should go back downstairs," said Zoe. "My

parents get paranoid if they can't pinpoint my location. I think they'd like to put a tracking device on me."

Frances sighed. "I guess I should too." But she didn't move. She gave Zoe a quizzical look. "Do *you* think we're all going to be 'transformed' by the end of this thing?"

"Not really," said Zoe. "What do you think?"

"I don't know," said Frances. "I feel like Masha could do anything. She scares the life out of me."

Zoe laughed and then they both startled at the clamorous sound of a gong being struck repetitively and aggressively from somewhere within the house.

They jumped to their feet and Frances grabbed Zoe's arm. "Oh God, it's just like boarding school! Do you think we're in trouble? Or maybe there's a fire and we're all evacuating?"

"I think it probably just means the silence is starting again."

"Yes, you're right. Okay, we'll go back together. I'll go first; I'm older, I'm not scared of her."

"Yes you are!"

"I know, I am, terrified! Quick, let's go! I'll see you on the other side of the silence."

"I'll read your book." Zoe held up the paperback as they left the Lavender Room and headed back downstairs. It was a crazy thing to say, she had no interest in reading a romance book, but whatever, she liked Frances.

"You're not meant to read in the silence."

"I'm a rebel," said Zoe. She shoved the book under her top and into the waist of her bike pants. "I'll be in an alliance with you."

She was just making a weak joke in reference to Frances's comment earlier about *Survivor*, but Frances stopped in her tracks and turned around with a radiant smile. "Oh, Zoe, I would *love* to be in an alliance with you."

And all of a sudden it felt like they were.

13

Masha

Two guests, Zoe Marconi and Frances Welty, had excused themselves from the meditation room and not yet come back. The silence had been broken and one guest, Tony Hogburn, was now demanding his money back and threatening to report Tranquillum House to the Department of Consumer Affairs, blah, blah, blah, Masha had heard it all before, while the remaining guests looked on with curiosity or concern.

Masha saw poor Yao shoot her an anxious look. He was a worrier. There was no need for stress. She could handle the childlike tantrums of one unhappy, unhealthy man. Solving unexpected problems energized her. It was one of her strengths.

"I am very happy to give you a full refund." She fixed Tony with her eyes like a pin through a butterfly. "You are free to pack your bags and leave immediately. May I suggest you drive yourself to the nearest village, where you will find a fine pub called the Lion's Heart? Their menu includes something called a

'Mega Monster Burger' with unlimited fries and soft drink. Does that sound delicious?"

"Sure does," said Tony truculently.

And yet he didn't get to his feet. *Oh, my sweetie pie, you need me. You know you need me. You don't want to be you anymore. Of course you don't. Who would?*

He tried to wriggle free of her gaze but she wouldn't let him. "I understand that you are not happy that we searched your bags, but the terms and conditions of your wellness contract clearly state that we have the right to search luggage and confiscate all contraband."

"Seriously? Did anyone else read that?" Tony looked around the room.

Napoleon raised his hand. His wife, Heather, lifted her eyes to the ceiling.

"It must have been buried in the fine print," said Tony. His face had turned mottled red, the color of uncooked steak.

"Growth can be painful," Masha told him, her voice gentle. He was a child. An enormous sulky child. "There will be parts of this experience that may be uncomfortable or unpleasant at times. But it's only ten days! The average person lives around twenty-seven thousand days."

Tony's outburst was actually a serendipitous opportunity to shape all their expectations and mold their future behavior. She spoke as if only to him, but the message was for them all.

"You are free to leave at any time, Tony. You are not a prisoner! This is a health resort, not a jail!"

A few people chuckled.

"And you are not a child! You can drink what you want to drink, eat what you want to eat. But there is a reason why you came here, and if you choose to stay, I ask you to commit fully to your journey and to put your trust in me and the other staff at Tranquillum House."

"Yeah, fine, that's . . . I mean, I obviously didn't read the fine print properly." Tony scratched hard at the side of his unshaved face and tugged at the fabric of his dreadful hot heavy blue jeans. "I just didn't appreciate my bags being searched." The aggression was draining from his voice. Now he sounded embarrassed. His eyes peered out at her from within the prison of his poor, tortured body from which he so desperately needed rescue.

She'd won. She had him. He would be beautiful when she finished with him. They would all be beautiful.

"Are there any more areas of concern before we resume the silence?"

Ben raised his hand. Masha observed his wife flash him a look of horror and move slightly away.

"Um, yeah, I have just one question. Are the cars parked under cover?"

She looked at him for a moment, long enough to help him see the sadness of this deep attachment to his earthly possessions.

He shifted uncomfortably.

"They are parked under cover, Ben. Please don't worry, they are perfectly safe."

"Okay, but, um, *where* are the cars? I've walked

around the property and I just can't see where . . ." As he spoke he removed his cap and briskly rubbed the top of his head.

For the briefest of moments, Masha saw another boy wearing a baseball cap walking toward her, so strange and yet so familiar. She felt the love rise within her chest and she crossed her arms so she could secretly pinch the flesh on her arm, hard enough to hurt, until the vision vanished, and all that was left was here and now and the important tasks that lay ahead.

"As I said, Ben, everyone's cars are perfectly safe."

He opened his mouth to speak yet again and his wife hissed something inaudible through her teeth. He closed his mouth.

"So, if everyone is in agreement, I would like to recommence the noble silence and begin our guided meditation. Yao, perhaps you could ring the gong to let our missing guests know we would appreciate their return?"

Yao struck the gong with a mallet, perhaps a little more forcefully than Masha would have done, and within only a few moments Frances and Zoe had returned, their faces apologetic and guilty.

It was clear to Masha that they had been chatting, forming a friendship perhaps, which would need to be monitored. The point of the silence was to prevent this. She smiled benignly at them as they returned to their mats. Zoe's parents sagged with relief.

"Although I will be your guide today," she said, "meditation is a *personal* experience. Please release your expectations and open yourself to all possibilities. This is called a guided sitting meditation but that doesn't mean you must sit! Please find the most natural, relaxed position for you. Some of you may like to sit cross-legged. Some of you may like to sit on a chair with your feet flat on the floor. Some of you may prefer to lie down. There are no hard-and-fast rules here!"

She watched as they chose their positions with self-conscious faces. Frances lay flat on her back. Tony went and sat on a chair, as did Napoleon. The rest remained cross-legged on their mats.

Masha waited until they were all settled. "Let your eyes drift closed."

She could sense their fluttering spirits: their anxieties, hopes, dreams, and fears. She was so *good* at this. It was a pleasure to excel.

Interviewers would one day ask, "Were you nervous when you first introduced the new protocol?" Masha would answer, "Not at all. We'd done our research. We knew from the beginning it would be a success." It might be better to admit to a little nervousness. People in this country admired humility. The biggest compliment you could give a successful woman was to describe her as "humble."

She looked at her nine guests, all of whom now had their eyes obediently closed as they awaited her instructions. Their destinies were in her hands. She was going to change them not just temporarily, but forever.

"We will begin."

14

Frances

It was the end of her first day at Tranquillum House and Frances lay in bed, willfully reading while she drank her "evening smoothie." No one could be expected to give up wine *and* books at the same time.

None of the four novels she'd packed to get her through the next ten days had been confiscated, unlike her wine and chocolate—presumably because books weren't on the "contraband list" (she would never have come here if so)—but a small slip of paper had been placed inside the front cover of each of them: *A gentle reminder that we recommend no reading during the noble silence.*

What an absolute joke. She didn't know how to go to sleep without reading. It wasn't possible.

The book she was reading now was a debut novel that had received rave reviews. There was a lot of "buzz" about it. It was described as "powerful, muscular" and it was written by a man Frances had met at a party last year. The man had been pleasant, shy, and bespectacled (not especially muscular), so Frances was trying to forgive him for his lavish descriptions of beautiful corpses. How many more beautiful young women had to die before they could get on with the job of tracking down their murderer? Frances made little "tch" sounds of disgust.

Now the craggy detective was drunk on single-malt whisky in a smoke-hazed bar and a long-legged girl half his age was whispering into his ear, without quotation marks (this being powerful, literary fiction): *I want to fuck you so bad*.

Frances, who had reached her limit, threw the book across the room. *In your* dreams*, buddy!*

She lay back with her hands clasped across her chest, and reminded herself that her own debut novel featured a piano-playing, poetry-reciting firefighter. It was *cute* that the bespectacled author imagined twentysomething girls ever whispered "I want to fuck you so bad" into the ears of fiftysomething men. She would give the author a consoling little pat on the shoulder next time she saw him at a festival.

Anyway, what did she know? Maybe twentysomething girls did that all the time. She would ask Zoe.

She certainly would not ask Zoe.

She reached for her phone on the bedside table to check the news and the weather for tomorrow.

No phone.

Of course. Well. Fine.

The bed was a luxurious one: a good mattress, the

sheets crisp with a high thread count. Her back hurt, but maybe a little less thanks to Jan's giant hands.

She attempted to quiet her "monkey brain," as per the rules.

In fact, her mind felt stuffed with new faces and new experiences: the long drive here; screaming on the side of the road; the serial killer on vacation (it was that damned book's fault for making her think of serial killers); Ben and Jessica in that car; Yao unexpectedly filling a test tube with her blood; Masha and her near-death experience; chatty Napoleon and his intense wife; lovely young Zoe with her multiple piercings and long smooth brown legs, sitting in the Lavender Room telling Frances about her dead brother. That's why Zoe's mother had looked so sad on the stairs. She probably wasn't intense at all. Just sad. The tall, dark, and handsome man who'd cried, "Gesundheit!" and the flustered lady with Frances's glasses.

A lot for one day. Stimulating and distracting. She hadn't had time for any more existential crises, so that was something. She hadn't even thought much about Paul Drabble, apart from when she was telling Jan and Zoe about what had happened. She'd be over her internet scam by the time she left. Over the review. Over everything.

And thin! She'd be so thin! Her stomach rumbled. She was starving. Dinner tonight had been possibly the most excruciating meal of her life.

When she took her place at the long dining room table, she picked up a small card propped in front of her plate:

At Tranquillum House we recommend MINDFUL EATING. Please take small bites of your food. After each mouthful, place your cutlery back on the table, close your eyes, and chew for at least fourteen seconds, slowly and pleasurably.

Oh God, she thought. *We're going to be here forever.*

She put down the card and looked up to share a "Can you believe this?" glance with someone. The only ones prepared to meet her eyes were the astonishingly handsome man, who *possibly* winked at her, and Zoe, who definitely grinned, and responded with a look that said, "I *know*. I can't believe it either."

Masha wasn't in the dining room, but her presence was felt, like that of a managing director or schoolteacher who could turn up at any moment. Yao and Delilah were there but they didn't sit down to eat with the guests. Instead they stood at the side of the room, at either side of a large candelabra on an ornate sideboard. The lighting in the room was muted and the candelabra had three lit candles.

They sat in silence for at least *ten . . . endless . . . minutes* before the meals came out, delivered by a briskly smiling gray-haired lady in a chef's hat. She didn't say a word but nevertheless exuded goodwill. It felt so rude not to thank her. Frances tried to convey warm gratitude with a nod of her head.

Every person at the table received a different meal. Both Heather and Zoe, who sat next to Frances, received delicious-looking *steaks* together with baked potatoes. Frances's meal was a quinoa salad. It was excellent, but in Frances's world she'd call that a "side," and by the time she'd masticated each mouthful for fourteen seconds it had lost all flavor.

Napoleon, who sat opposite Frances, received some sort of lentil dish. He leaned forward over the bowl and waved the rising steam toward his nose, enjoying the scent. It was clear the poor man was desperate to chat. Frances would bet that in normal circumstances he would have been discussing the history of the lentil.

The serial killer studied his giant bowl of green salad mournfully before picking up his cutlery and stabbing three cherry tomatoes onto his fork with an air of tragic resignation.

The flustered lady with the quirky glasses received fish, to her apparent delight.

The astonishingly handsome man was assigned chicken and vegetables, which he appeared to find mildly amusing.

Ben received a vegetable curry and finished his meal well before the rest of the table.

Jessica was given a really delicious-looking stir-fry, which was the wrong dish for the poor girl. She spent ages laboriously twirling the long noodles around her fork and then dabbing worriedly at her face with her napkin for splashes of food.

Nobody broke the silence or made eye contact. When Napoleon sneezed again, nobody responded in any way. How quickly people adapted to strange rules and regulations!

Heather ate less than half her steak before putting down her knife and fork with a little puff of irritation.

Frances had to restrain herself from leaping on it like a wolf.

Throughout the meal, Yao and Delilah stood silent and unmoving. They were like footmen, except you couldn't snap your fingers and tell them to let Cook know that my lady could do with a larger portion of quinoa, and perhaps a medium-rare sirloin.

The sound of strangers chewing and clinking and scraping their cutlery just about did Frances's head in. Hadn't she once read there was an actual disorder where people suffered real psychological distress at the sound of others eating? There was a name for it. Frances probably had that disorder and had never been diagnosed because you were meant to *talk* while you dined. Something else to remember to Google once she got her phone back.

Eventually they were done, and they all pushed back their chairs and returned to their rooms. You couldn't even say, "Goodnight! Sleep well!"

Now, as Frances drank the last of her evening smoothie, she thought about the number of silent in-sufficient meals ahead of her and considered leaving in the morning.

"No one leaves early, Frances," Yao had said today. Well, Frances could be the first. Set a new precedent.

She thought of her massage therapist's whispered warning just before the silence began: *Don't do anything you're not comfortable with.* What did she mean by that? Frances would certainly not do anything she didn't feel comfortable with.

She recalled what Ellen had said when she suggested

this place. "Their approach is really quite unconventional." Ellen was her friend. She wouldn't send her somewhere *dangerous* . . . would she? Just to lose three kilos? You'd want to lose a lot more than three kilos if they were doing something dangerous. What could it be? Walking across burning coals for enlightenment? Frances would absolutely not do that. She didn't even like walking across hot sand at the beach.

Ellen would have told her if there was walking across hot coals. Ellen was a dear friend.

"I've never trusted that Ellen," Gillian once said, darkly and knowledgeably, but Gillian was always making dark, knowledgeable comments about people, as if everyone had secret Mafia connections that only Gillian knew about.

Frances missed her greatly.

A wave of exhaustion hit her, not surprising after that long drive. She switched off her bedside lamp, and fell instantly sound asleep, flat on her back like a sunbather.

A light shone in her face.

Frances woke with a gasp.

15

Lars

"What the actual fuck?"

Lars sat up, his heart hammering. A figure stood at the end of his bed shining a small flashlight in his face like a nurse doing hospital rounds.

He switched on his bedside lamp.

His "wellness consultant," the delectable Delilah, stood next to his bed holding up the Tranquillum House dressing gown with one hand. She didn't speak. She lifted one finger and beckoned, as if he would just obediently and silently follow her instructions.

"I'm not going anywhere, sweetheart," he said. "It's the middle of the night and I like my sleep."

Delilah said, "It's the starlight meditation. It's always on the first night. You don't want to miss it."

Lars lay back in bed and shielded his eyes. "I do want to miss it."

"You'll like it. It's really beautiful."

Lars removed his hand from his eyes. "Did you even

knock before you came in to my room without permission?"

"Naturally I knocked," said Delilah. She held up the dressing gown again. "Please? I'll lose my job if you don't come down for it."

"You will not."

"I might. Masha wants all the guests there for it. It only takes half an hour."

Lars sighed. He could refuse on principle, but it was such a first-world, privileged principle he couldn't be bothered. He was awake now anyway.

He sat up and held out his hand for his dressing gown. He slept naked. He could have just leaped from the bed in all his glory to make the point that this was what happened when you woke your sleeping guests in the middle of the night, but he was too well mannered. Delilah averted her eyes as he threw back the sheet, although he didn't miss the quick downward flick. She was only human.

"Don't forget the silence," she said as she stepped into the corridor.

"How could I forget the beautiful noble silence?" said Lars.

She put her finger to her lips.

It was a clear night, the stars were out in force, and a perfect half-moon illuminated the garden with silvery light. The balmy air was a soft caress against his skin after the hot day. It was, he had to admit, all very pleasant.

Nine yoga mats had been placed in a circle and guests wearing the Tranquillum House dressing gowns lay with their heads facing the center of the circle, where their striking leader Masha sat cross-legged on the grass.

Lars saw there was only one empty yoga mat. He was the last guest to arrive. He wondered if he'd made the most fuss about being dragged from his bed. He never ceased to be amazed by the obedience of people at these places. They allowed themselves to be dipped in mud, wrapped in plastic, starved and deprived, pricked and prodded, all in the name of "transformation."

Of course, Lars did too, but he was prepared to draw the line when necessary. For example, he drew the line at enemas. Also, he did not want to ever, ever discuss his bowel movements.

Delilah led Lars to a mat in between the lady who got the giggles when Lars said, "Gesundheit!" earlier and the giant lump of a man who had complained about his contraband being confiscated.

There was something familiar about the big guy with the contraband. It had been hard not to stare at him through dinner. Lars couldn't shake the irritating feeling that he knew him from somewhere, but he couldn't work out where.

Was he one of the husbands? If he was one of the husbands, would he recognize Lars and come after him, like that time he was boarding a plane and a guy in the economy line saw Lars and went nuts? He shouted, "YOU! You're the reason I'm flying cattle class!" Lars had taken extra pleasure in his Perrier-Jouët on that flight (and walked briskly off the plane toward the priority queue at customs). The big guy didn't *look* like one of the husbands, but Lars knew he knew him from somewhere.

He wasn't good with faces. Ray was great with them. Every time they started a new series Lars would sit up on the couch, point at the screen, and say, "*Her! We know her! How do we know her?*" Ray normally had it within seconds: "*Breaking Bad*. The girlfriend. Walt let her die. Now shut up." It was a real skill. On the rare occasions that Lars worked it out before Ray he got very excited and demanded high fives.

Lars lay down on the mat between the big guy and the giggling lady. She reminded Lars of one of Renoir's women: small-faced and round-eyed with curly hair piled on top of her head, creamy-skinned, plump, and bosomy, possibly a little vacuous, but he thought they would probably get on. She looked like a fellow hedonist.

"Namaste," said Masha. "Thank you for leaving your beds for tonight's starlight meditation. I am grateful to you for your flexibility, for opening your hearts and minds to new experiences. I am proud of you."

She was *proud* of them. How condescending. She didn't even know them! They were her clients. They were paying for this. And yet Lars felt a sense of satisfaction in the garden, as if everyone wanted Masha to be proud of them.

"The retreat you are about to undertake combines ancient Eastern healing wisdom and herbal treatments with the latest cutting-edge advances in Western medicine. I want you to know that although I am not a practicing Buddhist, I have incorporated certain Buddhist philosophies into our practices here."

Yeah, yeah, East meets West, never heard that before, thought Lars.

"This won't take very long. I'm not going to say much. The stars will do the talking for me. Isn't it funny how we forget to look up at the stars? We scurry about like ants in our day-to-day lives and look, just *look*, what's up above our heads! All your life you look down. It's time to look up, to see the stars!"

Lars looked at the sky emblazoned with stars.

The big guy on his left gave a chesty cough. So did the busty blonde on his right. Jesus. He should be wearing some sort of sanitation mask. If he came back from this thing with a cold, he wouldn't be happy.

Masha said, "Some of you may have heard of the word *koan*. A koan is a paradox or puzzle that Zen Buddhists use during meditation to help on their quest toward enlightenment. The most famous one is this: *What is the sound of one hand clapping?*"

Oh Lord. The website had given the impression that this place leaned more toward *luxury* wellness. Lars had a daily yoga and meditation practice, but he preferred his health retreats to avoid too much embarrassing cultural appropriation.

"While you look at the stars tonight I want you to reflect on two koans. The first one is this: *Out of nowhere the mind comes forth*." Masha paused. "And the second: *Show me your original face, the one you had before your parents were born*."

Lars heard the big guy next to him make a wheezy exhalation that caused him to start rolling about coughing.

"Do not struggle to find answers or solutions," said Masha. "This is not a quiz, my people!" She chuckled a little.

The woman really was quite a strange mix of charismatic leader and enthusiastic nerd. One moment a guru, the next the newly appointed CEO of a telecommunications company.

"There is no right or wrong answer. Simply look at the stars and reflect without straining for a solution. Just breathe. That's all you need to do. Breathe and watch the stars."

Lars breathed and watched the stars. He did not think of either of the koans. He thought of Ray, and how, early on in their relationship, Ray had convinced him to go camping with him (never again). They had lain together on a beach, holding hands and looking at the stars, and it had been beautiful, but something had built up and up in Lars's chest until he couldn't take it anymore and he'd jumped up and run into the ocean, *whooping* and tearing off his clothes, pretending he was the type of guy who whooped, the type of guy who didn't think about sharks or the temperature of the ocean in October. He smiled a bit, because he knew he couldn't get away with that now. Ray knew about his shark phobia.

Ray had asked if he could join him on this retreat. Lars couldn't work out his motivation. He'd never wanted to come to one before. Lars did a couple of retreats a year, but Ray always said they sounded hellish. Why did he suddenly want to come along on this one?

Lars thought of Ray's face when he said he'd rather go alone. There was a micro-moment when it looked like Lars had slapped him, but then Ray shrugged, smiled, and said that was fine, he was going to eat lasagne every night while Lars was gone and watch nothing but sports on TV.

Ray's lifestyle was already squeaky clean and in-corporated vegetable juices and smoothies and protein shakes. It wasn't necessary for him to come along to this. Lars needed his time alone.

Did he *want* Lars to feel like shit? Was it somehow related to the text Ray's sister, Sarah, had sent earlier today: *Can you at least think about it?*

She must have sent it without Ray's knowledge. Lars was sure Ray had accepted that his decision about chil-dren was final. It wasn't like he hadn't been up-front about his lack of interest in having a family. He had never said otherwise.

"Did I ever say otherwise?" he'd said to Ray, and he'd come close to raising his voice, which was not something he could countenance. He could not be in a relationship with the crassness and indignity of raised voices. It made him shudder to think of it. Ray knew this.

"You never said otherwise," Ray had responded evenly, and he didn't raise his voice. "You never misled me. I'm not saying that. I guess I just hoped you might change your mind."

Sarah, all shiny-eyed and sincere, had offered to help them have a baby. Ray's family was so liberal and lovely and loving. It was fucking annoying.

Lars had recoiled, literally physically recoiled, at the thought. "God no," he'd said to Ray and his sister. "Just . . . no." He'd felt terrified and suffocated by the thought of all the earnest love he'd have to endure if they had a baby. There would be no escaping it. All those family functions! Ray's mother would never stop crying.

It was not happening. Never. *Out of nowhere the mind comes forth.*

A Zen koan. *Give me strength.*

If Ray really wanted to be a father, should Lars let him go be one with someone else? But wasn't that up to Ray? If Ray couldn't live without children, then he was free to leave. They weren't married. The house was in both their names, but they were both financially secure and sufficiently intelligent people to work all that out. Obviously Lars could handle a fair division of property.

Was it the only way forward? Had their relationship reached an impossible impasse because, either way, one of them had to make an impossible sacrifice? Whose sacrifice was worse?

But Ray had stopped asking! He'd accepted it. Lars felt that Ray wanted something *else* from him. What was it? Permission to leave? He didn't want Ray to leave.

Something tumbled in the sky. A falling star, for God's sake. How had Masha managed that? Lars heard everyone exhale with the wonder of it.

He closed his eyes and all of a sudden it came to him exactly how he knew the big guy on his left and he wished Ray was here so he could tell him, *I got it, Ray, I got it!*

16

Jessica

The author, Frances Welty, who lay on the yoga mat next to Jessica, was fast asleep. She wasn't snoring but Jessica could tell she was asleep by the way she breathed. Jessica considered giving her a gentle nudge with her foot. She'd just missed seeing a falling star.

On reflection, Jessica decided not to bother her. It was the middle of the night. People her age really needed their sleep. If Jessica's mother had a bad night's sleep the bags under her eyes made her literally look like something from a horror movie, though she just laughed when Jessica tried to teach her about concealer. It wasn't *necessary* to look that bad. It was stupid. If Jessica's dad left her for his PA, Jessica's mother would have no one to blame but herself. Under-eye concealer was invented for a reason.

Jessica rolled her head and looked at Ben on the other side of her. He was staring up at the stars with a glazed expression, as if he were considering those Zen riddles, when really he was probably just counting down the hours until he could get out of here and back behind the wheel of his precious car.

He turned his head and winked at her. It made her heart lift, as if her crush had winked at her in the classroom.

Ben looked back up at the stars and Jessica touched her face with her fingers. She wondered if her skin looked bad without makeup in the moonlight. There had been no time to put on foundation. They were just dragged from their beds. They could have been having sex when that girl came into their bedroom, with just the gentlest knock on their door and without even waiting for them to say, "Come in," before she marched on in and shone a light in their eyes.

They hadn't been having sex. Ben had been asleep and Jessica had been lying next to him in the darkness, unable to sleep, missing her phone so badly it felt like she'd had something amputated. When she couldn't sleep at home she simply picked up her phone and scrolled through Instagram and Pinterest until she got tired.

She looked at her scarlet toenails in the moonlight. If she had her phone with her right now she would have photographed her feet, together with Ben's feet, and tagged it #starlightmeditation #healthretreat #learningaboutkoans #wejustsawafallingstar #whatisthesoundofonehandclapping.

That last hashtag would have made her look quite intellectual and spiritual, she thought, which was good, because you had to be careful not to come across as superficial on your socials.

She couldn't shake the feeling that if she didn't record this moment on her phone then it wasn't really happening, it didn't count, it wasn't real life. She knew that was irrational but she couldn't help it. She literally felt *twitchy* without her phone. Obviously she was addicted to it. Still, better than being addicted to heroin, though these days no one was sure about Ben's sister's most recent drug of choice. She liked to "mix it up."

Jessica sometimes wondered if all their problems led back to Ben's sister. She was always there, a big black cloud in their blue sky. Because, apart from Lucy, honestly, what did they have to worry about? Nothing. They should have been as happy as it was possible to be. Where had they gone wrong?

Jessica had been so *careful*, right from day one. What was that stupid thing her mother said? "Oh, Jessica, darling—this sort of thing can ruin people."

She said that, all frowny-faced, on what should have been the most spectacular day of Jessica's life. The day that split her life in two.

It was two years ago now. A Monday evening.

Jessica had come home from work in a hurry because she was going to try to make the 6:30 P.M. spin class. She rushed into the tiny kitchen with its ugly laminate countertops to fill her water bottle and there was Ben sitting on the floor, his back up against the dishwasher, his legs splayed, phone held limply in his hand. His face was dead white, his eyes glassy. She got down on the floor next to him, her heart pounding, barely breathing, hardly able to speak. The uppermost thought in her mind was, "Who? Who?" Her first thought was Lucy, of course. Ben's sister flirted with death on a daily basis. But something told her it wasn't Lucy. He seemed too shocked and Lucy's death was never going to come as a surprise.

He said, "Do you remember how Mum sent us that card?"

Jessica's heart contracted because she thought it must have been his mother who had died and she loved Ben's mum.

"How?" she said. "How did it happen?" How was it *possible* that Donna had died? She played tennis twice a week. She was healthier and fitter than Jessica. It was probably the stress over Lucy.

"You remember the card she sent?" Ben repeated obliviously. "Because we were so upset about the robbery?"

Poor Ben. He was obviously mad with grief and for some reason he was clutching on to this memory.

"I remember the card," she said gently.

It came in the mail. It had a cute puppy on the front with a speech bubble coming out of his mouth, saying, "Sorry to hear you're feeling low," and a lottery ticket inside. Donna's message said, *You two deserve some good luck*.

Ben said, "The ticket won."

Jessica said, "What's happened to your mum?"

"Nothing. Mum is fine," said Ben. "I haven't told her yet."

"You haven't told her what?" Jessica's brain couldn't seem to keep up with the words she was hearing and she was suddenly angry. "*Ben*. Has anybody died or not?"

Ben smiled. "Nobody has died."

"You're sure?"

"Everybody is in perfect health."

"Right," she said. "Well, good." As the adrenaline left her body she was suddenly exhausted. She didn't think she could do her spin class now.

"The ticket won. The ticket that Mum gave us after the robbery. That was the lottery office. We won the grand prize. We just won twenty-two million dollars."

She said tiredly, "Don't be stupid. We did not."

He turned to look at her, and his eyes were red and watery and fearful. He said, "We have."

If only they'd known in advance: you're going to win the lottery tomorrow. Then they might have acted like proper lottery winners. But it took a long while for it to feel like a fact. Jessica checked and double-checked the numbers on the internet. She called the lottery office back herself to confirm.

It became more real with each phone call they made to their family and friends, and then they finally started doing the screaming and jumping and crying and laughing expected of lottery winners and invited everyone over to celebrate with the most expensive champagne they could find in the liquor store.

They toasted those pathetic thieves, because if it wasn't for the robbery, they would never have won the lottery!

Ben's mother couldn't get over it. "It would never

even have crossed my mind to buy you a lottery ticket! That's the first lottery ticket I've ever bought in my life! I had to ask the lady at the newsagent how it worked!" She seemed to want to make sure that no one forgot that she bought the ticket. She didn't want a share in the prize (although obviously they ended up giving her money), she just wanted everyone to know of her crucial role in this glorious event.

It was like a better version of their wedding day. Jessica felt special. The center of attention. She smiled so much her cheeks ached. The money made her instantly more intelligent and beautiful and stylish. People treated her differently because she *was* different. When she looked at her own face in the bathroom mirror that night, she could already see it: she glowed with money. Instant wealth was like the best facial ever.

But even on that first night, even while Ben and his brothers argued drunkenly over which luxury cars to buy, Jessica could sense Ben's fear growing.

"Make sure it doesn't change us," he slurred, just before they fell asleep that night, and Jessica thought, *What are you talking about? It's already changed us!*

Then there was Jessica's mother, who acted as if the win were a catastrophe.

"You have to be *so* careful, Jessica," she said. "This kind of money can send people off the rails."

It was true that there had been some unexpected difficulties with this new life. Some tricky situations they were still trying to unravel. Friendships they'd lost. One family estrangement. Two family estrangements. No. Three.

Ben's cousin, who thought they should have paid off his mortgage. They gave him a car. Jessica thought that was generous! Ben liked his cousin, but he barely saw him before the win. In the end, they *did* pay off his mortgage, but "the damage had been done." For God's sake.

Jessica's younger sister. They gave her a *million dollars* but she kept asking for more, more, more. Ben said, "Just give it to her," and they did, but then one day Jessica went out to lunch with her and didn't offer to pay the bill, and now they weren't talking. Jessica's heart clenched as she thought about it. She always paid the bill. Always. It was the one time she didn't and supposedly that was unforgivable.

Ben's stepdad, because Ben's stepdad was a financial planner and he'd assumed that he'd manage all their finances now that they *had* finances—but Ben thought his stepdad was an idiot and didn't want him near their money, so that was awkward. Ben could have kept his opinions about his stepdad a secret forever if it wasn't for winning the lottery.

And of course, Ben's sister. How could they give her money? How could they not give her money? Ben and his mother had agonized over what to do. They tried to do it all the right way, the careful way. They set up a trust fund. They never gave her cash, but cash was all she wanted. When they bought her a car she sold it within two weeks. She sold anything they bought her. She screamed ugly words at poor Ben: *You rich prick with your fancy car, you won't even help out your own family.* They spent thousands and thousands on expensive rehab programs that Ben's mother had once dreamed about, assuming those exclusive programs would be the answer, if only they had the money. But once they had the money they found out that those weren't the answer. It just went on and on. Ben kept thinking there had to be a solution. Jessica knew there was no solution. Lucy didn't want help.

And it wasn't just their immediate family who thought Ben and Jessica should give them money. Every day they were contacted by long-lost relatives and friends, and friends of friends, asking for "loans" or a "helping hand" or wanting Ben and Jessica to support their favorite charity, their local school, their kids' soccer club. Family members they hadn't seen in years got in touch. Family members they didn't know existed got in touch. The requests often had a passive-aggressive edge: "Ten thousand dollars is probably small change to you but it would mean a *huge* amount to us."

"Just give it to them." That was Ben's constant refrain, but sometimes it got Jessica's back up. The *nerve* of these people.

It was bewildering to Jessica that she and Ben fought more about money now that they had an abundance of it. It was impossible to even imagine they'd once felt so upset about the arrival of unexpected bills.

Becoming instantly wealthy was like starting a really stressful, glamorous job for which they had no qualifications or experience, but still, it was a pretty great job. It was hardly something to complain about.

There was no need to *ruin* it, as Ben seemed intent on doing.

She sometimes wondered if Ben regretted winning the money. He told her once that he missed working. "Start your own business then," she said. They could do anything! But he said he couldn't compete with Pete, his old boss. He was like his sister; he didn't want a solution to his problems.

He said that he didn't like their "snooty new neighbors" and Jessica pointed out that they didn't even know them and offered to invite some of them over for drinks, but Ben looked horrified at the idea. It wasn't like they'd really known their neighbors back at the old flat. Everyone worked full-time and kept to themselves.

He enjoyed the luxury holidays they took, but even the travel didn't truly make him happy. Jessica remembered a night watching the sun set in Santorini. It was incredible, gorgeous, and she'd just bought a stunning bracelet for herself, and she'd looked across at Ben, who was deep in what seemed like profound thought, and she said, "What are you thinking about?"

"Lucy," he answered. "I remember she used to talk about traveling to the Greek islands."

It made her want to scream and scream because *they could afford to send Lucy to Santorini* and put her up at a great hotel, but that wasn't possible because Lucy preferred to stick needles in her arms. So fine, let her ruin her own life, but why did she have to ruin their lives as well?

The car was the one thing about the lottery win that

made him happy. He didn't really care about any of the other things—not the beautiful house in the best part of Toorak, the concert tickets, the designer labels, the travel. Only the car. His dream car. God, how she hated that car.

Jessica realized with a start that people were standing, straightening their unflattering gowns, suppressing yawns.

She got to her feet and looked at the starry sky one last time, but there were no answers up there.

17

Frances

It was only eight in the morning and Frances was hiking.

It was going to be another hot summer's day, but the temperature at this hour was perfect, the air silky-soft on her skin. There was no sound apart from the occasional sweet piercing call of a bellbird and the cracks and rustles of sticks and rocks beneath her feet on the rocky trail.

She felt like she'd been up for *hours*, which in fact she had been.

Today, her first full day at Tranquillum House, had begun before dawn (*before dawn!*) with a firm knock at her bedroom door.

Frances stumbled out of bed and opened the door to find the corridor empty and a silver tray on the floor, with her morning smoothie and a sealed envelope containing her "personalized daily schedule."

Frances had gotten back into bed to drink the smoothie with a pillow propped up behind her back

while she read her schedule with equal parts pleasure
and horror:

DAILY SCHEDULE FOR FRANCES WELTY

Dawn: Tai chi class in the rose garden.
7 A.M.: Breakfast in the dining room. (Please re-
member to continue to observe the silence.)
8 A.M.: Walking meditation. Meet at the bottom
of Tranquillity Hill. (This will be a slow, silent,
mindful hike giving you plenty of time to stop and
contemplate the magnificent views. Enjoy!)
10 A.M.: One-on-one exercise class. Meet Delilah
at the gym.
11 A.M.: Remedial massage with Jan in the spa.
12 noon: Lunch in the dining room.
1 P.M.: Guided sitting meditation in the yoga and
meditation studio.
2–4 P.M.: FREE TIME.
5 P.M.: Yoga class in the yoga and meditation
studio.
6 P.M.: Dinner in the dining room.
7–9 P.M.: FREE TIME.
9 P.M.: LIGHTS OUT.

Lights out! Was that a suggestion or an order? Frances hadn't been to bed at 9 P.M. since she was a child.

But then again, maybe she'd be ready for bed by then.

She'd yawned her way through the tai chi class in
the rose garden with Yao, silently eaten her first breakfast in the dining room (very good, poached eggs and
steamed spinach, although it felt kind of pointless without the essential accompaniment of sourdough toast

and a cappuccino), and now here she was with the other guests participating in the "walking meditation," which was basically a slow uphill hike on a bushland track a short distance away from the house.

The two wellness consultants, Yao and Delilah, were with them. Delilah led the group at the front and Yao was at the back. The pace, set by Delilah, was extremely slow, almost *agonizingly* slow, even for Frances, and if she found it difficult to walk this slowly, she suspected the Marconis—"exercise fanatics," according to Zoe—were just about losing their minds.

Frances was in the middle of the group, behind Zoe, whose glossy ponytail swung as she walked behind her dad. The serial killer was directly behind Frances, which was not the ideal position for a serial killer, but at least he'd be obliged to kill her in mindful slow motion, so she'd have plenty of time to escape.

At random intervals the group came to a stop, and they then had to stand and gaze silently at some fixed point on the horizon for what felt like an extraordinary length of time.

Frances was all for a leisurely hike with lots of rests to enjoy the view, but at this rate they would never get to the top.

Slowly, slowly, *slowly*, they filed up the hiking trail and slowly, slowly, *slowly*, Frances felt her mind and body adjust to the pace.

Slow was certainly . . . slow . . . but also it was quite . . . lovely.

She considered the pace of her life. The world had begun to move faster and faster over the last decade.

People spoke faster, drove faster, walked faster. Everyone was in a rush. Everyone was busy. Everyone demanded their gratification instantly. She'd even begun to notice it in the editing of her books. *Pace!* Jo had begun to snap in her editorial comments, where once she would have written: *Nice!*

It seemed to Frances that readers once had more patience, they were content for the story to take its time, for an occasional chapter to meander pleasurably through a beautiful landscape without anything much happening, except perhaps the exchange of some meaningful eye contact.

The path steepened, but they were walking so slowly that Frances's breathing stayed steady. The trail curved and slivers of views appeared like gifts between the trees. They were getting quite high up now.

Of course, Jo's editing had probably taken on that frenetic tone in response to Frances's declining sales. No doubt Jo could see *the writing on the wall* and that accounted for her increasingly feverish pleas: *Add some intrigue to this chapter. Maybe a red herring to throw the reader off the scent?*

Frances had ignored the comments and let her career peacefully pass away, like an old lady in her sleep. She was an idiot. A deluded fool.

She walked faster. The thought came to her that she might be walking a little too quickly at the exact moment her nose slammed straight into Zoe's shoulder blades.

Zoe had stopped dead. Frances heard her gasp.

Heather had somehow veered off the trail and onto a

large rock that overhung the steep side of the hill. The ground fell away directly in front of her. Another step and she would have gone over.

Napoleon had his wife's arm in a fierce grip. Frances couldn't tell if his face was white with anger or fear as his hand closed around her thin upper arm and he hauled her back onto the hiking trail.

Heather didn't thank her husband or smile at him or even meet his eyes. She extricated herself from Napoleon's grasp with an irritated shrug of her shoulder and walked ahead, tugging the sleeve of her threadbare T-shirt straight. Napoleon looked back at Zoe and his chest rose and fell in tandem with his daughter's audibly ragged breathing.

After a moment both father and daughter lowered their heads and continued their slow hike up the trail, as if what Frances had just witnessed had been of no consequence at all.

18

Tony

Tony Hogburn had just returned to his room after yet another hellish experience of a "guided sitting meditation." How much more meditation could a man do?

"Breathe in like you're breathing through a straw." Jesus wept, what a load of absolute horseshit.

He was humiliated to realize that his legs ached from the excruciatingly slow *walking* meditation they'd done this morning. Once upon a time he could have *run* that trail, no problem at all, as a *warm-up*, and now his legs felt like jelly after walking it at the pace of a hundred-year-old.

He sat on the balcony outside his room and yearned for an ice-cold beer and the feel of an old collie's silky, hard head under his hand. It should have been a mild desire for a beer and a sad ache for a beloved pet, but it felt like a raging thirst in the desert and the deepest of heartaches.

He went to stand up for the two hundredth time to

get relief for this pain from the fridge before remembering for the two hundredth time that there was no relief to be found. No refrigerator. No pantry. No TV to turn on for a distracting documentary. No internet to surf mindlessly. No dog he could summon with a whistle, just to hear the obedient patter of paws.

Banjo made it to fourteen years old. Good innings for a collie. Tony should have been ready for it, but it seemed he wasn't. In the first week, great gusts of grief hit him whenever he put his key in the lock of his front door. A grief hard enough to buckle his knees. Contemptible. A grown man brought to his knees by a dog.

He'd lost dogs before. Three dogs over the course of his life. It was part of being a dog owner. He didn't get why he was taking Banjo's death so hard. It was six months now, for Christ's sake. Was it possible that he grieved the loss of this damned dog more than any human he'd lost in his lifetime?

Yes, it was possible.

He remembered when the kids were little and the Jack Russell they gave their youngest, Mimi, for her eighth birthday escaped from the backyard and got hit by a car. Mimi had been devastated, crying on Tony's shoulder at the "funeral." Tony had cried too, feeling horrible guilt for missing that hole in the fence and sadness for that poor little dumb dog.

His daughter had been such a sweet little thing back then with her soft round cheeks and pigtails, so easy to love.

Now Mimi was a twenty-six-year-old dental hygien-
ist and she looked just like her mother: skinny, with
a pinlike head and a rapid way of talking and walking that exhausted Tony. She was hygienic and busy,
Mimi, and maybe not so easy to love, although he did
love her. He'd die for his daughter. But sometimes he
wouldn't pick up the phone for her. Being a dental hy-
gienist meant that Mimi was used to delivering mono-
logues without fear of interruption. She was closer to her
mother than to him. All three kids were. He hadn't been
around enough in their childhood. Next thing, they were
grown-ups and he sometimes got the feeling that they
were doing "Dad duty" when they called or turned up
for a visit. Once, Mimi left a sweet, cooing message
on his phone for his birthday, and then right at the end
of the message he heard her say in an entirely different
tone of voice to someone else, "Right, that's done, let's
go!" as she hung up.

His sons didn't remember his birthday—not that he
expected them to remember it; he barely remembered it
himself, and he only remembered theirs because Mimi
texted him a reminder on the mornings of her brothers'
birthdays. James lived in Sydney, dating a different girl
every month, and his oldest, Will, had married a Dutch
girl and moved to Holland. Tony's three granddaughters,
whom he only saw in real life every couple of years and
Skyped with at Christmas, had Dutch accents. They
felt entirely unrelated to him. His ex-wife saw them all
the time, traveled over there twice a year and stayed for
two, three weeks. His oldest granddaughter excelled at
"Irish dancing." (Why were they doing *Irish* dancing in

Holland? Why were they doing Irish dancing at all? No one else seemed to find this strange. According to his ex-wife, children were doing Irish dancing all around the world. It was good for their "aerobic fitness" and co-ordination or something. Tony had seen footage on her phone. His granddaughter wore a *wig* and danced like she had a giant ruler duct-taped to her back.)

Tony never expected being a grandfather to be like this: funny-accented little girls talking to him on a screen about things he didn't understand. When he'd imagined being a grandfather, he'd imagined a small sticky trusting hand in his, a slow dawdling walk to the corner shop to buy ice creams. That never happened, and the corner store wasn't even there anymore, so what the hell was wrong with him?

He stood. He needed something to eat. Thinking of his grandchildren had created a crater of misery in his stomach that could only be filled with carbohydrates. He would make a grilled cheese—*Jesus Christ*. No bread. No cheese. No toaster. "You might experience something we call 'snack anxiety,'" his wellness consultant, Delilah, had told him with a gleam in her eyes. "Don't worry, it will pass."

He slumped back in his chair and thought back to the day he booked this hellhole. That moment of temporary insanity. His appointment with the GP had been at eleven A.M. He even remembered the time.

The doctor said, "Right. Tony." A beat. "About those test results."

Tony must have been holding his breath because he took an involuntary gusty gulp of air. The doctor studied the paperwork for a few moments. He took off his glasses and leaned forward, and there was something in his eyes that reminded Tony of the vet's face when he told him that it was time to let Banjo go.

Tony would never forget the shocking clarity of the moment that followed.

It was like he'd been walking around in a daze for the last twenty years and suddenly he was awake. He remembered how his mind had raced on the drive home. He had been so clear and focused. He needed to act. Fast. He could not spend the short time he had left working and watching TV. But what to do?

So he Googled. "How to change . . ." Google finished the sentence for him. *How to change my life*. There were a trillion suggestions, from religion to self-help books. That's when he came across an article about health resorts. Tranquillum House was top of the list.

A ten-day cleanse. What could be so hard about that? He hadn't taken a break in years. He ran a sports-marketing consultancy and he'd made one of the few excellent decisions of his life when he hired Pippa as an office manager. She was better than him at basically every aspect of his job.

He would drop some weight. He would get himself together. He would make an action plan. On the drive from the airport he'd felt almost *optimistic*.

If only he hadn't made that stupid last-minute decision to stock up on emergency supplies. He'd already taken the turnoff to Tranquillum House when he did a U-turn and headed back to the nearest town, where he'd seen a drive-through bottle shop. All he'd got was a six-pack of beer (*light* beer) and a bag of chips and some crackers (what the hell was wrong with *crackers*?).

If he hadn't turned around he would never have met Loony Woman on the side of the road. He'd thought she was in some kind of trouble. What other logical reason would there be to sit on the side of the road screaming and banging her horn? When she opened the window and he saw her face, she had looked seriously ill. Was menopause really that bad or was this woman a hypochondriac? Maybe it was that bad. Once he got out of here he'd ask his sister.

Now she appeared perfectly normal and healthy. If he hadn't seen her on the side of the road, he would have picked her as one of those bright-eyed, bushy-tailed "super mums" who bounded about like Labradors when Tony's kids were at school.

He was kind of terrified of her. She'd made him feel like a moron. It brought back a long-buried memory of a humiliating incident from childhood. He'd had a thing for one of his older sister's friends and something happened—he'd said something or done something, he couldn't quite remember—but he knew it was to do with periods and tampons, something he hadn't understood at the age of thirteen, something innocent and trite that had seemed like the end of the world at the time.

Now he was fifty-six years old. A grandfather! He'd seen his wife give birth to their three children. He was beyond feeling embarrassed by the dark mysteries of a woman's body. Yet that's how Loony Woman had made him feel.

He stood, agitated, his chair scraping back. There were two hours of "free time" to fill before dinner. At home the hours between work and bed glided by in a haze of beer and food and television. Now he didn't know where to go. This room felt too small for him. There were too many cutesy ornaments. Yesterday he'd turned around and knocked a vase off a side table, shattering it, causing him to swear so loudly whoever was in the room next to his probably heard. He hoped it wasn't an antique.

He leaned over the balcony and studied the grounds. Two kangaroos stood in the shade of the house. One of them was grooming itself, twisting around in a very human way to scratch. The other one sat still, ears alert; it looked like it was carved in stone.

He could see the gleaming aquamarine of a huge kidney-shaped pool. Maybe he'd go for a swim. He couldn't remember the last time he'd been for a swim. The beach used to be such a big part of his life when the kids were little. He took all three to Nippers every Sunday morning for years, where they learned how to be surf-safe. Meanwhile, his three pale-skinned grandchildren had probably never caught a wave in their sad little Dutch lives.

He went to his suitcase and pulled out his board shorts, trying not to think of a stranger's hands rifling through his clothes, searching for contraband, noting his faded underwear. He needed new clothes.

His ex-wife used to buy all his clothes. He never asked her to buy his clothes, she just did it, and he wasn't interested in clothes, so he got used to it. Then, years later, during the divorce, it appeared that was one of the many, many things she did for which she felt "taken for granted." He "never once said thank you." Didn't he? Could that be true? Jesus. And if it was true, why wait twenty-two years to mention it? Surely he said thank you. But why not tell him he was being an ungrateful pig *at the time*, so he didn't have to feel like the worst man in the world sitting there in front of that counselor all those years later? He felt so ashamed at that moment he literally couldn't speak. This turned out to be an example of him "shutting down," "being emotionally distant," "not giving a shit"—and on it went until he no longer did give a shit and he was numbly signing the papers.

What was that phrase his wife used to describe him? As if it were funny? "Amateur human being." She'd even said it to the counselor.

A few months after that counseling session it occurred to him that there were various things he'd done in that marriage for which he was pretty sure he'd never been thanked or acknowledged. He took care of everything to do with her car, for example. The amateur human being kept her car filled with petrol. He'd often wondered if she thought it had some sort of self-filling mechanism. He got her car serviced once a year. Did her tax return.

Wasn't it possible they both took each other for granted? Wasn't it possible that taking each other for granted was one of the benefits of marriage?

But it was too late by then.

Now it was five years since the separation and they

were the best five years of his ex-wife's life. She was back in touch with her "true self." She lived on her own and did evening courses and went on weekends away with a gaggle of blissfully divorced women. In fact, they often came to places like this. His ex now had a "daily meditation practice." "How long do you practice before you get it right?" Tony had asked, and she'd rolled her eyes so hard it was a wonder they didn't get stuck there. Whenever she talked to Tony these days she kept stopping to breathe deeply. Come to think of it, she looked like she was breathing through a straw.

Tony pulled up his board shorts.

Jesus Christ.

They must have shrunk badly. He'd probably washed them the wrong way. In cold water. Or hot water. The wrong water. He tugged at the fabric with all his strength and slid the button through the buttonhole.

Done. Except he couldn't breathe.

He coughed and the button pinged free, skittering across the floorboards. He laughed out loud with disbelief and looked down at the huge hairy bulge of his stomach. It seemed to belong to someone else.

He remembered a different body. A different time. The almighty roar of an ecstatic crowd. The way the sound used to vibrate in his chest. Once there had been no barrier at all between his mind and his body. He thought "run" and he ran. He thought "jump" and he jumped.

He rolled down his shorts so that they sat beneath his belly, and thought of his ex-wife, six months pregnant, doing the same thing with an elastic-waisted skirt.

He picked up his room key and put a white bath

towel over his shoulder. Were these towels allowed outside? There was probably a clause in the contract about
it. Old mate the beanstalk would be able to tell him.
Presumably a lawyer. Tony knew all about lawyers.

He left his room. The house was as quiet and still as
a church. He opened the front door and walked out into
the afternoon heat and down the paved path that led to
the pool.

A woman walked back toward him in the opposite
direction wearing a sporty black swimsuit and a sarong
tied at her waist. The one with the chunky plait of hair
like a horse's tail and brightly colored cat's-eye glasses.
Tony had her pegged: intellectual left-wing feminist. She
would write Tony off after five minutes of conversation.
Still, he'd rather be ignored by the feminist than interact
with Loony Woman.

The path was too narrow for them to pass each other,
so Tony stood to one side, which hopefully would not
offend her feminist principles, like that time when he'd
held open a door for a woman and she'd hissed, "I can
open it myself, thanks." He'd thought about letting it
slam in her face, but he didn't, of course, he just smiled
like a gormless goon, because not every man was capable of violence toward women even if they did have
the occasional violent thought.

This woman didn't make eye contact, but lifted her
hand in thanks as if she were lifting it from the steering
wheel of a car to thank him for letting her into his lane,
and it was only after she'd gone past him that he realized she was weeping quietly. He sighed. He couldn't
stand to see a woman cry.

He watched her go—not a bad figure—then walked on toward the pool, tugging at his shorts to make sure they didn't fall at his feet.

He opened the gate.

For fuck's sake.

Loony Woman was in the pool, bobbing about like a cork.

19

Frances

For heaven's sake, thought Frances. The serial killer.

The mechanisms of the pool gate had bamboozled her for about five minutes but naturally he had no problem at all. He lifted the little black knobby thing with one meaty hand and kicked the gate hard with the ball of his foot.

Frances had already had to endure Flustered Glasses powering up and down the pool creating a wake like a speedboat. Now *him.*

The serial killer dropped his bath towel on a deck chair (you were meant to use the stripy blue-and-white towels from reception, but rules didn't apply to him), walked straight to the edge of the pool and, without even bothering to put in his toe to check the temperature, dived straight in. Frances did a sedate breaststroke in the other direction.

Now she was stuck in the pool because she didn't want to get out in front of him. She would have thought she was too old to worry about her body being observed and judged in a swimsuit, but apparently this neurosis began at twelve years old and *never ended.*

The problem was that she wanted to convey strength in all her future interactions with this man, and her soft white body, especially when compared to Masha's Amazonian example, damn her, didn't convey anything much except fifty-two years of good living and a weakness for Lindt chocolate balls. The serial killer would no doubt be the type to rank every woman based on his own personal "Would I fuck her?" score.

She remembered her first-ever boyfriend of over thirty years ago, who told her he preferred smaller breasts than hers, while his hands were *on* her breasts, as if she'd find this interesting, as if *women's body parts were dishes on a menu and men were the goddamned diners.*

This is what she said to that first boyfriend: "Sorry."

This was her first boyfriend's benevolent reply: "That's okay."

She couldn't blame her upbringing for her pathetic behavior. When Frances was eight years old, a man patted her mother's bottom as he walked past them on a suburban street. "Nice arse," he said in a friendly tone. Frances remembered thinking, *Oh, that's kind of him.* And then she'd watched in shock as her five-foot-nothing mother chased the man to the corner and swung a heavy handbag full of hardback library books at the back of his head.

Right. Enough was enough. She would get out of the pool, at her own pace. She would not rush to grab up her towel to throw over her body.

Wait.

She didn't *want* to get out of the pool! She was here first. Why should she get out just because he was here? She would enjoy her swim and *then* she would get out.

She dived down and swam along the pebbly bottom of the pool, enjoying the dappled light and relishing the ache in her legs from the hike that morning. Yes, this was so lovely and relaxing and she was fine. Her back felt quite good—after her second massage with Jan— and she was definitely a little transformed already. Then, apropos of absolutely nothing, the words of the review slithered snakelike into her mind: *Misogynistic airport trash that leaves a bad taste in your mouth.*

Frances thought of how Zoe had said she would read *Nathaniel's Kiss* just to be nice. The last thing that sad beautiful child needed to read was misogynistic trash. Had Frances accidentally been writing misogynistic trash for the last thirty years? She came to the surface with an undignified gasp for air that sounded like a sob.

The serial killer stood at the opposite side of the pool, breathing hard, his back against the tiles, his arms resting on the paving. He stared straight at her with something like . . . *fear.*

For God's sake, she thought. *I may not be twenty years old, but is my body really so unattractive it actually scares you?*

"Um," he said out loud. He grimaced. He actually *grimaced*. That's how disgusting he found her.

"What?" said Frances. She squared her shoulders and thought of her mother swinging her handbag like a discus thrower. "We're not meant to be talking."

"Um . . . you're . . ." He touched under his nose.

Did he mean, "You smell"?

She did not smell!

Frances put her fingers to her nose. "Oh!"

Her nose was bleeding. She'd never had a bloody nose in her life. That review had *given her an actual bloody nose.*

"Thank you," she said coldly. Both times she'd interacted with this man she had been at a terrible and most mortifying disadvantage.

She tipped her head back and dog-paddled toward the steps.

"Head forward," said the serial killer.

"You're meant to put your head back," snapped Frances. She waded up the stairs, trying to stop her swimsuit from riding up with one hand while attempting to stem the flow of blood with the other. Great clots of blood slid from her nose into her cupped hand. It was disgusting. Unbelievable. Like she'd been *shot.* She was not good with blood. Not really very good with anything remotely medical. It was one of the reasons why having babies had never appealed to her. She looked up at the blue sky and a wave of nausea hit her.

"I think I'm going to faint," she said.

"No, you're not," he said.

"I have low blood pressure," she said. "I faint a lot. I could *easily* faint."

"I've got you," he said.

She clutched his arm as he helped her out of the pool. He wasn't rough exactly, but there was a detachment to his touch, and a kind of concentrated grunting effort, like he was moving an ungainly piece of furniture through a narrow doorway. A refrigerator, perhaps. It was depressing to be treated like a refrigerator.

The blood continued to gush from her nose. He led her to the deck chair, sat her down, put one towel around her shoulders and the other in front of her nose.

"Firmly pinch the bridge of your nose," he said. "Like this." He pinched her nose and then directed her hand into the same spot. "That's it. You'll be all right. It'll stop."

"I'm sure you're meant to put your head *back*," protested Frances.

"It's forward," he said. "Otherwise the blood runs down the back of your throat. I'm not wrong on this."

She gave up. Maybe he was right. He was one of those definite people. Definite people were often annoyingly right about things.

The nausea and dizziness began to ease. She kept pinching her nose and chanced an upward glance. He stood solidly in front of her so she was at eye level with his belly button.

"You okay?" he said. He coughed his phlegmy plague-ridden cough.

"Yes, thank you," she said. "I'm Frances." She kept one hand on her nose and held out her other hand. He shook it. Her hand disappeared into his.

"Tony," he said.

"Thanks so much for your help," she said. He was probably a nice man, even if he had treated her like a refrigerator. "And you know—for stopping on the road when I was . . ."

He looked pained by the memory.

"I've never had a bloody nose before," she told him. "I don't know what brought it on, although I guess I have had a bad cold. Actually, *you* sound like you've had quite a bad—"

"I might get going," Tony interrupted her impatiently, aggressively, as if she were an old lady who had accosted him at a bus stop and wouldn't let him get a word in edgewise.

"Places to go, people to see?" said Frances, deeply offended. She'd just been through a *medical crisis.*

Tony met her gaze. His eyes were light brown, almost gold. They brought to mind a small endangered native animal. A bilby, for example.

"No," he said. "I just thought I should . . . get dressed for dinner."

Frances grunted. They had plenty of time before dinner.

There was an awkward moment of silence. He didn't leave.

He cleared his throat. "I don't know if I'm going to survive this . . . experience." He touched his stomach. "It's not really my kind of thing. I didn't expect quite so much hippy-dippy stuff."

Frances softened, smiled. "You'll be fine. It's only ten days. Nine to go now."

"Yeah," said Tony. He sighed and squinted off at the blue-hazed horizon. "It *is* beautiful here."

"It is," said Frances. "Peaceful."

Tony said, "So you're okay? Keep pinching your nose until it stops."

"Yup," said Frances.

She looked down at the scarlet droplets on her towel and found another, cleaner section of fabric to plug her nose.

When she looked up Tony was already walking toward the pool gate. As he lifted his arm to open it, his shorts suddenly slid down to his knees to reveal the entirety of his buttocks.

"Fuck!" he said with deep feeling.

Frances stared. What in the world? The man had tattoos of *bright yellow smiley faces* on both his butt cheeks. It was extraordinary. It was like discovering he was wearing a secret clown suit beneath his clothes.

She ducked her head. A second later she heard the pool gate slam. She looked up and he was gone.

Smiley-face tattoos. How drunk must he have been? It kind of changed her entire view of the man. No longer the arrogant sneering man. He was *Tony*. Tony with smiley-face tattoos on his butt.

Tony, the smiley-face-tattoo-butted serial killer?

She chuckled, sniffed, and tasted quite a lot of blood.

20

Masha

Another email from him. In just a matter of days. Masha stared at her ex-husband's name on her computer screen. The subject heading of this one read: POZHA-LUYSTA PROCHTI MASHA.

Please read, Masha.

It was as if he were speaking directly to her. There was an attachment to the email. She heard herself make a noise, a silly pathetic little squeak, like the sound of someone standing on a child's toy.

She remembered the weight and warmth of his arm across her shoulders as they sat on an awful Soviet-made couch, in a flat that looked identical to their own, except that this one had something extraordinary: a VCR.

If not for that wonderful, terrible VCR, where would she be right now? *Who* would she be? Not here. Not this person. Maybe they would still be together.

She deleted the email then went straight to her deleted items folder and deleted it there too.

This was a crucial moment in her professional life. Focus was essential. People were depending on her: her guests, her staff. She did not have time for so-called . . . what was that rhyming phrase Delilah used? Blasts from the past. She did not have time for blasts from the past.

And yet her stomach continued to lurch about like the sea. She needed to practice detachment. First, she needed to identify the emotion she was experiencing, observe it, label it, let it go. She looked for a word that could describe how she felt and could only find one from her native language: *toska*. There was no adequate English word to describe the kind of anguished longing she felt for something she could not have and did not even want. Maybe because English-speaking people did not experience that feeling.

What was going on? This was not like her! She stood and went to the exercise mat on the floor of her office and did push-ups until her forehead was covered in sweat.

She returned to her desk, breathing hard, and opened the security program on her computer to check on the location and activities of her guests, her mind focused once again. She had installed CCTV cameras around the property for security reasons, and right now she could see most of her guests.

The young couple walked down the back footpath toward the hot springs. Jessica was in front, her head bowed, Ben a few steps behind, studying the horizon.

The Marconi family appeared to have split up. Napoleon was in the rose garden. He was down on his knees,

sniffing a rose. Masha smiled. He was literally stopping to smell the roses.

Meanwhile, his wife was out running. Heather was
nearly at the top of Tranquillity Hill. Masha watched
for a moment, impressed by her pace on the steep section. Not as fast as Masha, but fast.

Where was the daughter? Masha clicked through
grainy black-and-white images and found her in the gym,
lifting weights.

Tony Hogburn was leaving the pool area, where Frances Welty sat on a deck chair, dabbing at her face with
a towel.

Lars Lee lay in a hammock in the pergola with some
sort of drink he'd obviously persuaded the kitchen staff
to give him. He would have used sign language and his
good looks. Masha had his number.

No one else? She clicked through the upstairs cor-
ridors and came across a woman wearing a sarong,
walking briskly. Carmel Schneider. The other single
woman.

Carmel took off her glasses and rubbed her face.
Possibly crying?

"Deep breaths," murmured Masha as Carmel struggled with her room key and banged her fist with frustration against the door.

Eventually, Carmel opened the door and almost
fell inside. If only Masha could see what she did once
she was in her room. People were so prudish. Yao and
Delilah got worked up about legalities. Masha had no
interest in seeing the naked bodies of her guests! She

simply wanted to gain *knowledge* in order to do her job to the best of her ability.

She would have to rely on audio only. She turned a dial on her screen and keyed in Carmel's room number.

A woman's tear-choked voice emerged loud and clear from Masha's monitor.

"Get a grip. Get a grip. Get a grip."

21

Carmel

Carmel stood in her room and slapped her own face. Once. Twice. Three times. The third time she slapped herself so hard her glasses flew off.

She picked them up, went to the bathroom, and looked at her flushed cheek in the mirror.

For a moment there, when she was in the pool, swimming her laps, endorphins zipping through her body after that fantastic bushwalk, she felt fine, more than fine—she felt exultant. It had been years since she'd had time to do laps.

As she swam she gloried in the fact that there was nowhere to be, nothing to do, no one to worry about. No jazz pickup or karate drop-off, no homework to supervise, no birthday gifts to buy, no doctors' appointments to book; the endless multitude of teeny-tiny details that made up her life. Each obligation on its own seemed laughably easy. It was the sheer volume that threatened to bury her.

Here, she didn't even have to do her own laundry.

Carmel simply had to put her washing outside her door in a little cloth bag and it would be returned to her, laundered and ironed, within twenty-four hours. She'd literally cried with happiness when she read that.

She had set herself a goal of fifty laps of freestyle, faster and faster with each lap. She was going to get so, so fit here! She could almost feel that excess weight falling off her. All she'd ever needed was *time* to exercise and a pantry free of treats. As she swam, she silently chanted in time with her strokes: *I'm so happy, I'm so happy, I'm so happy,* breathe, *I'm so happy, I'm so happy, I'm so happy,* breathe.

But then that tiny voice beneath the exultant chanting, just the faintest whisper, had begun: *I wonder what they're doing now.*

She'd tried to ignore it, chanting louder: *I'm so HAPPY, I'm so HAPPY.*

The voice got louder until it became a shout: *No, but seriously, what do you think they're doing RIGHT NOW?*

That's when she'd felt her sanity come loose. The feeling of panic reminded her of one of those recurring dreams in which she'd lost all four of her daughters in some bizarrely negligent way, such as leaving them on the side of the road, or just forgetting they existed and going out dancing.

She'd tried to calm herself with rational thoughts. Her children were not lost on the side of the road; they were with their father and Sonia, his perfectly lovely new girlfriend, soon to be wife. Carmel knew from the itinerary that today they were in Paris, staying in a "wonderful" Airbnb flat. Sonia, who "just loved to travel," had stayed there before. It would be cold, of course, in January, but the kids had new jackets. They were on the trip of a lifetime. They were having a wonderful educational experience while their mother had a wonderful break to "recharge."

Their father loved them. Their father's new girlfriend loved them. "Sonia said she loves us more than life itself," Rosie told Carmel after only the *third time* she met the woman, and Carmel said, "Well, *she* sounds like a total nutcase!" but only in her head. Out loud she said, "That's so nice!"

It was an amicable divorce. Amicable on Joel's part, anyway. On Carmel's part, it felt like a death no one acknowledged. He just fell out of love with her, that's all. It must have been so hard for him, living with a woman he no longer loved. He really struggled with it, poor man, but he had to be true to himself.

It happens. It happens a lot. It's essential the discarded wife remain dignified. She must not wail and weep, except in the shower, when the kids are at school and preschool, and she's alone in the suburbs with all the other weeping, wailing wives. The discarded wife must not be bitchy or unkind about the new and improved wife. She must suck it up but without developing a sour face. It is better for all concerned if she is thin.

Carmel had touched the side and turned to do another lap when she saw that someone had joined her in the pool. The friendly-looking older blond woman. Carmel almost said, "Hi," before remembering the silence and ignoring her.

She'd kept swimming and thought about how that woman's hair was a similar shade to Sonia's hair. No doubt they both paid handsomely for it.

Carmel's daughter Lulu was fair-haired. Lulu looked entirely unrelated to Carmel, which had never mattered until the day Lulu told her that when Daddy and Sonia took them out to dinner a lady stopped by the table and said to Lulu, "You've got beautiful hair just like your mummy, haven't you?"

Carmel said, in a high, strained voice, "Huh, that's funny. Did you tell her that Sonia wasn't your mummy?"

Lulu said that Daddy had said it wasn't necessary to always point out that Sonia wasn't her real mother, and Carmel had said, "Of course it's necessary, darling, you should point it out *every single time* in your loudest voice," but only in her head. Out loud she said, "It's time to clean your teeth, Lulu."

Remembering this, she'd picked up speed, her arms and legs chopping through the water, harder and harder, faster and faster, but she couldn't sustain it, she wasn't fit enough, she was so unfit, and fat, and lazy, and *disgusting*. And she thought of her four girls on the other side of the world, in Paris, where Carmel had never been, having their hair done by Sonia, and probably sitting still for her, and suddenly she swallowed a giant mouthful of water.

She'd hopped out of the pool, without making eye contact with the friendly blond lady, as per the rules, fortunately, because she was crying like a fool, and she'd cried all the way to her room. There was no way the big man coming down the pathway to the pool hadn't noticed.

"Get a grip," she said now to her reflection in the mirror.

She wrapped her arms around her body.

She missed her children. It hit her like a sudden fever. She longed for the comfort of their four beautiful little-girl bodies and their heedless, proprietorial use of *her* body: the way they plonked themselves on her lap as if she were a chair, the way they burrowed their hot little heads into her stomach, her breasts. She was always yelping at someone, "Get *off* me!" When she was with her children, she was needed—essential, in fact: everything relied on her. Someone was always saying, "Where's Mummy?" "I'm telling Mum what you just said." "Mummmmmy!"

Now she was untethered by obligations, as loose and free as a balloon.

She undid the tie of her swimsuit and let it fall in a heap on the bathroom floor while she studied her naked body in the mirror.

"I'm so sorry. I still care very deeply for you, but we've always valued honesty in our relationship, haven't we?" Joel said to her a year ago, while he poured her a glass of wine. "It really hurts me to say this but, the thing is, I'm just not attracted to you anymore."

He truly thought he was being kind and ethical. He believed himself to be a man who did the right thing. He would never have cheated on her. He simply left her, went straight onto a dating website, and replaced her. His conscience was perfectly clear. He'd always liked to keep his possessions well maintained, and if they couldn't be repaired to "as new" then he updated them.

Carmel lifted her breasts in both hands to where they used to be, when they were "as new." She looked at the stretch marks on her wobbly stomach and thought of some sappy Facebook post she'd read about how stretch marks were beautiful because of what they represented, creating new life, blah blah blah. Maybe stretch marks could be considered beautiful if the father of your babies still loved your body.

When Joel asked if he and Sonia could please take the girls on a trip to Europe over the January school holidays—Disneyland in Paris! Skiing in Austria! Ice-skating in Rome!—Carmel had said, "Are you kidding me? You're going on the trip we used to talk about doing? But you're doing it without me?" but only in her head. Out loud she said, "That sounds like so much fun!" And then she arranged all their passports.

She'd told her sister that she was going to spend the time they were away eating paleo and doing cardio and weights and yoga. The plan was to transform her body.

She didn't want Joel back. All she wanted was for his mouth to drop open when he saw her. She didn't need him to *gape*, although that would be nice. She simply wanted her body to look as good as it was physically possible for her to look, and then maybe, possibly, probably not, but possibly, she herself might check out one of those dating websites where you went to replace your spouse.

"There's not a damned thing wrong with your body.

You are *average-sized*, you deluded fool! You are an attractive, intelligent woman, you idiot! You should spend January lying in a hammock and eating cheese," said Carmel's sister Vanessa, who was furious with Joel and the fat-shaming patriarchy.

Carmel let her breasts drop and put a hand to the curve of her stomach. Average wasn't good enough. Average was too big. Everyone knew that. There was an obesity crisis in this country! She didn't want to fat-shame other people, but she certainly wanted to fat-shame herself because she deserved to be shamed. She used to be two sizes smaller and the reason she was now two sizes larger was not because of her four daughters; it was because she didn't "take care of herself." Women were meant to "take care of themselves." That's what men said on dating websites: *I'd like a woman who takes care of herself.* They meant: *I want a thin woman.*

And it wasn't like the information wasn't available on *how* to take care of yourself! Everyone knew you simply cut out carbs and sugar and trans fats from your diet! Celebrities generously revealed their secrets. They snacked on a "handful of nuts" or "two squares of dark antioxidant-rich chocolate"! They drank a lot of water, stayed out of the sun, and took the stairs! It wasn't rocket science! But did Carmel ever take the stairs? No, she didn't.

It was true that she often had the kids with her, and if they walked up too many stairs one of them was liable to run too far ahead while another one sat down and announced that her legs no longer worked, but still, there must have been times when Carmel could have built some "incidental exercise" into her lifestyle. And yet she hadn't. She neglected her body, she didn't get her hair cut for months on end, her eyebrows were left unplucked, she forgot to shave her legs, and it was no surprise her husband left her, because, as she tried to teach her children, *actions had consequences.*

She thought of the long sculpted lines of Masha's body.

She imagined *Masha* living Carmel's life, standing at the front door when Joel and Sonia dropped off the girls. Joel wouldn't have left Masha in the first place, but say he did, then Masha's heart wouldn't hammer with pain and humiliation at the sight of her ex-husband and his new girlfriend. Masha wouldn't curve her body around the door at a strange angle as if to hide it from Joel. Masha would stand tall and proud. She wouldn't hunch her body to protect her raw, broken heart.

Her sister said Joel's so-called "lack of attraction" was Joel's problem, not hers. Her sister said Carmel should learn self-love and texted her links to articles about "intuitive eating" and "healthy at any size." Carmel knew these articles were written by fat people to make fat people feel better about their sad fat lives.

If she could transform her body, she could transform her life, and she could move on from her failed marriage. That wasn't deluded. That was a fact.

Her sister, who was both wealthy and generous—a most excellent combination—gave Carmel a card for her birthday that said: *Carmel, I don't think you need to lose weight. You're beautiful and Joel is a shallow idiot and you should give ZERO FUCKS what he thinks. But if you're determined to go on a health kick, I want you to do it in style and comfort. I've booked you into Tranquillum House for their ten-day cleanse while the kids are away. Enjoy! Ness xx PS And then come home and eat cheese.*

Carmel hadn't been that happy to receive a gift since she was a child.

Now she thought of Masha's words: "In ten days, you will not be the person you are now." The word "please" filled her mind. Please, please, please, let that be true, please, please, please, let me become someone other than this. She looked at her stupid, dopey, pleading face in the mirror. Her skin was rough and red like an old washerwoman's hands. There was a picket fence of tiny lines neatly indented across her top lip, which was so thin it disappeared when she smiled. The only part of her body that was thin was her top lip. Lips were meant to be plump rosebuds, not mean thin disappearing lines.

Oh, Carmel, of course he stopped being attracted to you! What were you thinking? How could he possibly be attracted to someone who looks like *you?* She lifted her hand to slap her face once more.

There was a gentle knock on the door. Carmel jumped. She pulled on the Tranquillum House dressing gown and went to open the door.

It was Yao. His head was bowed. He didn't make eye contact or say a word. He held out a small card.

Carmel took it and Yao immediately backed away. She closed the door.

It was a square of thick, creamy cardboard like a

wedding invitation. The handwriting was in thick black authoritative ink.

> *Dear Carmel,*
> *Although you are currently scheduled for free time, we ask that you please report immediately to the spa for the Tranquillum House Ultimate Relaxation and Rejuvenation Signature Facial. It's a ninety-minute treatment and will be completed just before dinner. Your therapist is waiting for you.*
> *Yours,*
> *Masha*
>
> *PS Yao is your assigned wellness consultant, but please know that I will also be doing everything in my power to deliver you the health, healing, and happiness you need and deserve.*

It was at this moment that Carmel Schneider gave herself to Masha with the same voluptuous abandon that novice nuns once surrendered themselves to God.

22

Yao

It was 9 P.M. The guests had all been fed and were safely in their rooms, hopefully sleeping soundly. Yao, Masha, and Delilah sat at a round table in the corner of Masha's office with notepads in front of them. They were having their daily staff meeting, at which Yao and Delilah were required to give status updates.

Masha tapped her fingertips on the table. There was always a discernible difference in her demeanor at these meetings. You could see her former corporate identity in the language she chose, the crispness of her speech, and the stiffness of her posture. Delilah found it laughable, but Yao, who had never worked in that world, found it charming.

"Right. Next item on the agenda. The silence. Has anyone broken it today?" asked Masha. She seemed brittle. It must be nerves about the new protocol. Yao was nervous himself.

"Lars broke it," said Delilah. "He was trying to get out of the daily blood tests. I told him not to be a baby."

Yao would never say that to a guest. Delilah just said what she was thinking, whereas Yao, *sometimes*, felt just a little . . . fraudulent. Like a performer. For example, he would be helping an ill-mannered guest do a plank and giving them gentle, patient encouragement—"You've got this!"—while thinking, *You're not even trying, you rude lazy motherfucker.*

"Frances wrote me a note," said Yao. "She asked if she could please skip the blood test as she'd had a bloody nose. I told her that was all the more reason to do the test."

Masha grunted. "Nobody likes blood tests," she said. "I don't like them! I hate needles." She shuddered. "When we were applying to come here all those years ago we had to do *many* blood tests: for AIDS, for syphilis. Your government wanted us for our brains but our bodies had to also be perfect. Even our teeth were checked." She tapped her finger against her white teeth. "I remember my friend said, '*It's like they are choosing a horse!*'" Her lip curled at the memory, as if her pride had been hurt. "But you do what you have to do," she said, without looking at either of them. It was as if she were speaking to someone else not in the room.

Yao looked at Masha's collarbone beneath the straps of her simple white sleeveless top. He had never thought the collarbone to be an especially sensual part of a woman's body until he met Masha.

"Are you in love with this woman or something?" his mother had said to him on the phone, just last week. "Is that why you work like a dog for her?"

"She's nearly the same age as you, Mum," Yao told her. "And I don't work like a dog for her."

"More like a *puppy*," Delilah told him. "You have a crush on her." They were in bed at the time. Delilah was beautiful and sexually very skilled and he liked her very much, but their hook-ups always felt kind of transactional, even though no money changed hands.

"I'm grateful to her," Yao said, his hands behind his head as he looked at the ceiling, considering this. "She saved my life."

"She didn't save your life. You saved *her* life."

"My supervisor saved her life," said Yao. "I didn't know what the hell I was doing."

"And now you loooooove her," said Delilah, putting her bra back on.

"Like a sister," said Yao.

"Yeah right," said Delilah.

"Like a cousin."

Delilah snorted.

He did care very deeply for Masha. Was that so strange? To love your boss? Surely not so strange when you lived and worked together, and when your boss looked like Masha. She was interesting and stimulating. He found her exotic accent as attractive as her body. He would admit he had a significant crush on her. Perhaps his crush was strange and indicated some flaw in his personality or dysfunctional consequence of his childhood, even though it was just the ordinary, happy childhood of a shy, earnest boy who could get a little too intense about things but mostly slipped under the radar. His parents were softly spoken, humble people who never pushed him. Yao's parents believed in keeping expectations low to avoid disappointment. His father *said* that out loud once, without irony: "Expect to fail, Yao, then you will never be disappointed." That's why Yao found Masha's egotism so refreshing. She was bigger than life. Self-deprecation was something she had never practiced and did not understand in other people.

And Masha *had* saved his life.

After her heart attack, she had written letters to both Finn and Yao, thanking them and talking about how her "near-death experience" had changed her forever. She said that while she floated above them, she had seen the tiny red birthmark on Yao's scalp. She had described it perfectly: strawberry shaped.

Finn never answered Masha's letter. "She's a nutter. She didn't need to float above our bloody heads to see your birthmark. She probably saw it when she was sitting at her desk, before she collapsed."

But Yao was intrigued by her near-death experience. He emailed her, and over the years they kept up a sporadic correspondence. She told him that after she recovered from her heart surgery, she'd given up her "highly successful" (her words) corporate career and cashed in her company shares to buy a famous historic house in the countryside. She was going to put in a swimming pool and restore the house. Her initial plan had been to start an exclusive bed-and-breakfast, but as her interest in health had developed, she changed her mind.

She wrote, *Yao, I have transformed my body, my mind, my soul, and I want to do the same for others.*

There was an element of grandiosity to her emails he found amusing and endearing, but really she was not especially important to him. Just a grateful ex-patient with a funny turn of phrase.

And then, just after his twenty-fifth birthday, all his dominos toppled: bam, bam, bam. First, his parents announced they were divorcing. They sold the family home and moved into separate apartments. It was confusing and distressing. Then, in the midst of all that drama, his fiancée, Bernadette, broke off their engagement. It came without warning. He thought they were deeply in love. The reception and honeymoon were booked. How was it possible? It felt like the foundations of his life were collapsing beneath his feet. A breakup wasn't a *tragedy* and yet, to his shame, it felt cataclysmic.

His car got stolen.

He began to suffer from stress-related dermatitis.

Finn moved away and the ambulance service transferred Yao to a regional area where he knew no one, where the call-outs mostly involved violence and drugs. One night a man held a knife to his throat and said, "If you don't save her, I'll slit your throat." The woman was already dead. When the police came, the man lunged at them with the knife and he was shot. Yao ended up saving *his* life.

He went back to work. Then two days later he woke up just a few minutes before his alarm, as usual, but the moment it went off something catastrophic happened to his brain. He felt it implode. It felt physical. He thought it was a bleed on the brain. He ended up in a psychiatric ward.

"It sounds like you've been under a lot of pressure," said a doctor with dark shadows under his eyes.

"Nobody died," said Yao.

"But it feels like they did, doesn't it?" said the doctor.

That was exactly how it felt: like death after death after death. Finn was gone. His fiancée was gone. His family home was gone. Even his *car* was gone.

"We used to call this a nervous breakdown," said the doctor. "Now we'd call it a major depressive episode."

He gave Yao a referral for a psychiatrist and a prescription for antidepressants. "A well-managed breakdown can turn out to be a good thing," he told Yao. "Try to see it as an opportunity. An opportunity to grow and learn about yourself."

The day after he got home from the hospital he received an email from Masha in which she said that if he ever needed to escape "the rat race," he was very welcome to visit and try out her new guest rooms.

It felt like a sign.

Your timing is good, I haven't been well, he wrote to her. *I might just come for a few days for a rest.*

He didn't recognize Masha when he arrived at the house and a goddess in white walked out onto the veranda; a goddess who took him into her arms and said into his ear, "I will make you well."

Each time he walked out of Tranquillum House to greet new guests he wanted to create that same experience for them: like the sight of land when you've been lost at sea.

Masha nurtured Yao like a sick bird. She cooked for him and taught him meditation and yoga. They learned tai chi together. They were alone in that house for three months. They didn't have sex but they shared *something*. A journey of some kind. A rejuvenation. During that time his body changed; it hardened and strengthened as his mind healed. He became someone else entirely as he experienced a kind of peace and certainty he'd never known in his life. He shed the old Yao like dead skin.

The old Yao only exercised sporadically and ate too much processed food. The old Yao was a worrier and an insomniac who often woke up in the middle of the night thinking of all the things that *could* have gone wrong in his working day.

The new Yao slept throughout the night and woke up in the morning refreshed. The new Yao no longer thought obsessively about his fiancée in bed with another man. The new Yao rarely thought of Bernadette at all, and eventually completely eradicated her from his thoughts. The new Yao lived in the moment and was passionate about "wellness," inspired by Masha's vision for Tranquillum House. Instead of just patching people up, like Yao had done as a paramedic, the plan was to *transform* people, in the same way that he himself had been transformed. It felt like religion, except everything they did was based on science and evidence-based research.

His parents visited separately and told him it was time to return to Sydney and get his life back on track, but within six months of his arrival Masha and Yao opened the doors of Tranquillum House for their first guests. It was a success. And fun. A lot more fun than being a paramedic.

A few days had become five years. Delilah joined the staff four years ago, and together the three of them had all learned so much, constantly refining and improving their retreats. Masha paid generously. It was a dream career.

"Tomorrow, I begin one-on-one counseling sessions," said Masha. "I will share my notes with you."

"Good, because the more we know about each guest the better," said Yao.

This particular retreat would set new precedents for the way they did business. It was natural to be nervous.

"I want to learn more about Tony Hogburn's past," said Delilah. "There's something about him. I can't put my finger on it."

"It's going to be fine," murmured Yao, almost to himself.

Masha reached across the table and grabbed him by the arm, her incredible green eyes ablaze with that energy and passion he found so inspiring.

"It's going to be more than *fine*, Yao," she said. "It's going to be beautiful."

23

Frances

It was now day four of the retreat.

Frances found she had settled into the gentle rhythm of life at Tranquillum House with surprising ease. She rarely had to make decisions about how to spend her time.

Every morning began with tai chi in the rose garden with Yao. Her schedule always included at least one, sometimes *two*, remedial massages with Jan. Some days she had to go to the spa on multiple occasions—if, for example, she was "assigned" a facial. She did not find this onerous. The facials were divinely scented, dreamlike experiences that left Frances rosy and glowing, with her hair sticking up like the petals of a flower. There were yoga classes in the yoga and meditation studio and walking meditations through the surrounding bushland. The walking meditations got brisker and faster and steeper each day.

In the early evening, when it got cooler, some guests went running with Yao (the Marconi family seemed to do nothing *but* run, even during free time; Frances would sit on her balcony and watch the three of them pelting up Tranquillity Hill as if they were running for their lives) while others did a "gentle" exercise class in the rose garden with Delilah. Delilah seemed to have made it her personal mission to get Frances to do push-ups on her toes like a man, and because Frances wasn't allowed to speak, she couldn't say, "No thank you, I've never seen the point of push-ups." She now understood that the point of push-ups was to "work every muscle in her body," which was supposedly a good thing.

Frances meekly allowed Yao to take her blood and check her blood pressure each day, before hopping mutely on the scale so he could record her weight, which she still avoided looking at but which she assumed was *plummeting*, probably in *free fall*, what with all the exercise, and the lack of calories and wine.

The noble silence, which seemed so flimsy and silly in the beginning, so arbitrary and easily breakable, somehow gained in strength and substance as the days passed, like the settling in of a heat wave, and in fact the summer heat had intensified. It was a dry, still heat, bright and white, like the silence itself.

At first, without the distraction of noise and conversation, Frances's thoughts went around and around on a crazy endless repetitive loop: Paul Drabble, the money she'd lost, the surprise, the hurt, the anger, the surprise, the hurt, the anger, Paul's son, who was probably not even his son, the book she'd written with delusional love in her heart, which had subsequently been rejected, the career that was possibly over, the review that she should never have read. It wasn't that she'd found any solutions or experienced any earth-shattering revelations, but the act of observing her looping thoughts seemed to slow them down, until at last they came to a complete stop, and she'd found that for moments of time she thought . . . nothing. Nothing at all. Her mind was quite empty. And those moments were lovely.

The other guests were silent, not unwelcome figures in her peripheral vision. It became perfectly normal to ignore people, to not say hello when you found someone else sitting in the hot spring you were visiting but to instead step silently into the bubbling, eggy-scented water with your face averted.

Once, she and the tall, dark, and handsome man sat in the Secret Grotto hot spring for what seemed like an eternity together, neither saying a word, both gazing out at the valley views, lost in their private thoughts. Even though they hadn't spoken or even looked at each other, it felt like they'd shared something spiritual.

There had been other pleasant surprises too.

For example, yesterday afternoon, as she passed Zoe on the stairs, the girl brushed against her and pressed something into the palm of her hand. Frances managed to keep her eyes ahead and not say anything (which was remarkable, as she was very bad at that sort of thing—*both* her ex-husbands had informed her that they could think of no one who would make a worse spy than her while they, in spite of their differing personalities, were both apparently eminently qualified to join the CIA at a moment's notice) and when she got to her room she had found a Reese's Peanut Butter

Cup in her hand. She had never tasted anything more divine. Apart from Zoe, Frances didn't have much interaction with anyone else. She no longer startled when Napoleon sneezed. She noted that Tony's hacking cough gradually lessened and lessened until it disappeared, and indeed her own cough disappeared around the same time. Her breathing became beautifully clear. Her paper cut vanished and her back pain got better every day. It really was a "healing journey." When she got home she was going to send Ellen an effusive thank you card for suggesting this place.

According to today's schedule she had a one-on-one counseling session with Masha straight after lunch. Frances had never had any form of *counseling* in her life. She had friends for that. They all counseled each other and it was generally a two-way process. Frances couldn't imagine sitting and telling anyone her problems without then listening to their problems and offering her own sage advice in return. She generally felt that the advice she offered was superior to the advice she received. Other people's problems were so simple; one's own problems tended to be so much more *nuanced*.

But the silence and the heat and the daily massages had all combined to create a peaceful sense of resignation. Masha could "counsel" Frances if it made her happy.

Frances's lunch that day was a vegetarian curry. She had stopped noticing the sound of everyone chewing and had begun to take the most extraordinary pleasure in her food—extraordinary because she thought she already took quite substantial pleasure in her food! The curry, which she savored tiny mouthful by tiny mouthful, had a hint of saffron that just about blew her mind. Was saffron always that good? She didn't know, but it felt like a religious experience.

After lunch, while still reflecting on the wonder of saffron, Frances opened the door marked PRIVATE then climbed up two flights of stairs to the princess tower at the top of the house and knocked on the door of Masha's office.

"Come in," said a voice, a little peremptorily.

Frances entered the room, reminded of visits to the principal's office when she was at boarding school.

Masha was writing something down and she gestured toward the seat in front of her to indicate that Frances should sit while she finished what she was doing.

Her demeanor would normally have made Frances bristle, and she wasn't yet quite so Zen that she didn't note the fact that she had the *right* to bristle. She was the paying guest turning up at the appointed time, thank you very much, not the hired help. But she didn't sigh or clear her throat or wriggle because she was very nearly transformed, definitely thinner, and yesterday she did two push-ups *in a row* on her toes. She'd probably look very similar to Masha quite soon.

A wave of laughter rose in her chest and she distracted herself by studying the room.

She'd love an office like this. If she had an office like this, she would probably write a masterpiece without chocolate. There were huge glass windows on all four sides, giving Masha a three-hundred-and-sixty-degree view of the soft, rippling green countryside. It looked like a Renaissance painting from up here.

In the same way that the silence didn't apply to Masha, it seemed that neither did the "no electronic devices" rule. Masha did not seem averse to the very latest in technology. She had not one but two very smart-looking oversized computer monitors on her desk, as well as a laptop.

Was she surfing the *internet* up here while all her guests digitally detoxed? Frances felt her right hand twitch. She imagined grabbing a mouse, spinning a monitor around to face her, and clicking on a news site. What had happened in the last four days? There could have been a zombie apocalypse or a significant celebrity couple breakup and Frances would have no idea.

She dragged her eyes away from the seductive computer screens and looked instead at the few items on Masha's desk. No photo frames revealing anything personal. There were a few lovely antiques that Frances coveted. Her hand crept out to touch a letter opener. The gold handle had an intricate design with pictures of . . . elephants?

"Careful," said Masha. "That letter opener is as sharp as a dagger. You could murder someone with that, Frances."

Frances's hand flew back as fast as a shoplifter's.

Masha picked up the letter opener and removed it from its sheath. "It is at least two hundred years old," she said. She pressed her thumb to the sharp point. "It has been in my family for a long time."

Frances made an interested murmur. She wasn't sure if she was allowed to break the silence, and suddenly she was irritated by that.

"I assume the noble silence doesn't apply right now?" she said, and her unused voice sounded strange and unfamiliar to her ears. She'd been so good! She hadn't even talked to *herself* when she was alone in her room, and normally she was very chatty when alone, cheerfully narrating her own actions and engaging in friendly dialogue with inanimate objects. "Where are you hiding, O peeler of carrots?"

"Ah, you are a person who likes to follow the rules, are you?" Masha rested her chin in both hands and studied her. Her eyes really were a remarkable shade of green.

"Generally," said Frances.

Masha didn't break eye contact.

"As I'm sure you know, I did have some banned items in my luggage," said Frances. She was happy with her cool tone, but her face was hot.

"Yes," said Masha. "I am aware of that."

"And I'm still *reading*," said Frances defiantly.

"Are you?" said Masha.

"Yes," said Frances.

"Anything good?" Masha replaced the letter opener on her desk.

Frances thought about this. The book was meant to be another murder mystery but the author had introduced far too many characters too early, and so far everyone was still alive and kicking. The pace had slowed. Come on now. Hurry up and kill someone. "It's quite good," she told Masha.

"Tell me, Frances," said Masha. "Do you *want* to be a different person when you leave here?"

"Well," said Frances. She picked up a colored glass ball from Masha's desk. It felt vaguely bad-mannered—you didn't pick up other people's belongings—and yet she couldn't help it. She wanted to feel the cool weight of it in her hand. "I guess I do."

"I don't think you do," said Masha. "I think you are here for a little rest, and you are quite happy with the way you are now. I think this is all a little bit of joke to you. You prefer not to take things too seriously in your life, yes?" Her accent had deepened.

Frances reminded herself that this woman had no *authority* over her.

"Does it matter if I'm just here for a 'little rest'?" Frances put the glass ball back down and pushed it away from her, causing a moment's panic when it began to roll. She stopped it with her fingertips and placed her hands in her lap. This was ridiculous. Why did she feel ashamed? Like a teenager? This was a *health resort*.

Masha didn't answer her question. "I wonder, do you feel that you've ever been truly *tested* in your life?"

Frances shifted in her seat. "I've suffered losses," she said defensively.

Masha flicked her hand. "Of course you have," she said. "You are fifty-two years old. That is not my question."

"I've been lucky," said Frances. "I know I have been very lucky."

"And you live in the 'lucky country.'" Masha lifted

her arms to encompass the countryside that surrounded them.

"Well, that phrase about us being the lucky country,
it's kind of misused." Frances heard a pedantic tone
creep into her voice, and she wondered why she was
parroting her first husband, Sol, who always felt the
need to point this out smugly when someone referred
to Australia as being the lucky country. "The author
who wrote that phrase meant to imply that we hadn't
earned our prosperity."

"So Australia is not so lucky?"

"Well, no, we *are,* but . . ." Frances stopped. Was
that exactly the point that Masha was trying to make?
That Frances hadn't earned her prosperity?

"You never had children," said Masha, referring to
an open file on the desk in front of her. Frances found
herself craning to look, as if her file would reveal a
secret. Masha only knew she didn't have children because Frances had indicated that when she filled in the
booking form. "Was that decision made by choice? Or
was it forced upon you by circumstance?"

"Choice," said Frances. *This is none of your business,
lady.*

She thought of Ari and the PlayStation games he was
going to show her when she got to America. Where was
Ari now? Or the boy who pretended to be Ari? Was he
on the phone with some other woman?

"I see," said Masha.

Did Masha think she was selfish for not wanting
children? It wouldn't be the first time she'd heard that
accusation. It had never especially bothered her.

"Do *you* have children?" Frances asked Masha. She was allowed to ask questions. This woman was not her therapist. She probably had no qualifications whatsoever! She leaned forward, curious to know. "Are you in a relationship?"

"I am not in a relationship and I do not have children," said Masha. She had become very still. She looked very steadily at Frances—so steadily that Frances couldn't help but wonder if she was lying, although it was impossible to imagine Masha in a relationship. She could never be *half* of any relationship.

"You mentioned losses," said Masha. "Tell me about those losses."

"My father died when I was very young," said Frances.

"Mine also," said Masha.

Frances was taken aback by this unasked-for personal revelation.

"I'm sorry," said Frances. She thought of her last memory of her dad. It was summer. A Saturday. She was going out to her part-time job as a checkout girl at Target. He was sitting in their living room playing *Hot August Night*, smoking a cigarette, eyes closed and humming along with deep feeling to Neil Diamond, whom he considered to be a genius. Frances kissed him on the forehead. "See you, darling," he said, without opening his eyes. For her, the smell of cigarettes was the smell of love. She dated far too many smokers for that reason.

"A lady driving a car didn't stop at a pedestrian crossing," said Frances. "The sun was in her eyes. My father was going for a walk."

"My father was shot in a market by a hitman for the Russian Mafia," said Masha. "Also an accident. They thought he was someone else."

"*Seriously?*" Frances tried not to look too avid for more exotic detail.

Masha shrugged. "My mother said my father had too common a face. Too plain. Like anybody's, like everybody's. She was very angry with him for his plain face."

Frances didn't know whether to smile. Masha didn't smile, so Frances didn't either.

Frances offered up, "My mother was angry with my father for going for a walk. For years she said, 'It was so hot that day! Why didn't he just stay inside like a normal person? Why did he have to *walk* everywhere?'"

Masha nodded. Just once.

"My father should not have been at the market," she said. "He was a *very* clever man, he had a very senior position for a firm that made vacuum cleaners, but after the fall of the Soviet Union, when inflation went . . ." She made a whistling motion and pointed up. "Our entire savings, gone! My father's company could not pay him cash. They paid him in vacuum cleaners. So . . . he went to the market to sell the vacuum cleaners. He should not have had to do that. It was beneath him."

"That's awful," said Frances.

For a moment it felt as if the giant chasm that separated their different cultures and childhoods and body types could be bridged by the commonality of the loss of their fathers, through terrible chance, and their bitter grieving mothers. But then Masha sniffed, as if suddenly disgusted by some unmentionable behavior. She closed the file in front of her. "Well. It has been nice to chat with you, Frances, to get to know you a little bit."

She made it sound as if she now knew everything there was to know about Frances.

"How did you end up in Australia?" asked Frances, suddenly desperate for the conversation not to end. She didn't want to go back to the silence now that she'd experienced the pleasure of human interaction, and it was fine if Masha didn't want to know more about Frances, but Frances most certainly wanted to know more about her.

"My ex-husband and I applied to different embassies," said Masha coldly. "The U.S. Canada. Australia. I wanted the U.S., my husband wanted Canada, but Australia wanted us."

Frances tried not to take this personally, although she had a feeling that Masha wanted her to take it personally.

Also, ex-husband! They had divorce in common too! But Frances could tell she wouldn't get anywhere trying to exchange divorce stories. There was something about Masha that reminded Frances of a friend from university who had been both deeply egocentric and deeply insecure. The only way to make her open up was with flattery: extremely *careful* flattery. It was like dismantling a bomb. You could accidentally offend them at any time.

"I think it's a very brave thing to do," said Frances. "To start a new life in a new country."

"Well, we did not have to travel the open seas in a

rickety boat, if that's what you are thinking. The Australian government paid our airfares. Picked us up at the airport. Paid for our accommodation. You *needed* us. We were both very intelligent people. I had a degree in mathematics. My husband was a talented, world-class scientist." Her eyes looked back into a past Frances longed to see. "Extremely talented."

The way she said "extremely talented" didn't make her sound like a divorced wife. She sounded like a widow.

"We're lucky you came then," said Frances humbly, on behalf of the Australian people.

"Yes. You are. Very lucky," said Masha. She leaned forward, her face suddenly alight. "I'll tell you why we came! Because of a VCR. It all starts with the VCR. And now nobody even has a VCR! Technology . . ."

"The VCR?" said Frances.

"Our neighbors in the flat next to ours got a VCR. Nobody could afford such a thing. They inherited money from a relative who died in Siberia. These neighbors were good friends of ours and they asked us over to see movies." Her gaze became unfocused, once again remembering.

Frances didn't move; she didn't want Masha to stop this sudden sharing of confidences. It was like when your uptight boss goes to the pub with you and loosens up over a drink and suddenly starts chatting to you like you're an equal.

"It was a window into another world. Into a capitalist world. It all seemed so different, so amazing, so . . . *abundant*." Masha smiled dreamily. "*Dirty Dancing*,

Desperately Seeking Susan, The Breakfast Club—not that many, because the movies were insanely expensive, so people had to swap them. The voices were all done by the same person holding his nose to disguise his voice because it was illegal." She held her nose and spoke in a nasal voice to demonstrate.

"If it wasn't for that VCR, for those movies, we might not have worked so hard to leave. It was not easy to leave."

"Did the reality live up to your expectations?" asked Frances, thinking of the glossy, highly colored world of eighties films and how bland suburban Sydney would feel when she and her friends emerged blinking from the cinemas. "Was it as wonderful as in the movies?"

"It was as wonderful," said Masha. She picked up the glass ball that Frances had put down and held it in the flat palm of her hand as if daring it to roll. It stayed completely still. "And it was not."

She put the ball back down decisively. Suddenly she seemed to remember her superior status. Like when your boss remembers you have to work together the next day.

"So, Frances, tomorrow we will officially break the silence and you will get to know the other guests."

"I'm looking forward—"

"Enjoy your evening meal because there will be no meals served at all tomorrow. Your first light fast will begin."

She held out her hand in such a way that Frances found herself automatically rising to her feet.

"Have you done much fasting before?" Masha

looked up at her. She said "fasting" as if it were an exotic, delightful practice, like belly dancing.

"Not really," admitted Frances. "But it's just a *light* fast, right?"

Masha smiled radiantly. "You may find tomorrow a little testing, Frances."

24

Carmel

"You have already lost some weight, I see." Masha opened Carmel's file to begin her counseling session.

"*Have* I?" said Carmel. She felt like she'd won a prize. "How much?"

Masha ignored the question. She ran her finger down a sheet of paper in the file.

"I thought I might have lost some—but I wasn't sure." Carmel heard her unused voice tremble with pleasure. She hadn't dared to hope. It seemed that Yao deliberately stood in such a way that she couldn't see that dreaded number on the scale each day.

She put a hand to her stomach. She had suspected it was getting flatter, her clothes looser! She'd been secretly touching her stomach, like when she was pregnant for the first time. This retreat was just like that euphoric time: the feeling that her body was changing in new and miraculous ways.

"I guess I'll probably lose even more when we start the fast tomorrow?" Carmel wanted to demonstrate her enthusiasm and commitment to the retreat. She would do whatever it took.

Masha said nothing. She closed Carmel's file and balanced her chin on her folded hands.

Carmel said, "I hope it's not just fluid loss. They say that in the first few days of a diet you mostly just lose fluid."

Masha still said nothing.

"I know the meals here are all calorie-controlled. I guess the challenge will be maintaining my weight loss when I go home. I'd be really grateful for any nutrition advice you can give me going forward. Maybe a recipe plan?"

"You do not need a recipe plan," said Masha. "You are an intelligent woman. You know what to do to lose weight, if that's what you want. You are not especially fat. You are not especially thin. You want to be thinner. That is your choice. I find this not so interesting."

"Oh," said Carmel. "Sorry."

"Tell me something about yourself that is not related to your weight," said Masha.

"Well, I have four daughters," said Carmel. She smiled at the thought of them. "They're aged ten, eight, seven, and five."

"I know this already. You are a mother," said Masha. "Tell me something else."

"My husband left me. He has a new girlfriend now. So that's been—"

Masha waved that away irritably as if it were of no relevance. "Something else."

"There *is* nothing else right now," said Carmel.

"There's no time for anything else. I'm just a normal busy mum. An overweight stressed-out suburban mum." As she spoke she scanned Masha's desk for family photos. She must not have children. If she did, she would know how motherhood swallowed you up whole. "I work part-time," she tried to explain. "I have an elderly mother who is not well. I am always tired. Always, always tired."

Masha sighed, as if Carmel was not behaving.

"I know I need to work more exercise into my schedule?" offered Carmel. Was that what she wanted to hear?

"Yes," said Masha. "Yes, you do. But I find this also not so interesting."

"When the kids are older I'll have more time to—"

"Tell me about when you were schoolgirl," interrupted Masha. "What were you like? Smart? Top of class? Bottom of class? Naughty? Loud? Shy?"

"I was mostly near the top of the class," said Carmel. Always. "Not naughty. Not shy. Not loud." She thought about it. "Although, I *could* be very loud. If I felt strongly about something."

She remembered a heated argument with a teacher who wrote "the thunder boomed, the lightening flashed" on the blackboard. Carmel stood up to correct the teacher's spelling of "lightning." The teacher didn't believe her. Carmel wouldn't back down, even when the teacher yelled at her. She was all-powerful when she knew without doubt that she was in the right. But how often did you know for sure that you were right? Hardly ever.

"Interesting," said Masha. "Because right now you do not seem like a very loud person."

"You should see me in the morning when I yell at my kids," said Carmel.

"Why have I not seen this 'loud' Carmel? Where is she?"

"Um—we're not allowed to speak?"

"That is a good point. But see—even then, when you make a very valid point, you said it like a question. You put this questioning sound at the end of your sentences. Like this? Your voice goes up? Like you are not really sure? Of everything you say?"

Carmel squirmed at Masha's imitation of her speech patterns. Was that really how she sounded?

"And your walk," said Masha. "That is the other thing: I don't like the way you walk."

"You don't *like* the way I *walk*?" spluttered Carmel. Wasn't that kind of rude?

Masha stood and came out from behind her desk. "This is how you walk right now." She rounded her shoulders, dropped her chin, and did a scurrying kind of side step across the room. "Like you are hoping no one sees you. Why do you do that?"

"I don't think I exactly—"

"Yes, you do." Masha sat back down. "I don't think you always walked like this. I think once you walked properly. Do you want your daughters to walk like you walk?" It was obviously a rhetorical question. "You are a woman in the prime of your life! You should march into a room with your head held high! Like you are walking onto a stage, a battlefield!"

Carmel stared. "I'll try?" she said. She coughed, and remembered to turn it into a statement. "I will try. I will try to do that."

Masha smiled. "Good. At first it will feel strange. You will have to fake it. But then you will remember. You will think, 'Oh, that's right, this is how I talk, this is how I walk. This is me, Carmel.'" She knocked her closed fist against her heart. *"This is who I am."*

She leaned forward and lowered her voice. "I will tell you a secret." Her eyes danced. "You will look thinner if you walk like that!"

Carmel smiled back. Was she joking?

"Everything will become clearer over the next few days," said Masha, with a gesture that made Carmel stand up quickly, as if she'd outstayed her welcome.

Masha pulled a notepad toward her and began to write something down.

Carmel hovered. She tried to put her shoulders back. "Could you just tell me how much weight I've lost so far?"

Masha didn't look up. "Close the door behind you."

25

Masha

Masha studied the large man who sat on the other side of her desk, his feet planted solidly on the floor, his hands curled in meaty fists on his thighs, as if he were a prisoner hoping for parole.

Masha remembered how Delilah had implied there was something unusual or secretive about Tony Hogburn. Masha did not agree. The man was not especially complex. He seemed to her to be a simple, grumpy fellow. He had lost weight already. Men who drank a lot of beer always did lose weight when they stopped, whereas women like Carmel, who had much less weight to lose, took much longer. In truth, Carmel hadn't lost any weight at all, but there was no benefit in Carmel hearing that.

"How did you come across Tranquillum House, Tony?" Masha asked him.

"I Googled 'how to change your life,'" said Tony.

"Ah," said Masha. As an experiment, she sat back, crossed her legs, and waited for his eyes to travel down her body, which they did, of course (the man was not dead yet), but not for very long. "Why do you want to change your life?"

"Well, Masha, life is short." His gaze moved past hers to the window behind her head. Masha noted that he seemed much calmer and more confident now than when he had complained about his contraband being confiscated. The positive effects of Tranquillum House! "I didn't want to waste the time I had left."

He looked back at her. "I like your office. It's like you're on top of the world up here. I get claustrophobic down in that yoga studio."

"So how do you hope to change your life?"

"I just want to get healthier and fitter," said Tony. "Drop some weight."

Men often used that phrase: "drop some weight." They said it without shame or emotion, as if the weight were an object they could easily put down when they chose. Women said they needed to "lose weight," with their eyes down, as if the extra weight was part of them, a terrible sin they'd committed.

"I used to be very fit. I should have done this sooner. I really regret . . ." Tony stopped, cleared his throat, as if he'd said more than he wanted.

"What do you regret?" asked Masha.

"It's not anything I've done. It's more everything I *haven't* done. I've just kind of moped about for twenty years."

It took a fraction of a second to translate the English word "moped"—a word she didn't hear much.

"Twenty years is a long time to *mope*," said Masha.

Foolish man. She herself had never moped. Not once. Moping was for the weak.

"I kind of got into the habit of it," said Tony. "Not sure how to stop."

She waited to hear what he would say next. Women liked to be asked questions about themselves but with men it was better to be patient, to be silent and see what eventuated.

She waited. The minutes passed. She was considering giving up when Tony shifted in his chair.

"Your near-death experience," he said, without looking at her. "You said you no longer feared death, or something like that?"

"That's right," said Masha. She studied him, wondering about his interest in this subject. "I no longer fear it. It was beautiful. People think death is like falling asleep but for me it was like waking up."

"A tunnel?" said Tony. "Is that what you saw? A tunnel of light?"

"Not a tunnel." She paused, considered changing the subject and putting the focus back on him. She had already revealed too much of her personal life earlier to that Frances Welty, with her bouncy hair and red lipstick, nearly knocking Masha's glass ball off the desk, like a child, asking her greedy, nosy questions, making Masha forget her position.

It was hard to believe Frances was exactly the same age as Masha. She reminded Masha of a little girl in her second-grade class. A plump, pretty, vain little girl who always had a pocket filled with Vzletnaya candies. People like Frances lived candy-filled lives.

But she did not feel that Tony had lived a candy-filled life. "It was not a tunnel, it was a lake," she told him. "A great lake of shimmering colored light."

She had never told a guest this before. She had told Yao about it, but not Delilah. As Tony ran a hand over his unshaven jaw, considering her words, Masha saw again that incredible lake of color: scarlet, turquoise, lemon. She hadn't just seen that lake, she had experienced it with all her senses: she had breathed it, heard it, smelled it, tasted it.

"Did you see . . . loved ones?" asked Tony.

"No," lied Masha, even as she saw an image of a young man walking toward her through the lake of light, color streaming off him like water.

Such an ordinary but exquisite young man. He wore a baseball cap, like so many young men did. He took it off and scratched his head. She had only ever seen him as her baby, her beautiful fat-cheeked toothless baby, but she knew immediately that this was her son, this was the man he would have and should have become, and all that love was still within her, as fresh and powerful and shocking as it had been when she'd held him for the first time. She did not know if it had been a precious gift or a cruel punishment to have experienced that love again. Perhaps it was both.

She saw her son for what could have been a lifetime, or what could have been a few seconds. She had no concept of time. And then he was gone, and she floated near her office ceiling, above the two men working on her lifeless body. She could see a button on the floor where they had ripped open her silk shirt. She could see one of her legs splayed at a strange angle, as if she'd landed there after falling from a great height. She could see the top of another young man's head, the white part in his dark hair revealing a tiny strawberry-shaped birthmark, the dampness of his forehead as he sent electrical pulses through her body, and somehow she felt everything he felt: his fear, his focus.

Her next conscious memory was the following day. She was back in the drab confines of her body and a tall beautiful nurse was saying, "Hello there, sleeping beauty!" It was like being returned to jail.

Except it wasn't a nurse. This woman was the doctor who had performed her heart surgery: a quadruple bypass. In the years to come Masha often considered how her life would have been different if her heart surgeon had looked like the vast majority of heart surgeons. Her prejudices would have made her dismiss everything he had to say, no matter the accuracy. She would have put him in the same category as the gray-haired men who worked for her. She knew better than all of them. But this woman made Masha snap to attention. She felt strangely proud of her. She too was a woman at the top of her profession in a man's world, and she was *tall;* it somehow mattered that she was tall like Masha. So Masha listened attentively as she talked about reducing her risk factors when it came to diet and exercise and smoking, and she listened when the doctor said, "Don't let your heart be a casualty of your head." She wanted Masha to understand that her state of mind was just as important as the state of her body. "When I was on the wards in my first term of cardiac surgery we had something called the 'beard sign,'" she said. "Meaning that if one of our male patients was so miserable he couldn't even be bothered to shave, his chances of recovery were not as good. You must take care of your whole self, Masha." Masha shaved her legs the very next day for the first time in years. She went to the cardiac rehabilitation exercise program suggested by the doctor determined to top the class. She *attacked* the challenge of her health and her heart in the same way that she had once attacked challenges at work, and naturally she over-achieved beyond all expectations. "Good God," said the surgeon when Masha went to her for her first checkup.

She never once moped. She re-created herself. She did it for the tall attractive doctor. She did it for the young man in the lake.

"My sister also had a near-death experience," said Tony. "A horse-riding accident. After her accident, she changed. Her career. Everything about her life. She got right into *gardening*." He gave Masha an uneasy look. "I didn't like it."

"You don't like gardening?" said Masha, teasing a little.

He gave her a half smile, and she saw a flash of a more attractive man.

"I think I just didn't want my sister to change," he said. "It felt like she'd become a stranger. Maybe it felt like she'd experienced something I couldn't understand."

"People are frightened of what they don't understand," said Masha. "I never believed in life after death before that. Now I do. And I live a better life because of it."

"Right," said Tony. "Yeah."

Again Masha waited.

"Anyway . . ." Tony exhaled and patted his thighs, as if he were done. Masha would get nothing else of interest out of him. It did not matter. The next twenty-four hours would tell her so much more about this man. He would learn things he did not know about himself.

A glorious sense of calm settled upon her as she watched him leave the room, hitching up his pants with one hand. Those last remnants of doubt were gone. Maybe it was because of the thoughts of her son.

The risks were calculated. The risks were justified.

No one ever ascended a mountain without risk.

26

Napoleon

It was dawn at Tranquillum House. The fifth day of the retreat.

Napoleon parted the wild horse's mane three times both sides.

He enjoyed the soft swooping moves of tai chi, and this was one of his favorite moves, although he heard his knees crunch like a tire on gravel as he bent his legs. His physio said it was nothing to worry about: people Napoleon's age crunched. It was just middle-aged cartilage.

Yao led this morning's class in the rose garden, quietly and calmly naming each move for the nine guests who stood in a semicircle around him, all wearing their green Tranquillum House dressing gowns. People seemed to be wearing the robes more often than not now. On the horizon behind Yao, two hot-air balloons ascended so slowly above the vineyards it looked like a painting. Napoleon and Heather had done that once, on a romantic weekend away: wine tasting, antiques shops; multiple lives ago, before children.

It was interesting: when you have children you think your life has changed forever, and it's true, to an extent, but it's nothing compared to how your life changes after you lose a child.

When Masha, an extraordinarily fit and healthy-looking woman, clearly passionate about what she did (his wife mistrusted passion and Zoe was young enough to still find it embarrassing, but Napoleon found it admirable), had spoken on the first day about how this experience would change them "in ways they could never have imagined," Napoleon, once a believer in self-improvement, had felt an unusual sensation of bitter cynicism. He and his family had already been transformed in ways they could never have imagined. All they needed was peace and quiet, and certainly an improvement in their diets.

While I admire and salute your passion, Masha, we do not seek or desire further transformation.

"The white crane spreads its wings," said Yao, and everyone moved in graceful unison with him. It was quite beautiful to see.

Napoleon, who stood at the back, as always (he'd learned to stand at the back of every audience once he hit six foot three), watched his wife and daughter lift their arms together. They both bit their bottom lips like chipmunks when they concentrated.

He heard the knees of the guy next to him crunch too, which was pleasing, because Napoleon guessed he was at least a decade younger than him. Even Napoleon could see this guy was notably handsome. He looked at Heather to see if she was maybe checking out the good-looking guy, but her eyes were opaque, like a doll's eyes; as usual, she was somewhere deep and sad within herself.

Heather was broken.

She had always been fragile. Like a piece of delicate china.

Early on in their relationship, he thought she was feisty, funny, a tough chick, athletic and capable, the sort of girl you could take to the football or camping, and he was right, she *was* exactly that type of girl. She was into her sport, she loved camping, and she was never high-maintenance or needy. The opposite: she found it hard to admit she needed anyone or anything. When they first started going out, she broke her toe trying to move a bookshelf on her own, when Napoleon was on his way over and could have lifted that piece of plywood junk with one hand. But no, she had to do it herself.

The fragility beneath that feisty demeanor came out slowly, in odd ways: a peculiar attitude toward certain foods that may have just been a sensitive stomach, but may have been something more; an inability to make eye contact if an argument got too emotional or to say "I love you" without bracing her chin, as if she were preparing to be punched. He'd thought, romantically, that he could keep her funny, fragile little heart protected, like a tiny bird in the palm of his hand. He'd thought, full of love and testosterone, that he would protect his woman from bad men and heavy furniture and upsetting food.

When he first met her odd, detached parents he

understood that Heather had grown up starved of love, and when you're starved of something you should receive in abundance, you never quite trust it. Heather's parents weren't abusive, but they were just chilly enough to make you shiver. Napoleon became excessively loving in their presence, as if he could somehow *make* them love his wife the way she should be loved. "Doesn't Heather look great in this dress?" he'd say. "Did Heather tell you she came top in her midwifery exams?" Until one day Heather mouthed the words: *Stop it.* So he stopped it, but he still touched her more than usual whenever they visited her family, desperate to convey through his touch: *You are loved, you are loved, you are so, so loved.*

He'd been too young and happy to know that love wasn't enough; too young to know all the ways that life could break you.

Their son's death broke her.

Maybe a son's death broke any mother.

The anniversary was tomorrow. Napoleon sensed its dark, malignant shadow. It was irrational to feel frightened of a day. It was just a sad day, a day they were never going to forget anyway. He reminded himself that this was normal. People felt like this on anniversaries. He'd felt this same impending sense of doom last year. Almost as if it was going to happen again, as if this were a story he'd read before and he knew what lay ahead.

He'd hoped that doing this retreat might make him feel calmer about the approach of the anniversary. It was a marvelous house, so peaceful and, yes, "tranquil," and the staff seemed kind and caring. Yet Napoleon felt skittish. At dinner last night his right leg began to tremble uncontrollably. He'd had to put a hand on his thigh to still it. Was it just the anniversary? Or the silence?

Probably the silence. He didn't like having all this time with only his thoughts, his memories and regrets.

The sun rose higher in the sky as the Tranquillum House guests moved in unison with Yao.

Napoleon caught a glimpse of the profile of the big chunky guy who had tried to smuggle in the contraband. It had seemed like he might be a troublemaker, and Napoleon had kept his teacher's eye on him, but he appeared to have settled down, like one of those students you thought was going to be your nemesis for the whole year but then turned out to be a good kid. There was something about this guy's profile that reminded Napoleon of somebody or something from his past. An actor from some old TV show he used to enjoy as a child, perhaps? It felt like a good memory, there was something pleasant about the feelings he invoked, but Napoleon couldn't put his finger on it.

Somewhere in the distance a whipbird called. He loved the sound of the whipbird: that long musical crack of the whip that was so much a part of the Australian landscape you had to leave the country to realize how much you missed it, how it settled your soul.

"Repulse the monkey," said Yao.

Napoleon repulsed the monkey and remembered three years ago: this day, this time. The day before.

It was around this time three years ago that Napoleon was making love to his sleepy wife for the last time in their marriage. (He assumed it was the last time, although he hadn't given up entirely. He would know if she was ever ready. All it would take would be a look. He understood. Sex felt cheap now, tawdry and tacky. But he'd still be up for some cheap, tawdry sex.) She'd fallen asleep again—she used to love her sleep back then—and Napoleon had quietly left the house and headed for the bay. He kept the surf ski on the roof rack of his car throughout the long summer holiday. When he came back, Zach was eating breakfast at the sink, shirtless—he was always shirtless—hair sticking up in tufts. He looked up, grinned at his father, and said, "No milk," meaning he'd drunk it all. He said that he might come with Napoleon for a paddle the next day. After that Napoleon worked for a few hours in the garden and cleaned the pool, and Zach went to the beach with his friend Chris, and then Napoleon fell asleep on the couch, and the girls went out—Heather to work, Zoe to a party. When Zach came home, Napoleon did ribs on the barbecue for the two of them, and afterward they had a swim in the pool and talked about the Australian Open, and Serena's chances, and conspiracy theories (Zach liked conspiracy theories), and how Chris had told Zach he wanted to go into gastroenterology. Zach was gobsmacked by the bizarre specificity of Chris's career plans because Zach didn't even know what he wanted to do *tomorrow*, let alone for the rest of his life, and Napoleon told him that was fine, there was plenty of time to settle on a career, and these days no one had just one career anyway (he absolutely told him it was fine; he'd double-checked his memory about a thousand times), and then they played table tennis in honor of the tennis—best of three, Napoleon won two—and then they watched a movie, *The Royal Tenenbaums*. They both loved the movie. They laughed a lot. They stayed up too late watching the movie. That's why Napoleon was tired the next morning. That's why he hit the snooze button on his phone.

It was a split-second decision he would regret until the day he died.

Napoleon knew everything about that day because he'd examined his memories over and over, like a homicide detective combing through the evidence. Over and over he saw it: his hand reaching for the phone, his thumb on the snooze button. Over and over he saw the other life, where he made a different decision, the right decision, the decision he normally made, where he didn't hit snooze, where he turned off the alarm and got out of bed.

"Grasp the bird's tail," said Yao.

It was Heather who found Zach.

The sound of his wife's scream that morning was like no sound he'd ever heard before.

His memory of running up the stairs: it seemed like it took a lifetime, like running through mud, like something from a dream.

Zach had used his new belt to make the noose.

It was a brown leather belt from R.M. Williams that Heather had bought him for Christmas, only a few weeks earlier. It cost ninety-nine dollars, which was ridiculous. "Expensive belt," Napoleon had said to Heather when she showed it to him. He remembered fishing the receipt from the plastic bag, raising his eyebrows. She shrugged. Zach had admired it once. She overspent every Christmas.

You broke your mother, mate.

The kid did not leave a note or a text. He did not choose to explain his actions.

"Carry the tiger over the mountain," said Yao, who was a young man, maybe only ten years older than Zach. Zach could have worked somewhere like this. He could have grown his hair long. He would have looked good with one of those beards they all had these days. He could have lived a fantastic life. So many opportunities. He had the brains, the looks, the facial hair. He was good with his hands. He could have done a trade! He could have done law or medicine or architecture. He could have traveled. He could have done drugs. Why didn't he just do drugs? How wonderful to have a son who made bad choices but not irreversible bad choices; a kid who did drugs, who *dealt* drugs even, who got arrested, who went off the rails. Napoleon could have got him back on the rails.

Zach never even owned his own car. Why would you choose to die before you knew the pleasure, the spectacular pleasure, of owning your own car?

Apparently, that young bloke in front of him drove a *Lamborghini*.

Zach had chosen to turn his back on this beautiful world of whipbirds and Lamborghinis, long-legged girls and hamburgers with the lot. He chose to take a gift from his mother and use it as a murder weapon.

That was a bad choice, son. It was the wrong thing to do. It was a really bad choice.

He heard a sound and realized it was him. Zoe turned to look at him. He tried to smile at her reassuringly. *I'm fine, Zoe, just yelling at your brother.* His eyes blurred.

"Needle at the bottom of the sea," said Yao.

My boy. My boy. My boy.

He was not broken. He would never stop grieving for Zach, but he had made a decision in the week after the funeral. *He must not break.* It was his job to heal, to be there for his wife and his daughter, to get through this. So he studied the literature, he bought books online and read every word, he downloaded podcasts, he Googled the research. He attended the Tuesday night Survivors of Suicide group as faithfully as his mother once went to Sunday mass, and now he ran the group. (Heather and Zoe thought he talked too much, but that was only in social situations. On Tuesday nights he hardly spoke a word; he listened and he listened on his foldout chair and did not flinch while a tsunami of pain crashed all around him.) He gave speeches to parent groups and schools and did radio interviews and edited an online newsletter and helped with fundraising.

"It's his new hobby." He'd overheard Heather say that on the phone one night to someone, he never found out to whom because he never mentioned it, but he never forgot it, or the bitter tone; it sounded close to hatred. It hurt because it was both a malicious lie and the shameful truth.

He could find hatred in his heart for her, too, if he went looking for it. The secret of a happy marriage was not to go looking for it.

He saw his wife's thin arms curved up toward the sun to "master its life force" and his heart filled with painful tenderness for her. She could not heal and she refused to even try. She never went to the support group except for that one time. She did not want to hear from other parents who had lost sons because she believed Zach was superior to their stupid sons. Napoleon thought Zach was superior to their stupid sons too, but he still found solace in giving back to this community he had never asked to join.

"The white crane spreads its wings."

Sometimes there are no signs.

That's what he told the newly grieving parents at the Tuesday night group. He told them there was research to suggest that teenage suicide was often the consequence of an impulsive decision. Many had suicidal thoughts for only eight hours before their attempts. Some idiotic kids put as little as *five minutes' thought* into their catastrophic choice.

He did not tell them other things he had learned from his research, such as that suicide survivors often reported that their first thought after they'd swallowed the pills, after they'd jumped, after they'd cut, was a version of: *My God, what have I done?!* He did not tell them that many survivors of suicide are transformed by their experience and go on to live happy lives, sometimes with little psychiatric intervention. He didn't tell them that if the decision to take their lives was in some way thwarted, if the means was removed, their suicidal thoughts often disappeared with time and never returned. He didn't tell them how Britain's national suicide rate dropped by a third when coal gas was phased out, because once people no longer had the option to impulsively stick their head in the oven, there was time for their dark and dreadful impulses to pass. He didn't think it was helpful for parents to know just how much bad luck was involved in the loss of their children; that perhaps all they'd needed was a well-timed interruption, a phone call, a distraction.

But Napoleon knew it, because that was Zach. *Impulsive.* The absolute definition of impulsive. He never thought things through. He never thought of the consequences of his actions. He lived in the moment, as you were meant to do. He practiced mindfulness. No yesterday. No tomorrow. Just now. *I feel this now, so I will do this now.*

If you chase the waves along the beach your new sneakers will get wet and they will stay wet for the rest of the day. If you run about outside when the pollen count is high (even though we told you to stay indoors), you will have an asthma attack. If you give up your life, you won't get it back, kid, it's gone.

"Zach, you've got to think!" Napoleon used to yell at him.

That's why Napoleon knew without a doubt that if he'd got up at the time he'd originally planned, if he hadn't pressed the snooze button on his alarm that morning, if he'd knocked on Zach's door and said, "Come paddling with me," then right now he'd have a wife who wasn't broken and a daughter who still sang in the shower and a son about to celebrate his twenty-first birthday.

Napoleon was meant to be the one who knew and understood boys. He had a drawer full of cards and letters from the boys he'd taught over the years, and their parents, all telling him how very special he was, how much he'd contributed to their lives, that they would never forget him, that he'd pulled them back from some terrible brink, a wrong path, that they'd be eternally grateful to their wonderful teacher, Mr. Marconi.

Yet he'd somehow failed his own boy. The only boy in the world who mattered.

For a year he'd searched for answers. He'd talked to every friend, every teammate, every teacher, every coach. None of them had answers. There was nothing more to know.

"Fan through the back," said Yao.

Napoleon fanned through the back and felt his muscles stretch and the sun warm on his face as he tasted the sea from the tears that ran heedlessly down his face.

But he wasn't broken.

27

Zoe

Zoe saw the tears slide down her father's face and wondered if he knew he was crying. Her dad cried a lot without seeming to realize he was doing it, like a scratch he didn't know was bleeding, as if his body excreted grief without his knowledge.

"Touch the sky," said Yao.

Zoe followed the graceful arc of Yao's arms and turned now in her mother's direction, and saw the deep crevices in her mother's face and heard once more the sound of her mother's scream that awful morning. Like the scream of an animal caught in a trap. A scream that tore straight through Zoe's life like a razor blade.

Tomorrow it would be three years. Would it ever get any easier for her parents? Because it sure didn't look like it was getting any easier. There was no use hoping that once they got through this next anniversary things would get better, because she'd thought that the last two anniversaries. She knew that when they went back home it would all be just the same.

It felt like her parents were sick with a terrible, incurable disease that ravaged their bodies. It felt like they'd been assaulted. As if someone had come after them with a baseball bat. She had not realized that grief was so physical. Before Zach died, she thought grief happened in your head. She didn't know that your whole body ached with it, that it screwed up your digestive system, your menstrual cycle, your sleep patterns, your skin. You wouldn't wish it on your worst enemy.

Sometimes it felt like Zoe was just *waiting out* her life now, enduring it, ticking off events and days and months and years, as if she just had to get herself through something unspecified and then things would be better except she never got through it and it never got better and she would never forgive him. His death was the ultimate "fuck you."

At least you weren't close, said her friend Cara in her head.

At least we weren't close. At least we weren't close. At least we weren't close.

28

Heather

Heather didn't see Napoleon's tears as they did tai chi.

She was remembering something that had happened last week, after a long exhausting night shift when she'd helped to deliver two baby boys.

It was impossible not to think of Zach every time she held another newborn baby boy and stared into those sad wise eyes. All babies had that same wise look, as if they'd just come from another realm where they'd learned some beautiful truth they couldn't share. Every day brought an endless stream of new life.

Heather had gone to get her coffee from the hospital café after her shift and run into a familiar face from the past. There was no time to turn away and pretend she hadn't seen. She recognized her instantly. One of the soccer mums. Before Zach gave it up. Lisa Somebody. A friendly, bubbly lady. It had been years. Lisa Somebody's face lit up when she saw Heather. *Oh, I know you!* And then, as so often happened, a moment later her face fell, as she remembered what she'd heard on the grapevine. You could virtually read her thoughts: *Oh fuck, she's that mother, but no time to look away!*

Some people crossed the street to get away from her. She'd seen them do it. Some people recoiled. They literally recoiled, as if what happened to Heather's family was vile and shameful. This woman was one of the brave ones. She didn't duck or hide or pretend.

"I was so sorry to hear about Zach," she said. She even said his name without lowering her voice.

"Thank you," said Heather, longing for coffee. She looked at the boy standing next to her on crutches. "This must be . . . Justin?" The name came to her on a flood of memories of shivering Saturday mornings on the soccer field, and suddenly, without warning, the anger exploded in her chest, and this kid, this living stupid kid, was her target.

"I remember you," she hissed at him. "You were the kid who never passed to Zach!"

He stared at her with blank, slack-jawed horror.

"You never passed to Zach! Why didn't you pass?" Heather turned to Lisa. "You should have made him pass!" Her voice rose beyond the bounds of what was acceptable in a public place.

Most people would have made their excuses and scurried away. Some people might have retaliated. *Your dead son doesn't give you the right to be rude.* But this Lisa, this woman Heather barely knew, a woman who (Heather now remembered) had once taken Zoe home to her place and fed her lunch after Zach had an asthma attack on the field, just looked at Heather steadily and sadly and said, "You're right, Heather, I should have made him pass."

And then Justin, who had been *nine years old* when he played with Zach, had spoken up in his deep young man's voice and said, "Zach was a great striker, Mrs. Marconi. I should have passed to him more. I used to be really bad at passing the ball."

The generosity, the kindness, the maturity that young man showed that day. Heather had looked at his face—the freckles on his nose, the tiny black whiskers around his young boy's mouth—and seen the grotesque face of her son on the last day of his life.

"I'm so sorry," she'd said, weak and trembling with regret, and she'd left without making further eye contact with either of them, without picking up her coffee. Yet again she'd turned the anger that should have been directed only at herself on someone else.

"Snake creeps through the grass," said Yao.

She saw herself sitting alone in Zach's room, her hand opening the drawer of his bedside cabinet. Heather was the snake that crept through the grass.

29

Frances

It was nearly 3 P.M. as Frances made her way, with some eagerness, downstairs to the meditation studio for the breaking of the silence. She hadn't eaten anything solid since the night before and she was very hungry. When the breakfast and midday bells had rung today, Frances had gone to the dining room to find a row of smoothies set out on the sideboard, labeled by name. Frances had found hers, and tried to drink it slowly and mindfully, but it was gone before she knew it, and her stomach had begun to rumble, loudly and embarrassingly.

She was not really starving, but she was yearning; not so much for food, but for the ritual of food. Maybe if she'd been at home, running around doing errands, it would be easy to skip a few meals (not that she ever did, she'd always had difficulty comprehending the phrase: "I forgot to eat lunch"), but here, especially during the silence, meals were crucial to break up the day.

She'd tried to distract herself by reading in the

hammock but her book had taken an outlandish turn which she couldn't handle on an empty stomach.

Her spirits lifted when she walked into the studio. The lights had been turned off and the room was illuminated by clusters of flickering candles. It was cool down here, some sort of essential-oil burner was pumping out a heady mist, and spine-tingling music was being piped through invisible speakers.

Frances always appreciated a little effort when it came to ambience. She noted low camplike beds had been set out around the sides of the room, with blankets and pillows. Headphones and eye masks were laid out on the pillows, with water bottles alongside, like business-class seats thoughtfully arranged for a long-haul flight.

Masha, Yao, and Delilah sat cross-legged in the middle of the room, along with the three members of the Marconi family and the tall, dark, and handsome man.

"Welcome, please join the circle," Masha said as more people filed into the room behind Frances.

Masha wore a long white sleeveless satin and lace dress somewhere between a wedding dress and a nightgown. She'd made up her eyes, so that they were even more prominent. Yao and Delilah, extremely attractive young people, looked almost ordinary and washed-out next to this celestial being.

Within a few moments, everyone was there. Frances was seated with Heather on one side, and young Ben on the other. She wondered how Ben was feeling. Probably missing his car. She studied his tanned hairy leg in the candlelight—not in a sexual way, thank the

Lord, just in a kind of fascinated way, because all this silent mindful meditating over the last few days made everything fascinating. Each individual hair on Ben's leg was like a *tiny tree* in a *dear little forest*—

Ben cleared his throat and shifted his leg. Frances straightened and met the eyes of the tall, dark, and handsome man seated on the opposite side of the circle. He sat straight-backed and solemn, yet somehow in a manner that conveyed he wasn't taking any of this too seriously. She automatically went to look away but he held her gaze and winked. Frances winked back and he looked startled. She was a terrible winker; she found it hard to close only one eye and had been told that her attempt looked like an extraordinary facial spasm.

"And so we come to the end of our noble silence," said Masha. She grinned and punched the air. "We did it!"

Nobody said a word, but there was a gentle murmur of sound: exhalations, the shifting of bodies, and half chuckles of acknowledgment.

"I'd like us to now slowly reintroduce conversation and eye contact," said Masha. "We shall each take a turn to introduce ourselves and speak for just a few moments about whatever comes to mind: perhaps why you chose to come to Tranquillum House, what you're enjoying most about your experience so far, and what you've found most challenging. Are you dying for a cappuccino or glass of sauvignon blanc? I get it! Share your pain with the group! Are you missing a loved one? Tell us about that! Or maybe you'd just prefer to deliver straight-up facts: your age, your occupation, your hobbies, your star sign."

Masha smiled her extraordinary smile and everyone smiled back.

"Or recite a line of poetry, if you like," she continued. "It doesn't matter what you say. Simply enjoy the experience of speaking, connecting, and making eye contact with your fellow guests."

People cleared their throats, adjusted their posture, and stroked their hair in preparation for public speaking.

"While we get to know each other, Yao and Delilah will distribute your afternoon smoothies," said Masha.

Such was Masha's charismatic charm that Frances hadn't even noticed Yao and Delilah stand up. Now they began to glide about the room distributing tall glasses. This afternoon's smoothies were all the same emerald-green color. *Spinach?* thought Frances with alarm, but when she took hers and had a sip she tasted apple, honeydew melon, and pear, with undertones of moss and bark. It brought to mind a walk by a babbling brook in a dappled green forest. She tossed it back like tequila.

"Why don't you go first, Frances?" said Masha.

"Oh. Okay. Well, I'm Frances. Hi." She put down her empty glass, dipped her head, and licked her teeth for lipstick. She realized she was automatically adopting her professional public-speaking persona: warm, humble, gracious, but a little standoffish in order to repel any huggers in the signing line.

"I came to Tranquillum House because I was kind of in a bad way: my health, my personal life, my career." She allowed her gaze to travel the circle. It felt strangely intimate, looking everyone in the eye again. "I write romance books for a living and my last one got rejected. I also got badly burned in a romance scam. So."

Why was she telling them all about the scam? Blab, blab, blab.

Tony looked steadily back at her. He had more stubble than before, and his face seemed more defined. Men always lost weight so easily, the fuckers. She faltered a little. Was he sneering again? Or was he just . . . looking at her?

"So the first five days have been good!" All at once she was desperate to talk. She didn't care if she gave them "too much information." The words spilled from her mouth. It was like that greedy feeling of sitting down to an excellent meal when you were very hungry and after the first mouthful you were suddenly shoveling food into your mouth like a machine.

"I enjoyed the silence more than I thought I would, it did seem to calm my thoughts. In addition to being rejected I was very upset about this really very nasty review, I was thinking about it obsessively in the beginning, but I'm not even thinking about it at all now, so that's good, and, well, I miss coffee and champagne and the internet and . . ." *Shut up, Frances.* "And, you know, all the normal luxuries of normal life."

She sat back, her face warm.

"I'll go next," said the tall, dark, and handsome man. "I'm Lars. I'm a health-retreat junkie. I indulge and atone, indulge and atone. It works for me."

Frances looked at his chiseled cheekbones and golden-toned skin. *It certainly does work for you, lovely Lars.*

"I'm a family lawyer, so I need to drink a lot of wine after work." He paused as if to allow time for his audience to laugh, but no one did.

"I always do a retreat in January because February is my busiest time of year. The phone starts ringing the day the new school year starts. You know, Mum and Dad realize they can't spend another summer together."

"Oh dear," said Napoleon somberly.

"As for Tranquillum House, I love the food, love the location, and I'm doing fine. I don't miss anything much except for my Netflix account." He lifted his smoothie glass as if it were a cocktail and toasted the room.

Flustered Glasses lady spoke up next, although she was noticeably less flustered than the first day.

"I'm Carmel. I'm here to lose weight. Obviously."

Frances sighed. What did she mean, *obviously*? Carmel was thinner than her.

"I love everything about this place," said Carmel. "*Everything.*" She looked at Masha with a degree of intensity that was unsettling. She lifted her smoothie glass and drank deeply.

Jessica spoke up next, eagerly, as if she couldn't wait for her turn. "So, my name is Jessica."

She sat cross-legged, her hands placed on her knees like a kid in a school photo, and Frances could see the cute little girl she had been not all that long ago, before she succumbed to the temptation of all those cosmetic procedures.

"We came here because we've been having really very serious troubles with our marriage."

"We don't need to tell everyone that," muttered Ben into his chest.

"No but, babe, you know what? You were right when you said I'm too obsessed with appearances." She turned to look at him intently. "You were *right*, babe!" Her voice skidded up to an uncomfortably high pitch.

"Yeah but . . . Okay, Jesus." Ben subsided. Frances could see the back of his neck turning red.

"We were heading for a *divorce*," continued Jessica, with touching earnestness, as if the word "divorce" would be shocking to all.

"I can give you my card," said Lars.

Jessica ignored him. "This noble silence has been really good for me, really great, really *clarifying*." She turned to Masha. "It's like, I had so much noise in my head before I came here. I was, like, obsessed with social media, I admit it. I just had this constant chit-chat going on." She opened and closed her hand next to her ear to demonstrate. "And now I see everything more clearly. It all started with the money. We won the lottery, you see, and everything changed and it really fucked us up."

"You won the lottery?" said Carmel. "I've never known anybody who won the lottery."

"We were actually going to keep that kind of . . . shush-shush," said Jessica. She pressed her fingertip to her lips. "But we changed our mind."

"Did we?" said Ben.

"How much did you win?" asked Lars, and then he immediately held up his palm. "Inappropriate! Don't answer that! None of my business."

"How did you find out you'd won?" asked Frances. "Tell us the story." She wanted the story of the moment their lives changed forever.

"I'm so glad to hear that the silence has given you clarity, Jessica," Masha interrupted before the conversation could take a turn toward this exit. She had a remarkable ability to ignore what didn't interest her. "Who else?"

Ben spoke up. "Yeah. I'm Ben. Jessica's husband. Jessica covered why we're here. I'm fine. The silence has been fine. The food is better than I expected. I'm not sure what we're achieving, but it's all good. I guess I miss my new car."

"What sort of car, mate?" asked Tony.

"Lamborghini," said Ben, tender-eyed, as if he'd been asked the name of his newborn son.

Tony smiled. It was the first time Frances had seen him smile and it was the most unexpected, apple-cheeked smile. It entirely transformed his face. It was like a baby's smile. His eyes disappeared into a mass of wrinkles. "No wonder you miss it," he said.

"If I won the lottery I always thought I'd get a Bugatti," mused Lars.

Ben shook his head. "Overrated."

"*Overrated,* he says! The most stunning car in the world is *overrated*!"

"If I ever won the lottery I'd get a cute little red Ferrari," offered Zoe.

"Yeah, well the Ferrari is—"

Masha cut off the sports-car conversation. "Who haven't we heard from yet? Tony?"

"You all know me as the desperado who tried to bring in the contraband," said Tony. He smiled again. "Here for weight loss. I miss beer, pizza, ribs with plum sauce, wedges with sour cream, family-sized chocolate bars—you get the picture." His initial enthusiasm waned and he lowered his eyes, clearly keen for everyone to stop looking at him.

"Thank you," he said formally, to the floor.

Frances didn't believe him. There was more to his decision to come here than just weight loss.

Napoleon raised his hand.

"Go ahead, Napoleon," said Masha.

He lifted his chin and recited. "*It matters not how strait the gate, How charged with punishments the scroll, I am the master of my fate, I am the captain of my soul.*" His eyes gleamed in the shadows from the candlelight. "That's, ah, from Nelson Mandela's favorite poem, 'Invictus.'" He looked uncertain for a moment. "You said we could recite poetry."

"Absolutely I did," said Masha warmly. "I love the sentiment."

"Yes, well, it just came into my head. I'm a high school teacher. The kids like to hear that they are masters of their own fates, although . . ." He laughed a strange sort of a laugh. Heather, who sat next to him, placed a gentle hand over his jiggling kneecap. He didn't seem to notice it. "Tomorrow is the third anniversary of our son's death. That's why we're here. He took his own life, so that's how *my* kid chose to be master of his own fate."

The room became very still as if, for just a moment, they all held their breath. The tiny gold flames on the candles trembled.

Frances compressed her lips so no words would escape. She felt as if all feelings were too big and unwieldy for her body, as if she might burst into tears or burst out laughing, as if she might say something overly sentimental or intimate. It was like she'd drunk too much in an inappropriate setting, a business meeting with publishing executives.

"I'm so sorry for your loss, Napoleon," said Masha and she reached out her hand as if she wanted to touch Napoleon, but he was too far away. "So very sorry."

"Why thank you, Masha," said Napoleon chattily.

If Frances didn't know better she would have thought *he* was drunk. Had he got stuck into Zoe's smuggled wine? Was he having a nervous breakdown? Or was this just a natural response to the breaking of the silence?

Zoe looked at her father, her forehead creased like that of an elderly woman, and Frances tried to imagine the missing boy who should have been sitting next to her. *Oh, Zoe,* thought Frances. She had thought it might have been suicide when Zoe didn't say how he died. Her friend Lily, who used to write beautiful historical romances, had lost her husband ten years ago and all she had told people was that "Neil died unexpectedly" and everyone understood what that meant. Lily hadn't written since.

"Who else would like—"

But Napoleon interrupted Masha. "Got it!" he cried. "I know who you are!" he said to Tony. "It's been driving me mad. Heather, darling, do you see who it is?" Napoleon turned to his wife.

Heather looked up from the empty smoothie glass she'd been studying. "No."

"I know who he is," said Lars proudly. "I worked it out on the very first day."

Frances looked at Tony, who was looking awkwardly down at his glass with an expression of discomfort, but not confusion, as if he knew what they were all talking about. Who *was* he? A *famous* serial killer?

"Heather!" cried Napoleon. "You know him! I promise you know him!"

"From . . . school? Work?" Heather shook her head. "I don't . . ."

"I'll give you a clue." Napoleon chanted, *"We are the Navy Blues!"*

Heather studied Tony. Her face cleared. "Smiley Hogburn!"

Napoleon pointed at Heather as if she'd correctly guessed his charade. "Exactly! It's Smiley Hogburn!" Then he seemed to doubt himself. "Aren't you?"

Tony looked strained. "Years ago I was," he said. "Thirty kilos ago."

"But Smiley Hogburn played for Carlton," said Jessica. *"I'm* a Carlton supporter! Aren't you, like, a total legend?" She said it like there must have been a mix-up.

"It was probably before you were born," said Tony.

"Carlton is a *football* team, right?" whispered

Frances to Ben. She was very ignorant of anything to do with sports; a friend once told her it was like she'd lived her whole life in a bunker.

"Yep," said Ben. "Aussie Rules."

"That's the jumping one?"

Ben chortled. "They do jump, yeah."

Smiley Hogburn, thought Frances. There *was* something blurrily familiar about that name. She felt her perception of Tony shift. He was a man who used to be someone, like Frances used to be someone. They had that in common. Although Frances's career was slowly fading away, whereas presumably Tony's had ended officially, probably with an injury of some sort—all that jumping!—and he was no longer leaping about the football field.

"I knew you were Smiley Hogburn!" said Lars again. He seemed to be looking for some sort of recognition that he wasn't getting. "I'm not normally good with faces but I worked out who you were straightaway."

"Did you have to finish up playing because of a sporting injury?" asked Frances. She felt that was quite a knowledgeable, empathetic question to ask a sportsperson. It was probably something to do with *ligaments*.

Tony looked mildly amused. "I had multiple injuries."

"Oh," said Frances. "I'm sorry to hear that."

"Two knee reconstructions, hip replacement . . ." Tony seemed to be doing a sad assessment of his body. He sighed. "Chronic ankle issues."

"Were you called Smiley Hogburn because you *did* smile a lot, or because you *didn't*?" asked Zoe.

"Because I did smile a lot," said Tony unsmilingly. "I was kind of a simple guy back then. Happy-go-lucky."

"*Were* you?" said Frances, unable to hide her surprise.

"I was," said Tony. He smiled at her. He seemed to find her funny.

"Weren't you the one with the smiley-face tattoos on your butt?" said Lars.

"I've seen them!" cried Frances before she could help herself.

"Have you now?" said Lars suggestively.

"*Frances*," said Tony, and he put a finger to his lips as if they had something to hide. Wait! Was he flirting with her?

"Oh no, not in *that* way," said Frances. She looked nervously at Masha. "I saw them accidentally."

"My brother used to have your poster in his bedroom!" It was Delilah, breaking ranks and speaking like a human being. "The one where you're jumping six feet in the air and the other player is pulling down your shorts and you can see your tattoos! Hilarious!"

"Fancy that. We have a famous athlete in our midst." There was an edge to Masha's voice. Maybe she wanted to be the only athlete in their midst.

"Former athlete," Tony corrected her. "It was a long time ago."

"So . . . who haven't we heard from yet?" said Masha, clearly keen to change the subject.

"Post-sport depression," said Napoleon. "Is that what you've got? I've read about it. It affects a lot of elite sportspeople. You've got to focus on your mental health, Tony . . . Smiley . . . Tony—I hope you don't mind if I call you Smiley—you really do, because depression is an *insidious*—"

"Who's next?" interrupted Masha.

"I'll go next," said Zoe. "I'm Zoe."

She seemed to gather her thoughts. Or was she nervous? *Oh, sweetheart.*

"As Dad already said, we decided to come to Tranquillum House because we can't stand to be at home in January, because that's where my brother hanged himself."

Masha made a strange startled sound and pressed her hand to her mouth. It was the first time Frances had observed Masha show any sign of weakness. Even when she spoke about her father, whom she clearly grieved, she'd still been controlled.

Frances watched Masha swallow convulsively for a few seconds, as if she were choking, but then she regained her composure and carried on listening to Zoe, although her eyes looked a little watery, as if she really had just choked on something.

Zoe looked at the ceiling. The circle of people seemed to tilt toward her with the weight of their useless sympathy.

"Oh wait, Dad probably didn't say that Zach hanged himself, but if you were wondering, like, what was his *method of choice*, that was it! It's popular."

She smiled and rocked in tiny circles. The silver studs along her ears gleamed.

"One of his friends said that was so 'brave' of Zach—to choose that way to kill himself. Instead of

pills. Like, he'd been bungee jumping. God!" She blew
out a puff of air and her hair lifted from her forehead.

"*Anyway*, once we became, like, total experts on suicide, we stopped telling people how he did it. Because
of suicide contagion. Suicide is really contagious. My
parents were terrified I'd catch it too. Like chicken pox.
Ha ha. I never caught it though."

"Zoe?" said Napoleon. "Darling, maybe that's
enough."

"We weren't close," said Zoe to the group. She
looked at her hands and said it again. "Like, sometimes
people think because we were twins we were really
close, but we went to different schools. We had different interests. Different *values*."

"Zoe," said her mother. "Maybe now is not the—"

"He got up really early that morning." Zoe ignored
her mother. She fiddled with one of the many earrings
in her earlobe. Her empty smoothie glass lay on its side
against her thigh. "He hardly ever got up early. He took
out the recycling bin, because it was his turn, and then
he went back upstairs and killed himself." She sighed,
as if she were bored. "We took it in turns to take out
the bins. I don't know if he was making some kind
of point by doing that. It really pissed me off. Like,
thanks so much for that, Zach, good on you, that makes
up for you killing yourself."

"Zoe?" said Heather sharply.

Zoe turned in her mother's direction, but very
slowly, as if she had a stiff back. "What?"

Heather took the smoothie glass and placed it upright

on the floor, out of the way. She leaned toward her daughter and brushed a lock of hair out of Zoe's eyes.

"Something is not quite . . ." Heather's gaze traveled around the circle of people. "Not quite right."

She turned to Masha. She said, "Have you been medicating us?"

30

Masha

Focus. Only. On your breathing. Focus. Only. On your breathing.

Masha was fine, perfectly fine, she was under control. For a moment there, when Zoe said what she said, Masha had very nearly lost her focus completely; time slipped. But now she was back, her breathing steady, she was in control.

This information about the brother should have come out in her one-on-one counseling sessions with the Marconi family. They had all freely said they were here for the anniversary of his death, but none had mentioned he took his own life. Masha should have seen through their evasive behavior. It was not like her to miss this. She was extremely perceptive. They had deliberately misled her and as a result she had been unprepared. She had felt *blindsided*.

And now this question from Heather: "Have you been medicating us?"

Before Heather spoke, Masha had been observing the group, watching their mannerisms become freer, their pupils dilate and tongues loosen. They were clearly losing their inhibitions, speaking fluidly, with refreshing honesty. Some, like Napoleon, fidgeted, whereas others, like Frances, were very still. Some were flushed, others pale.

Right now, Heather was both: pasty white with hectic spots of color on her cheeks.

"Have you?" she demanded. "Have you been medicating us?"

"In a manner of speaking," said Masha calmly.

Heather's question was not ideal and not anticipated, although perhaps it should have been, because Heather was a midwife, the only one of the guests, as far as Masha knew, with any medical expertise. But Masha would handle this.

"What do you mean, 'in a manner of speaking'?"

Masha did not like Heather's tone. Snappy. Disrespectful.

"Well, *medicating* implies . . ." Masha searched for the right words. "A dulling of the senses. What we're doing here is *heightening* the senses."

"You need to tell us exactly what you've been giving us! Right now!" Heather moved up onto her knees, as if she were ready to leap to her feet. Masha was reminded of a ferocious little dog. One she'd quite like to kick.

"Hang on, what's going on here?" said Napoleon to Heather.

Masha flashed a look at Yao and Delilah: *Be ready if needed*. They gave her barely perceptible nods, both gripping the discreet medical pouches they had clipped around their waists.

This was not how it was supposed to go.

31

Lars

In his long history of health resorts Lars had experienced some bizarre and unusual practices, but this was a first. It was ironic because one of the side benefits of coming here was to cut *down* on his recreational drug use.

"It's called micro-dosing and it's perfectly safe," said their esteemed leader, who, as always, sat cross-legged and straight-backed, her incredible long white legs so entwined that sometimes Lars got distracted trying to work out where each leg started and ended.

"There are multiple benefits: higher levels of creativity, increased focus, heightened spiritual awareness, improved relationships—I could go on and on. Basically, you function just a little better than a normal person. The doses are about a tenth of a normal dose of LSD."

"Wait . . . what?" asked Frances. She laughed uncertainly, as if she'd heard a joke she didn't quite get. Lars liked her already. "Sorry. You're not saying that *we've* been taking *LSD*?"

Lars saw most of his fellow guests were staring at Masha with dull incomprehension. This was surely too conservative a crowd to cope with a revelation about drugs, even taking into account the popularity of cocaine in the suburbs. Lars himself dabbled with coke, Ecstasy, and pot, but never LSD.

"As I said, it's called micro-dosing," said Masha.

"It's called spiking our smoothies with a hallucinogenic drug," snapped Heather.

Heather. Before today, Lars would never have picked Heather as her name. It was far too soft a name for this skinny, tanned woman with quadriceps that looked like machine parts and a permanent pained squint as if she were peering straight into the sun. Every time Lars had looked at her during the silence, he'd imagined pressing his thumbs to the point between her eyebrows and saying, "Chill." Now he felt bad about feeling aggravated, because she'd lost her son. The woman was allowed to frown.

"It's called outrageous," continued Heather. She wasn't squinting now. Her eyes were ablaze with fury.

"I don't quite understand," said her adorably addled husband, a long celery stick of a man, so dorky he was cool. His name was *Napoleon*, which just added to his marvelousness.

Lars didn't think he was high. He'd been feeling great, but he generally did feel good on any sort of cleanse. Perhaps the doses were too small to affect him, or he'd built up a tolerance. He surreptitiously ran a finger around the edge of his smoothie glass and licked it. He thought about how, on the first day, he'd drunk his smoothie and said to Delilah, "This is so good. What's *in* this stuff?" and Delilah had said, "We'll give you the recipes when you leave." Lars had been imagining the recipes would specify the number of teaspoons of chia, not how many milligrams of LSD.

"But . . . but . . . we're here to detoxify!" said Frances to Masha. "You're saying we've cut out caffeine and replaced it with *acid*?"

Tony, aka Smiley Hogburn, said, "I can't believe you confiscated my beer and now you've given me drugs. I've never taken drugs!"

"You don't think alcohol is a drug?" said Masha. "LSD has been ranked one-tenth as harmful as alcohol! What do you think of that?"

"I guess LSD has no calories," said Carmel. It was easy to remember her name because Lars had a friend called Carmel who was also boringly convinced she was fat. Carmel's glasses sat crookedly on her face but she didn't seem aware of it. She had been mooning about for the last five days with that recently-kicked-in-the-face look Lars knew so well from his clients. The one that ignited a deep burn of rage in his belly; the rage that had fueled his entire career. He'd put a million bucks on her husband having left her for a trophy wife.

"Does LSD also speed up the metabolism?" Carmel asked hopefully. "I really feel like my metabolism might be speeding up. I've never had drugs either, but I'm completely fine with this. I have total respect for you and your methods, Masha."

Getting thin won't help you feel better, honey. Take

the fuckwit to the cleaners. Lars would talk to her later. See who represented her.

"I can't believe you've been giving my underage daughter LSD," said Heather.

"I'm not underage, Mum," said Zoe. "I'm feeling pretty good right now; better than I've felt in a while. They're only micro-doses. It's all good."

"It's not all good!" her mother sighed. "For Christ's sake."

Napoleon spoke earnestly. "Masha, listen, I had a terrible experience with drugs when I was a teenager. It was a 'bad trip,' as they say. One of the worst experiences of my life and I always told my kids that's when I swore off drugs forever. So I appreciate what you're saying, but I'm not taking anything."

"My God, Napoleon, you've already *taken* it!" said Heather through gritted teeth. "Are you not listening?"

"This is bullshit," said the lottery-winner kid. What was his name again? A good wholesome straight-boy name. What was it? The kid trembled with so much suppressed rage it looked like he was having a seizure and he spoke through clenched teeth. "*I did not choose this.*"

His young wife spoke up. "Ben is, like, full-on anti-drugs."

Ben, thought Lars. That was it. Ben, and his cosmetically enhanced wife was . . . *Jessica.* Ben and Jessica. No chance those two had a pre-nup, and now there was significant money at stake if the marriage fell apart. They'd be the type to lose it all to their lawyers.

"He doesn't even like taking aspirin," said Jessica.

"His sister is an addict. A proper addict. This is not good." She put her hand on her husband's shoulder. "I don't see how this is going to help our marriage. I'm not feeling very happy about this either. Not happy at all."

Her poor little Barbie-doll face did look very unhappy. Lars felt something unfurl in his chest: a deep rich welling of sympathy for poor Jessica. Poor, poor little plastic Jessica. Confused little rich girl. All that money and no idea how to spend it, except on cosmetic procedures that were doing her no favors.

"I understand your fear," said Masha. "You've been brainwashed because of the misinformation spread by governments."

"I have not been *brainwashed*," said Ben. "I have *seen* it for myself."

"Yes, but those are street drugs, Ben," said Masha. "The problem with street drugs is you can't control the content or dosage."

"I cannot believe this." Ben got to his feet.

"LSD has actually been used very successfully to treat drug addiction," said Masha. "Your sister could benefit from it. In the right setting."

Ben smacked his hands to his face. "Unbelievable."

Masha said, "Do you know, there was a great man. His name was *Steve Jobs*."

Lars, who had been expecting her to say the Dalai Lama, snickered.

"I always admired him greatly," said Masha.

"Not sure why you took all our iPhones away then," muttered Tony.

"Do you know what Steve Jobs said? He said that taking LSD was one of the most important, profound experiences of his life."

"Oh well then," said Lars, greatly amused. "If Steve Jobs said we should all take LSD, then we really should!"

Masha shook her head sadly at them, as if they were misguided but lovable children. "The side effects of psychedelic drugs are *minimal*. Respected researchers at Ivy League universities are doing clinical trials as we speak! The results have been excellent! Micro-dosing has allowed you to focus on your meditation and yoga practices over the last week, as well as alleviating the withdrawal symptoms you would otherwise have suffered by cutting out far more dangerous substances, like alcohol and sugar."

"Yes, but, Masha . . . ," said Heather. She sounded calmer than before. She splayed her fingers on both hands as if she were waiting for a fresh manicure to dry. "The effects I'm feeling right now, the effects I suspect we are now all beginning to feel, that has to be more than just a micro-dose."

Masha smiled at Heather, as if she couldn't be happier with her. "Oh, Heather," she said. "You are a smart lady."

"That last smoothie was different," said Heather. "Wasn't it?"

"You are right, Heather," said Masha. "I was about to explain this but you keep racing me to the punch!" She corrected the phrase almost instantly. "*Beating* me to the punch!" Her strong white teeth gleamed in the candlelight. It was hard to tell if it was a smile or a grimace.

"What's happening now is the next step in a rigorously planned and executed new protocol." She looked around the room, giving everyone tiny nods, as if dispensing affirmative answers to their unspoken questions. *Yes, yes, yes*, she seemed to be saying. "You are about to embark on a *truly* transformative experience. We've never done this before at Tranquillum House and we're all so excited about it. You are the first nine guests to have this extraordinary opportunity."

A glorious sense of well-being spread like honey throughout Lars's body.

"For most of you, your last smoothie contained both a dosage of LSD and a liquid form of psilocybin, a naturally occurring substance found in certain mushrooms."

"*Magic mushrooms*," said Tony with disgust.

"Oh my goodness," said Frances. "It's like I'm back doing my arts degree again."

Lars was so happy he'd chosen Tranquillum House for this cleanse. What a truly wonderful place. How innovative and cutting-edge.

"But that's what caused my bad experience," said Napoleon. "My bad trip. It was a magic mushroom."

"We won't let that happen, Napoleon," said Masha. "We are trained medical professionals and we're here to help and guide you. The drugs you have taken have been tested to ensure they are in their purest form."

Lovely, top-quality, pure drugs, thought Lars dreamily.

"It's called guided psychedelic therapy," said Masha. "As your ego dissolves you will access a higher level of consciousness. A curtain will be drawn back and you will see the world in a way you've never seen it before."

Lars had a friend who had traveled for days in the Amazon to take part in an ayahuasca ceremony, where he'd vomited repeatedly and been eaten alive by bugs in his search for enlightenment. This was delightfully civilized in comparison. Five-star enlightenment!

"What a load of bullshit," said Tony.

"But I lost my mind," said Napoleon. "I honestly lost my mind, and I did not like losing my mind."

"That's because you weren't in a safe, secure environment. The experts call it 'set and setting,'" said Masha. "For a positive experience you need the right mind-set and a controlled environment like we've created here today." She gestured about the room. "Yao, Delilah, and I are here to guide you and keep you safe."

"You know you're going to get sued for this," said Heather serenely.

Masha smiled at her tenderly. "In a moment, I'm going to ask you to move to one of the stretchers, where you may lie down and enjoy what I can assure you will be a truly transcendent experience."

"And what if we don't want this experience?" said Tony.

"I think we're all strapped into the spaceship now." Lars nudged Tony's big beefy shoulder with his own. "All you can do is sit back and enjoy the ride. I find your smile very charming, by the way."

"Oh, so do I!" said Frances. "I love his smile! It's like his whole head kind of crumples up like a . . . like a . . . crumpled tissue."

"Jesus," said Tony.

"You yourself are very handsome," said Frances to Lars. "Devastatingly handsome, in fact."

Lars always felt fondly toward people who were unequivocal in their acknowledgment of his looks.

"That's kind of you," he said modestly. "I can't take credit for it. I come from a long line of devastatingly handsome men."

"I feel like giving us drugs without our permission must be against the law," said Jessica.

Of course it's against the law, you twit, thought Lars.

"Please don't call me a twit," said Jessica.

Lars's blood ran cold. She could read his mind and she was extraordinarily wealthy. She now had the capacity to take over the world for her own nefarious purposes.

"We're here for couples counseling," said Jessica to Masha. "We paid for couples counseling. This is all just pointless for us."

"This will have a profound impact on your marriage," said Masha. "You and Ben won't be separated on your journey. You will sit together and experience this as a couple." Masha indicated one of the clusters of cushions in the corner. "Your smoothies contained a different formula from everyone else's. We studied the research carefully and we found that MDMA was the best—"

"Ecstasy," snapped Heather. "She means Ecstasy. She's given you a *party drug*. Unbelievable. Kids die every year after taking Ecstasy tablets, but don't let that bother you."

"You're being kind of a downer about all this, Mum," said Zoe.

"Let's go," said Ben to Jessica. He held out his hand to his wife and looked at Masha. "We're leaving."

"Just . . . hold on." Jessica didn't take his hand.

"Again, when used in a controlled environment, MDMA is perfectly safe. It has been trialed for prescription psychotherapy with great success to treat PTSD, social anxiety, and for couples therapy!" said Masha. "There has never been a single death or even a single adverse reaction to a clinically administered dose of MDMA."

"This is not a clinical setting!" cried Heather.

Masha ignored her. "MDMA is an empathogen. It produces feelings of empathy and openness."

"It *is* a very nice experience, you guys," said Lars lovingly.

Masha gave him a disapproving look. "But this is not about dancing all night at a club. This is *guided therapy*. You will find, Ben and Jessica, that you become more sensitive to feelings and more accepting of each other's views. You're about to communicate in a way you've probably never communicated before."

"Consent," said Napoleon. "I feel like that's what's missing here. I feel like . . . I'm pretty sure . . ." He held up a finger. "I read the paperwork very carefully, and I feel certain we did not consent to this."

"No, we fucking did not," said Tony.

Jessica stuck one of her long fake fingernails in her mouth and chewed.

Careful, thought Lars. *Those things look sharp.*

"What things look sharp?" Jessica frowned at Lars, and then turned to Ben. "Maybe we should give it a go?"

Ben, who was still on his feet, shook his head, his eyes fixed on a far-off horizon only he could see. "I did not choose this," he said again. "Drugs are dangerous. Drugs are *bad*. Drugs *ruin lives*."

"I know, babe," said Jessica, looking up at him. "But maybe we should just go with it?"

"I think you two should go for it," said Lars. "I've seen a lot of bad marriages, but I think your marriage has . . ." There was a fine word he needed to finish his fine sentence but it had escaped his brain.

The word swooped about between Jessica and Ben like a frisky butterfly before it landed, quivering, on Tony's hand. Lars leaned forward and read it.

"*Potential!*" he said. "I think your marriage has potential."

Time slowed, and then snapped back to normal pace.

Delilah stood right in front of him. She'd teleported herself, the clever minx.

"It's time to lie down now, Lars," said Delilah. Teleporting was a handy skill that Lars would like to develop. He would order *Teleporting for Dummies*. He felt like that was the kind of witticism his new friend Frances would appreciate, but he saw that Frances was with Yao, lying down on one of the stretchers, trustingly lifting her head as Yao placed a mask over her eyes.

"Up you get." Delilah offered her hand. Lars was momentarily transfixed by a thick lustrous curl of black hair that fell over her shoulder. He studied it for an hour and then he took her hand.

"I know all about bad marriages," Lars explained as he let her haul him to his feet. Delilah was as strong and powerful as Wonder Woman and she also strongly resembled Wonder Woman. She was quite wondrous in many ways, although he would not let her near his hair.

"Let's talk about that more in a moment," said Delilah as she led him to a stretcher. "We can explore it during your guided therapy."

"No thank you, sweetheart, I've already done years of therapy," said Lars. "There is nothing I don't already know about my psyche."

He thought of all those fat files crammed with pages of handwritten words about the Great Mysteries of Lars, which could in reality be summed up in a few paltry paragraphs.

When Lars was ten his father left his mother for a woman called *Gwen*. There may have been nice Gwens in the world, but Lars doubted it. His mother was screwed in the financial settlement. Now Lars spent his days eviscerating wealthy men who left their wives: an endless, pointless revenge fantasy against his long-dead father, a job which he found emotionally and financially satisfying.

He was a control freak because he'd lost control of his life when he was a kid, and weird about money because he'd grown up with none, and he wasn't sufficiently *vulnerable* in his relationships because . . . he didn't want to be vulnerable. He loved Ray, but there was a part of himself he withheld, because Ray had had a happy, functional childhood, and it seemed Lars subconsciously wanted to punch him in the face for having the happy childhood that Lars didn't get. That was it. Nothing more to know, nothing more to learn. A few years ago Lars swapped therapy for health resorts, and Ray took up cycling and got skinny and obsessed like all city cyclists. Life was good.

"You haven't done this sort of therapy," said Delilah.

"No thank you," said Lars firmly and politely. "I'll just take the trip."

Lars lay down and got himself comfortable. Big Tony, Smiley Hogburn, lay on the stretcher next to his. Masha kneeled by his side, tucking him in with swift, sure movements like he was a giant, grizzled baby. Lars met Tony's eyes just before Masha covered them with a mask. It was like looking into the terrified eyes of a prisoner. Poor Tony. *Just relax and enjoy it, big man.*

Delilah leaned in close to Lars, her breath warm and sweet. "I'm going to leave you for a moment, but I'll be back to check in on you and to talk about whatever is on your mind."

"There's nothing on my mind," said Lars. "Don't you touch my hair while I'm asleep, Delilah."

"Very funny. I've never heard that joke before. Masha and Yao are here too. You're not on your own. You're in safe hands, Lars. If there is anything you need, just ask."

"That's sweet," said Lars.

Delilah put the mask over his eyes and headphones over his ears.

"Look for the stars," said Delilah.

Classical music cascaded from the headphones directly into his brain. He could hear each note separately, in its entirety, with absolute purity. It was extraordinary.

A little boy with dark hair and a dirty face said to Lars, "Come with me. I've got something to show you."

"No thanks, buddy," said Lars. "I'm busy right now."

He recognized this little kid. It was his boyhood self, little Lars, trying to give him a message.

"Please," said the little boy, and he took Lars's hand. "I've got something I need to show you."

"Maybe later," said Lars, pulling his hand free. "I'm busy right now. You go play."

Remember this, he thought. *Remember it all.* He would tell Ray all about it when he got home. Ray would be interested. He was always interested in everything that happened to Lars. His face so earnest and open and hopeful.

Ray didn't want to *take* anything from him. All Ray wanted was his love.

For a moment that simple thought was everything, it hung there suspended in his consciousness, the answer to every question, the key to every lock, but then his mind exploded into a billion purple petals.

32

Zoe

Zoe's dad was refusing to lie down and put on his head-phones, and those were the *rules*, but her Dad didn't want to follow them and that was the first time in Zoe's life that she had ever seen her dad break the rules and it was so funny and awesome.

Zoe carefully pressed each of her fingertips against her thumbs as she watched Masha try to convince her dad to lie down. Her mum was shouting: "Illegal . . . Unconscionable! . . . Appalling!"

She was a savage little spitball of rage. It was cute. What did Zach used to say when Mum got mad? "Mum's being a savage cabbage."

She closed her eyes. *Mum is being such a savage cabbage right now.*

Thought you weren't talking to me. His voice was clear as a bell in her ear.

I'm not. I hate you. I can't stand you.

Yeah. I can't stand you either. Why do you keep telling people we weren't close?

Because we weren't. Before you died, we hadn't talked in, like, a month.

Because you were being a bitch.

No, because you were being a total loser.

Fuck off.

You fuck off. I downloaded your Shakespearean Insult Generator.

I know you did. It's funny, right? Do you like it? You pribbling half-faced harpy.

And I broke your electric guitar.

I saw that. You threw it across the room. You spleeny milk-livered lewdster.

I'm so angry with you.

I know.

You did it on purpose. To get back at me. To win.

Yeah, no. I can't even remember what we were arguing about.

I miss you every single day, Zach. Every single day.

I know.

I'll never be a normal person ever again. You took that away from me. You made me ABNORMAL and it's lonely being abnormal.

You were already kind of abnormal.

Very funny.

I think the parents want us over there.

What?

Zoe opened her eyes and the yoga studio was a million miles wide and her mum and dad were tiny specks in the distance, beckoning to her. "Come sit with us."

33

Frances

Frances felt the soft, frosty tickle of snowflakes on her face as she and her friend Gillian flew across a star-studded sky in a sleigh drawn by white horses.

A pile of books filled her lap. They were all the books she'd ever written, including foreign-language editions. The books were open at the top like cereal boxes. Frances dipped her hand into each book and pulled out great handfuls of words to scatter across the sky.

"Got one!" said Sol, from the back of the sleigh, where he and Henry sat smoking cigarettes and killing off unnecessary adjectives with catapults.

"Leave them be," said Frances snappily.

"Let's get all those adverbs too!" said Sol happily.

"Even the rhyming ones?" asked Henry affably.

"That's an imperfect rhyme," pointed out Frances.

"They're just words, Frances," said Gillian.

"So profound, Gillian," said Sol.

"Shut up, Sol," said Gillian.

"She never liked you," Frances told Sol.

Sol said, "That sort of woman always secretly wants an alpha male."

Frances smiled fondly at him. Egotist but sexy as hell. "You were my first-ever husband."

"I was your first-ever husband," agreed Sol. "And you were my second-ever wife."

"Second wives are so young and pretty," said Frances. "I liked being a second wife."

"By the by, Gillian kissed me once," said Henry. "At someone's thirtieth birthday party."

"She was drunk," said Frances. "Don't get a big head about it."

"I was drunk," agreed Gillian. "I felt bad about that until the day I died."

"Henry, you were my second husband," said Frances. "But I was your *first* wife. Therefore not as pretty."

Gillian said, "Why do you keep identifying your husbands?"

"Readers get impatient if they have trouble working out which character is which," explained Frances. "You've got to help them out. None of us is getting any younger."

"Except this isn't a book," said Gillian.

"I think you'll find it is," said Frances. "I'm the protagonist, obviously."

"I feel like that tall Russian lady is giving you a run for your money," said Gillian.

"She is not," said Frances. "It's all about me. I'm just not sure of my love interest yet."

"Oh my God, it's so obvious," said Gillian. "Blind

Freddy could pick it." She shouted at the sky, "You knew it from day one, right?"

"Gillian! Did you just try to break the fourth wall?" Frances was shocked.

"I did not," said Gillian, but she looked guilty. "I'm sure no one noticed."

"How tacky," said Frances. "How very gimmicky."

She dared to look up and the stars were a million darting eyes on the lookout for rule-breaking in her story: sexism, ageism, racism, tokenism, ableism, plagiarism, cultural appropriation, fat-shaming, body-shaming, slut-shaming, vegetarian-shaming, real-estate-agent-shaming. The voice of the Almighty Internet boomed from the sky: *Shame on you!*

Frances hung her head. "It's just a story," she whispered.

"That's what I'm trying to tell you," said Gillian.

An endless gossamer-like sentence embroidered with jewel-like metaphors, far too many clauses, and a meaning so obscure it had to be profound wrapped itself around Frances's neck, but it really didn't suit her, so she wrenched it off and flung it into space, where it floated free until at last a shy author on his way to a festival to accept a prize grabbed it from the sky and used it to gag one of his beautiful corpses. It looked lovely on her. Gray-bearded critics applauded with relief, grateful it hadn't ended up in a beach read.

"Will younger readers even recognize the term 'Blind Freddy'?" asked Jo, who floated alongside Frances doing a line-edit. She sat astride a giant lead pencil. "Could it be ableist?"

"What's interesting is that I'm a fictional character," said her internet scammer from the back of the sleigh, where he sat between Henry and Sol, his arms around their shoulders. "Yet she loved me more than either of you."

"You're nothing but a scam," said Sol. "She never even met you, let alone fucked you, cocksucker!"

"!!!!" cried Jo.

"I agree. Delete," advised Gillian. "My mother reads your books."

"As her loving ex-husbands, it's our duty to beat you to a pulp," said Henry to Paul Drabble. "Scram, scam."

"Life is nothing but a scam," said Gillian. "It's all just a giant illusion."

"Scram, scam," chuckled Sol. "Good one."

He and Henry fist-bumped.

"You're both far too old for fist-bumping," sighed Frances, but her ex-husbands were busy bonding. She always knew they'd like each other if they ever met. She should have invited them both to her fiftieth.

She realized that Paul Drabble had vanished, as easy as that. There was no pain in the empty space he'd left behind. It turned out he'd meant nothing at all. Not a thing.

"He was just a credit on my bank balance," she told Gillian.

"Debit, you idiot," said Gillian.

"Debit, credit," said Frances. "Whatever. I am completely over him."

"I was the one who meant something," said a child's voice. It was Ari, Paul Drabble's son.

Frances didn't turn around. She could not look at him.

"I thought I was going to be his mother," she said to Gillian. "It's the only time in my life I even considered being a mother."

"I know," said Gillian.

"So embarrassing," whispered Frances. "I am so deeply embarrassed."

"It's a loss, Frances," said Gillian. "You're allowed to grieve your loss even if it's embarrassing."

The snow fell silently for days as Frances grieved her loss of an imaginary boy and Gillian sat beside her, head bowed in sympathy, until they were frozen snow-covered figures.

"What about my dad?" asked Frances in the spring, when the snow melted, butterflies danced, and bees buzzed. "Why isn't he here on my trip? I'm the one writing this thing, Gillian, not you. Let's get Dad on board."

"I'm here," said her dad from the back of the sleigh.

He was alone, wearing the khaki safari suit he wore for Christmas lunch 1973, captured forever in the framed photo on her writing desk. She reached back and took his hand. "Hello, Dad."

"You were always so crazy about the boys." Her dad shook his head. Frances smelled his Old Spice after-shave.

"You died when I was too young," said Frances. "That's why I made such bad choices in men. I was trying to replace you."

"Cliché?" asked Jo from astride her lead pencil, which was bucking like a horse. "*Whoa*, boy!"

"Stop editing me," said Frances to Jo. "You're retired. Go look after your grandchildren."

"Don't even pretend you have unresolved daddy issues—you do not," said Gillian. "Take responsibility."

Frances pinched Gillian on the arm.

"Ouch!" said Gillian.

"Sorry. I didn't think it would hurt. It's not like any of this is real," said Frances. "It's just a story I'm making up as I go along."

"Speaking of which, I always thought your plots could be better structured," said Gillian. "The same goes for your life. All this chopping and changing of husbands. Maybe you could think about planning ahead for the final chapters. I never had the courage to say that when I was alive."

"You actually did say that when you were alive," said Frances. "More than once, as a matter of fact."

"You're always acting like you're the heroine of one of your own novels. You just fall into the arms of the next man the narrator puts in front of you."

"You told me that too!"

"Did I?" said Gillian. "That was impolite of me."

"I always thought so," said Frances.

"I could have been kinder," said Gillian. "I may have been on the spectrum."

"Don't think you're getting any more character development now you're dead," said Frances. "You're done. Let's focus on *my* character development."

"You're easy: you're the princess," said Gillian. "The passive princess waiting for yet another prince."

"I could kill the emu," said Frances.

"Well, we'll see, won't we, Frances? We'll see if you can kill the emu."

"Maybe." Frances watched the emu, alive again, but still incapable of flight, run across the star-studded sky. "I really miss you, Gillian."

"Thanks," said Gillian. "I would say I missed you too, but that would not strictly be true as I'm actually in a constant state of bliss."

"I'm not surprised. It's so beautiful," said Frances. "It's kind of like the northern lights, isn't it?"

"It's always there," said Gillian.

"What is? The northern lights? They are not always there. Ellen paid a fortune and didn't see a thing."

"This, Frances. This beauty. Just on the other side. You just have to be quiet. Stay still. Stop talking. Stop wanting. Just be. You'll hear it, or feel it. Close your eyes and you'll see it."

"Interesting," said Frances. "Did I tell you about my review?"

"Frances, *forget* the review!"

Gosh. Gillian sounded quite cranky for someone who didn't have anything to do except lie back and enjoy the exquisite beauty of the afterlife.

34

Yao

"Where are you now, Frances?" asked Yao.

He sat on the floor next to her stretcher, and removed her headphones so she could hear him.

"I'm in a story, Yao," said Frances. He couldn't see her eyes because of the mask but her face was animated. "I'm writing the story and I'm *in* the story. It's quite a nice story. I've got a kind of magic-realism vibe going, which is new for me. I like it! Nothing needs to make sense."

"Okay," said Yao. "Who else is in the story with you?"

"My friend Gillian. She died. In her sleep, when she was forty-nine. It's called Sudden Adult Death Syndrome. I thought it was just for babies. I didn't even know it was possible."

"Does Gillian have anything to say to you?"

"Not really. I told her about the review."

"Frances, *forget* the review!"

It wasn't professional but Yao couldn't hide his frustration. Frances kept talking on and on about the review. Shouldn't authors be used to bad reviews? Wasn't it just an occupational hazard?

Try being a paramedic. See how you go when a psycho husband holds a knife to your throat while you're trying to save his wife's life, which you can't save, because she's already dead. Try that, Frances.

Frances pushed up her mask and looked at Yao. Her hair stuck up comically as if she'd just got out of bed.

"I'll have the seafood linguine. Thank you so much." She snapped an imaginary menu shut, pulled her mask back over her eyes, and began to hum "Amazing Grace."

Yao checked her pulse and thought of a long-ago night after a university party when he'd looked after a drunk girl in someone's bedroom. Yao had listened to her incoherent, slurred rambling for hours and made sure she didn't choke on her vomit, before he finally fell asleep and woke up at dawn to her face inches away from his, and her sick-sweet breath in his nostrils. "Get out," she said.

"I never touched you," Yao told her. "Nothing happened."

"Get the fuck out," she said.

He felt like he *had* taken advantage of her, raped an unconscious girl. It didn't matter that he would never do such a thing, that he wanted to make a career out of healing; at that moment he was the representative for his gender and he had to cop it on the chin for all their sins.

Guiding Frances on her psychedelic therapeutic

journey was nothing like looking after a drunk girl.
And yet . . . it kind of felt like looking after a drunk
girl.

"I haven't had sex in so long," said Frances. White
spittle gathered at the corner of her mouth.

Yao felt a little ill. "That's too bad," he said.

He looked over at Masha, who sat with Ben and Jessica, their three shadows enormous on the wall. Masha
nodded as the couple spoke. It seemed like their therapy was going well. Delilah was talking to Lars, who
had sat up from his stretcher and was chatting calmly
with her, as if they were both guests at a party.

All his patients were fine. He had a crash cart on
standby. They were all being monitored. There was
nothing to worry about, and yet it was so strange because right now all his senses were screaming one
inexplicable word: *Run*.

35

Tony

Tony ran across an endless field of emerald green carrying an oddly shaped football that weighed as much as three bricks. His arms ached. Footballs weren't normally that heavy.

Banjo ran along beside him, he was a puppy again, bounding along with the same joyful abandon as a toddler, getting in between Tony's legs, tail wagging.

Tony understood that if he wanted to be happy again, he simply needed to kick this strange misshapen football through the goal. The football represented everything he hated about himself: all his mistakes, his regrets and his shame.

"Sit!" he said to Banjo.

Banjo sat. His big brown eyes looked up at Tony trustingly.

"Stay," he said.

Banjo stayed. His tail whooshed back and forth across the grass.

Tony saw the white goalposts rise like skyscrapers above him.

He lifted his foot, made contact. The ball sailed in a perfect arc across a clear blue sky. He knew immediately it was good. That rollercoaster feeling in his stomach. There was nothing better. Better than sex. It had been so long.

The crowd roared as the ball went straight through the middle of the goalposts and the euphoria blasted like rocket fuel through his body as he leaped high in the sky, one fist raised like a superhero.

36

Carmel

Carmel sat on a plush velvet couch in a snooty fashion shop specializing in the latest designer bodies.

Carmel wasn't wearing a body. It was so wonderful and relaxing not wearing a body. No thighs. No stomach. No bum. No biceps. No triceps. No cellulite. No crow's feet. No frown marks. No cesarean scar. No sun damage. No fine lines. No seven signs of aging. No dry hair. No frizzy hair. No gray hair. Nothing to wax or color or condition. Nothing to lengthen or flatten, conceal or disguise.

She was just Carmel, without her body.

Show me your original face, the one you had before your parents were born.

Her little girls sat on either side of her on the couch, waiting for her to choose a new body. They were all quietly reading age-appropriate quality chapter books and eating freshly cut fruit. No devices. No sugary snacks. No arguing. Carmel was the best mother in the history of mothering.

"Let's find you a divine new body for your divine new life," said Masha, who was the manager of the shop. She was dressed as a Disney princess.

Masha ran her finger along a rack filled with different bodies on hangers. "No, no, maybe . . . oh, now *this* one is nice!" She draped the body over one arm. "This would look lovely on you. It's very fashionable, and such a flattering shape!"

It was Sonia's body. Her sleek blond hair. Her trim waist.

"I don't like the ankles," said Carmel. "I prefer a more finely tapered ankle. Also, my husband's new girlfriend has that exact same body."

"We don't want that one then!" said Masha. She hung it back up and selected another one from the rack. "How about this one? So striking. You'll turn heads wearing this one."

It was Masha's body.

"It's amazing, but honestly, I don't think I can carry it off," said Carmel. "It's kind of too dramatic for me."

Her daughter Lulu put down her book. She had peach smeared around her mouth. Carmel went to wipe it away but then she remembered she had no fingers. Fingers were useful.

"That's your body there, Mummy," said Lulu, and she pointed at Carmel's body sagging on a door handle, without even a hanger.

"That's my old body, darling," said Carmel. "Mummy needs a new one."

"It's yours." Lulu was implacable as always.

Masha held up Carmel's old body. "It does look very comfortable," she said.

"Could we at least take it in a few inches?" said Carmel.

"Of course we can." Masha smiled at her. "We'll make it beautiful. Here. Try it on."

Carmel sighed and put back on her old body.

"It really suits you," said Masha. "Just some minor adjustments."

"I quite like the ankles," admitted Carmel. "What do you think, girls?"

Her daughters threw themselves at her. Carmel marveled at the blue veins in her hands as she cupped her daughters' heads, the thump of her heart and the strength of her arms as she hefted a little girl on each hip.

"I'll take it," she said.

"You're going to love your body," said Masha.

37

Masha

My God, it is all going incredibly well, thought Masha. The therapy was working exactly as the research said it would. Carmel Schneider had just made a breakthrough in relation to her body-image issues. There had been a moment where for some reason she kept trying to take her clothes off, but Masha had put a stop to that and she'd just had a very good conversation with her about body acceptance.

The triumph was as tangible as a trophy, solid and gleaming gold in Masha's hands.

38

Napoleon

Napoleon sat with his back against a wall of the studio, watching the floor breathe in and out with the rapid heartbreaking vulnerability of a sleeping baby.

This happened last time, he reminded himself. It was just an optical illusion. Walls and floors did not breathe. And so what if they did breathe? What was so bad about that?

The walls of that seedy smoky club had breathed too, and he'd become convinced he was trapped within an amoeba hurtling through space. It had made perfect sense at the time. The amoeba had swallowed him whole like the whale swallowed Jonah and he was stuck in that amoeba for a thousand years.

Twenty years old and he was so sure his brain had been fried, and he took such pride in his brain, and the only way to comfort himself in the bleak days that followed was by chanting: *Never again, never again, never again.*

And yet here he was, trapped once more.

I'm not in an amoeba, he told himself. *I'm at a health resort. They have given me drugs without my permission and I'm just going to have to wait this out.*

At least he was in this very pleasant, nice-smelling, candlelit studio, not that packed bar with all those looming faces.

He held hands with his girls. Heather's hand in his left. Zoe's in his right. Napoleon had refused to lie down on one of those stretchers or put on the mask and headphones. He knew the only way to keep a good firm grip of his mind was to sit upright with his eyes open.

Masha pretended she was fine with that, but Napoleon knew she was annoyed that they weren't following the correct procedure for "optimum results."

Napoleon recognized the moment she made the decision not to push the issue. It was like he could read her mind. *Pick your battles*, she thought. Napoleon had to pick his battles with his students. He was good at picking his battles. He used to do the same with the kids.

"Pick your battles," he said softly. "Pick them carefully."

"I know which battle I'm picking—I will not rest until that woman is behind bars," said Heather. She was watching Masha move about the room, chatting to her guests, placing the back of her hand against their foreheads.

"Look at her, sashaying about as if she's fucking Florence Nightingale," said Heather. "Psychedelic therapy, my foot."

Napoleon wondered if there was some sort of professional jealousy going on here.

"Can you see the walls breathing?" he asked, to take her mind off things.

"It's just the effects of the drugs," said Heather.

"Well, I know that, darling," said Napoleon. "I just wondered if you were experiencing the same effects."

"I can see the walls breathing, Dad," said Zoe. "They look like fish. It's awesome. Are you seeing the colors?" She glided her hands back and forth as if through water.

"I am!" marveled Napoleon. "It's like phosphorescence."

"Great. A nice druggy dad-and-daughter bonding experience," said Heather.

Napoleon noted that she was in a very bad mood.

"Zach would think this was hilarious," said Zoe. "All of us getting high together."

"He's here actually," said Napoleon. "Hi, Zach."

"Hey, Dad." It didn't even seem that remarkable that Zach was sitting right in front of him, wearing shorts and no shirt. The kid never wore a shirt. It just felt like everything was right again, the way it used to feel, the four of them hanging out together, taking each other's existences for granted, just being a family, a run-of-the-mill family.

"Do you see him?" said Napoleon.

"Yes," said Zoe.

"I see him too," said Heather, her voice full of tears.

"Your turn to take out the recycling, Zach," said Zoe.

Zach gave his sister the finger and Napoleon laughed out loud.

39

Frances

Frances sat up on her stretcher, pushed back her head-phones, and pulled her eye mask down around her neck.

"Thank you," she said to Delilah, who sat next to her, smiling at her in a way that could be called condescending, as a matter of fact. "That was lovely. Quite an experience. I feel like I learned a great deal. How much do I owe you?"

"I don't think you're done yet," said Delilah.

Frances looked around the room.

Lars and Tony were on stretchers next to each other. Tony's head lolled to one side, his feet splayed in a V shape. Meanwhile, Lars's profile looked like that of a Grecian god and his feet were neatly crossed at the ankles, as if he were napping on a train while listening to a podcast.

Ben and Jessica were in a corner of the room kissing like young lovers who have just discovered kissing and have all the time in the world. Their hands moved over each other's bodies with slow passionate reverence.

"Goodness," said Frances. "*That* looks like fun."

She continued to survey the room.

Carmel lay on her stretcher, her thick black hair spread like seaweed around her head. She held up her hands and wiggled her fingers as if she were trying to see them through her eye mask.

Napoleon, Heather, and Zoe sat in a row with their backs against the wall, like young travelers stranded at an airport. There was a boy sitting in front of them. He stuck his finger up at Zoe.

"Who is that boy?" said Frances. "The boy without the shirt?"

"There is no boy," said Delilah. She reached for Frances's headphones.

"He's laughing," said Frances. She tried and failed to grab at Delilah's arm to stop her pulling the eye mask back over her eyes. "I think I'll go say hello."

"Stay with me, Frances," said Delilah.

40

Heather

Heather focused on her breathing. She was determined to keep a tiny part of her brain safe and sober and in charge of monitoring the effects of the psilocybin and LSD; one brightly lit office window in a dark office tower.

She knew, for example, that in reality her son rotted beneath the earth; he was not really there with them. And yet he seemed so real, and when she reached out to touch his arm, it was his flesh: firm and smooth and tanned. He tanned easily and he was hopeless about putting on sunscreen, even though she nagged.

"Don't go, Zach." Napoleon jerked upright and reached out his hands.

"He's not going, Dad," said Zoe. She pointed. "He's still right there."

"My boy," sobbed Napoleon. His body convulsed. "He's *gone*." His sobs were guttural, uncontrolled. "My boy, my boy, my boy."

"Stop that," said Heather. This was not the place, not the time.

It was the drugs. Not everyone reacted the same way to drugs. Some laboring mothers got plastered on just one whiff of nitrous oxide. Others screamed at Heather that it wasn't working.

Napoleon had always been susceptible. He couldn't even cope with coffee. One long black and you'd think he'd taken speed. An over-the-counter painkiller could send him loopy. The only time he ever had a general anesthetic, which was for a knee reconstruction the year before Zach died, he'd had a bad reaction when he came out of it and scared a poor young nurse to death by supposedly "speaking in tongues" about the Garden of Eden, although it wasn't clear how she understood what he was saying if he was *speaking in tongues*. "She must be fluent in tongues," Zach had said, and Zoe had laughed so much, and there was no greater pleasure in Heather's life than watching her children make each other laugh.

Watch your husband, she thought. *Monitor him*. She narrowed her eyes and clenched her jaw to maintain focus, but she felt herself drift hopelessly, inevitably away on a sea of memories.

She is walking down the street pushing her two babies in a big double stroller and every single old lady stops to make a comment and Heather is never going to make it to the shops.

She is a little girl staring at her mother's stomach wishing she could make a baby grow in there so that she can have a brother or sister but the wishing doesn't work, wishing never works, and when she grows up she will never have an only child, a lonely only.

*She is opening the door of her son's bedroom be-
cause she's going to do a load of washing and she may
as well scrape up some of the layer of clothes on his floor
and her whole body resists what she is seeing and she
thinks, I'm doing a load of washing, don't do this, Zach,
I want to do laundry, I want to keep this life, please,
please let me keep this life, but she hears herself screaming because she knows it's too late, there is nothing to
be done, the life of one second ago is gone.*

*She is at her son's funeral and her daughter is de-
livering a eulogy, and afterward people keep touching
Heather, so much touching, everyone wants to paw at
her, it is repulsive, and they are all saying, Oh, you
must be so proud, Zoe spoke so beautifully, as if it's
fucking school speech night, not her son's funeral, and
can't you see my daughter is alone now, how can she
live without her brother, she never even existed without him, and who cares if she spoke beautifully, she
can't even stand, her father is holding her upright, my
daughter can't even walk.*

*She is watching Zoe take her first steps at only eleven
months, and Zach, who has never even considered such
a thing, is shocked, he can hardly believe it, he is sitting on the carpet with his little plump legs stuck out in
front of him and he is looking up at his sister with big
astonished eyes and you can see he is thinking, What
is she DOING? and she and Napoleon are laughing so
hard, and maybe wishes do come true because this is
family, this is what she never had, never knew, never
dreamed, this is a moment so perfect and funny and
this is her life now, just a string of perfect, funny mo-*

ments one after the other, like a string of beads that will go on forever.

Except that it won't.

She is alone in Zach's bedroom crying, and she thinks that Napoleon and Zoe are somewhere in the house crying too, all alone crying in separate rooms, and she thinks families are probably meant to grieve together but they aren't doing it right, and to distract herself she goes through Zach's drawers for the hundredth time, even though she knows there is nothing to find, no note, no explanation, she knows exactly what she will find—except that this time, she does find something.

She was back.

Napoleon still rocked and sobbed.

Had she been gone for a second or an hour or a year? She didn't know.

"How are the Marconi family feeling right now?" Masha sat in front of them. "Could this perhaps be a good opportunity for a family therapy session about your loss?"

Masha had multiple arms and multiple legs but Heather refused to acknowledge her multiple limbs because it was not real, people simply did not have that many limbs. Heather had never once delivered a baby with that many limbs. She was not falling for it.

"When you say it's your fault, Napoleon, are you referring to Zach?" asked Masha, all faux concern.

Heather heard herself hiss, "Jesus fucking Christ."

Heather was a snake with a long forked tongue that could whip from her mouth and pierce Masha's skin, shooting venom through her veins, poisoning her, the same way Masha had poisoned Heather's family. "Don't you dare talk about our son! You know nothing about our son."

"My fault, my fault, my fault." Napoleon banged his head against the wall. He was in danger of concussing himself.

Heather gathered up all her mental strength to focus her mind and crawled around to face Napoleon on her hands and knees. She grabbed his head between her hands. She could feel his ears against her palms, the warmth of his stubbled skin.

"Listen to me," she said in the loud carrying voice she used to cut through the screams of a woman in labor.

Napoleon's eyes rolled about, bulging and veined with blood, like a frightened horse.

"I pressed snooze on my alarm," he said. He repeated it over and over. "I pressed snooze on my alarm. I pressed snooze on my alarm."

"I know you did," said Heather. "You've told me so many times, darling, but it wouldn't have made a difference."

"It wasn't your fault, Dad," said Zoe, her lonely only, and it seemed to Heather that she spoke very much like a zombie, not a university student, and that her young beautiful mind was already fried like an egg, sizzled to a crisp. "It was my fault."

"Good," said Masha. The Poisoner. "This is so good! You are all speaking from your hearts."

Heather turned and screamed in her face. "Fuck off!"

A pellet of Heather's spittle flew in a slow arc from her mouth and hit the target of Masha's eye.

Masha smiled. She wiped her eye. "Excellent. Release all that rage, Heather. Let it all out." She stood, and her multiple limbs drifted about her like an octopus's tentacles. "I will be back momentarily."

Heather turned back to her family. "Listen," she said. "Listen to me."

Napoleon and Zoe made eye contact with her. They were all three in a temporary air pocket of clarity. It wouldn't last. Heather had to speak fast. She opened her mouth and began to tug an endless tapeworm from deep down in her throat, and it was making her gag and vomit, but there was relief in it too, because at last she was wrenching it free from her body.

41

Zoe

The walls no longer breathed. The colors were fading. Zoe felt like she was sobering up. It was like that feeling at the end of a party when you walked out of a stuffy room into the night air and your mind cleared.

"Zach was on medication," said Zoe's mother. "For his asthma."

Why did that matter? Zoe could tell that her mother thought she was sharing something momentous here but she had learned that what was momentous to your parents was often not that momentous to you, and what was momentous to you was often not that momentous to your parents.

"I like to call it Zachariah's Theory of Momentousity," said Zach, who was still there with them.

"Don't tell me your theories. I'm all alone, taking care of the parents," said Zoe. "And it's an onerous responsibility, thou fuckwit, because they are both cray-cray."

"I know, I'm sorry, thou mangled pox-marked clack dish," said Zach.

"I need you to concentrate, Zoe," said her mother.

"I know he was on medication for his asthma," said her dad. "A preventative. So what?"

"One of the side effects can be depression and suicidal thoughts," said Heather. "I told you the specialist wanted to prescribe it to him and you said, 'Are there any side effects?' and I said . . . I said . . . 'No.'"

The regret dragged at her face like claw marks.

"You said no," repeated Zoe's father.

"I said no," said her mother. Her eyes were pleading for forgiveness. "I'm so sorry."

A cliff face of momentous-ity loomed in front of Zoe.

"I hadn't even read the leaflet in the box," said her mother. "I knew Dr. Chang was the best, I knew he wouldn't prescribe anything with dangerous side effects, I trusted him, so I just said, 'No. It's all fine. I've checked.' But I lied to you, Napoleon, I lied."

Zoe's dad blinked.

After a while, he said slowly, "I would have trusted him too."

"You would have read the leaflet. You would have gone through it so carefully, reading every word, asking me questions, driving me crazy. I'm the one with the medical training but I didn't even read it. I thought I was so busy at that time. I don't know what I thought I was so busy doing." Her mother rubbed her hands down her cheeks as if she were trying to smear herself away. "I read the leaflet about six months after he died. I found it in his bedroom drawer."

"Well, darling, it wouldn't have made any difference,"

said her dad dully. "We needed to get the asthma under control."

"But if we'd known depression was a possibility we would have monitored him," said Zoe's mother. She looked desperate to make him understand the full breadth of her guilt. "*You* would have, Napoleon, I know you would have!"

"There were no signs," said her dad. "Sometimes there are no signs. No signs at all. He was perfectly happy."

"There were signs," said Zoe.

Her parents turned to her, and their faces were like those clown faces at an amusement park, turning back and forth, mouths agape, waiting for the ball to drop.

"I knew he was upset about something."

She remembered walking by his bedroom and registering the fact that Zach was lying on his bed but he wasn't looking at his phone or listening to music or reading, he was just *lying there*, and that was not Zach. Zach didn't just lie on his bed and stare at the ceiling.

"I thought something was going on at school," she told her parents. "But I was angry with him. We weren't talking. I didn't want to be the first one to talk." Zoe closed her eyes so she could not see the disappointment and pain on her parents' faces. She whispered, "It was a competition to see who would be the first one to talk."

"Oh, Zoe, sweetheart," said her mother from far, far away. "It's not your fault. You know it's not your fault."

"I was going to talk on our birthday," said Zoe. "I was going to say, 'Happy birthday, loser.'"

"Oh, Zoe, you stupid-head," said Zach.

He put his arm around her. They never hugged. They weren't that sort of brother and sister. Sometimes when they passed each other in the hallway they randomly shoved each other for no reason at all. Like, hard enough to hurt. But now he was hugging her, and talking in her ear, and it was him, it was Zach, it was absolutely him, he smelled of that stupid Lynx body-wash which he said he used ironically but he totally used because he believed the ads about how it made the girls think you were hotter.

Zach pulled her close and whispered in her ear. "It was nothing to do with you. I didn't do it to get at you." He gripped her arm to make sure she got his point. "*I wasn't me.*"

42

Napoleon

He would do anything for his girls, anything, so he took the dreadful, heavy secrets they'd been carrying and he saw the relief with which they handed them over, and now he had his own secret, because he would never tell them how angry their secrets made him, never ever, never ever ever.

The walls continued to pulsate as his wife and daughter held his hands and he knew this nightmare would last an eternity.

43

Masha

Ben and Jessica sat cross-legged on cushions facing each other. Their hands gripped each other's forearms as if they were on a narrow beam and trying to maintain their balance. It was glorious to see. Ben spoke directly from his heart and Jessica listened, transfixed by his every word.

Masha guided only when necessary. The MDMA was doing exactly what it was meant to do: dissolving barriers. They could have spent *months* in therapy to get to this point. This was an instant shortcut.

"I miss your face," Ben said to Jessica. "Your beautiful face. I don't recognize you. I don't recognize us or anything about our lives. I miss our old flat. I miss my job. I miss the friends we lost because of this. But most of all I miss your face."

His words were crisp and clear. There was no slurring. No equivocation.

"Good," said Masha. "Wonderful. Jessica, what do you want to say?"

"I think that Ben is body-shaming," said Jessica. "I'm still me. I'm still *Jessica*. I'm still in here! So what if I look a bit different? This is the fashion. It's just fashion. It's not important!"

"It's important to me," said Ben. "It feels like you took something precious and fucked it up."

"But I feel beautiful," said Jessica. "I feel like I was ugly before and now I'm beautiful." She stretched her arms above her head like a ballerina. "The question is: Who gets to decide if I'm beautiful or not? Me? You? The internet?"

Right now, she did look beautiful.

Ben considered for a moment.

"It's your face," he said. "So I guess you should decide."

"But wait! Beauty is . . ." Jessica pointed at her eye. She began to laugh. "Beauty is *in the eye of the beholder*."

She and Ben laughed and laughed. They clutched each other, repeating "beauty is in the *eye* of the beholder" over and over, and Masha smiled at them uncertainly. Why was that funny? Perhaps it was an inside joke. She began to feel impatient.

At long last they stopped laughing and Jessica sat up and touched her lower lip. "Look. Fair call. I might have overdone it on the lips last time."

"I liked your lips before," said Ben. "I thought you had beautiful lips."

"Yeah, I get it, Ben," said Jessica.

"I liked our life before," said Ben.

"It was a shitty little life," said Jessica. "An ordinary shitty little life."

"I don't think it was shitty," said Ben.

"I feel like you love your car more than me," said Jessica. "I'm jealous of your car. *I* was the one who scratched it. That was me. Because I feel like your car is a slutty girl having an affair with my husband, and so I scratched her slutty face."

"Wow," said Ben. He put both hands to the top of his head. "*Wow.* That is . . . wow. I can't believe you did that." He didn't sound angry. Just amazed.

"I *love* the money," said Jessica. "I love being rich. But I wish we could just be rich and still be us."

"The money," said Ben slowly, "is like a dog."

"Mmm," said Jessica.

"A great big out-of-control pet dog."

"Yeah," said Jessica. "Yeah. That's right." She paused. "Why is it like a dog?"

"So, it's like we got a dog, and it's the dog we always wanted, we dreamed of this dog, this dog is our dream dog, but it's changed everything about our lives. It's, like, really distracting, it barks all through the night wanting our attention, it won't let us sleep, we can't do *anything* without taking into account the dog. We have to walk it, and feed it, and worry about it, and . . ." He scrunched up his face, working it out. "See, the problem with this dog is that it *bites*. It bites us, and it bites our friends and family; it's got a really vicious streak, this dog."

"But we still love it," said Jessica. "We love the dog."

"We do, but I think we should give the dog away," said Ben. "I think it's not the right dog for us."

"We could get a labradoodle," said Jessica. "Labra-doodles are so cute."

346 Liane Moriarty

Masha reminded herself that Jessica was very young.

"I think Ben is using the dog as a . . . story to explain how the lottery win has impacted your lives," she said. "A metaphor, that is." The word metaphor came to her a fraction later than she would have liked.

"Yeah," said Jessica. She gave Masha a sly, shrewd look and tapped her nose with her forefinger. "If we're going to get a dog we should get it before the baby comes."

"What baby?" said Masha.

"What baby?" said Ben.

"I'm pregnant," said Jessica.

"You are?" said Ben. "But that's awesome!"

Masha reeled. "But you never—"

"You gave my pregnant wife drugs," said Ben to Masha.

"Yeah, I kind of feel really angry about that," said Jessica to Masha. "Like, I think you should go to jail for a very long time for this."

44

Heather

Heather woke but did not open her eyes.

She was lying on her side, on something thin and soft, her hands pillowed beneath her head.

Her body clock told her it was morning. Maybe around 7 A.M., she would have guessed.

She was no longer high. Her mind felt clear. She was in the yoga and meditation studio at Tranquillum House and today was the anniversary of Zach's death.

After years of nausea she'd vomited up her secret and now she felt shaky, strange and empty, but also better. She felt *cleansed*, which, funnily enough, was exactly what Tranquillum House had promised. Heather would have to write them a glowing testimonial: *I feel so much better after my time at Tranquillum House! I especially enjoyed "tripping" with my husband and daughter.*

Obviously they would leave this place immediately. They would not eat or drink anything provided by Masha. They would go straight to their rooms, pack, get in the car, and leave. Perhaps they would go to a café in the nearest town and order a big fried breakfast in Zach's honor.

Heather wanted to spend this year's anniversary alone with her family talking about Zach, and tomorrow, she wanted to somehow mark her children's twenty-first birthday in a way that wasn't about shame or grief, or everyone pretending to forget that this was Zoe's birthday too.

Napoleon had been saying it for so long: we have to separate Zach from the way he chose to end his life. There was so much more to Zach than his suicide. One memory should not eclipse all the other memories. But she hadn't listened. She had somehow thought that his unhappiness that one day nullified everything else that he did in his life.

Now, all at once, she knew that Napoleon was right. Today they would mark the anniversary of his death by pooling their best memories of his eighteen years of life, and the grief would be unbearable, but Heather knew better than anyone that the unbearable could be borne. For the last three years she'd been grieving Zach's suicide. Now it was finally time to grieve his loss. The loss of a beautiful, silly, smart, impetuous boy.

She hoped that his sister would cope today. All that rubbish about "not being close" to Zach. Heather's heart ached for her. The child adored her brother. They were ten years old before they stopped creeping into each other's beds at night when they had nightmares. Heather would need to tell her over and over that it wasn't her fault. It was Heather's failure alone. Her failure to notice her son's change in behavior and her failure to give anyone, *including Zach himself*, a reason to look for it.

And at some point today they would report the mad-woman's actions to the police.

Heather opened her eyes, and saw that she was lying on a yoga mat, face-to-face with her sleeping daughter. She was still asleep, her eyelids fluttering. Heather was close enough to feel Zoe's breath on her face. She put her hand to her cheek.

45

Frances

Frances pulled the headphones from her head. They got caught in her hair. She tugged them free, her eyes still shut.

She was on a flight. The only time she fell asleep wearing headphones was on a flight.

She could hear the sound of far-off construction. A drill. A jackhammer. A digger. Some such thing. It was an intermittent mechanical roar. A lawn mower? A leaf blower. She lay on her side, drew the blanket up over her shoulders, and tried to make herself sink back into deep, delicious sleep. But no, there was the sound again, pulling her inexorably up, up, up, and it wasn't a machine, it was the sound of a man snoring.

Had she got drunk and slept with a stranger last night? Good Lord, surely not. It had been decades. She didn't feel any of the symptoms of a hangover, or the shame of a seedy sexual encounter. Her mind felt clear and bright, as if it had been pressure-cleaned.

Her memory clicked into place in one solid block.

She was in the yoga and meditation studio at Tranquillum House, and yesterday she'd drunk a delicious smoothie containing hallucinogenic drugs resulting in an extremely beautiful, remarkably vivid dream that had lasted forever, about Gillian and her dad and her ex-husbands, with many symbols and visual metaphors which she looked forward to interpreting. Yao, and sometimes Delilah, and sometimes Masha, had kept interrupting her lovely dream, asking irritating questions and trying to steer her in certain directions. Frances had ignored them, she was having too much fun, and they were aggravating her. She sensed that after a while they gave up on her.

She'd been in space.

She'd been an *ant*.

Also a butterfly!

She'd been on a sleigh ride with Gillian across a stunning starlit sky, and more, much more.

It was like waking up the first morning back home in your own bed after a long international holiday to multiple exotic locations.

She opened her eyes to darkness and remembered her eye mask. The sound of snoring got even louder as she pulled it off. Her eyes didn't feel gritty or blurry. Everything was in crisp color. She could see the vaulted stone ceiling above her. Rows of downlights. They were all switched on.

She sat up and looked around.

The man snoring was Lars. He lay on the stretcher next to hers, flat on his back, still wearing his eye mask, a blanket pulled up to his chin, his mouth wide open. His body twitched in tandem with each snore. It was pleasing to hear someone so good-looking with such a loud, unpleasant snore. It kind of redressed the balance.

Frances reached over with her bare foot and gave his leg a gentle shove. Henry was a snorer. Once, toward the end of the marriage, he was wearing shorts, and he'd looked down and said confusedly, "I don't know why I'm always getting these bruises right here on my calf. It's like I keep bumping into something." *My right foot*, thought Frances. She felt terrible about that right up until their last day together when they fought over the division of cutlery.

She scanned the room.

Tony—she would not be calling him "Smiley"—had just sat up on his stretcher. It looked like he had a headache by the way he rested his forehead in his hands.

Carmel was also upright and was attempting to comb her fingers through her black frizzy hair, which stood out in a wild halo around her head.

She met Frances's eye. "Bathroom?" she mouthed, although she'd been in the studio as often as Frances.

Frances pointed to the toilets at the back of the cellar and Carmel got to her feet, staggering a little.

Ben and Jessica sat shoulder to shoulder against a wall, drinking bottled water.

Heather and Zoe lay face-to-face where they had fallen asleep on a yoga mat. Heather was absently caressing Zoe's hair.

"Need water?" Napoleon crouched down with difficulty on his long legs in front of Frances and offered her a bottle of water. "I'm assuming it's not spiked with drugs," he said. "I guess if we're worried we could just drink from the tap, although they could do something to the water supply if they really wanted."

"Thank you." Frances accepted the water, suddenly desperate for it, and drank nearly the whole bottle in one go. "Just what I needed," she said.

"I guess it's a good sign that they left us with water," said Napoleon. He straightened. "They haven't completely abandoned us."

"What do you mean?" asked Frances. She stretched luxuriously. She was *really* looking forward to breakfast.

"We're locked in," said Napoleon apologetically, as if he were the one responsible. "There doesn't seem to be a way out."

46

Carmel

"I'm sure this is all just part of the process," said Carmel. She didn't know why everyone looked so worried. "They're not going to leave us down here for much longer. It's all fine."

The time, according to Napoleon, the only one among them with a watch, was coming up to 2 P.M., and they had still not heard from any of the staff at Tranquillum House. They had been down here for close to twenty-four hours now.

They all sat in a circle similar to the one from the previous day, when they'd introduced themselves. Everyone looked exhausted and grimy. The men needed shaves. Carmel was desperate to brush her teeth, but she wasn't especially hungry, even though she hadn't eaten for coming up to *forty-eight hours*, so that was kind of wonderful. If appetite suppression was one of the side effects of last night's perfectly enjoyable drug experience, then she was all for it.

Each of them had confirmed for themselves that the

only access point to the room was the heavy oak door at the bottom of the stairs, and that the door was undeniably, irrefutably locked with what looked to be a brand-new gold security keypad next to the door handle. Presumably there was a code that would unlock the door, but multiple combinations of numbers had been attempted with no success.

Frances had suggested that the code might be the same as the one given at the front gate of Tranquillum House.

Napoleon said he'd already thought of that but had no memory of the number.

Carmel had no memory of it either. She'd been crying when she arrived at Tranquillum House, suddenly struck by a memory from her honeymoon when they'd stayed at a hotel with a similar-looking intercom. It seemed stupid now. Her honeymoon hadn't been *that* great. She'd gotten a terrible UTI.

Ben thought he remembered the access code for the front gate, but if he did, the number didn't work.

Tony thought he remembered too, although he remembered one digit different from Ben's, but that number didn't work either.

Carmel suggested the phone number for Tranquillum House, which for some reason she was able to recite, but they had no luck with that.

Frances wondered if the code was related to the letters of the alphabet. They tried various words: Tranquillum. Cleanse. Masha.

Nothing worked.

Zoe wondered if it was meant to be a kind of a game.

An "escape room." She told them there was a bizarre craze where people *allowed* themselves to be locked up in a room for the pleasure of trying to work out how to escape. Zoe had been to one before. She said it was great fun, with multiple clues concealed in what looked like normal objects. For example, Zoe and her friends had to find and assemble the parts of a flashlight hidden around the room. The flashlight could then be used to shine a light on a secret message in the back of a wardrobe with further instructions. A timer counted down the minutes on a wall, and Zoe said they got out just seconds before the timer went off.

But if this was an escape-room game it seemed it was a very tricky one. The yoga studio was virtually empty. There were towels, yoga mats, stretcher beds, water bottles, headphones, eye masks, and burnt-out candles from the night before and that was it. There were no bookshelves with messages in books. No pictures on the wall. There was nothing that could feasibly represent a clue.

There were no windows that could be smashed in either the men's or the women's toilets. No manholes, no air-conditioning ducts.

"It's like we're trapped in a *dungeon*," said Frances, which Carmel thought was melodramatic but then the woman wrote romantic fiction for a living so you had to allow for an overactive imagination.

Eventually, they'd sat back down, dispirited and disheveled.

"Yes, this is all just part of the process," said Heather to Carmel. "Spiking our drinks with illegal drugs, locking us up, and so on and so forth. Nothing to worry about, it's all fine."

She was using a very sarcastic, familiar tone for someone Carmel had only just met.

"I'm just saying we should trust the process." Carmel tried to remain reasonable.

"You're as deluded as her," said Heather.

So that was definitely rude. Carmel reminded herself that Heather had lost her son. She spoke evenly. "I know we're all tired and stressed, but there's no need to get personal."

"This *is* personal!" shouted Heather.

"Sweetheart," said Napoleon. "Don't." The gentle way he scolded his wife made Carmel's heart ache.

"Do you have children, Carmel?" asked Heather in a more civilized tone.

"I have four little girls," said Carmel carefully.

"Well, how would you feel if someone gave your children drugs?"

It was true that she wouldn't want a single drug to cross their precious lips. "My children are very little. Obviously Masha would never—"

"Do you have any idea of the serious long-term health consequences we could all be facing?" interrupted Heather.

"I feel worse than I've ever felt in my entire life," said Jessica.

"There you go," said Heather with satisfaction.

"Well, I feel *better* than I've ever felt in my entire life," said Carmel. It wasn't entirely true, there was the teeth situation, but she did feel quite good. Her mind was filled with images she hadn't yet had a chance to interpret, as if she'd just spent a day at some incredible immersive art exhibit.

"I feel pretty good so far," admitted Frances.

"I do have a significant headache," said Lars.

"Yeah, me too," said Tony.

"I feel like I might be down a dress size." Carmel pulled at the loose waistband of her leggings. She frowned, trying to remember some important revelation she'd come to last night about her body. It didn't matter . . . it did matter . . . it was the only one she had? Somehow it didn't seem quite so profound and transcendent a revelation when she tried to pin it down with ordinary words. "Although I'm not trying to change my body *completely*. I'm just here to get healthy."

"Healthy?!" Heather banged her palm against her forehead. "This place has gone way beyond bloody dieting!"

"Mum." Zoe put her hand on her mother's knee. "Nobody died. We're all still here. Just . . . please, relax."

"Relax?!" Heather took Zoe's hand in hers and shook it. "*You* could have died! Any one of us could have died! If there was anyone with underlying mental-health issues that could have been exacerbated, or heart issues! Your dad has high blood pressure! He should never have been given drugs."

"People probably think you're the one with mental-health issues," murmured Zoe.

"That's not helping," said Napoleon.

"Can't we just pick the lock on the door?" said Frances, and she looked hopefully at Tony.

"Why are you looking at me? Do I look like I have a lot of break-and-enter experience?" he said.

"Sorry," said Frances. Carmel could see her point. Tony *did* look like someone who might have dabbled in a bit of breaking-and-entering in his youth.

"We could try. We'd need something to pick it with," said Ben. He patted himself down and came up with nothing.

"I'm sure there's no need to panic just yet," said Napoleon.

"It's obviously a kind of problem-solving exercise and eventually she'll realize that we can't solve it." Lars yawned, then lay down on a yoga mat and shielded his eyes with his arm.

"I think they're watching us in here," said Jessica. She pointed to a corner of the ceiling. "Isn't that a camera up there?"

They all looked up at the tiny security camera with a flashing red light above the blank television screen.

"Yao told me they had some kind of security inter-com system," said Frances.

"Me too," said Carmel. "On the first day."

It felt like a hundred years ago.

Heather leaped to her feet and addressed the camera. "You let us out immediately!" she shrieked. "We did not come here to spend the anniversary of our son's death *locked in a room with strangers*!"

Carmel flinched. She had forgotten the anniversary was *today*. The woman was allowed to snap and snarl as much as she wanted.

There was silence. Nothing happened.

Heather stamped her foot. "I can't believe we're *paying* for this."

Napoleon stood and pulled Heather into his arms. "It doesn't matter where we are today," he said.

"It does," Heather cried quietly into his shirt. Suddenly she seemed diminished, all the rage gone, just a tiny, sad, traumatized mother.

"Shhh," said Napoleon.

She was saying something over and over and it took a moment for Carmel to distinguish the words: "I'm sorry, I'm sorry, I'm sorry."

"It's okay," said Napoleon. "We're fine. Everything is fine."

Everyone looked away from what seemed like an unbearably private moment. Zoe avoided looking at her parents also. She went to a corner of the room, put one palm against a wall, stood on one leg, and held her ankle in the other hand, doing a yoga class for one.

Carmel looked at the blank screen of the television, suddenly desperate to be far, far away from this family's pain, which so dwarfed her own. She felt a sharp stab of homesickness. Her home was beautiful. She recalled this as if it were brand-new information. Not a mansion by any means, but a comfortable, sunshine-filled family home, even when it had been trashed by four little girls. She'd been the one to renovate it, to make it beautiful. People said she had "an eye." When she got home she would remember to enjoy it.

"I might see if I can kick that door down," said Tony.

"*Great* idea," said Carmel. People were always kicking down doors in the movies. It seemed quite simple.

"I'll do it," said Ben.

"Or I'll ram it." Tony limbered up, rolling his shoulders.

"*I'll* ram it," said Ben.

"The door opens inward," said Lars.

There was a pause. "Does that matter?" asked Frances.

"Think about it, Frances," said Lars.

Tony looked deflated. "Let's try to pick the lock then." He put his fingertips to his forehead and breathed deeply. "I'm starting to feel a little . . . claustrophobic. I want to get out of here."

So did Carmel.

47

Frances

They collected everything they could find that would work as a possible lock pick: one hairclip, one belt buckle, one bracelet. It was Frances's bracelet and she had nothing else to contribute except ignorant enthusiasm, so she stayed out of the way and the lock-picking committee became Ben, Jessica, Napoleon, Tony, and Carmel. They seemed to be enjoying themselves destroying her bracelet and discussing exactly what was needed: "teeth to push the pins out" or some such thing.

She went instead to talk to Zoe, who sat in the corner of the room, hugging her knees.

"You okay?" Frances asked, sitting down next to her and putting a tentative hand on the curve of her back.

Zoe lifted her head and smiled. Her eyes were clear. She looked lovely. Not like someone who had spent the previous night tripping. "I'm fine. How was your . . . experience last night?"

Frances lowered her voice. "I don't approve of what Masha did, outrageous etcetera, your mother is right, drugs are bad, illegal, wrong, just say no and all that . . . but I have to admit, I'm with Steve Jobs: it was one of the most fantastic experiences of my life. What about you?"

"There were good and bad parts," said Zoe. "I saw Zach. We all saw Zach. You know . . . hallucinated him, we didn't really see him."

"I thought I saw him too," said Frances without thinking.

Zoe turned her head.

"I saw a boy," said Frances. "With you and your mum and dad."

"You saw Zach?" Zoe's face lit up.

"Sorry," said Frances. "I hope you don't think that's disrespectful. Obviously, I never knew your brother. It was just my imagination, creating his image."

"It's fine," said Zoe. "I like that you saw him. You would have liked him. He would have talked to you. He talked to anyone." She stopped. "I don't mean that in a bad way—"

"I know what you're saying." Frances smiled.

"He was interested in everyone," said Zoe. "He was like Dad. Chatty. He would have asked you about, I don't know, the publishing industry. He was the biggest nerd. He liked watching documentaries. Listening to these obscure podcasts. He was fascinated by the world. That's why . . ." Her voice broke. "That's why I could never believe he'd choose to give it up."

She banged her chin against her propped-up knees. "When he died we weren't talking. We hadn't been talking for, like, weeks. We used to have these really big screaming arguments over . . . lots of things: the bathroom, the television, the charger. It all seems stupid now."

"That's what siblings do," said Frances, seeing a flash of her own sister's pursed lips.

"We had this thing where if the fight got really bad we'd stop talking to each other and it was like a competition to see who would talk first, and the person who talked first was *kind of* saying sorry without saying sorry, if you know what I mean, so I didn't want to be the one to talk first." She looked at Frances as if she were telling her something truly terrible.

"I used to have a very similar arrangement with my first ex-husband," said Frances.

"But I could tell there was something not quite right with him," said Zoe. "That week. I could tell. But I didn't ask him. I didn't say anything. I just ignored him."

Frances kept her face neutral. There was no point saying, You mustn't feel responsible. Of course she felt responsible. Denying her regret would be like denying her loss.

"I'm so sorry, darling." She wanted to envelop the child in a big, probably unwelcome hug but she settled for placing a hand on her shoulder.

Zoe looked over at her mother. "I've been so angry with him. It felt like he did it on *purpose* just to make me feel bad forever, and I couldn't forgive him for that. It just felt like the meanest, cruelest thing he'd ever done to me. But last night . . . this sounds stupid, but last night, it felt like we talked again."

"I know," said Frances. "I talked to my friend Gillian, who died last year. And my dad. It felt different from a dream. It felt so vivid. It felt realer than real life, to be honest."

"Do you think maybe we really *did* see them?" There was so much tremulous hope in Zoe's face.

"Maybe," lied Frances.

"It's just, I was thinking how Masha said that after her near-death experience she realized there was this other reality, and I just thought . . . maybe we sort of accessed it."

"Maybe," said Frances again. She didn't believe in alternate realities. She believed in the transcendent power of love, memory, and imagination. "Anything is possible."

Zoe lowered her voice so much that Frances had to lean in close to hear. "I feel like I've got him back now, in a weird sort of way. Like I could text him if I wanted."

"Ah," said Frances.

"I don't mean I *will* text him," said Zoe.

"No," said Frances. "Of course not. I understand what you're saying. You feel like you're not fighting anymore."

"Yeah," said Zoe. "We made up. I used to always be so relieved when we made up."

They sat in silence for a few comfortable minutes and watched the lock pickers crouched down next to the door.

"By the way, I forgot to tell you: I read your book during the silence," said Zoe. "I loved it."

"You loved it?" said Frances. "Really? It's fine if it wasn't your cup of tea."

"Frances," said Zoe firmly, "it was my cup of tea. I *loved* it."

"Oh," said Frances. Her eyes stung, because she could see that Zoe was telling the truth. "Thank you."

48

Zoe

She lied. The book was so, so sappy.

She had finished it yesterday morning (there was nothing else to do here), and it was fine, she kept turning the pages, but you knew from the very beginning that the girl would end up with the guy, even though they hated each other at first, and that there would be trials and tribulations but it would all work out fine in the end, so what was the actual point in reading it? At one stage the girl fainted into the guy's arms, which, like, was romantic or whatever, but did anyone ever really faint in real life? And if they did, was anyone ever really there to conveniently catch them?

Also, where was the *sex*? It took, like, three hundred pages to get to the first kiss, and the book was called *Nathaniel's Kiss*.

Zoe preferred books about international espionage.

"I thought it was a fantastic book," she told Frances, perfectly poker-faced. *Your country is depending on you, Zoe.*

"Maybe you're still high," said Frances.

Zoe laughed. Maybe she was. "I don't think so."

She couldn't believe she'd got high with her *parents*. That had been the freakiest part of the whole experience. The fact that her mum and dad were there with her. *Whoa*, she kept thinking. *There's Mum. Whoa. There's Dad*. Worlds collided with volcanic sparks and supersonic booms.

She felt like she could spend the rest of her life remembering everything that happened last night. Or it could all disappear. Either way was possible.

But one thing that wouldn't change when she left here was her mother's revelation.

She and her mother had barely spoken to each other this morning. Right now she was doing sit-ups, although Zoe noticed that she was doing them with less . . . *aggression* . . . than usual. In fact, as Zoe watched, she stopped and lay flat on her back with her hands on her stomach, staring at the ceiling.

All these years Zoe had longed for someone to blame other than herself. After Zach died, she'd been through all of his technology: his phone, his email accounts, his social media. She *wanted* to find evidence that he'd been bullied, that there was something going on in his life which was nothing to do with her that could explain his decision. But there was nothing. Her dad had done it too. He'd met up with every single one of Zach's friends, interviewing them, trying to understand. But nobody understood. All his friends were devastated, as baffled as his family.

Now it seemed possible that there was nothing going

on in the outside world. It was all in his head. It was the effects of the asthma medication making him temporarily lose his mind.

Maybe. She would never know for sure.

Her mother's revelation didn't exonerate Zoe, but it did give her someone with whom to share the blame. For just a moment, she allowed herself the pleasure of hating her mother. Her mother should not have let him take those stupid tablets. Her mother should have read that leaflet *like a responsible mother*. Like a mother with medical training.

But then she remembered the sound of her mother's scream that morning and she knew she could never truly blame her.

It had been so wrong, and almost *childish* of her mother to keep this a secret, but that very childishness made Zoe feel better. For the first time ever, she saw her mother as just a girl: a girl like her who made mistakes, who screwed things up, who was just making it all up as she went along.

Yes, her mum should have read the leaflet about the side effects, just like Zoe should have gone into her brother's bedroom when she saw him lying on his bed. She should have walked into his room, sat on the end of his bed, grabbed his gigantic foot, given it a shake, and said, "What's wrong with you, loser?"

Maybe he would have told her, and if he *had* told her, and if he'd made it seem serious enough, she would have gone to her dad and said, "Fix it," and her dad would have fixed it. She looked at her dad, the only innocent one in their family, on his hands and knees peering at the lock. He'd get them out of here. He could fix anything, given the opportunity. He just hadn't been given the opportunity to fix Zach.

It wasn't okay, it would never be okay, but it felt like hard knots in her stomach were loosening and she wasn't resisting. Other times when she'd started to feel better, when she'd found herself laughing or even looking forward to something, she had immediately pulled herself up. She had felt as though getting better would be forgetting him, betraying him, but now it seemed like there might be a way to remember not just the times they fought, but also the times they laughed so hard their faces hurt, to remember the times they stopped talking, but also the times they talked, about anything and everything, to remember the secrets they kept from each other but also the secrets they shared.

Zoe studied Frances's profile as she too watched the group of lock pickers. Frances looked younger today, without all that bright red lipstick she wore every day even when she was doing an exercise class. It was like she thought her red lipstick was a piece of clothing she couldn't be seen without.

Zoe felt all at once as if she *was* Frances, a middle-aged lady who wrote books about romance but fell for a romance scam; and she was her dad, who cried all the time without even knowing he did it, on his knees now trying to pick a lock; and she was her mum, so angry with the world but mostly with herself for the mistakes she'd made; and she was the hot guy who won the lottery but didn't seem that happy about it; and she was his wife with the incredible body; and she was the gorgeous gay divorce lawyer; and she was the lady who thought she was fat; and she was the man who used to smile and play football. She was all of them, and she was Zoe.

Wow. Maybe she *was* still high.

"It means a lot to me that you liked my book," said Frances, turning to face her, eyes shiny. It was sweet. It seemed like Zoe's opinion really mattered to her.

Well done, kid, said Zach. *Thou droning, dog-hearted dewberry.*

Zach was still there. He wasn't going anywhere. He was going to stick around while she finished uni and traveled and got a job and got married and got old. Just because he chose death didn't mean Zoe couldn't choose life. He was still there in her heart and her memory, and he was going to stay beside her, keeping her company right until the end.

49

Ben

They got nowhere trying to pick the lock. Ben could tell straightaway that it wasn't going to work. They didn't have the right tools and the locking mechanism was newly installed. There was some swearing and tetchy remarks: "You try it then!"

People kept coming up with suggestions for the security code, but that red light kept flashing its mean little *fuck you* rejection signal. Ben hated that red light.

He reckoned even his friend Jake, a locksmith, wouldn't be able to do it. He'd once asked Jake if he could pick any lock anywhere. "With the right tools," Jake had answered.

They didn't have the right tools.

Finally, Ben gave up. He left Carmel and the older men, Napoleon and Tony, to their useless endeavors and went and sat up against a wall with Jessica, who sat chewing on her false fingernails. She looked at him and smiled tentatively. Her lips were dry and chapped. They had kissed forever last night, in front of people.

Sometimes Masha had been there, sitting right next to them, and they just kept right on kissing, like two horny teenagers on public transport.

But it had felt different from being a horny teenager because there was no end goal. He wasn't doing the kissing just to get to the sex. The kissing was the point. Ben felt like he could have done it forever. It wasn't like sloppy drunken kissing, it was hyperreal, like every part of his body had been involved. He couldn't pretend he'd hated his first experience of drugs. It had been incredible. Was this what his sister had destroyed her life for?

Would Ben steal in order to experience that again?

He thought about it. No. He still didn't want to do it again, thank God. So he wasn't an addict from that one time he tried drugs.

His mother had been telling him that ever since he was ten years old, her face haggard with worry over his sister. "It only takes once, Ben, only once, and your life is ruined." He'd heard it over and over, like a bedtime story. The story was about how the beautiful princess, his sister, got taken away by the evil monster of drugs. "You must never ever, never ever, never ever," his mother would say, holding his arm so tight it hurt and looking at him with such terrified intensity he always wanted to look away, but he had to maintain eye contact because if he looked away she would start the *never ever, never ever, never ever* chant again.

He didn't need his mother to tell him that drugs ruined your life. The evidence was right there in front of his eyes. He was only ten when it started, and Lucy was five years older, but he still remembered the old Lucy, the first Lucy, the real Lucy who got taken away. The real Lucy played soccer and she was really good. She sat at the dinner table and ate her dinner and said stuff that made sense and laughed when something was *funny*, not for hours at a time at nothing, and if she lost her temper it was normal anger, not the anger that turned her eyes red and mean, like a demon's eyes. She didn't steal, she didn't break things, and she didn't bring home skinny, rat-faced boys with matching red demon eyes. He didn't need to be told never ever, never ever. He knew what the monster did.

Ben's poor mother would have a panic attack if she heard he'd been given drugs.

"It's okay, Ben," said Jessica quietly, as if she'd read his mind. "You're not an addict now."

"I know that." He put his hand over hers and wondered if maybe the couples counseling had worked. Although, if so, why didn't he feel more elated? Maybe it was the crash after the high. That's what got people addicted. The highs were so great, and the lows were so shit in comparison that you'd do anything to get back to the high.

He and Jessica had talked. He remembered that. They'd talked about so much. About everything. Maybe more than they'd ever talked in their entire relationship. They talked about the money. He remembered he'd told her he didn't like the way she'd changed her face and her body. It was strange, because that had seemed like such a big deal before, like the biggest deal ever, and now it seemed like absolutely nothing. Why had it mattered so much? So he didn't like her puffy new lips. Why was that the end of the world?

And the car. She'd been the one who scratched the car. That didn't seem to matter much either now. It was like those smoothies had sucked all the air out of their arguments, and now they were all wrinkled and deflated and kind of embarrassing. Like they'd both been making a whole lot of fuss about nothing.

There was something else they'd talked about too. Something he thought might have been more significant. He'd remember it in a moment.

Jessica pulled out her shirt and sniffed her cleavage. "I stink. I'm going to try and have a sponge bath at the bathroom sink."

"Okay," he said.

"I need to wash my face," said Jessica. She ran a hand over her cheek.

"Okay," said Ben. He glanced at her. "Not a single person in this room will care if you're not wearing makeup."

"There will be a single person who cares," said Jessica as she got to her feet. "Me. *I* care." But she didn't seem angry.

He watched her walk toward the bathroom.

Are we fixed? Do we have the right tools now?

He wanted a Bacon 'N Egg McMuffin. He wanted to be at work with the guys listening to FM radio, making cars beautiful again. He was going back to work when they got home. He didn't care if they didn't need the money; he needed the work.

How much longer would they be left down here? He

had to see *sky*. Even when he was working, he never spent a full day without going outside to eat his lunch.

He remembered a TV show he'd seen about a guy in jail who might have been wrongfully convicted and how he told his mother that he hadn't seen the moon in seven years. Ben experienced a full-body chill when he heard that. That poor, poor schmuck.

"Hey. Mind if I sit here?"

It was Zoe, the girl who was here with her parents.

She sat down next to him.

When he'd seen her over the last few days he'd wondered why someone of her age, who was obviously fit and sporty, would choose to come to a place like this. Now he knew.

"I'm sorry about your brother," he said.

She glanced at him. "Thank you." She pulled on her ponytail. "I'm sorry about your sister."

"How do you know about my sister?" asked Ben.

"Your wife mentioned it—when we heard about what was in the smoothies yesterday. She said she was an addict."

"Right," said Ben. "I forgot that."

"It must be hard," said Zoe. She flexed her toes.

"It's hard for Jessica," said Ben. "It's like she has to keep hearing the same old story. She never knew Lucy before the drugs, so to her, she's just a messed-up junkie."

"You never really get anyone else's family," said Zoe. "I broke up with my boyfriend because he wanted to go to Bali this week, and I said I couldn't go anywhere, I had to be with my parents for the anniversary of my brother's death. He was like, 'So are you going to have to spend that week in January with your parents *for the rest of your whole life*?' And I said . . . 'Uh, *yeah*.'"

"He sounds like kind of a jerk," said Ben.

"It's hard to pick the jerks," said Zoe.

"I bet your brother would have picked him for a jerk," said Ben, because it wasn't hard for a guy to pick the jerks, but then he wanted to kick himself. Was that an insensitive thing to say on the anniversary? And maybe her brother wasn't the type to be on the lookout for his sister.

But Zoe smiled. "Probably."

"What was your brother like?" asked Ben.

"He liked science fiction and conspiracy theories and politics and music that no one had ever heard of," said Zoe. "He was never boring. We disagreed on basically everything there is to disagree on." For a horrible moment he thought she might cry, but she didn't.

She said, "What was your sister like? Before the drugs? Or beneath the drugs?"

"Beneath the drugs," repeated Ben. He thought about it: *Lucy beneath the drugs.* "She used to be the funniest person I knew. Sometimes she still is. She's still a person. People treat addicts like they're not real people anymore but she's still . . . she's still a person."

Zoe nodded, just once, almost businesslike, as if she heard what he said and she got it.

"My dad just wanted to cut her off," said Ben. "Have nothing more to do with her. Pretend like . . . she never existed. He said it was a matter of self-preservation."

"How did that work out for him?" asked Zoe.

"It worked out great for him," said Ben. "He left. Mum and Dad got a divorce. He doesn't even ask about Lucy when I see him."

"I guess everyone has, like, different ways of coping with stuff," said Zoe. "After Zach died, my father wanted to talk about him all the time and my mother couldn't bear to say his name, so . . ."

They sat in silence for a few moments.

"What do you think is going on here?" asked Zoe.

"I don't know," said Ben. "I really don't know."

He watched Jessica walk out of the bathroom. She looked across at Ben and smiled, a bit self-consciously. It would be because she wasn't wearing makeup. These days he hardly ever saw her without that gunk plastered all over her face.

He looked at his wife and he knew that he loved her, but at the same time a thought occurred to him. All that kissing wasn't reconnecting. It was saying goodbye.

50

Frances

Nobody came. The hours passed as slowly as if they were passengers stuck on a plane not moving from the tarmac.

Everyone kept returning to the keypad and trying out random combinations of numbers over and over.

Frances tried the alphabet code with multiple words: LSD. Psychedelic (hard to spell). Unlock. Open. Key. Health.

That red light flashed again and again and it started to feel personal.

Moods began to fluctuate in odd and unexpected ways.

Heather became quiet and withdrawn, her limbs floppy. She went to a corner of the room, put three yoga mats on top of each other, curled up on her side, and fell asleep.

Lars sang. Endlessly. He had a deep, melodic voice but he changed from song to song as if someone was turning a dial looking for a particular radio station.

Eventually Tony said abruptly, "Christ Almighty, put a sock in it, mate," and Lars looked startled, and stopped in the middle of "Lucy in the Sky with Diamonds," as if he hadn't realized he'd been singing for all that time.

Carmel made an irregular *kwock* sound by clicking her tongue and Frances challenged herself to see how long she could put up with it. She was up to thirty-two *kwocks* when Lars said, "How long do you intend to keep that up for?"

Some people exercised. Jessica and Zoe practiced yoga poses together. Ben did an extraordinary number of push-ups, and finally stopped, breathing heavily, drenched in sweat.

"You should conserve your energy," suggested Napoleon mildly. "While we're fasting."

Fasting didn't feel like the right word to Frances. Fasting implied an element of choice.

Napoleon didn't speak as much as Frances would have expected. She had thought from their first meeting that he was a talker, but he was quiet and contemplative, frowning at his watch and then glancing up at the camera on the ceiling with a quizzical look, as if to say, "*Really?*"

"What if something has happened to them?" said Frances eventually. "What if they've all been murdered or kidnapped or fallen ill?"

"They've locked us in," said Lars. "So it seems like they planned this."

"Maybe they did plan it, but it was just meant to be

for an hour or so," said Frances. "And *then* something terrible happened to them."

"If that's the case, we'll be found eventually," said Napoleon. "Our friends and families will notice when we don't return from the retreat."

"So we could be here for another, what, four, five days?" said Frances.

"We'll be so thin," said Carmel.

"I might lose my mind," said Ben, and his voice sounded shaky, as if it were already happening.

"At least we have running water," said Napoleon. "And bathrooms. It could be worse."

"It could be better," said Tony. "Room service would help."

"I *love* room service," said Frances.

"Room service and a movie," sighed Tony.

They locked eyes and Frances looked away first because she was accidentally imagining herself in a hotel room with him. Those tattoos on his butt as he came out of the shower. That *smile*.

She gave herself a mental slap across the cheek, and thought of her dad sighing, "You were always so crazy about the boys." Fifty-two years old and still no sense. Just because they both liked room service didn't mean they were compatible. What would they talk about while they ate their room service? Football?

"We'll offer them *money*," said Jessica suddenly. "To let us out! Everyone has a price, right?"

"How much?" said Ben. "A million? Two million?"

"Steady on," said Lars.

"They're not going to let you out on a promise," said Tony, but Jessica had already walked to the middle of the room and was addressing the camera.

"We're prepared to pay a fee to get out of here, Masha!" She jammed her fists into her waist. "Money is no issue for us. We've got no shortage of cash. Honestly, we're happy to pay for . . . ah . . . an upgrade. We want to skip this part of the program, thanks, and we're happy to pay a penalty." She looked around the room uncomfortably. "For everyone, that is. We'll cover the cost for everyone to get out."

Nothing happened.

"I don't think Masha is motivated by money," said Napoleon quietly.

Frances thought, *What does motivate her?*

She remembered her counseling session and the way Masha's eyes had lit up when she spoke of how the VCR had once been a window into another world, but presumably movies no longer interested her. She had definitely wanted Frances to know that Australia needed her brains. Approval? Admiration? Was that it?

Or was it love? Was it that simple? She just wanted love, like everyone. But some people had such a peculiar way of manifesting that need.

"We don't even know if they're watching us," said Lars. "Maybe they've all got their feet up somewhere and they're watching *Orange Is the New Black*."

"We did not pay for shared accommodation!" Jessica jabbed her finger up at the camera. "I'm not sleeping in here again tonight! We paid for a double room and I want to be back in my room! I'm hungry, I'm tired!" She lifted up a strand of her hair and smelled it. "And I need to wash my hair right now!"

"Oh my God." Ben put both his hands on his temples. He ran about in a comical half circle. "I just remembered what you said! You're pregnant! You said last night you were pregnant!"

"Oh yeah," said Jessica, turning to her husband. "I forgot."

51

Delilah

"She's not pregnant." Yao's face was pasty with panic. "She is absolutely not pregnant."

Delilah, Masha, and Yao were in Masha's office, watching the live CCTV footage of their guests in the meditation room.

"I would never have allowed a pregnant woman to take those substances," said Yao. "Never."

"So why does she keep saying she is?" asked Masha.

They'd been here for hours. Masha and Yao stood and paced as they watched, but Delilah had finally sat down in Masha's chair.

Delilah was tired and hungry and kind of over it. Maybe she was kind of over being a wellness consultant. Four years now and the guests were all starting to blend together. They were all so self-absorbed, and sometimes she felt like she was a minor character in a story about everyone except her.

Over the years only a handful of guests had ever asked Delilah a single question about herself. Which, fine, the guests didn't have to talk to her at all if they didn't want, but they all assumed she would be so fascinated by *them*! The things they told her: about their marriages, their sex lives, their bowels! If she had to hear another story about someone's irritable bowel syndrome, she would slash her wrists.

And then there were the complaints that came thick and fast: the softness of their pillows, the temperature of their rooms, the *weather*—like she could control the weather.

It was nice when people seemed to truly believe they were "transformed" at the end of a retreat, but Delilah wasn't quite as evangelical about this whole transformation business as Masha and Yao.

Yes, she enjoyed yoga, her core strength was excellent, she had a six-pack and she liked having a six-pack, meditation was relaxing, mindfulness was great, and she had no problem introducing drugs into the equation, that made life interesting, and sure, it might give people some insights into their psyches, although, honestly, most of their psyches didn't seem that, you know, *complex*. This wasn't God's work. This was a health resort.

Delilah was skilled at giving the impression she cared as much as Masha and Yao. She could talk the talk, walk the walk. God, she'd done it with dairy products when she was Masha's executive PA. *Yes, yes, I'm just passionate about yogurt*. Then after Masha's heart attack she'd left dairy and done it with *insurance*. All those years working as a PA had been great training to be a wellness consultant: nod and smile and agree and make things happen behind the scenes and don't ask questions unless absolutely necessary. Masha paid well. Delilah had nearly reached her savings goal. She was going to travel for a year.

"I did pregnancy tests for all the women," said Yao. "Even the older women. She's not pregnant."

"So why did she say she was?" asked Masha again.

"I don't know," said Yao. He was very upset. Almost in tears.

"So she can sue us for giving her drugs," said Delilah.

"She doesn't need money." Masha gestured at the screen. "Like she said, money is no issue."

Delilah shrugged and sighed. "Maybe she just wants to make a point, like: 'What if I *was* pregnant and you gave me drugs!'"

"She's not pregnant," said Yao again.

"She doesn't know we know that," said Delilah. "And her husband's sister is an addict so, you know, they're really antidrugs. Pity we didn't know that."

Masha swung around. "But they should be happy, their therapy went so well! They kissed!"

"That's because they were high," said Delilah. Sometimes Masha had a bizarre innocence to her. Did she really think the kissing between those two *meant* something?

"They kissed for a very long time," said Masha to Delilah.

"Yes," said Delilah. "That's what happens when you take Ecstasy. That's why they call it the love drug."

The first time Delilah took Ecstasy she kissed Ryan, her boyfriend at the time, for over two hours straight, and it was incredible kissing, the best kissing of her entire life to date, but it didn't mean she wanted to *marry* the pompous British twat with his tight purple shirts. It was just kissing.

"It wasn't just the drug," said Masha. "I led them to many important breakthroughs."

"Mmm," said Delilah.

Like all of Delilah's bosses ever, Masha was a total narcissist. Delilah found it hilarious when Masha spoke so solemnly to guests about the "dissolving of the ego," as if her giant-sized ego could ever be dissolved. Over the last few years, Delilah had observed Masha's ego flourish, nurtured by the guests who hung on her every word and the doglike devotion of Yao.

"I have a gift for this," she said, straight-faced, when, really, what the hell would Masha know about relationships? In all these years Delilah had never known her to be in one. Delilah couldn't tell if she was straight or gay or bi or just had no sexual orientation whatsoever.

"I thought they would be more positive at this stage of their journeys," said Masha. "More *grateful*."

Delilah exchanged a look with Yao. Wow. That was *almost* an acknowledgment of a mistake. At the very least it was the acknowledgment of a moment of doubt.

Yao looked terrified, as if his whole world was falling apart. The dude was obsessed with Masha, probably in love with her. Delilah couldn't tell if his interest was sexual; it was more like the way a superfan behaves around a rock star, as if he couldn't quite believe he was allowed in the same room as her.

"It will all be fine," said Masha to Yao. "We just need to carefully consider how we proceed."

"We should feed them," said Delilah. She knew this from her waitressing days. Get some complimentary garlic bread out to the table. Stuff them with carbs and they'll stop complaining about the long wait on their mains.

"It hasn't even been forty-eight hours yet!" said Masha. "They all knew the retreat would include fasting."

"Yes, but they *didn't* know it would include LSD," said Delilah. "Or being locked up."

She thought that Masha had badly overestimated her guests' commitment to transformation. When people said they came to Tranquillum House to be "enlightened," what they really meant was "skinnier."

Anyway, as far as Delilah could see, no one in that room looked particularly *transformed*. There was no way in hell Heather Marconi was coming out of that room and giving them a five-star review on TripAdvisor.

Masha, being Masha, had never doubted that this new protocol was going to be a success. She had no concerns about the issue of consent. She said it was too risky to ask for it because the ones who most needed help would be the ones most likely to refuse. The glorious ends would justify the means. No one would complain once they experienced their personal transformations!

"Let's keep our focus on solutions," said Masha now as she contemplated her guests moving about their temporary prison. She didn't even look that tired.

Delilah remembered a night more than ten years earlier, when she was working as Masha's PA. Someone had discovered a major error in their analysis for the budget they were presenting to the board of directors the following day. Masha had worked thirty hours straight, right through the night, without stopping, to rectify the error. Delilah had stayed in the office with her, but she'd had a couple of power naps to keep herself going. The presentation was a triumph.

Six months later Masha had her heart attack.

Six years after that, when Delilah had honestly kind of forgotten Masha's existence, she called to ask Delilah if she'd like to train as a wellness consultant at a health resort she was starting up.

Masha liked to tell guests that they would hear about Delilah's supposed "wellness journey," but they never heard about it because there was no wellness journey. Delilah resigned from her job as PA for the chief executive douchebag at an insurance company. Her wellness journey was basically a train ride from Central Station to Jarribong.

"I think we should let them out," said Yao. "They were meant to be out by now."

"We have to be ready to adapt," said Masha. "I told you both that at the beginning. For dramatic results, you need dramatic action. I know this is uncomfortable for them, but that's the only way people *change*. They have water. They have shelter. We are taking them out of their comfort zone, that's all. That's when growth occurs."

"I'm just not sure that this is right," fretted Yao.

"Turn up the audio," said Masha.

"Obviously we're obligated to report this to the police as soon as we're out," said a woman.

"Who's that?" said Masha.

"Frances," said Yao, his eyes on the screen. Frances had her back to them. She was talking to Lars.

"*Frances!*" said Masha. "She loved her experience. She seemed to get so much out of it!"

Lars was saying, "Morally obligated. Legally obligated. We've got a duty of care. They'll kill someone eventually if we don't."

"I don't know if I'd want them to do actual jail time," said Frances. "I think their intentions were good."

"Right now, I'm deprived of my liberty, Frances," said Lars. "I'm not too worried if someone does a little jail time for this."

"Oh God." Yao moaned into his knuckles. "It's a disaster. They're not even . . . trying!"

"It's not a disaster," said Masha. "They'll work it out. It's just taking a little longer than we expected."

"They don't seem any different after the therapy," said Yao. "They just seem so . . . angry."

Delilah suppressed a sigh. It's called a hangover, you fools.

She said, "Would anyone like a green tea?"

"Thank you, Delilah, that's very thoughtful," said Masha gratefully, and she touched Delilah on the arm and smiled that soul-warming smile.

Even before, when Masha didn't look anything like a goddess, when she was just a frumpy high-level executive who was really good at her job, she had charisma.

You wanted to please her. Delilah had worked harder for Masha than she'd ever worked for anyone, but now it was time to close this chapter in her life.

Clearly the police were going to be involved. Delilah had been the one to access the drugs on the dark web, a process she had enjoyed and a new skill to add to her résumé along with PowerPoint. She thought her actions probably wouldn't be enough for her to go to jail, but they might be, and she felt like she wouldn't enjoy jail.

Part of her had known all along it was going to come to this. There was a kind of inevitability to it, from the moment Masha had first handed her the book about psychedelic therapy and said, "This is going to revolutionize the way we do business." Delilah remembered thinking, *This won't end well.* But she'd been feeling bored for a while. Experimenting with drugs was interesting and she'd kind of wanted to see the train wreck.

They micro-dosed guests' smoothies for over a year without ill effects. People had no idea. They believed it was the organic food and meditation that caused them to feel so great. They rebooked because they wanted to feel that great again.

Then Masha decided she wanted to do more than micro-dosing. She wanted to do something "revolutionary." She wanted to "push the envelope." She said they would be changing the course of history. Yao had argued. He didn't want to change the course of history. He just wanted to "help people." Masha said this would be helping people in a way that would truly change their lives forever.

The clincher had been when he'd tried the psychedelic therapy himself with Masha as his guide. Delilah
hadn't been there—it was her weekend off—but when
she saw Yao next he had an even crazier, more obsessive blaze in his eyes than before, and he was quot-
ing from the research as if it was the research that had
changed his mind when it was just the power of hallucinogenic drugs and the power of Masha.

Obviously Delilah tried the psychedelic therapy too.
Her experience had been awesome, but she wasn't stupid enough to think any of those feelings or so-called
"revelations" were *real*. They were just drugs. She'd
done magic mushrooms before. It was like mistaking
lust for love, or thinking that the sentimental feelings
you got when you heard a certain song were genuine.
Get real. Those feelings were *manufactured*.

When Yao had gone on and on about what he'd supposedly *learned* from his psychedelic therapy she kind
of wanted to slap him. It was just another example of
how that sweet stupid boy was addicted to Masha. He
was a lost cause. Nothing was ever going to change
there.

Delilah didn't go to the kitchen to make green tea.
She went straight to her room and collected her ID.
Everything else about this particular life—the white
uniforms, the sandalwood scent, her yoga mat—she
left behind.

Ever since she'd joined the workforce, she'd known
this about herself: she was, at heart, a PA. The smoother
of the way. Like a butler or a lady-in-waiting. Someone

seen and not heard. She wasn't the captain of this ship and she sure as hell wasn't going down with it.

Within five minutes she was behind the wheel of Ben's Lamborghini, driving toward the nearby regional airport where she would take the next available flight, wherever it was going.

The car drove like a dream.

52

Jessica

"How far along are you?" asked Heather from her position in the corner of the room. She sat up and rubbed her knuckles so hard into the sockets of her eyes that Jessica winced. You needed to be careful with the delicate skin around your eyes.

"Um, let's see. Two days," answered Jessica. She put a hand to her stomach.

"Two *days*?" said Carmel. "Do you mean your period is two days late?"

"No, I'm not late yet," said Jessica.

"So you haven't done a test?"

"No," said Jessica. Jeez. What was with the Spanish Inquisition? "How could I?"

This was so weird, all of them standing around in this small room like they were at an office party, but they were talking about her periods.

"So you might not be pregnant?" asked Ben. Jessica couldn't tell if his shoulders dropped with relief or disappointment.

"I am," said Jessica.

"What makes you think so?" asked Carmel.

"I just know," said Jessica. "I could tell. As soon as it happened."

"You mean you knew at the moment of *conception*?" said Carmel. Jessica saw her exchange a look with Heather, as if to say: *Can you believe this shit?* Older women could be so condescending.

"Well, you know, some mothers do say they could tell they were pregnant at the moment of conception," said Heather kindly. "Maybe she is."

"I bet a lot of women think they 'know' and then it turns out they're wrong," said Carmel.

"What's the big deal?" said Jessica. Why did this strange fuzzy-haired woman sound so angry with her? "I mean, I know, we weren't meant to be touching during the silence." She glanced up at the silent dark eye of the camera watching them. "We weren't meant to be taking drugs either."

The sex had happened in the dark on their second night at the retreat. Not a word spoken. It was all blind, silent touch, and it had been raw and real, and afterward she lay awake and felt a wave of peace wash over her, because if their marriage was over, so be it, but now there was going to be a baby, and even if they didn't love each other anymore, the baby was created from a moment of love.

"But wait, she's on the pill," said Ben to Heather and Carmel, as if Jessica wasn't even there. "Can that happen?"

"Only abstinence is one hundred percent effective,

but if she's . . ." Heather looked at Jessica. "If you've been taking the pill every day, at the same time, it's probably unlikely that you're pregnant."

Jessica sighed. "I went off the pill two months ago."

"Ah," said Heather.

"Without telling me," said Ben. "You went off the pill without telling me."

"Uh-oh," said Lars quietly.

"You didn't mention this last night," said Ben. "When we were 'speaking from our hearts.'"

He sarcastically quoted Masha, his face stone hard, and Jessica thought about last night, and how their words had flowed like water. But she hadn't told him last night about going off the pill. She'd still kept secrets even when she was high. Because she'd known it was a betrayal.

She *should* have said it last night, when his face was all soft and she felt like they were two halves of one person. She'd felt like that was a beautiful truth the drugs had helped her discover, but it had been a beautiful lie.

"Yeah," said Jessica. She lifted her chin and remembered the kissing and how, as they'd kissed, a single thought had blinked on and off like a neon sign in her head: *We're okay. We're okay. We're okay.*

But they weren't okay. Nothing she'd thought last night had been real. It was all just drugs. Drugs *lied.* Drugs fucked you up. She and Ben knew that better than anyone. Sometimes Ben's mother sat and cried over the pictures of Lucy before she fell for the lies of drugs. Now that was a "transformation."

"Don't waste your money on this stupid retreat,"

Jessica's own mother had said before they came here. "Give all that money to charity and go back to *work*. Then your marriage will be just fine. You'll have something to talk about at the end of the day."

Her mother seriously thought Jessica could go back and work in that shit-kicker job when she now earned more in bank interest in just one month than she used to earn in a whole year. Jessica couldn't make her mother understand that once you had that much money you were changed forever. You were worth more. You were better than that. You couldn't go *back* because you could never see yourself that way again. Rationally, she knew it was just dumb luck that had gotten her rich, but deep, deep down an insistent voice in her head told her: *I deserve this, I was meant for this, I AM this person, I was always this person.*

"Oh dear. Take it from someone who knows: getting pregnant is not the best way to try to save a marriage," said Carmel.

"Well, thanks, but I wasn't trying to save my marriage," said Jessica.

"What were you trying to do, Jess?" asked Ben quietly, and for a moment it was like last night, just the two of them together in their little boat floating down a river of Ecstasy.

"I wanted a baby," said Jessica.

She was going to document her journey on Instagram. Sideways shots of her "baby bump." A stylish gender-reveal party. Blue or pink balloons would fly out of a box. Hopefully pink. People would put heart emojis in the comments.

"I was scared you'd say no," she told Ben. "I thought if we were going to break up I'd better hurry up and get pregnant."

"Why would I say no? We always said we'd have children," said Ben.

"Yes, I know, but that was before we started to have . . . issues," said Jessica. She couldn't have borne to hear him say, "Are you kidding? Us?"

"So this baby isn't anything to do with me," said Ben. "You assumed we were breaking up and wanted to have a baby on your own?"

"Of course it's to do with you," said Jessica. "I only wanted your baby."

She could see him soften, but then, idiotically, without thinking, she said, "You're the father. You can see it whenever you want."

"I can see it whenever I want!" exploded Ben. You would think she'd said the worst thing in the world. "Gee. Thanks."

"No, I didn't mean—I just meant, *God*."

Their words no longer flowed like water. Now their conversations stopped and started in hard little jabs.

"It's probably premature to be sorting out custody visits," said Lars.

"I doubt she's even pregnant," said Carmel.

"I *am* pregnant," insisted Jessica. "I just hope these drugs haven't hurt the baby."

"You won't be the first or the last to have got drunk or high in the very early days of pregnancy," said Heather. "I'm a midwife, and the things some mothers have admitted to me, especially when the partners have left the room! If you *are* pregnant, there's a good chance your baby will be fine."

"So much for being the antidrug crusader, Mum," said Zoe.

"Well, there's nothing to be done now," said Heather under her breath, although Jessica could hear her perfectly well.

"I've been taking folate tablets," Jessica told her.

"That's great," said Heather.

"Yep, so great: folate, a little LSD, and some Ecstasy," said Ben bitterly. "The perfect start to life."

"Don't worry about it, she's probably not even pregnant," said Carmel in a low voice.

"What is your fucking *problem*?" Jessica's voice rose to an embarrassingly high pitch. She knew she shouldn't be swearing and showing her emotions like this, but she felt suddenly very upset.

"Hey now," said Napoleon soothingly.

Frances, the romance author, plonked herself down and went bright red in the face as if she'd never heard the f-word in her life.

"Sorry," said Carmel. She lowered her head. "It's probably just envy."

"Envy? You're, like, jealous of *me*?" said Jessica. Wasn't this woman too old to feel jealous? "Why?"

"Well . . ." Carmel laughed a little.

The money, thought Jessica. *She's jealous of the money*. It had taken her a while to realize that people of any age, people she considered grown-ups, of her parents' generation, who you would think wouldn't care that much about money because their lives were virtually done, could still be jealous and weird about it.

"Well, you're thin and beautiful," said Carmel. "I know it's embarrassing to admit this at my age—I've got four beautiful daughters, I should be way beyond this—but my husband left me for a . . ."

"Bimbo?" suggested Lars.

"Sadly not. She's got a Ph.D.," said Carmel.

"Oh, honey, you can still be a bimbo with a Ph.D.," said Lars. "Who represented you? I assume you're still in the family home?"

"It's fine. Thank you. I'm not complaining about the settlement." She stopped and looked at Jessica. "You know what? I'm probably jealous of you being pregnant."

"Haven't you got four children?" said Lars. "That seems like more than enough."

"I don't want any more children," said Carmel. "I just want to go back in time to when everything was beginning. Pregnancies are the ultimate *beginnings*." She put a hand to her stomach. "I always felt beautiful when I was pregnant, although I must admit my hair looked preposterous. I've got all this thick black Romanian hair, so when I was pregnant, it went wild."

"Wait, why did it go wild?" asked Jessica. She was not prepared for her hair to go wild, thank you very much. Surely there was a shampoo and conditioner to fix that.

"Your hair stops falling out when you're pregnant," said Heather. "So it gets thicker." She touched her own hair. "I loved my hair when I was pregnant."

"I'm sure you *are* pregnant, Jessica," said Carmel. "And I'm sorry." She paused. "Congratulations."

"Thank you," said Jessica. Maybe she wasn't pregnant. Maybe she'd just made a fool of herself in front of these people. She looked at Ben. He was studying his bare feet as if they had the answer. He had huge feet. Would their baby have huge feet too? Could they really be parents together? They weren't too young. They could afford a baby. They could afford a dozen babies. Why did it seem unimaginable?

Tony had gone to the bathroom and come back with a damp towel that he wordlessly handed to Frances. She pressed it to her forehead. She was sweating.

"Are you not well, Frances?" asked Carmel.

Everyone looked at Frances.

"No," said Frances. She waved a languid hand in front of her face. "Just . . . you know how you talked about how much you liked beginnings? I've got my own personal *ending* going on here."

"Ah," said Heather, as if that made perfect sense to her. "Don't think of it as an ending. Think of it as a beginning."

Carmel said, "When I was a teenager, my mother used to wear this pin that said, 'They're not hot flushes, they're power surges.' I was absolutely *mortified* by it."

The three of them laughed that self-satisfied middle-aged-woman laugh that made you want to stay young forever.

53

Frances

"You all right?"

Tony sat on the floor next to Frances, in that uncomfortable way men sat on the ground at picnics, as if they were looking for somewhere to stow their legs.

"I'm okay," said Frances. She pressed the damp towel to her forehead as the wave of heat continued to engulf her. She felt strangely sanguine, even though she was locked in a room with strangers having a hot flush. "Thanks for the towel."

She studied him. His face was pale and there were beads of sweat across his forehead too. "Are *you* okay?"

He patted his forehead. "Just a bit claustrophobic."

"You mean like properly claustrophobic? Not just *I really want to get out of here* claustrophobic?" Frances let the towel drop to her lap.

Tony tried to bend his knees up toward his chest, gave up, and stretched them out again. "I'm mildly claustrophobic. It's not that big a deal. I didn't like being down here even before we were locked in."

"Right then, I need to distract you," said Frances. "Take your mind off it."

"Go right ahead," said Tony. He smiled a half version of his full-on smile.

"So . . . ," said Frances. She thought about what Napoleon had said yesterday before their smoothies had had their full effect. "Did you suffer from that 'post-sports depression' when you gave up football?"

"That's a really sparkling topic of conversation to hit off with," said Tony.

"Sorry," said Frances. "I'm not at my best. Also, I'm interested. My career might be kind of ending right now."

Tony grimaced. "Well. They say that a sports star dies twice. The first time is when they retire."

"And was it like a death?" asked Frances. It would feel like a death if she had to stop writing.

"Well, yeah, kind of." He picked up a half-melted candle and pulled off a chunk of wax. "Not to be dramatic about it, but the game was all I knew for all those years, it's who I was. I was a kid straight out of school when I started playing professionally. My ex-wife would say I was still a kid when I finished. She used to say it stunted me. She had this phrase she'd picked up somewhere: professional sportsperson, amateur human being." He put the candle back on the floor and flicked away the piece of wax with his fingertips. "She used to repeat it every time I . . . demonstrated my amateur approach to life."

There was a hurt look in his eyes that belied his light humorous tone. Frances decided his ex-wife was a witch.

"Also, I wasn't ready to finish up. I thought I had one season left in me, but my right knee thought otherwise." He pulled up one leg and pointed at the offending knee.

"Stupid right knee," said Frances.

"Yeah, I was pissed off with it." Tony massaged his knee. "A sports-doctor friend told me that retiring is like coming off cocaine; your body is used to all those feel-good chemicals: serotonin, dopamine, and—*bam*—suddenly they're gone and your body has to readjust."

"I don't think I've ever experienced those feel-good chemicals doing exercise," admitted Frances. She picked up the candle he'd discarded and dug her thumbnail into the soft wax near the wick.

"You probably have," said Tony. "Doing certain types of exercise." He paused.

She blinked. Wait. Was that *innuendo*?

He continued talking. Maybe she'd got it wrong.

"You probably find this laughable but there were some games where we were all where we were meant to be and we all did what we were meant to do, and it all just came together, like a piece of music or poetry or . . . I don't know . . ." He met her eyes and winced, as if preparing himself for derision. "Sometimes it felt transcendent. Like drugs. It really did."

"That's not laughable," said Frances. "That makes me want to take up AFL."

He gave a deep appreciative chuckle.

"My ex-wife used to say that all I ever thought about was the game. It probably wasn't much fun being married to me."

"Oh, I'm sure it was," said Frances without thinking, and caught herself staring at his massive shoulders. She changed the subject hurriedly. "So what did you do after you stopped playing? How did you re-create yourself?"

"I set up a sports-marketing consultancy," said Tony. "It's done well—you know, for a business run by an amateur human being. I thought I was doing better than a lot of my teammates. Some of them really fucked up—I mean . . . stuffed up their lives."

"I feel like fucked up is the correct phrase to use there," said Frances.

He gave her his full "Smiley" grin. It really was the funniest smile.

"You're kind of annihilating that candle," he said.

She looked guiltily at the mess of wax in her lap. "You started it." She brushed the wax onto the floor. "Go on. So you set up this consultancy."

"I had one friend who said to me, 'Don't you hate the way that everyone only wants to talk about who you *used to be*?' but I honestly never minded that. I liked it when people recognized me; I never mind talking about the man I used to be. But anyway . . . late last year I started to get these symptoms, this incredible fatigue, I just felt something was wrong, even before I got on Dr. Google."

Frances felt herself go cold. She was at an age where

people in her circle didn't imagine serious illnesses, they got them. "And . . . ?"

"So, I took myself off to my GP, and he ran a lot of tests, and I could tell he was taking it seriously, and I said, 'Are you thinking pancreatic cancer?' Because that's what I was thinking—that's how I lost my dad, and I know it runs in families. And the GP just gave me this look, I've known him for years, and he said, 'I'm covering all bases.'"

Oh, damn it to hell.

"It was just before Christmas, and he called me in to give me the results. He pulled out the file and, afterward, I realized I had these words in my head, and I was saying them to myself, and it just . . . shocked the life out of me that I would think that."

"What words?" asked Frances.

"I was thinking, *Let it be terminal.*"

Frances blanched. "And . . . but . . . is it?"

"Oh, I'm fine," said Tony. "Nothing wrong with me, except that I obviously don't have a healthy lifestyle."

Frances exhaled. She hoped not excessively. "Well, thank goodness."

"But it shook me up—that I would think that, that I would *hope* for a terminal diagnosis. I thought, *Mate, how fucked-up is your head?*"

"Yeah, that's bad," said Frances. She felt energized in that bossy female way that she knew drove men crazy, but there was really nothing you could do about it once you felt that sense of righteousness surge through you, because they were such idiots. "So, right, you've got to get this fixed. You need—"

He held up his hand. "I've got it under control."

"It's really very bad that you thought that!"

"I *know* it is. That's why I'm here."

"So you probably need—"

He put his finger to his lips. "Shhh."

"Therapy!" she got in quickly.

"Shhh."

"And—"

"Zip it."

Frances zipped it. She held the wet towel to her face to hide her smile. At least he wasn't thinking about his claustrophobia now.

"Tell me about this bastard who scammed you," said Tony. "And then tell me where he lives."

54

Yao

"What's wrong with this one now? Is she sick? Why is she dabbing at her face like that?"

Masha's accent, usually just a flavor, sounded more pronounced than usual to Yao. Yao's parents were the same. They sounded extra Chinese when they were stressed about their internet service or health.

He should call his parents. "You are wasting your life with this woman!" his mother had said the last time they talked.

"Yao?" said Masha. She had sat down in the chair vacated by Delilah and was looking up at him, her big green eyes so worried and vulnerable. She was rarely vulnerable. It was exquisite torture to see her so.

"Frances is menopausal," said Yao.

Masha shuddered. "Is she?"

Yao knew Masha was a similar age to Frances, also in her fifties, but she was presumably not experiencing any symptoms of menopause. Masha was a puzzle Yao could never quite solve. She enjoyed discussing the most intimate intricacies of the digestive system, she had no shame when it came to nudity (why would she?) and often walked about naked when there were no guests on the property, but the word "menopause" caused her to shudder, as if something so distasteful could never happen to her.

Yao looked at the back of Masha's neck and saw a small inflamed lump: a mosquito bite. It was strange to see any form of blemish on her beautiful body.

She reached back with her hand and scratched it.

"You're making it bleed," he said. He put his hand over hers.

She waved him away irritably.

"Delilah is taking a long time," he said.

"Delilah is gone," said Masha, her eyes on the screen.

"Yes, she went to get you tea," said Yao.

"No, she is gone," said Masha. "She's not coming back."

"What are you talking about?"

Masha sighed. She looked up at him. "Have you not worked it out yet? Delilah looks after Delilah." She turned back to the screen. "You can go too, if you like. I will take responsibility for it all. The new protocol was my idea, my decision."

She could never have applied the new protocol without his medical expertise. If anyone should pay, it was Yao.

"I'm not going anywhere," he said. "No matter what happens."

Over a year ago now, Masha had come across an article about micro-dosing in Silicon Valley. White-collar professionals were using micro-doses of LSD to increase their productivity, alertness, and creativity. Micro-dosing was also being used with some success to treat mental illnesses like anxiety and depression.

Masha was fascinated in her typical Masha way. Yao loved her sudden wild enthusiasms and the fearless way she strode into unfamiliar territory. She tracked down the person who wrote that first article and phoned him. That's what led to her learning about psychedelic therapy, where people were given "full doses" of psychedelic drugs. Within a very short time, she became obsessed. She ordered books online. She made more phone calls to experts all around the world.

This was the answer, she said. This was what would take them to the next level. Psychedelic therapy, she said, was *the magic shortcut to enlightenment*. Scans showed that the brain activity of someone who had taken psilocybin bore striking similarities to the brain of an experienced meditator during deep meditation.

At first, Yao had just laughed in disbelief. He had no interest. When he was a paramedic he had seen the terrible impact of illegal drugs. The man who had held a knife to his throat had been suffering the psychotic effects of crystal meth. Yao had treated junkies. They were not a good advertisement for the wonderful effects of drugs.

But Masha chipped away at him, day by day.

"You're not listening. This is nothing like that," she said. "Would you not use penicillin because of heroin?"

"Penicillin does not affect brain chemistry."

"Okay, then, what about antidepressants? Antipsychotics?"

That low, persuasive, accented voice in his ear, those green eyes fixed on his, that body, that beautiful hold she had over him.

"At least study the research," she said.

So he did. He learned about the government-approved clinical trials of psychedelic drugs being used to help ease the anxiety of patients with terminal cancer. The results were overwhelmingly positive. So, too, were similar trials with war veterans suffering PTSD.

Yao became curious and intrigued. Eventually he agreed to try the therapy himself.

Delilah got the supplies on the dark web, including the drug-testing kits. Yao did all the testing.

He and Delilah both agreed to be the guinea pigs. Masha would be the psychedelic therapist. She herself, because of her medical history, could not do the therapy, but that was fine because she had already had transcendent experiences through her meditation and her famous near-death experience.

The psychedelic therapy had been, as Masha promised, transformative.

Even if medicating the guests turned out to be a mistake, he would never regret that.

It started with a journey down a tunnel that was possibly a waterslide (but the water was not wet, which was a brilliant idea) that ultimately spat him out in a cinema, where he sat on a red velvet seat and ate buttery popcorn while he watched as his whole life was played back to him, frame by frame, from the moment of his birth, right through school and university, up until the moment he arrived at Tranquillum House, except that he didn't just watch it happen, he re-experienced every incident, every failure, every success, and this time around he'd understood *everything*.

He understood that he'd loved Bernadette, his fiancée, more than she'd ever loved him and that she was never going to be the right woman for him. He understood that his parents had never been suited to each other either. He understood that he had the wrong personality to be a paramedic. (He was depleted, rather than energized, by bursts of adrenaline.)

Most significant of all, he learned that his phobia about mistakes had begun when he was a child.

It was an incident he was sure he had never heard about from his parents or remembered before, but under the influence of psychedelic drugs he re-experienced it in vivid detail.

He was no more than two or three years old, in the kitchen of their old house. His mother briefly left the room and he thought to himself, *I know! I'll help do the stirring*, and he'd carefully pulled a chair over to the stove, and he was so pleased with himself that he'd worked out this smart solution. He'd climbed up on the chair and he was about to reach out to the bubbling saucepan when his mother came back into the kitchen and *shouted* at him, so loudly, and his heart leaped out of his chest and he fell from the chair into endless space and his mother caught him, and shook him so hard his

teeth chattered. He understood at last that he had inter-
nalized his mother's terror at *her* mistake, not his.

Delilah, who refused to reveal much about her own
experiences, had been unimpressed by Yao's revelations. "So it's your mother's fault you're a nervous
Nellie? Because she saved you from being scalded?
What a terrible mother. No wonder you're so *damaged*, Yao."

Yao ignored her. Sometimes Delilah seemed angry
with him. He did not know why and he didn't care,
because the day after his psychedelic therapy he woke
dizzy with a new freedom: the freedom to make mistakes.

Perhaps this was his first mistake.

He looked at the screen showing nine people who
did not look to be transformed in any way. They looked
tired, agitated, and angry. They were meant to be out
by now, beginning the next stage of their "rebirth."

The "code-breaker puzzle" should have taken an
hour at most. It was meant to be a fun, stimulating
group activity to help them bond as a group. Back in
Masha's corporate days, she'd once been on a team-
building retreat where they'd done a similar exercise
and everyone had loved it. She said that people had
come out of the room laughing and high-fiving each
other.

Masha said she had come up with something sophisticated, subtle, and symbolic that would integrate
perfectly with their psychedelic experiences. ("Never
afraid to blow her own trumpet, is she?" Delilah had

said to Yao. Yao had put it down to jealousy. What woman wouldn't be jealous of Masha?)

Yao had worried that it was perhaps *too* subtle, but what did it matter? The code breaking wasn't integral to their transformations. If the guests couldn't break the code within the hour, they would let them out and lead them straight to the dining room for platters of fresh fruit and organic, sugar-free hot chocolate for breakfast. Yao had been looking forward to that part, imagining how everyone's faces would light up as he, Masha, and Delilah triumphantly entered the dining room, plates aloft. People would clap, he'd thought.

Yao had eaten a nectarine after his own psychedelic therapy session, and he could still remember the sensation of his teeth sinking into that sweet flesh.

Once they'd eaten, the group was to share what they'd learned through their experiences. After that, beautiful hardbound journals would be handed out, so that everyone could write down how they planned to integrate what they'd learned about themselves into their lives back home.

But nothing was going according to plan.

It felt like it had first gone off track with Heather's unexpected question, "Have you been medicating us?" which meant that Masha's presentation of the treatment had begun on a defensive note, although she'd responded brilliantly, even under attack. People had gotten so angry, as if they truly believed something sinister was going on, when this was all for their benefit.

Yao had checked and rechecked the dosages, the possible side effects, the guests' medical histories, their daily blood tests. There should have been only positive outcomes. He had checked everyone's vital signs throughout the night. Nothing had gone wrong. There had been no unexpected side effects. Napoleon had become agitated, but Yao had given him a dose of lorazepam and he'd calmed down.

It was true that the therapy side of it, from Yao's perspective at least, had been a little clunky. There was a disappointing banality to some of the insights the guests experienced, especially when compared to his own transcendent revelations. But Masha had been thrilled. After all the guests had fallen asleep, she'd locked the door of the meditation studio, flushed with success.

They had not imagined this.

As the time had passed, both Yao and Delilah had begun to say, "I think we should let them out. Or give them a clue."

But Masha was convinced that they would work it out. "This is essential to their *rebirthing*," she said. "They need to fight their way out like a baby squeezes its way out of the birth canal."

Delilah had made a small sound like a cough or a snort.

"We have given them so many hints," Masha kept saying. "Surely they are not so stupid."

The problem was that the longer they left them locked up, the hungrier and angrier and stupider they got.

"Even if they do work it out," said Yao now, "I think their primary emotion will still be anger."

"You may be right," said Masha. She shrugged. "We

may need to be more creative going forward. Let us see what happens."

Yao saw himself on that chair, his small pudgy hand reaching for the pot of boiling water.

"Look!" said Masha. She pointed at the screen. "*Finally*. We have progress."

55

Frances

Frances and Tony sat next to each other in companionable silence. Most people were sitting now, except for Napoleon, who paced constantly. No one was attempting to decode the security lock of the cellar door.

Someone hummed "Twinkle, Twinkle, Little Star." Frances thought it was Napoleon. She sang the words in her head along with him: *Up above the world so high, Like a diamond in the sky.*

She thought of the night of the starlight meditation and her sleigh ride across the starry sky with Gillian. Lars had been singing "Lucy in the Sky with Diamonds" before. That was the song that had been playing when she first lay down on the stretcher.

She mentally listed the other songs that had played through the headphones.

"Vincent."

"When You Wish Upon a Star."

Beethoven's *Moonlight Sonata*.

They all related to stars or the sky or the moon.

What had Masha said last night? Something like:
*All your life, you've been looking down. You have to
look up.*

"I think we're meant to look up," she said. She got
to her feet.

"What?" Lars propped himself up on his elbows.
"Look up where?"

"All the songs were about stars and the moon and
the sky," she said. "And Masha said that we have to
look up."

The younger ones caught on first. Zoe, Ben, and Jessica leaped to their feet and began to walk around the
room, craning their necks to study the vaulted stone
ceiling with curved wooden rafters. The older ones followed more slowly and warily.

"What do you think we're looking for?" asked
Napoleon.

"I don't know," said Frances.

After a moment, she said sadly, "Maybe I'm wrong."

"*There!*" Heather pointed. "See? Do you see?"

"I see it!" said Jessica.

Frances followed her gaze. "I don't actually see anything," she said. "My eyesight is terrible."

"It's a sticker," said Tony. "A sticker of a gold star."

"What good is a sticker?" asked Carmel.

"There's something above the sticker on the rafter
there," said Zoe.

"It's a package," said Napoleon.

"I still can't see it," said Frances.

"It's wrapped up in brown paper." Heather took Frances's hand and pointed it up to the ceiling, trying to get her to look in the right direction. "It's jammed into the little triangle where the two rafters meet, camouflaged against the wood."

"Oh yes, I see it," said Frances, although she didn't.

"Okay, so let's get it down," said Jessica to Ben. "Lift me up onto your shoulders."

"I'm not lifting you up, you're pregnant," said Ben. "You're possibly pregnant."

"Lift *me* up, Dad," said Zoe to her father. "You're the tallest."

"I don't think we'd get enough height." Napoleon tilted his head back, considering the distance. "Even if you stood on my shoulders you wouldn't reach it."

"The obvious thing to do is throw something up to knock it down," said Lars.

"I'll jump up and knock it down," said Tony. He looked up at the rafter with a gleam in his eye. "I just need a couple of you guys to give me leverage."

"You cannot possibly jump that high," said Frances.

"I got the mark of the year three times in a row," said Tony.

"I don't know what 'the mark of the year' means, but that's impossible," said Frances. It was like a joke to think of someone jumping that high. "You'll injure yourself."

Tony looked at her. "Have you ever watched a game of Aussie Rules in your life, Frances?"

"I understand that you leap about energetically—"

"Seriously," said Lars. "We just need to throw something up there, dislodge it from the rafters."

"We *leap about*," repeated Tony as if to himself. "We *leap about energetically*."

"It's *very* impressive leaping," said Frances. She remembered how she'd made the mistake of scoffing when Henry had started talking about how he wanted to learn to hang glide at the age of fifty. All her friends had shaken their heads. *Oh, Frances, you never tell a man in the middle of a mid-life crisis that he can't do something.* Henry did three months of hang-gliding lessons and suffered a chronic hip injury before he felt he'd proved his point.

"My highest mark ever was close to twelve feet." Tony looked up at the rafter. "I can reach that, no problem."

"Off the back of that Collingwood player, right?" said Heather. "Jimmy Moyes? Napoleon and I were at that game."

Napoleon recited, ". . . *the leap into heaven, into fame, into legend—then the fall back to earth (guernseyed Icarus) to the whistle's shrill tweet.*"

"Is that a poem about football?" asked Frances.

"It is, Frances," said Napoleon in a teacherly way. "It's called 'The High Mark' by Bruce Dawe. It's about how the mark is the manifestation of the human aspiration to fly."

"It's really lovely," said Frances.

"Oh my God, could we leave the poetry and the football and maybe just focus on getting out of here?" said Lars as he picked up an empty water bottle, aimed it like a javelin, and threw it up toward the ceiling. It hit the rafter and bounced back again.

"I'll get that parcel," said Tony, and his chest swelled and his shoulders went back like a superhero emerging from a telephone box.

56

Yao

"What are they *doing*?" asked Masha.

"I think Tony is going to try to launch off their backs like he's in a game of football," said Yao worriedly.

"That's crazy," said Masha. "He's too heavy! He will hurt them!"

"They're hungry and tired," said Yao. "They're not thinking straight."

"It's so obvious what they should do," said Masha.

"Yes," said Yao. Lars had the right idea.

"Why are they not building a simple human pyramid?" said Masha.

Yao looked at her to see if she was serious.

"They are just not that smart," said Masha. "This is the problem we face, Yao. They are not smart people."

57

Frances

Napoleon and Ben had positioned themselves beneath the rafter, their heads lowered, their bodies tensed.

"Should we jump at the same time?" suggested Napoleon. "Give you more height?"

"No," said Tony. "Just stand still."

"I don't think this is such a good idea," said Carmel.

"It's a ludicrous idea," said Lars.

"Now that you mention it," began Heather, but it was too late.

Tony ran from the doorway at full pace.

He leaped up vertically, one knee dug into Napoleon's back, the other into Ben's shoulder. For a fraction of a second, Frances saw the young man within the old. The athlete he'd once been was there in the length of his body and the resolve in his eyes.

He got up there! Impossibly high! He was going to do it! What a *hero*! One hand slapped the rafter, but then he crashed to the floor on his side with an almighty thud. Napoleon and Ben staggered in opposite directions, muffling curses.

"That wasn't at all predictable," sighed Lars.

Tony sat up, cradling one elbow, his face as white as toothpaste.

Frances got onto her knees next to him, to be supportive, even though her knees crunched. "Are you okay?"

"I'm fine," he said through gritted teeth. "I think I just dislocated my shoulder."

Frances's stomach turned at the sight of his shoulder protruding at a strange, distressing angle.

"Don't move it," said Heather.

"No," said Tony. "I need to move it. It's going to pop back in when I move it."

He moved his arm. There was an audible pop.

Frances toppled in a dead faint straight into his lap.

58

Zoe

Zoe's poor dad clutched his back where he'd just borne the entire weight of one Smiley Hogburn. She was kind of surprised that her mother had allowed that little exercise to go ahead. Maybe it was the drugs, or her crazy fury over the drugs, or maybe it was just that she and her dad were starstruck by meeting an AFL legend.

"Sorry, everyone," said Tony. "Last night I dreamed I was playing again. This felt . . . this felt like it would be easy." He gently patted poor Frances on the cheek. "Wake up, lady writer."

Frances sat up self-consciously from Tony's lap and pressed a single fingertip to the center of her forehead. She looked around her. "Did we get the package down?"

"Not quite," said Zoe's dad, who never wanted anyone to feel like a failure. "Very close!"

Zoe looked around for something to throw up at the rafter. She picked up a three-quarters-full bottle of water, held it in the palm of her hand, and took aim.

She hit the package straight on. It fell into Ben's hands.

"Nice shot." He handed it to her.

"Thanks," she said.

"Open it," instructed Jessica, as if Zoe had been intending to just look at it for a while.

The package had that firm, soft consistency of something encased in bubble wrap. She fumbled with the masking tape and tore at the brown paper.

"Careful," said her mother. "It might be breakable."

Zoe pulled at the tape on the bubble wrap and was reminded of opening a birthday gift, surrounded by people at a party, all eyes on her and Zach. Tomorrow was their twenty-first birthday. It might be time to reclaim it. She thought that maybe, once they got back to Melbourne, she would tell her parents that she wanted to go to La Fattoria for pizza to celebrate her twenty-first. It felt suddenly as if it might be possible to do some of the things they'd stopped doing after Zach died. It wouldn't be the same without him, it would never be the same, but it felt possible. She would still take off the olives and leave them along the edge of her plate for Zach.

And now she really, really felt like pizza. Her mouth watered at the thought of pepperoni. She would never take pepperoni for granted again.

She unrolled the bubble wrap. Inside was a small hand-painted wooden doll of a little girl wearing a scarf around her head and an apron around her waist. She had red circles on her cheeks and quizzically angled eyebrows. She seemed to be saying to Zoe, "Uh, hello?"

Zoe turned it around and held it upside down.

"It's a Russian doll," said her mother.

"Oh, right." Zoe twisted the top and bottom halves of the doll in opposite directions to reveal the smaller doll inside.

She handed the halves to her mother, and opened the next doll.

Within moments there was a row of five dolls of increasingly smaller sizes on the floor between them.

"Wait, is that the last one?" said Carmel. "It's empty. Normally there is a tiny final doll that you can't open."

"No message?" said Frances. "I thought the security code would be inside the last one!"

"So what the hell does that mean then?" said Ben.

"I don't know." Zoe tried to suppress a yawn. She was all at once exhausted. She longed for her own bed, for her phone, for pizza, for all this to be over.

"Okay, this is really starting to piss me off now," said Lars.

59

Masha

Masha saw Yao's smile of relief fade from his face as he watched the screen.

"But wait, why isn't the code in the doll?" He turned to Masha. "The plan was to put the security code in the doll!"

Masha lifted up the last tiny doll from where it sat on her keyboard and held it between her fingertips. "Yes, you're right, that was the original plan."

"So . . . but why isn't it there?" Yao's eyebrows were drawn together just like those of the doll.

"I had an epiphany," said Masha. "While I was meditating. Suddenly I knew what needed to be done in order for them to achieve true transformation after their psychedelic experiences. This—what is happening to these nine people right now—is quite literally a koan. It is a koan *in practice*." He must surely see the brilliance of it.

Yao stared at her without comprehension.

"A koan is a paradox that leads to enlightenment!"

said Masha. "A koan demonstrates the inadequacy of their logical thinking!"

"I know what a koan is," said Yao slowly.

"Once they surrender and accept that there is no solution, well then, they will be free. That is the central paradox of this koan," said Masha. *"The solution is no solution."*

"The solution is no solution," repeated Yao.

"Exactly. Do you remember this koan? A master who lived as a hermit on a mountain was asked by a man, 'What is the way?' and the master said, 'What a fine mountain this is.' The man felt frustrated. He said, 'I am not asking you about the mountain, but about the way!' The master said, 'So long as you cannot go beyond the mountain, my son, you cannot reach the way.'"

"So in this case the mountain is . . . the security door?"

"Take detailed notes," said Masha impatiently. She pointed at the screen and at his notepad. "Don't forget. This is very important for the book we will write."

"They've been in there for too long," said Yao. "They're hungry and tired. They are going to lose their minds."

"Exactly," said Masha. She herself had not eaten now for more days than she could remember and she had not slept since the night before the therapy sessions. She touched Yao lightly in the center of his chest with her finger. She knew the power of her touch on him. She had not yet fully exploited that power but she would if necessary. *"Exactly.* They must lose their

minds! You know this. The self is an illusion. The self does not exist."

"Sure, okay," said Yao. "But, Masha—"

"They must *surrender*," said Masha.

"I think they're going to report us to the police," said Yao.

Masha laughed. "Remember the Rumi quote, Yao. *Out beyond ideas of wrongdoing and rightdoing there is a field. I'll meet you there.* Isn't that beautiful?"

"I don't think the justice system is interested in fields," said Yao.

"We can't give up on them, Yao." Masha gestured at the screen. "They have all come so far."

"So how long are you planning on keeping them locked up?" Yao's voice sounded thin and strained, as if he'd become an old man.

"That's not the right question," said Masha tenderly, her eyes on the computer monitor, as some of the guests gathered around the door to the studio. They were taking it in turns to punch in different combinations of numbers. Lars punched the door with his fist like a spoiled child.

"I think I should let them out now," said Yao.

"They must open that door themselves," she said.

"They can't," said Yao.

"They can," said Masha.

She thought about the sunny Australian lives these people had been handed at birth. They had only ever known supermarket shelves that overflowed with choice. They had never seen an empty grocery store with nothing but boxes of Indian tea. They did not *need* attributes like ingenuity or resourcefulness. The clock struck five and they turned off their computers and went to the beach because they did not have a hundred university-educated candidates all too willing to take their job off their hands.

"Oh yes, I did that for U2 tickets once," an Australian woman at Masha's work said when Masha described the horrendous queues that lasted for days at the embassies and how she and her husband took turns to wait, and Masha said, "Yes, very much the same."

She remembered how, when they were right in the middle of the application process, her husband received a card in the mail to report to the KGB office.

"It will be fine," her husband said. "Do not worry."

It was like he was already an Australian, the phrase "no worries" built into his psyche before he even knew the words, but in the Soviet era people had received those cards and never come back.

When Masha dropped him off outside that tall gray building he kissed her and said, "Go home," but she didn't go home; she sat in that car for five hours, the simmering terror in her heart misting up the windows, and she would never forget the relief that detonated through her body when she saw him walking down the street toward her, grinning like a boy on an Australian beach.

Only a few months later she and her husband stood at the airport with American dollars hidden in their socks while a sneering customs officer upturned the entire contents of their carefully packed suitcases, because they were traitors betraying their country by leaving, and her grandmother's necklace broke and beads scattered like pieces of her heart.

Only those who have feared they will lose everything feel true gratitude for their lucky lives.

"We must terrify them," she told Yao. "That is what they need."

"Terrify them?" said Yao. His voice quavered. He was probably tired and hungry himself. "I don't think we should terrify our guests."

Masha stood. He looked up at her; like her child, like her lover. She could feel the unbreakable spiritual connection between them. He would never defy her.

"Tonight will be their dark night of the soul," she said.

"Dark night of the soul?"

"A dark night of the soul is essential for rapid spiritual progress," said Masha. "You've had your own dark night of the soul. I've had mine. We need to break them before we can make them whole again. You know this, Yao."

She saw the flicker of doubt in his eyes. She stepped closer to him, so close that they were almost touching.

"Tomorrow they will be reborn," she said.

"I just don't know—"

Masha stepped closer still and for the merest fraction of a second she let her eyes drop to his lips. Let the darling boy think the impossible was possible.

"We are doing something extraordinary for these people, Yao," said Masha.

"I'm going to let them out," said Yao, but there was no conviction in his voice.

"No," said Masha. She lifted her hand tenderly to his neck, careful not to reveal the silvery glint of the syringe. "No, you're not."

60

Frances

Frances twirled an empty water bottle on her finger, round and round, until it flew off and skittered across the floor.

"Stop that," said Carmel severely, and Frances could tell that was the voice Carmel used when one of her little girls was being annoying.

"Sorry," she said at the same time as Carmel said, "Sorry."

It was, according to Napoleon's watch, 9 P.M. They had been in here now for just over thirty hours. They hadn't eaten for over forty-eight hours.

People had begun complaining of headaches, light-headedness, fatigue, and nausea. Waves of irritability swept the room at intervals. People bickered, then apologized, then snapped again. Voices quivered with emotion and skidded into hysterical laughter. Some people drifted off to sleep and then woke with a loud gasp. Napoleon was the only one who stayed consistently calm.

It felt like he was their unofficially appointed leader, even though he wasn't issuing any instructions.

"Don't drink too much water," Heather had told Frances when she'd seen her returning from the bathroom after filling her water bottle yet again. "Only drink when you're thirsty. You can die from drinking too much water because you flush out all the salt in your system. You can go into cardiac arrest."

"Okay," said Frances resignedly. "Thank you." She'd thought drinking lots of water would stave off the hunger pangs, although she wasn't as hungry as she thought she would be. The desire for food had peaked just before they'd found the useless Russian-doll package and then gradually begun to wane until it became more abstract; she felt like she needed *something*, but food didn't seem to be the answer.

Her friend Ellen was a fan of intermittent fasting and she'd told Frances that she always experienced feelings of euphoria. Frances didn't feel euphoric, but her mind felt scrubbed clean, clear and bright. Was that the drugs or the fasting?

Whatever it was, the clarity was an illusion, because she was having difficulty differentiating what had and hadn't happened since she'd gotten here. Did she dream of her bloody nose in the pool? She hadn't really seen her dad last night, had she? Of course she hadn't. Yet the memory of talking with her father felt more vivid than her memory of the bloody nose in the pool.

How could that be?

Time slowed.

And slowed.

Slowed.

To.

A.

Point.

That.

Was.

So.

Slow.

It.

Was.

Unsustainable.

Soon time would stop, literally stop, and they would all be trapped in a single moment forever. That didn't seem too fantastical a thought after last night's smoothie experience, when time had elongated and contracted, over and over, like a piece of elastic being stretched and released.

There was a long heated discussion about when and if they should turn the lights out.

It had not occurred to Frances that there was no natural light down here. It was Napoleon who'd figured it out; he'd been the one to find the light switch this morning when he woke up. He said he'd crawled around the room on his hands and knees and run his hands around the walls until he found it. When he flicked the switch to demonstrate for them, the room was plunged into a thick impenetrable darkness that felt like death.

Frances voted for the lights to go off at midnight. She wanted to sleep: sleeping would pass the time, and she knew she'd never sleep with those blazing downlights.

Others thought that they shouldn't risk sleeping; they should be "ready to take action."

"Who knows what they're planning next?" Jessica shot a hostile look at the camera. At some point she had scrubbed off all her makeup. She looked ten years younger, younger even than Zoe; too young to be pregnant, too young to be wealthy. Without the makeup, the cosmetic enhancements looked like acne: a teenage blight that would pass when she grew up.

"I don't think anything sinister is going to happen in the middle of the night," Carmel said.

"We were woken up for the starlight meditation," said Heather. "It's entirely possible."

"I liked the starlight meditation," said Carmel.

Heather sighed. "Carmel, you really need to kind of reframe your thinking about what's going on here."

"I vote for lights off," said Frances in a low voice. Napoleon had showed them where the microphones were installed in the corners of the room. He'd told them all, in whispers, that if they wanted to share something they didn't want heard they should sit in the center of the room with their backs to the camera and keep their voices as low as possible. "I think we should give Masha the impression of total *acceptance*."

"I agree," whispered Zoe. "She's exactly like my year eleven maths teacher. You always had to let her think she'd won."

"I'd prefer lights on," said Tony. "We're at a disadvantage if we can't see."

In the end, there were more in favor of "lights on."

So here they all sat. Lights on. Occasional low

murmurs of conversation like you'd hear in a library or a doctor's waiting room.

Long periods of silence.

Frances's body kept twitching and then she would remember that there was no book to pick up, no movie to switch on or bedside lamp to switch off. Sometimes she'd be almost on her feet, before she realized that the decisive thing she was planning on doing was *leaving the room*. Her subconscious refused to accept her incarceration.

Carmel came and sat next to Frances. "Do you think we've gone into ketosis yet?" she asked.

"What's ketosis?" asked Frances. She knew perfectly well what it was.

"It's where your body starts to burn fat because—"

"You don't need to lose weight," interrupted Frances. She tried not to snap, but she had not been thinking about food and now she was.

"I used to be thinner," said Carmel. She stretched her perfectly normal legs out in front of her.

"We all used to be thinner," sighed Frances.

"Last night I hallucinated that I didn't have a body," said Carmel. "I feel like there was maybe a message my subconscious was trying to give me."

"It's so obscure. What could that message *possibly* be?" mused Frances.

Carmel laughed. "I know." She grabbed the flesh on her stomach and squeezed. "I'm stuck in this cycle of self-loathing."

"What did you do before you had children?" asked Frances. She wanted to know if there was more to

Carmel than just hating her body and having four children. Early in Frances's career, a friend complained that
the mothers in her books were too one-dimensional and
Frances had thought secretly, *Don't they only have one
dimension?* She'd tried to give them more depth after
that. She even gave them the leading roles, although it
was hard to know where to put the children while their
mothers were falling in love. When her editorial notes
came back, Jo had written all over the margins: *Who is
looking after the kids?* Frances had to go back through
the manuscript and make babysitting arrangements. It
was annoying.

"Private equity," said Carmel.

Goodness. Frances wouldn't have picked that. She
wasn't even quite sure what it *meant*. How were they
going to find a middle ground between private equity
and romance?

"Did you . . . like it?" Surely that was safe.

"Loved it," said Carmel. "*Loved* it. It was a long
time ago now, of course. Now, I've got a part-time,
entry-level job which is basically just data entry to
try to keep the cash coming in. But back then I was
kind of a high-flyer, or on my way to becoming one.
I worked long hours, I'd get up at five every day and
swim laps before work, and I ate whatever the hell I
wanted, and I found women who talked about their
weight excruciatingly boring."

Frances smiled.

"I *know*. And then I got married and had kids and
I got totally swallowed up by this 'Mum' persona. We
were only meant to have two, but my husband wanted a

son, so we kept trying, and I ended up with four girls—
and then out of the blue, my husband said he wasn't
attracted to me anymore and he left."

Frances said nothing for a moment as she considered
the particular cruelty of this kind of all-too-common
midlife breakup and how it crushed a woman's self-
worth. "Were you still attracted to *him*?"

Carmel thought about it. "Some days." She put her
thumb to the empty spot on her ring finger. "I still
loved him. I know I did, because some days I'd think,
Oh, what a relief, I still love him, it would be so inconvenient if I didn't love him."

Frances thought of all the things she could say: You'll
meet someone else. You don't need a man to complete
you. Your body does not define you. You need to fall
in love with you. Let's talk about something other than
men, Carmel, before we fail the Bechdel test.

She said, "You know what? I think you are most
definitely in ketosis."

Carmel smiled, and at that moment the room went
dark.

61

Napoleon

"Who turned the lights out?"

It was his angriest teacher voice; the one that got even the worst-behaved boy in a class to sit down and shut up. They had agreed the lights would stay on.

"Not me."

"Not me."

"Not me."

The voices came from all around the room.

The darkness was so complete Napoleon instantly lost all sense of up and down. He held out his hands in front of him blindly like he'd done this morning.

"Is that you?" It was Heather's voice. She had been sitting next to him. He felt her hand take his.

"Yes. Where's Zoe?"

"I'm here, Dad." Her voice came from the other side of the room.

"None of us was near the light switch," said Tony.

Napoleon felt the rapid beat of his heart and took

pleasure in his fear. It was a respite from the gray feeling that descended upon him the moment he woke up this morning. A thick fog had spread its soft fingers throughout his brain, his heart, his body, weighing him down so that it was an effort to speak, to lift his head, to walk. He was trying to pretend he was fine. He was fighting the fog with all his strength, trying to behave normally, to trick himself into getting better. It might be temporary. It might be just for today. Like a hangover. Tomorrow, perhaps, he would wake up and be himself again.

"Maybe Masha is telling us it's time to go to sleep now." It was Frances. He recognized her light, dry voice in the darkness. Before last night Napoleon would have said that he and Frances had similar personalities, in that they shared a certain base level of optimism, but not now. Now all his hope had drained away, it had seeped out of him and evaporated like sweat, leaving him empty and spent.

"I'm not tired," said Lars. Or maybe Ben.

"This is fucked." That was Ben. Or maybe Lars.

"I think Masha is about to do something," said Jessica, he was pretty sure. She sounded more intelligent when you couldn't see her face.

There was a moment of silence. Napoleon kept waiting for his eyes to adjust but they didn't. No figures emerged. The dark seemed to get darker.

"It's a bit creepy," said Zoe, with a tremor in her voice, and Napoleon and Heather both moved reflexively, as if they could make their way through the darkness to get to her.

"It's just dark. We're all here. You're safe." That was definitely Smiley Hogburn, comforting Zoe.

Napoleon wished he could tell someone that he'd kind of played football with Smiley Hogburn. He realized the person he wished he could tell was himself, the self who no longer existed.

The darkness settled.

It *was* creepy.

"Maybe Lars should sing," said Frances.

"At last, some appreciation for my talent," said Lars.

"We should all sing," said Carmel.

"No thanks," said Jessica.

"You and me, Carmel," said Lars.

He began to sing "I Can See Clearly Now" and Carmel joined in. She could sing beautifully. What a surprise to hear her voice rise in the darkness like that, holding the melody with such grace. How people could surprise you.

Napoleon had thought when he woke this morning that the feeling that permeated his body must be anger, because he had the right to be incandescent with anger at his wife for what she had concealed from him, and what she had chosen to finally reveal in the most nightmarish of settings, as his mind had struggled to separate ghastly fiction from reality—although now he thought he was free of the drugs, he did not have any doubt about what had and hadn't really happened. He'd dreamed of Zach, but he hadn't dreamed Heather's revelation.

He didn't remember asking her about the side effects of the asthma medication and yet he could imagine exactly how she would have replied: with unconcealed impatience, because *she* was the one in their family in charge of all decisions relating to health. Heather had the medical training, he was the teacher. He was in charge of homework. She was in charge of medication. She took pride in not questioning his decisions about education, although he would *happily* have been questioned by her, he was always eager for a debate, but she just wanted to get things ticked off the list. She liked to think of herself as the efficient, no-nonsense one in their relationship. The one who got things done.

Well, look what you got done, Heather.

She was right when she said that, given the opportunity, he would have read the leaflet that came with the medication, and yes, Napoleon would have monitored Zach, and he would have *told* him. He would have said, "This might affect your mood, Zach. You need to watch out for it and let me know," and Zach would have rolled his eyes and said, "I never get any of those side effects, Dad."

He could have, he would have, he should have, he might have saved him.

Every day for three years Napoleon had woken up each morning and thought, *Why?* And Heather knew why, or could take an educated guess at *one possibility* of why, and she had deliberately denied him the comfort of her knowledge, because of her guilt. Did she not trust his love? Did she think he would have blamed her, left her?

Not only that, they had an obligation to make this

known, to let the authorities know that this had happened. My God, there could be other children dying. They needed to make the community aware that those side effects should be taken seriously. It was incredibly selfish of Heather to have kept this to herself, to have protected herself at the risk of others. He would call Dr. Chang as soon as he got out of here.

And Zoe. His darling girl. The only one to see that something wasn't right because she knew Zach best. All she'd needed to say was: "Dad, something is wrong with Zach," and Napoleon would have acted because he knew how dangerous a boy's feelings could be.

He could have, he would have, he should have, he might have saved him.

They'd had *conversations* about depression around the dinner table. Napoleon knew all the conversations you were meant to have with your kids, and he made sure they had those conversations: don't give out your personal details on the internet, never get in the car with a driver who has been drinking, call us at any time of the night, tell us how you feel, tell us if you are being bullied, we can fix things, we promise we can fix things.

Am I angry? He had been asking himself that question all day, wondering if the fog was just anger masquerading as something else, but the feeling that had infiltrated all the cells of his body was something far more and something far less than anger. It was a dull nothingness with the weight and texture of wet cement.

As he sat there lost in the darkness, listening to

Carmel sing, as Lars lowered his voice and let her take the song, it occurred to him: *Maybe this was how Zach felt.*

Whether the asthma medication caused it, or whether it was teenage hormones run amok, or a combination of both, maybe this was how it felt: like his mind, body, and soul were shrouded in gray fog. Like there was not much point to anything at all. Like you could act and look exactly the same on the outside but on the inside everything was different.

Oh, mate, you were just a kid, and I'm a man, and it's been less than a day, and already I just want it to end.

He saw his son's face. The first rough graze of stubble, the curve of his eyelashes when he looked down, avoiding eye contact. He could never meet his father's eyes when he'd done something wrong. He hated to be in trouble and the poor kid was always in trouble. Zoe was smarter. She could twist her narrative to make it appear she'd done the right thing.

It looked like girls were controlled by their feelings but the opposite was true. Girls had excellent control of their feelings. They spun them around like batons: *Now I'm crying! Now I'm laughing! Who knows what I'll do next! Not you!* A boy's emotions were like baseball bats that blindsided him.

At that moment, that morning, three years ago, Zach didn't make a bad choice. He made what to him must have felt like the only choice. What else could you do when you felt like this? It was like asking those people in the burning towers not to jump. What else could you do if you couldn't breathe? You would do anything to breathe. Anything at all. Of course you jump. Of course you do.

He saw his boy looking at him with eyes pleading for understanding.

Zach was such a good kid. Of course Napoleon did not accept or condone the kid's decision, it was the wrong decision, it was a stupid decision, the worst decision, but for the first time ever he felt he might understand how he came to make it.

He imagined taking him onto his lap the way he'd once done when he was a little boy, holding him close, whispering into his ear:

You're not in trouble, Zach. I'm so sorry for yelling at you. I understand now, son. You're not in trouble, mate.

You're not in trouble.

You're not in trouble.

"Napoleon?" said Heather. He was squeezing her hand too tightly. He loosened his grip.

A black-and-white image flickered on the screen above their heads. Carmel broke off her singing.

"What the hell?" said Lars.

Masha's voice boomed at a volume that made Napoleon's ears throb. Her face filled the screen. She smiled at them, radiant with love. "Good evening, my sweetie-pies, my *lapochki*."

"My God," said Heather under her breath.

62

Frances

She's mad. She's crazy. She's nuts. She's unhinged.

It had all been a joke before. What Frances really meant was that Masha was odd, alternative, intense, excessively tall and exotic, and different in every way from Frances. She hadn't truly questioned Masha's state of mind. Part of her had wondered if Masha was a genius. Didn't all geniuses seem mad to mere mortals?

Even the drugs hadn't truly concerned her. The fact was that if Masha had asked, "Would you like to try this smoothie laced with LSD?" Frances might have said, "Sure, why not?" She would have been impressed by all the talk about "research," comforted by Yao's background as a paramedic, and intrigued by the possibility of a transcendent experience, and she would have been especially susceptible if someone else had said yes first. (As a teenager, her mother had once said to her, "If all your friends jumped off a cliff, would you jump too?" Frances had answered, without guile, "Of course.")

But now, sitting here in the dark, watching Masha's image on the screen, it was clear: Masha was not quite right. Her green eyes shone with an evangelical fervor that would not respond to logic or sense.

"Congratulations to all of you!" she said. "I am so pleased with your progress. You have all come so *far* from day one!" She clasped her hands together like an actress accepting an Oscar. "Your journeys are nearly complete."

The screen lit up the room in ghostly patches of light so that Frances could see everyone's faces as they all stared up at Masha.

"You need to let us out of here!" shouted Jessica.

"Can she hear us?" asked Carmel uncertainly.

"No need to shout, Jessica. Hello there, Carmel. I can see you, I can hear you," said Masha. "The magic of technology. Isn't it amazing!"

Her eyes looked off-center at the camera. It made it easier not to succumb to her madness.

"I was so happy when you solved the escape puzzle and found the *matryoshka*," said Masha.

"But we didn't solve it!" said Frances. She was personally offended by this. "We're still *here*. There was no damned code in the doll."

"Exactly," said Masha. "*Exactly.*"

"What?" said Frances.

"You worked as a team, though not quite to the extent I'd hoped. I assumed you would build a human pyramid to reach the doll—all of you!—rather than playing football." Her lip lifted in a sneer on the word "football." Frances felt defensive of Tony.

"When I was at school in Serov, many years ago, we made a human pyramid that was quite remarkable, I have never forgotten it." Her eyes lost their focus, and then she snapped back. "Anyway, that does not matter, you got there in the end, you found the doll and here we are."

"The doll told us nothing," said Jessica. "It was empty."

"That's right, Jessica," said Masha patiently, as if to a small child who does not understand the way the world works.

"She's not making any sense," muttered Ben.

"What I'd find truly transformative right now is a long hot shower," said Lars. He smiled up at Masha with the full force of his gorgeous face. It was like he was holding a glowing lightsaber up to the screen. Frances would bet that smile had opened many doors before.

But not this one. Masha just smiled back. It was an epic battle of beauty and charisma.

Lars held on for as long as he could before he surrendered. His smile vanished. "For God's sake, I just want to get out of here, Masha."

"Ah, Lars," said Masha. "You need to remember what Buddha said: 'Nothing is forever except change.'"

"This already feels like forever, Masha."

Masha chuckled. "I know you like your solitude, Lars. It is hard to find yourself having to interact with strangers all day long, yes?"

"Everyone is very nice," said Lars. "That's not really the point."

"We just want to go back to our rooms," said Heather. She sounded quite meek and reasonable. "The psychedelic therapy was wonderful, thank you, but—"

"It was wonderful, was it? You have changed your tune then, Heather!" A fine thread of aggression ran through Masha's words. "I hope you speak from the heart. I heard talk of reporting me to the police! I must confess that was hurtful to me."

"I was upset," said Heather. "As you know, today is the anniversary of my son's death. I wasn't thinking straight. Now I understand." She looked up at the screen with what appeared to be complete acquiescence. It was inspiring to see. "We *all* understand," continued Heather. "We're so grateful for what you've done for us. We would never have had this opportunity in our normal lives. But now we'd just like to go back to our rooms and enjoy the rest of the retreat."

Frances tried to put herself in Masha's position. It came to her that Masha considered herself an artist and, like any artist, she was starved for praise. She simply wanted recognition, respect, five-star reviews, gratitude.

"I think I speak for all of us when I say this has been an *incredible* experience," she began.

But she was interrupted by Tony.

"Is that Yao behind you?" He was on his feet, his eyes on the screen. "Is he all right?"

"Yao is here, yes," said Masha.

She moved to one side of her computer screen and gestured graciously, like a model on a game show indicating the prize.

The prize was Yao.

He was slumped forward in Masha's chair, asleep or unconscious on Masha's desk, one cheek squashed flat, while his arms formed a semicircle around his head.

"Is he breathing? What's wrong with him?" Heather also stood and moved to a position beneath the television screen. She dropped the fake acquiescent tone. "What has he taken? What have you given him?"

"Is he alive?" asked Frances in panic.

"He is just napping," said Masha. "He is so tired. He has been up all night, working hard for you!"

She caressed Yao's hair, and pointed at something they couldn't see on his scalp.

"That is Yao's birthmark. I saw it during my near-death experience." She smiled back at the camera and Frances shivered. "That is when I came face-to-face with my own mortality in the most remarkable and wonderful way." Her eyes shone. "This evening, you too will face your mortality. Sadly, I can't give you the privilege of looking death *directly* in the eyes, but I can give you a glance, a glimpse! An unforgettable glimpse that will . . ." She searched for the right word and found it with obvious satisfaction. "That will *amalgamate* all of your experiences so far: the silence, the psychedelic therapy, the escape puzzle."

"He doesn't look like he's napping," said Heather. "Have you given him something?"

"Ah, Heather," said Masha. "You are practically a doctor, aren't you? But I can assure you, Yao is simply napping!"

"Where is Delilah?" asked Ben.

"Delilah is no longer with us," said Masha.

"What do you mean, 'no longer with us'?" said Ben. "What does that mean?"

"She has left us," said Masha airily.

"Of her own *accord*?" asked Frances.

She thought about the other Tranquillum House staff: the lovely smiley chef who brought out the food; *Jan*, with her miraculous healing hands. Where were they, while the guests were locked up and Yao lay unconscious on Masha's desk?

"I need you all to listen carefully," said Masha, ignoring Frances's question about Delilah. She moved to the front of the camera again so that Yao's body was concealed. "We are now going to play a fun *icebreaker*!"

"I feel like the ice is well and truly broken, Masha," said Lars.

"Buddha said that we must 'radiate boundless love toward the entire world,' and that's what this exercise is all about. It's about love. It's about passion. It's about getting to know each other," said Masha. "I call it: 'Death Sentence!'"

She looked at them expectantly, as if waiting for an enthusiastic eruption of questions and comments.

Nobody moved.

"You like the name?" said Masha, lowering her head and lifting her eyes in a way that could almost be considered flirtatious.

"I do not like the name," said Napoleon.

"Ah, Napoleon, I like *you*. You are an honest man. Now, let me explain how this activity works," said

Masha. "Imagine this: You have all of you been sentenced to death! You are on death row! Maybe that would have been a better name? Death Row." She frowned. "I think that is better. We will call it *Death Row*."

Carmel began to weep softly. Frances put her hand on her arm.

"So how does this game Death Row work? Let me explain. If you are sentenced to death, what happens? You need someone to argue on your behalf, don't you? To argue for clemency, for a stay of execution. Obviously that person is your . . ." Masha raised encouraging eyebrows.

"Lawyer," finished Jessica.

"Yes!" cried Masha. "Your lawyer who defends you! The person who says to the judge, 'No, this person does not deserve to die! This is a good person, Your Honor! An upstanding member of the community with so much to offer!' You see what I'm saying? So, you are all lawyers and you each have a client. You understand?"

Nobody spoke.

"I have assigned your clients. Let me read out the names to you."

She held up a piece of notepaper and read out: "Frances defends Lars. Lars defends Ben." She looked up at them. "You're listening? I will only say this once."

"We're listening," said Napoleon.

"Heather defends Frances, Tony defends Carmel, Carmel defends Zoe, Zoe defends Jessica, Jessica defends Heather, Ben defends Napoleon, and . . ." she took an exaggerated breath, ". . . Napoleon defends

Tony! Whew! That's all of you!" She looked up from the paper. "Do you all know who you are defending?"

Nobody answered. They all looked dumbly back at the screen.

"Tony, who are you defending?" asked Masha.

"Carmel," said Tony evenly.

"And Zoe, what about you?"

"I'm defending Jessica," said Zoe. "I don't really understand what crime she's committed."

"The crime is not relevant. We've all committed crimes, Zoe," said Masha. "I think you know that. No one is innocent."

"You're a psychotic—"

"So presumably you are the judge, Masha?" Napoleon spoke loudly over the top of his wife.

"That's right! I will be the judge!" said Masha. "You will each have just five minutes to defend your client. It's not long—but it's long enough. Don't waste time with waffle! Make sure that every word packs a punch." She curled her hand into a fist.

"You will have the night to prepare. Presentations will be at dawn. You must ask yourself, Why does my client deserve to live?"

"Because *everyone* deserves to live," said Tony.

"But why your client in particular? Let's say there is only one parachute left! Only one place left in the lifeboat! Why should your client take that parachute over someone else?" said Masha.

"Then it's women and children first," said Tony.

"But what if you are all the same gender? All the same age? Who lives? Who dies?" said Masha.

"Is the game called 'Last Parachute' now?" said Lars, his face hard with bitter mockery. "So we're all going to sit around and discuss ethical dilemmas like first-year philosophy students while Yao lies there comatose on your desk? Wonderful, this is all just so transformative."

"Careful," said Tony under his breath.

"This is an important *exercise*!" shouted Masha. The tendons on her neck were rigid with rage.

Frances felt sick. She was going to lose this game. She always performed poorly in these kinds of "activities" and now her "client," Lars, had already got off on the wrong foot with the judge.

Ben spoke up in a placatory manner. "So, could you just explain, please, Masha, what happens if—according to you, our judge—we *don't* successfully defend our clients?"

Masha breathed in deeply through her nostrils. "Well, obviously we don't *generally* execute our guests! That's not good for business!" She laughed gaily.

"So this is all just . . . hypothetical?" said Ben.

"That's enough questions!" screamed Masha so loudly that Carmel took a step back and landed quite hard on Frances's toe.

"This is totally ludic—" began Heather. Napoleon grabbed her arm.

"We're all going to take part in the exercise, Masha," he said loudly. "It sounds very . . . stimulating."

Masha nodded graciously. "Good. You're going to find it transformative, Napoleon. You really are. Now, I must give you light for this enlightening exercise!"

She reached out her hand and the lights came back on, causing everyone to blink and stare dazedly at each other.

"Once we've defended our 'clients,' will you let us out?" asked Carmel, rubbing her eyes, her voice hoarse.

"You're asking the wrong questions, Carmel," said Masha. "Only *you* can set yourself free. Remember, I talked to you just a few days ago about impermanence. Nothing lasts forever. Do not cling to happiness *or* suffering."

"I just really want to go home right now," said Carmel.

Masha clucked sympathetically. "Spiritual awakenings are rarely easy, Carmel."

Frances raised a hand. "I need a pen. I can't prepare a presentation if I can't write it down!" She patted the empty pockets of her sweatpants. "I have nothing to write with!"

Masha behaved as if Frances hadn't spoken. "Now, my sweetie pies, I wish you the best of luck. I shall be back at dawn. Remember to focus your thoughts. Ask the right questions of your clients, and listen with your heart. Convince me why each of *you* deserves to live."

She looked fondly at Yao if he were her sleeping child, patted his head, and then looked back at the screen. "Let me leave you with these words: 'Ardently do today what must be done. Who knows? Tomorrow death comes.' The Buddha." She put her hands together in prayer and lowered her head. "Namaste."

63

Lars

The guests of Tranquillum House stood in a huddled, whispering group in the center of the studio, their heads bent, like a cluster of banished smokers outside their office on a chilly day. Lars could smell acrid sweat and stale breath. Ben and Jessica held hands. Carmel and Frances both chewed at their fingernails. Tony tugged aggressively at his bottom lip, as if he could somehow contort his mouth into providing the correct answers, while Zoe kneaded her stomach and studied her feet, and her parents both studied her.

"I'm sure Yao is fine, don't you think? And Delilah? There is no way Masha would really hurt anyone," said Frances. "No way in the world. She sees herself as a healer."

Lars could tell Frances was trying to convince herself. The longer they were in here, the more stripped back she got. Her red lipstick was gone and her blond hair, which had been in a bouncy circa 1995 ponytail, was now slicked back against her head. Lars liked

Frances, but she wasn't the lawyer he would have retained, given a choice, if he was on death row. He didn't know who he would have chosen out of this motley lot. He wasn't sure how much it really mattered. Masha was going to do what she was going to do.

"We just need to make it look as if we're going along with the madness," he said to the group.

"I agree," said Napoleon. "We have to play along and take the first opportunity we can to find a way out of here."

"I believed in her," said Carmel sadly. "I believed in this." She indicated her surroundings. "I thought I was being transformed."

"So I'm representing you," said Frances to Lars anxiously. "We need to talk. God, I would do anything for a *pen*."

"Well, supposedly I'm representing you, Frances, in this grotesque . . . *game*," sighed Heather. "So I guess we need to talk too."

"Okay, yes, yes, but just let me talk to my client first," said Frances, breathing fast. She put a hand to her chest to try to calm herself. Lars smiled at her. She would be the sort to play a game of charades with endearing seriousness and little skill, as if it were a matter of life and death, and now that it truly might be a matter of life and death (surely not!), she was in danger of hyperventilating.

"Let's go have a chat, Frances," said Lars soothingly. "And then you can go convince Heather why you should live."

"This is pathetic," said Heather as they split up into pairs.

"We're an odd number," said Napoleon. "I'll wait for my turn." He lowered his voice even further. "I'll just keep looking around for a way out of here." He wandered off, his hands shoved in the pockets of his dad shorts.

Lars and Frances went to sit in a corner.

"Right." Frances sat cross-legged in front of Lars. She frowned intensely. "Tell me *everything* about your life, your relationships, your family."

"Tell her I'm a philanthropist, I do a lot of things for the community, volunteer work . . ."

"Do you?" interrupted Frances.

"You write fiction!" said Lars. "Let's just make it up! It doesn't actually matter what you say as long as it looks like we're going along with the exercise."

Frances shook her head. "That woman might be crazy, but she can smell insincerity a mile off. I am going along with the exercise and I'm doing it properly. You tell me everything, Lars, right now. I'm not kidding."

Lars groaned. He ran his fingers through his hair. "I help women," he said. "I only represent women in divorce cases."

"Seriously?" said Frances. "Isn't that discriminatory?"

"I get my clients by word of mouth," said Lars. "They all know each other, these types of women, they play tennis together."

"So you only represent wealthy women?" said Frances.

"I'm not doing it for *love*," said Lars. "I make good

money. I just make sure a certain type of man pays a fair price for his sins."

Frances tapped her thumbnail against her front teeth like an imaginary pen. "Are you in a relationship?"

"Yes," said Lars. "We've been together for fifteen years. His name is Ray and he would probably prefer I wasn't 'sentenced to death.'"

He felt a sudden burst of longing for Ray and for home, for music and the sizzle of garlic, for Sunday mornings. He was done with health resorts. When he got out of here he was going to book a holiday for him and Ray, a gastronomic tour of Europe. The man had gotten too skinny. His eyes looked huge in his face. All that obsessive bike riding. Legs spinning in a blur, up and down the hills of Sydney, faster and faster, trying to get those endorphins flooding his body, trying to forget that he was in a relationship where he gave more than he got.

"He's a good person," said Lars, and he was surprised to find himself close to tears, because it occurred to him that if he were to die, Ray would be snatched up like a too-good-to-be-true deal at the supermarket, and someone else could very easily love him the way he deserved to be loved.

"Poor Ray," murmured Frances, as if she knew what he was thinking.

"Why do you say that?" said Lars.

"Oh, it's just you're so good-looking. I was briefly in love with a handsome man in my youth and it was awful, and you're just . . ." she gestured at him, ". . . ridiculous."

"That's kind of offensive," said Lars. There was a lot of prejudice against people who looked like him. People had no idea.

"Yeah, yeah, get over it," said Frances. "So . . . no kids?"

"No kids," said Lars. "Ray wants children. I don't."

"I never wanted children either," said Frances.

Lars thought of Ray's mother at Ray's thirty-fifth birthday last month. As usual she'd had "one too many glasses of champagne," which meant she'd had two glasses. "Can't you let him have *one* baby, Lars? Just one itsy-bitsy baby? You wouldn't have to lift a finger, I promise."

"Did your psychedelic therapy give you any special insights into your life?" asked Frances. "Masha would probably like it if I mentioned that."

Lars thought about last night. Some parts had been spectacular. At one point, he realized he could *see* the music coming through his headphones in waves of iridescent color. He and Masha had talked, but he didn't think there had been any particular insights. He'd told her at length about the color of the music and he felt like she might have gotten bored, which he'd found insulting because he'd been speaking very eloquently and poetically.

He didn't think he'd told Masha about the little boy who kept appearing in his hallucinations last night. She would have liked that.

He knew that the dark-haired, dirty-faced kid who kept grabbing Lars's hand was there to remind Lars of something significant and traumatic from his childhood, one of those formative memories that therapists were always so excited about dredging up.

He had refused to go with the young Lars. "I'm busy," he kept telling him, as he lay back down on a beach to enjoy the colors of the music. "Ask someone else."

I don't care what my subconscious is trying to tell me, thanks anyway.

At one point in the night he got into a conversation with Delilah that didn't feel therapeutic, more like shooting the breeze; in fact, he was pretty sure he could feel a sea breeze while they chatted.

Delilah said, "You're just like me, Lars. You don't give a shit, do you? You just don't care."

Did she have a cigarette in her hand at that point? Surely not.

"What do you mean?" Lars had said lazily.

"You know what I mean." Delilah had sounded so sure of herself, as if she knew Lars better than he knew himself.

Frances banged her knuckles in rapid motion against her cheekbones.

"Stop hitting yourself," said Lars.

Frances dropped her hand. "I've never represented anyone in court before," she said.

"This isn't court," he said. "This is just a silly game."

He looked over at Jessica, supposedly pregnant.

"Tell Masha that my partner and I are planning to have a baby," he said flippantly.

"We can't lie," said Frances. She was clearly exasperated with him, poor woman.

The expression on her face made him think of Ray when Lars had done something to annoy or frustrate him. The compressed lips. The resigned slump of his shoulders. Those disappointed eyes.

He remembered the impish face of that little boy from last night and realized with a start that it wasn't his younger self at all. The kid had hazel eyes. *Ray's* eyes. Ray and his sister and mother all had the same eyes. Eyes that made Lars want to close his own because of all that terrifying love and trust and loyalty.

"Tell Masha if I don't live I'll take out a wrongful death lawsuit against her," Lars told Frances. "I'll win. I guarantee you I'll win."

"What?" Frances frowned. "That doesn't even make sense!"

"None of this makes sense," said Lars. "None of it."

He saw again the dark-haired little boy with the hazel eyes, felt the tug of his hand and heard his insistent voice: *I've got something to show you.*

64

Jessica

Jessica and Zoe sat opposite each other, cross-legged, on a yoga mat, as if they were about to do a joint Pilates exercise.

Jessica would have given anything to be in a Pilates class right now. Even the cheap one she did before they won the money, in that drafty community hall, with all the local mums.

"Do you think this is, I don't know, serious?" Zoe's eyes darted over to her parents and back. Jessica couldn't help but notice Zoe had great natural eyebrows.

"Ah, yeah, I kind of do," Jessica answered. "I feel like Masha is, like, totally capable of anything. She seems very unstable." She tried to control her breathing. The fear kept rising and then receding in her stomach, like bouts of nausea on an amusement park ride.

"She wouldn't really, like, *execute* anyone of course," said Zoe, smiling fiercely, as if determined to show she was making a joke.

"Of course not," said Jessica, but how did she know

what this woman could do? She'd given them drugs without their consent, and who knew what she'd done to Yao and Delilah. "It's an exercise, that's all, to make us think. It's just a really stupid exercise."

"I'm worried my mother might antagonize Masha. She's not taking it seriously enough." Zoe shot a look at Heather.

"Don't worry, I'll do a really good job defending her," said Jessica. "Your mother is a *midwife*. She helps bring new life into the world. Also, I was on the debating team. First speaker." *Jessica is a conscientious student.* That was the comment she used to see most often on her report cards.

"And I'll do a good job defending you!" Zoe sat up straighter, with the air of a fellow conscientious student. "So, okay, I thought, first of all, I should obviously mention your pregnancy, right? You can't execute a pregnant woman. That would be against some convention or something, right?"

"That's true," said Jessica doubtfully, although she wasn't sure why she felt doubtful. Was it because the pregnancy wasn't confirmed? Because it seemed like that was exploiting a loophole? She only deserved to live because her innocent child deserved to live?

And if she wasn't pregnant, why *should* she live? Just because she really *wanted* to live? Because her parents loved her? Because she knew her sister loved her too, even if they were currently estranged? Because her Instagram followers often said she "made their day"? Because last financial year her charitable donations were higher than what had once been her annual income?

"When we won the money, we really tried to, you know, not be *selfish*," she told Zoe. "To share it, to give to charity." She ran her fingers through her hair like a comb and lowered her voice. "But we didn't give it *all* away."

"No one would expect that," said Zoe. "It was your prize."

"That's one thing I miss about our old life," admitted Jessica. "Before we got rich we didn't ever have to think about whether we were 'good' people, because we didn't have time to be good. We were just paying the bills, getting by, living our lives. It was kind of easier." She winced. "That makes it sound like I'm complaining and I promise you I'm not."

"I've read about lottery winners who go on crazy spending sprees and their relationships end and they lose the lot and end up on benefits," said Zoe.

"I know!" said Jessica. "When we won, I did a lot of research about lottery winners. So I, like, knew the pitfalls."

"I reckon you've done a good job of it," said Zoe.

"Thank you," said Jessica gratefully, because sometimes she had longed for someone to give her a good mark for how well she'd handled the prize money.

She'd tried so hard to be a well-behaved lottery winner. To invest properly, to share appropriately, to get tax advice, to go to posh fundraiser balls where terrifyingly elegant people sipped French champagne while they bid obscene amounts of money on obscure items at charity auctions: "All for a good cause, ladies and gentlemen!" She thought of Ben tugging at his bow tie, muttering, "Who the fuck *are* these people?"

Should she have spent more at those charity balls? Less? Not gone at all? Sent a check? What would have made her a better person, more deserving of life right now?

If this had happened before the win, what would Zoe have said? Jessica deserves to live because she works really hard at her boring-as-batshit job and she's never even flown business class in her life, let alone first class, so what sort of life is that?

The money defined her now. She didn't even know who she was before the money.

"Ben didn't want to make any decisions except for which car to buy," she told Zoe. "He didn't want anything to change . . . and that's just not possible."

She touched her lips and looked down at her boobs, which were objectively awesome.

Would her defense case be better if she didn't look like this? If she hadn't spent so much money on her body?

"Why would you *want* to look like one of those dreadful Kardashians?" her mother had once asked her.

Because Jessica thought those dreadful Kardashians were stunning. It was her prerogative to think so. Before the money Ben had drooled over images of luxury cars and Jessica had drooled over pictures of models and reality stars, that were maybe photoshopped, but she didn't care. He got his car, she got her body. Why was her new body more superficial than his new car?

"Sorry." She looked back up at Zoe and remembered that this girl's brother had committed suicide. Zoe had probably never met anyone as superficial as Jessica in her life. "None of that helps you build my case, does it? Why should this girl live? Oh, because she tried really hard when she won the lottery."

Zoe didn't smile but gave Jessica a very serious, focused look. "Don't worry, I can put a good spin on this."

She looked up at the television screen where Masha's face had loomed. "What do you think will happen next? After we've played her stupid game?"

"I don't know," said Jessica honestly. "It feels like anything could happen."

65

Masha

Masha collected a cushion from the Lavender Room. Yao made no sound as she lifted his head from her desk and slid the cushion beneath his cheek. His fluttering eyelids were not fully closed, revealing the shimmery slivers of his eyes.

She remembered adjusting a blanket around a small sleeping form. It felt like a memory that belonged to someone else, although she knew it was hers. The memory had no texture to it, no smell or color; it was like the scenes from the security cameras around the building.

That was not correct. She could give the memory color and texture if she so chose.

The blanket was yellow. The smell was No More Tears baby shampoo. The sound was the tinkling tune of the Brahms lullaby as a mobile with dangling toys turned in slow circles. The touch was of soft warm skin beneath her fingertips.

But she did not choose to remember that right at this moment.

She switched off the monitor so she could no longer see or hear her guests. She needed a break from them. The pitch of their voices was like fingernails on a blackboard.

The sedative she'd given Yao was one they'd prepared in case a guest had a bad reaction to yesterday's smoothies and became so violent or agitated as to be a danger to themselves or others. Masha understood that Yao would sleep for a few restful hours and then he'd be fine. It was Yao himself who had taught both Masha and Delilah how to urgently administer the injection in the event of an emergency.

This had not been planned, but it had become clear to her that Yao's loss of confidence in the protocol was a serious liability. He needed to be temporarily removed from the strategic decision-making process. She needed to act fast and she did, in the same way that she had once culled nonperforming staff or even entire divisions. Her ability to make swift decisions and execute those decisions in the face of change had been one of her strengths throughout her working life. *Agility.* That's what it was. She was both metaphorically and literally agile.

But once Yao slept, she felt oddly alone. She missed him. She missed Delilah too. Without Yao or Delilah here there was no one to mentor, no one observing her actions, no one to whom she needed to explain herself. It was strange. She had lived alone for large chunks of her life. When she was renovating Tranquillum House and creating and refining the personal-development plan that resulted in her incredible physical and spiritual transformation, she had spent months at a time without seeing a soul, and she had not felt the loss of company at all. But her life was different now. She was rarely alone. There were always people in the house: her staff, her guests. This reliance on people was a weakness. She needed to work on that. She was a work in progress.

Nothing stays the same.

It was a hypothetical exercise she had set for the guests, but their fear needed to be real. She had not seen enough fear. She had seen cynicism and doubt. These people were disrespectful. Ungrateful. Quite unintelligent, to be frank.

Those drugs weren't cheap. They had cut into her profit margins. She had been prepared to take less profit for their benefit. Dear Yao had worked so hard to ensure the correct dosages for each guest. There had been many late nights getting this right!

The new protocol was meant to be Masha's career pivot. She was ready to be part of a bigger world again. She missed the public recognition she had enjoyed in her corporate life: the profiles in business magazines, the invitations to deliver keynote addresses. She wanted to publish articles and deliver speeches at conferences and events. She had already put the word out about a potential book deal. The response had been positive. *Personal transformation is a topic of perennial interest*, wrote one publisher. *Keep us posted.*

Masha had enjoyed the thought of her previous colleagues seeing her reincarnation. They would probably not recognize her at first, and then they would respond with awe and envy. She had escaped the rat race and look what she had achieved. There would be magazine profiles and television interviews. She planned to employ a publicist. She certainly intended to mention Yao in the acknowledgments of her book and would even consider promoting him to a more senior position at Tranquillum House while she was busy on the speaking circuit.

Masha's glittering, glorious future lay ahead and these ungrateful dolts stood in the way of it. Masha had anticipated yearlong waiting lists after the news of their success got out. Prices would rise to reflect the demand. These people had been offered this incredible program for a bargain-basement price and they did nothing but moan.

They thought they were hungry! Had they ever known true hunger? Had they ever lined up *for more than five minutes* to buy basic food supplies?

Masha considered the blank computer monitor and thought about turning it back on, but she didn't want to see them right now. She was too angry with them. That Heather Marconi was so disrespectful. Masha did not like her.

If any one of them had a brain, they could be out of that room right now and on their way to the police to make their complaints about how *poorly* they had been treated, when the truth was they had been lovingly nurtured.

Masha took a key from her top drawer and unlocked the cupboard beneath her desk.

For a moment she sat and studied the contents. Her mouth filled with saliva. She lunged forward and grabbed a bag of Doritos and a jar of salsa. The bag was fat and smooth and crackled in her hand.

She remembered the woman who would come home late at night from the office after working a sixteen-hour day and sit in a dark room in front of the television to mindlessly eat Doritos and salsa. That had been Masha's evening meal. She had not cared about her body. Her body meant nothing. She just bought bigger- and bigger-sized clothes when she noticed. All she cared about was work. She smoked and did no exercise. As that doctor had said, she was a heart attack or a stroke waiting to happen.

She opened the pack and breathed in the scents of fake cheese and salt. Her mouth watered. Her stomach churned with self-disgust. It had been over a year since she had last indulged in this depraved, disgusting act. This was all because of her ungrateful guests.

Last time she ate Doritos it had also been a guest's fault. He had put a one-star review on TripAdvisor about Tranquillum House and written a litany of lies. He said they had bedbugs. He posted a photo of the bites. There were no bedbugs. He made it all up because Masha told him on the last day that he was a candidate for a heart attack or a stroke unless he continued to change his lifestyle when he got back home. She knew this because she *recognized* him as the person she had once been.

Yet she offended him by using the word "fat." He *was* fat. Why the surprise? Wasn't that why he came here?

Masha put the first Dorito on her tongue and her whole body trembled with the chemical reaction it invoked. She knew exactly how many calories she was about to consume and how much exercise she was going to need to do to burn them off. (Alternatively she could vomit.)

She crunched the Dorito between her teeth and opened the jar of salsa with one hard twist of her wrist. Once, she had weak, useless arms that would have struggled to open this jar. That sad fat woman in front of the television used to swear and tap away at the lid with a spoon, trying to loosen it.

In the life before that, there had been a man for opening jars. She used to call for her husband sharply like he was a servant, and he would open the jar, smile, and touch her. He was always touching her. Every single day for years and years she was touched.

But that was someone else. It had been decades now since she was touched with love.

She thought briefly of Yao's hand tonight touching hers, and she took another Dorito from the pack and scooped out the red glistening salsa.

Yao made a tiny sound like a child. His cheeks were flushed. He looked like a feverish baby.

Masha put the back of her hand to his forehead and held it there for a moment. He did feel hot.

She shoved the Dorito in her mouth and began to eat faster and faster, yellow crumbs falling all over her desk and her dress, as she allowed herself to remember the last day of that life of so long ago.

It was a Sunday. Her ex-husband was out being a "laid-back" Australian. Australians liked to call themselves "laid-back," as if that were a good thing. He had accepted an invitation from his work colleagues to play a game where they shot each other with balls of paint. It would be "fun" and "a lot of laughs."

Yes, it sounded very laid-back: running around shooting each other. The other wives were going but Masha stayed home with the baby. She had nothing in common with those women and they dressed so badly it made her depressed and homesick. Masha was a working mother. She had work to do. She was ten times smarter than all the men at the company where she worked, but she had to work ten times harder for the recognition she deserved.

She was too tall. Sometimes her colleagues pretended not to understand her and sometimes she could tell they really didn't understand, even though she spoke better English than them. She didn't appreciate their humor—she never laughed on time—and they didn't appreciate hers. When she made a joke, often a very funny, sophisticated, intelligent joke, they stared at her with confused, blank faces.

At home she had many friends, but here she experienced a strange kind of shyness. It made her angry and resentful to feel that way, because back home she would never have been called shy. She held herself stiffly because she could not stand to be laughed at, and here there was always the possibility that she might misunderstand or be misunderstood. Her husband didn't care when that happened. He found it funny. He had fearlessly dived straight into the social scene before he knew the rules, and people loved him. Masha was proud of him for that, although also a little envious.

Once, Masha and her husband were invited to her boss's home for what Masha assumed was a dinner party. She dressed very nicely, very sexy, high heels and a dress. Every single woman but Masha wore jeans.

The invitation said "bring your own meat." Masha confidently told her husband: "No, no, that is a joke! An Australian joke. Not very funny but most definitely a joke." They would not make the embarrassing mistake of taking it seriously.

But it was not a joke. The women in jeans carried plastic shopping bags looped over their arms. The bags contained packages of uncooked meat. Just enough for two. Two steaks. Four sausages. Masha could not believe her eyes.

Her husband was quick. He slapped his hand to his forehead. "Oh no, we left our meat at home!" he told the host.

"No worries," said the host. "We've got plenty to spare."

So generous of him to spare a little meat for the guests he'd invited to his home.

The moment they walked through the front door, the women and men split into different groups as if they were banned from talking to each other. The men stood around a barbecue overcooking the meat for what seemed like hours. The food was inedible. There were no chairs. People sat anywhere. Three women sat on a *retaining wall*.

After that day, Masha decided not to concern herself with establishing a social circle in Sydney. What was the point? She had an eleven-month-old baby and a demanding full-time job and a husband. Her life was busy and satisfying and she was truly happy, happier than she'd ever been in her life. It was gratifying to have a baby so clearly superior to other babies in terms of both beauty and intelligence. This was an objective fact. Her husband agreed. Sometimes she felt sorry for other mothers when they saw her baby, sitting so dignified and upright in his stroller, his fair hair shining in the sun (so many other babies were bald, like old men), his little head swiveling from side to side as he observed the world with his big green eyes. When he found something funny, as he often did (he got that from his father), he chuckled, right from his belly, surprisingly deep, and everyone in hearing distance had to laugh too, and at that moment, as Masha exchanged smiles with those around her, real smiles, not polite smiles, she wasn't isolated at all; she was a Sydneysider, a mother out with her child.

That Sunday, she had nearly finished her work when the baby woke up. He no longer cried when he woke up. Instead he made a musical "aaaah" sound as if he was playing with his voice. He let the sound go up and down, up and down. He was as happily tone deaf as his father singing as he stirred a pot on the stove.

At one point he called out, "Ma-ma! Ma-ma!" He

was so smart. Many children of that age did not have a single word in their vocabulary.

"I'm coming, my *lapochka*!" she called back. She only needed five minutes more and she would be done.

He became quiet again. She finished what she was doing. It took less than five minutes. Maybe four.

"Did you get tired of waiting for me, little bunny?" she said as she opened the door of his bedroom. She thought he might have fallen back asleep.

He was already dead.

He'd strangled himself playing with a long white cord from the window blind. It was not an uncommon accident, she later learned. Other women had seen what she saw that day. Their trembling fingers had untangled their precious babies.

These days there were warning tags on blind cords. Masha always saw them when she walked into a room, even from very far away.

Her husband said it was an accident and there was nothing to forgive as he stood in the hospital wearing the paint-splattered overalls from his game. She remembered the fine spray of blue dots across his jaw, like blue rain.

She remembered also one strange moment when she had looked at the strangers all around her and wanted her mother, a woman who had never really liked Masha, let alone loved her, and who would provide no comfort. Yet, for just one moment in her grief, Masha had craved her presence.

She refused her husband's forgiveness. Her son called for her and she did not go to him. It was unacceptable.

She let her husband go. She insisted he find another life and he did eventually, although it took much, much longer than Masha wanted. It was such a relief when he was gone, when she no longer had to experience the pain of seeing the face that so resembled that of their beautiful son.

Although she refused to read the emails he sent and wanted to know nothing about him, she accidentally discovered many years ago, when she came across a man in a food court who was still friends with her husband—a man who was there on the day they shot the balls of paint—that her husband was healthy and happy, that he had married an Australian girl and had three sons.

Masha hoped that he still sang when he cooked. She thought that he probably did. In her research, she had read of the hedonic treadmill theory, which said that people returned to a certain pre-set level of happiness regardless of what happened to them, whether it was very good or very bad. Her husband had been a simple happy man whereas Masha was a complex unhappy woman.

Masha's son would have been twenty-eight this August. She probably would have had a difficult relationship with him if he had lived. They probably would have fought like Masha had once fought with her mother. Instead he would always be her singing, chuckling baby and a beautiful young man wearing a baseball cap walking toward her through a lake of color.

She should have been allowed to stay with him.

Masha looked at the empty bag of Doritos. Her fingertips were stained yellow the way her father's had once been stained by nicotine. She ran the heels of her hands over her mouth and turned the monitor back on to observe her guests.

They were all awake, she saw. They sat in small groups, chatting, in that laid-back Australian way. They were too relaxed. This was no dark night of the soul. It could have been a barbecue. These people did not truly believe they were facing death sentences.

Never once had a member of staff defied her the way these people were defying her.

The screen of her monitor pulsed as if it were alive. Was there some sort of malfunction? She put her finger to it and felt it quiver like a dying fish.

She was momentarily confused before she remembered she had earlier taken seventy-five milligrams of LSD to improve her decision making and mental clarity. This was simply a hallucination. She needed to relax and allow her brain to find all the right connections.

She looked around the room and noticed a vacuum cleaner sitting quietly in the corner of her office. It was not pulsating. It was quite real. She had just not noticed it before. The cleaners must have left it. They had excellent cleaners here. She only recruited and employed the best. It was important to maintain quality standards at all levels of your business.

There was something so familiar about the vacuum cleaner.

"*Oh!*" she said, for her father was picking up the vacuum cleaner, clumsily, with both hands. It was such a cumbersome thing. He walked toward the door with it.

"*No, no, no!*" she screamed. "*Papochka!* Put it down! Do not go!"

But he looked back at her sadly and smiled, and he was gone and no man would ever love her the way her father had loved her.

He was not real. She knew this. It was very easy to see what was real and what was not. Her mind was very sharp, sharp enough to differentiate.

She closed her eyes.

Her baby's voice was calling for her. *No. Not real.*

She opened her eyes and he was crawling across her office floor, babbling nonsense to himself.

She closed her eyes quickly. *No. Not real.*

She opened her eyes. A cigarette would calm her.

She opened her secret cupboard once more and removed an unopened packet of cigarettes and a lighter. The geometry of the pack enthralled her. Each of its four mathematically aligned angles was so pleasing.

She opened the pack, removed a cigarette, and rolled its cylindrical shape back and forth between her fingertips. The lighter was orange, a color of such depth and beauty it astonished her.

She ran her thumb across the tiny rough-edged wheel of the lighter. A gold flame burst forth, instantly and obediently.

She let it go and did it again.

The lighter was a miniature factory producing perfect flames on demand. There was such beauty in the efficient production of goods and services.

A thought of crystalline clarity: Masha should forget the wellness industry completely and return to the corporate world. Forget pivoting. She should *jump*. It would simply be a matter of reactivating her LinkedIn account and within a very short time she would be head-hunted, fielding offers.

The boy in the baseball cap sat on the other side of her desk, dripping puddles of iridescent color all over her floor.

"What do you think?" she asked him. "Should I do that?"

He didn't speak, but she could tell he thought it was a good idea.

No more entitled, ungrateful *guests*. She would once again conduct multiple departments of a company like an orchestra: accounting, payroll, sales, and marketing—it was all coming back to her, the glorious unassailable solidity of a documented reporting structure with her name at the top. She would micro-dose daily to optimize her productivity. Ideally her staff would do the same, although the people in HR would have all sorts of objections.

She had begun a new life when she emigrated, when her son died, and again when her heart stopped. She could do it again.

Sell this property and buy an apartment in the city.

Or . . .

She studied the tiny flickering flame. The answer was right there.

66

Ben

"So, Napoleon, I've got you," said Ben, walking next to the older man as he strode up and down the length of the cellar. "I mean, I'm defending you."

He felt like he should call him Mr. Marconi or sir. He had that teacher-ish manner. The sort of teacher you still wanted to impress even after you'd left school and bumped into him at the shops looking startlingly short. Not that he could imagine Napoleon ever looking short.

"Thank you, Ben," said Napoleon, as if Ben had been given a choice.

"So, okay," said Ben. He rubbed his stomach. He had never been so hungry in his life. "I guess it's pretty simple why you deserve a stay of execution. You're a husband and a father, and, well, I hope it's okay to include this in my speech—but your wife and daughter have already lost enough, haven't they? They couldn't lose you too."

"You can say that if you like." Napoleon smiled sadly. "That's true."

"And you're a teacher," said Ben. "So kids depend on you."

"They do. Yep." Napoleon rapped his knuckles on the brickwork. Ben had seen him do this a hundred times since they'd been down here, as if he were hoping that he'd find a loose brick that would give them a way out. Ben knew it was hopeless. There was no way out of here except that door.

"Anything else I should say?" asked Ben, and his voice cracked. When he had had to deliver the toast at Pete's wedding he thought he might pass out. And now it was his job to defend this man's *life*?

Napoleon turned away from the wall and looked at Ben. "Mate, I don't think it matters what you say. I wouldn't take it too seriously." He clapped him on the shoulder. "I think we need to take *Masha* seriously, but not the game itself."

"You've got yourself a dud defense lawyer here," confessed Ben. "I got lucky. Lars is defending me and he's *appeared* in court."

When Lars had his "meeting" with Ben, he only asked two or three quick questions before he said, "How about this?" And then he launched into an eloquent speech, like something on *television*, all about how Ben was a morally upstanding young man standing on the very cusp of adulthood, about to become a father, deeply committed to his marriage, with so much to give to his wife, his family, his *community*, and so on and so forth. It all just flowed out, without a single "um" or "ah."

"Think that will do the trick?" he asked at the end.

"Sure," marveled Ben.

And then Lars had gone off to the bathroom to fix his hair in preparation for his "appearance."

"I get so terrified of public speaking, I can't even breathe," Ben told Napoleon.

"Do you know the only difference between fear and excitement is the exhalation?" asked Napoleon. "When you're afraid, you hold the air in the top part of the lungs. You need to exhale. Like this. *Ahhhhh.*" He put his hand to his chest and demonstrated with a long slow breath out. "Like that sound people make after a firework explodes. *Ahhhhh.*"

Ben did it with him. "*Ahhhhh.*"

"That's it," said Napoleon. "Tell you what—I'll go first. I'm defending Tony, so I'll bore Masha to death speaking about his football career. I plan to do a rundown of every game he played. That'll show her." He stopped at the beam near the inscribed brick in the wall. "You saw this?"

"The convict graffiti?" Delilah had shown it to them on their first tour of the house. Ben and Jessica hadn't really been that interested.

Napoleon grinned. "Fascinating, eh? I read up on the history of this place before we came. These brothers eventually got their tickets of leave and ended up becoming very respectable, highly sought-after stonemasons. Far more successful than they would have been back home in England. They've got thousands of descendants in this area. When they were sentenced to be transported to Australia I bet they were devastated. They probably felt like it was the end of the world. But it turned out to be the making of them. The lowest point of your life can lead to the highest. I just find that so . . ." For a moment he looked profoundly sad. "Interesting."

Ben didn't know why he suddenly felt in danger of crying. It must be hunger. It occurred to him that when he got home he owed his dad a visit. Just because his dad had given up on Lucy didn't mean Ben should give up on him.

Ben put his fingers to the inscription. He thought about how everyone said it was such fantastic luck that he and Jessica won the lottery, but sometimes it didn't feel that way.

He looked over at Jessica. Was he really going to be a dad himself? How could he advise a kid on how to live his life when he hadn't yet worked it out himself?

"Remember the exhale, mate," said Napoleon. "Just breathe out the fear."

67

Heather

"I'm quite a good friend," said Frances to Heather. "You could mention that." She chewed a fingernail. "I remember birthdays."

"I'm hopeless at birthdays," said Heather. In reality she was hopeless at friends, and after Zach died she could see no point to them at all. Friends were an indulgence.

Frances winced. "I did totally forget a good friend's birthday this year, but that was because I was caught up in this internet scam and I was so distracted that day, and then it got to midnight, and I thought, Oh my God, *Monica*! but it was too late to text, so—"

"What about your family?" Heather interrupted, before she heard this Monica's life story. She found Frances to be quite flaky. "Do you have family?"

Heather looked over Frances's shoulder at her own family. Zoe was sitting with Jessica, their heads bowed close, as if they were two friends sharing secrets. Napoleon and Ben walked as they talked, Ben listening intently and nodding respectfully like he was one of Napoleon's best students. She didn't know what was going on with Napoleon right now. It was like an imposter was doing an excellent job performing the role of Napoleon. He was saying and doing all the right things and nearly getting away with it, but there was something just not quite right.

"Yes," said Frances. "I have family." She looked uncertain. "I guess I'm not that close to my immediate family. My father died and my mother remarried and moved overseas. The South of France. I have a sister, but she has a lot on her plate. Their day-to-day lives wouldn't be impacted that much if I was gone."

"Of course their lives would be impacted," said Heather.

"Well . . ." Frances gave the blank screen a nervous look. "I'm not saying they'd dance on my grave."

Heather looked at her, surprised. The woman looked genuinely frightened. "You do know you're not really on death row, don't you? This is just a stupid power game for that maniac."

"Shhh," hissed Frances. "She could be listening."

"I don't care," said Heather recklessly. "I'm not scared of her."

"I kind of think you *should* be." Frances shot another uneasy look at the screen.

"It's fine, I'm going to play along," said Heather, to comfort the poor woman. "I don't think you should be executed."

"Thanks so much," said Frances.

"So what else should I say?"

"Appeal to her ego," said Frances. "Start out by saying that it's true that Frances's life didn't mean all that much until this point, but now she has done this retreat, she has been rehabilitated."

"Rehabilitated," said Heather.

"That's right." Frances was as jittery as a junkie. "Make sure you use the word 'rehabilitated.' I think she'll like that. Make it clear that I've seen the error of my self-indulgent ways. I'm going to exercise. Eat clean. No more preservatives. I'm going to *set goals*."

"*Good morning, my sweetie pies!*"

Masha's voice boomed through the room as her image flickered to life once more on the screen.

Frances gasped and swore, clutching Heather's arm.

"It is time!" cried Masha. She took a long deep drag of a cigarette and blew the smoke out the side of her mouth. "It is time to play Death Sentence. Wait. We're not calling it that, are we? It is time to play Death Row. A much better name! Who thought of that name?"

"But it's not time yet!" Napoleon looked at his watch.

Heather stared at the screen. Masha was *smoking*. She didn't know why she was so surprised after everything else that had happened, but it was shocking and distressing, like seeing a nun lifting her habit to reveal suspenders.

"You're smoking!" accused Jessica.

Masha laughed and took another deep drag. "I am smoking, Jessica. Occasionally, in times of stress, I smoke."

"You're high," said Ben tiredly, sadly, and Heather

could hear in his voice the years of resigned disappointment suffered by an addict's relative. Ben was right. Masha's eyes were glassy, and her posture was strange and stiff, as if her head wasn't attached to her body and she was worried it would roll off.

Masha held up an empty smoothie glass. "I have taken steps to reach a higher level of consciousness."

"Is Yao okay?" asked Heather. She tried to keep her tone respectful, even though her throat burned with hatred. "Could we please see Yao?"

The screen of the camera seemed to be angled differently from the previous time. Masha stood in front of a window in what looked like her office, although it was dark outside, so it was impossible to tell for sure.

"He is not your concern right now," said Masha. "It is time for you to present your cases for your clients. Will they live? Will they die? This is such a stimulating and thought-provoking exercise, I think."

"It's only three A.M., Masha!" Napoleon tapped the face of his watch. "It's not dawn. You said we'd do this at dawn."

Masha lunged at the screen and pointed her cigarette at him. "Guests should not wear watches during retreats!"

Napoleon reeled back. He held up his wrist. "I've been wearing it the whole time. Nobody said I couldn't wear a watch."

"The watch should have been handed in with the other devices! Who was your wellness consultant?"

"It's my fault, Masha. I take responsibility for this." He unbuckled his watch.

"It was Yao, wasn't it?" screamed Masha. She looked demonic. Her scream reverberated through the room. Flecks of her saliva dotted the screen.

"Jesus Christ," said Tony quietly.

Zoe came to stand next to Heather and took her hand, something she hadn't done since she was a very little girl. It felt like no one breathed.

Heather squeezed Zoe's hand and, for the first time since they'd been trapped down here, she experienced true dread.

She thought of those times throughout her working life when the atmosphere in a labor ward went from focused to hyper-focused, because a mother's or a baby's life hung in the balance and every member of staff in that room knew the next decision made had to be the right one. Except in this case she had no training or experience to fall back upon. She longed to *act*, but she was impotent, and the overwhelming powerlessness reminded her of that nightmarish moment when she found Zach, her fingers looking for a pulse she already knew she wouldn't find.

"I am *very* disappointed in Yao!" raged Masha. "That was an unacceptable mistake! I shall make sure HR knows! A note will go in his file. He will receive a formal letter of warning."

Napoleon held up his watch by the strap and showed it to Masha. "I'm taking it off."

Zoe squeezed Heather's hand convulsively.

"I'm sorry. It was my fault," said Napoleon in the slow careful tone of someone placating a crazed gunman.

"I'm going to destroy it." He dropped the watch to the ground and went to put his foot over it.

Masha switched tone. "Oh, stop being so dramatic, Napoleon, you could cut your foot!" She waved her cigarette about gaily, as if she were in animated conversation at a party, a glass of wine in the other hand.

Heather heard Zoe take a shaky breath and the thought of her daughter's fear made her want to hurt this madwoman.

"I am not the sort to become too obsessive about bureaucratic rules. I am flexible! I am big picture!" Masha took a long drag of her cigarette. "On the Myers-Briggs personality test I am the Commander! I think you will not be surprised to hear that."

"This is not good." Lars peered up at the screen through splayed fingertips.

"She's off with the fairies," murmured Tony.

"Nothing is forever," said Masha irrelevantly. "Remember that. It's important. Now, who will be presenting first?" She looked around as if searching for something. "Does everyone have coffee? Not yet? Don't worry. Delilah will have it all under control."

She smiled and held out her arms as if she were sitting at the head of a conference table.

Heather shuddered with a sudden sense of overwhelming fear. *She's hallucinating.*

At that moment Masha's attention was caught by the cigarette between her fingers. Minutes passed and she continued to stare at the cigarette.

"What's she *doing*?" whispered Carmel.

"It's the LSD," said Lars in a low voice. "She can't believe she's never noticed the innate beauty of the cigarette."

Finally, Masha looked up. "Who is presenting first?" she asked again calmly. She flicked the ash from her cigarette onto a windowsill.

"I will," said Tony.

"Tony! Excellent," said Masha. "Who are you defending?"

"Carmel," said Tony. He gestured at Carmel, who made a strange, awkward movement as if she couldn't decide whether to curtsey or hide behind Lars.

"Go ahead, Tony."

Tony cleared his throat. He stood with his hands clasped and looked respectfully up at the screen. "I'm representing Carmel Schneider today. Carmel is thirty-nine years old, divorced, with four young daughters. She is their primary caregiver. She is also very close to her older sister, Vanessa, and her parents, Mary and Raymond."

Masha looked bored. She sniffed.

Tony's voice trembled. "Carmel's mother Mary is not in good health and Carmel normally takes her to her doctors' appointments. Carmel says that she's just an ordinary person, doing the best she can, but I think anyone bringing up four little girls on her own is pretty special." He pulled nervously at the collar of his T-shirt as if he were adjusting a tie. "Carmel also volunteers at her local library teaching English to refugees. She does this once a week. She's been doing this since she was eighteen, which I think is very impressive." He clasped his hands in front of him. "Thank you."

Masha yawned theatrically. "Is that it?"

Tony lost his temper. "For Christ's sake, she's a young mother! What else do you want to hear? Obviously she doesn't deserve to die."

"But where is your USP?" said Masha.

"USP?" asked Tony blankly.

"You've forgotten the basics, Tony! What is your unique selling proposition? What makes Carmel unique and special?"

"Well," said Tony desperately, "she is very special because . . ."

"I also wonder why you did not begin with a basic analysis of strengths, weaknesses, opportunities, and threats? It's not rocket science, people! And visual aids! I see no visual aids! A simple PowerPoint slideshow would have helped support your arguments."

Heather made eye contact with Napoleon: *What do we do?* She saw the confusion and fear on his face and that made her panic grow, because if Napoleon had no answers they were in trouble. She thought of those times in hospital emergency waiting rooms with Zach when they realized they were dealing with a numbskull of a triage nurse, how they would exchange looks over Zach's head, and how they both knew exactly what to do and say to act as advocates for their child. But they had never dealt with this dizzying lack of logic.

"I'm sorry," said Tony humbly. "Obviously, PowerPoint would have helped support my argument. Yes."

"Sorry doesn't cut it!" snarled Masha.

"Could I go next?" A loud voice cut unexpectedly through Masha's.

Heather saw with a start that it was Carmel, her chin lifted, her eyes unflinching.

"I've prepared a *strategic analysis* on behalf of Zoe Marconi, and what we should be doing, ah, going forward, and I'd really like your buy-in on this, Masha."

Masha's face smoothed. She lifted a hand. "Go ahead, Carmel."

Carmel strode to the center of the room and straightened an imaginary suit jacket, even though she was wearing leggings and a pink singlet top emblazoned with the sequined word HAWAII. "I know you wanted me to really drill down on this, Masha, and think outside the box."

It was hard to reconcile this woman of such confidence with the Carmel who had just a few hours earlier begged so pathetically to go home. Now you could practically see her power suit. Was she an *actress*? Or was she calling on the memory of a previous profession? Whatever it was, it was impressive.

"Absolutely." Masha made a brisk chopping motion with the side of her hand. "*This* is more like it. We need to push the envelope. This is very impressive, Carmel."

It could almost be amusing if it wasn't so terrifying.

"The way I see it, we've got a real window of opportunity here to leverage Zoe's core competencies," said Carmel, "and achieve, ah . . . best-practice solutions."

"Oh well *done*," whispered Frances.

"That's right." Masha nodded. "We should always be aiming for best practice."

It was bizarre to see how well she responded to this meaningless corporate-speak, like a baby responds to the sound of its mother's voice.

"The question is this," said Masha shrewdly. "Does it align with our corporate values?"

"Exactly," said Carmel. "And once we have all our ducks in a row, we need to ask this: Is it scalable?"

"Is it?" said Masha.

"*Exactly*," said Carmel. "So what we're looking for is . . ." She faltered.

"Synergies," murmured Lars.

"Synergies!" said Carmel with relief.

"Synergies," repeated Masha dreamily, as if she were saying, "Paris in spring."

"So to sum up, we need a synergistic solution that dovetails—"

"I've heard all I need to hear," said Masha briskly. "Action that please, Carmel."

"Will do," said Carmel.

Masha stubbed out her cigarette on the windowsill behind her. She leaned back against the window. "Welcome to Tranquillum House."

Oh dear God, thought Heather. *We've lost her again.*

Masha smiled. No one smiled back. Heather saw that every face in the room was slack with exhaustion and despair, like the face of a woman who has innocently prepared a "natural birth plan," created a playlist, and who, after thirty hours of labor, is told that she must now have an emergency cesarean.

Masha said, "I promise you this: in ten days, you will not be the person you are now."

"Fuck," said Jessica. "Fuck, fuck, fuck."

"It's just the drugs," said Lars. "She doesn't know what she's saying."

"That's not the problem," said Ben. "She doesn't know what she's *doing*."

Masha lowered her head and put her fingertips to the neckline of her dress.

"We will all do push-ups now," she said. "Push-ups are the perfect functional integrated-resistance exercise. It's the only exercise that works every single muscle in your body. Twenty push-ups! Now!"

No one moved.

"Why do you ignore me?" Masha jabbed a finger at the screen. "Push-ups! Now! Or I will be forced to take action!"

What action could she possibly take? But they didn't wait to find out. They dropped to the floor like soldiers.

Heather tried to lift and lower her tired hungry body in a parallel line as Masha counted out loud, "One, two, three! Drop those hips! No Harbor Bridges!"

Was she still in her hallucinogenic state, where she seemingly believed they all worked for her? Did she plan to kill them all? Heather felt a sudden, wild panic. She'd brought her daughter to this place. Zoe's life could rest in the hands of this mad, drug-affected woman.

She looked around her. Frances did girl push-ups on her knees. Jessica cried as she, too, gave up and went from her toes to her knees. Tony, the former athlete, dripped sweat as he did perfect form push-ups at twice the speed of almost everyone else, in spite of having just popped his shoulder. Heather noted that her own darling husband kept pace.

"Eighteen, nineteen, twenty! Relax! Excellent!"

Heather collapsed onto her stomach and looked up. Masha had pressed her face so close to the screen that all they could see was a magnified image of her nose, mouth, and chin.

"I'm just wondering," said the disembodied mouth. "Can you smell it yet?"

It was Napoleon who answered in the calm, gentle voice he would use for a toddler. "Smell what, Masha?"

"The smoke."

68

Tony

The screen turned to static but Masha's voice continued to ring through the room.

"Deep transformation is possible but you must *detach from your beliefs and assumptions*!"

"I *can* smell smoke," said Zoe, her face white.

"That's right, Zoe, you can smell smoke, for this house, my house, is burning to the ground as we speak," said Masha. "Possessions mean nothing! Will you rise from the ashes? Remember, Buddha says, 'No one saves us but ourselves!'"

"Look," whispered Frances.

Wisps of black smoke drifted sinuously beneath the locked heavy oak door.

"Let us out!" Jessica screamed so loudly her voice turned hoarse. "Can you hear me, Masha? You let us out right now!"

The screen turned black.

Masha's absence was now as terrifying as her presence.

"We need to block that doorway," said Tony, but Heather and Napoleon were way ahead of him, returning from the bathroom carrying dripping-wet towels that they were rolling into tight cylinders, as if this was their job, as if they'd been expecting exactly this situation.

As they got to the door the volume of smoke increased suddenly and frighteningly, pouring into the room like water. People began to cough. Tony's chest tightened.

"Everybody get back!" shouted Napoleon as he and Heather shoved the rolled-up towels between the door and the floor, forming a tight seal.

The low level of claustrophobia Tony had been experiencing ever since they first discovered the locked door threatened to turn into full-blown panic. He felt his breathing become ragged. Oh God, he was going to lose it in front of all these people. He had no job to do. He couldn't even put the towels at the door because Heather and Napoleon were already doing it. He couldn't help. He couldn't kick down that door because it opened inward. He couldn't fight anyone. He couldn't do a damned thing.

He coughed so violently his eyes filled with tears.

Frances grabbed his hand and pulled. "Get away from the door."

He let her pull him back. She didn't let go of his hand. He didn't let go of hers.

Everyone huddled at the point in the room furthest away from the door.

Napoleon and Heather came and stood with them,

their eyes already bloodshot from smoke. Napoleon pulled Zoe close to him and she buried her face in his shirt. "The door didn't feel hot," he said. "That's a good sign."

"I think I can hear it," said Carmel. "I can hear the fire."

They all went quiet. It sounded at first like heavy settled rain, but it wasn't rain; it was the unmistakable crackle of flames.

Something heavy and huge crashed to the ground above them. A wall? There was a dramatic whoosh of air, like wind in a storm, and then the flames grew louder.

Jessica made a sound.

"Are we all going to die down here?" asked Zoe. She looked up at her father with disbelief. "Is she seriously going to let us die?"

"Certainly not," said Napoleon, with such matter-of-fact grown-up assurance Tony wanted to believe Napoleon had special knowledge, except that Tony was a grown-up too, and he knew better.

"We'll all put wet towels over our heads and faces to protect us from smoke inhalation," said Heather. "Then we'll just wait this thing out."

She sounded as calm and assured as her husband. Maybe Tony would be the same if one of his kids or grandkids were here.

He thought of his children. They would grieve for him. Yes, of course his children would grieve for him. They wouldn't be ready to lose him, even though he didn't see them that often these days. This knowledge felt like a surprise, as if he'd spent the last few years pretending his children didn't love him, when he knew they loved their dad, for Christ's sake. He knew that. Late last year, Will forgot about the time difference and rang in the middle of the night from Holland to tell him about his latest promotion at work. "Sorry," he said. "I wanted to tell you first." Thirty years old and he still wanted his dad's praise. According to Mimi, James was always posting pictures from Tony's football career online. "He shows off about you," Mimi said, rolling her eyes. "Exploits your fame to pick up girls." Then there was Mimi herself, his baby, bustling about his house, setting things right. Every time she broke up with another dickhead she turned up at his house to "give him a hand." She couldn't lose her dad right now, when she was still dating dickheads.

He wasn't ready to die. Fifty-six years wasn't long enough. His life felt suddenly incredibly rich and abundant with possibility. He wanted to repaint the house, get another dog, a puppy; it wouldn't be betraying Banjo to get a puppy. He always got another puppy in the end. He wanted to go to the beach, eat a big breakfast at the café down the road while he read the paper, listen to music—it was like he'd forgotten music existed! He wanted to travel to Holland and see his granddaughter perform in one of those stupid Irish dancing competitions.

He looked at Carmel, who he had written off as a kooky intellectual because of her glasses. He'd asked her how she came to teach English to refugees and she explained that her dad was a refugee from Romania back in the fifties and a next-door neighbor took it upon herself to teach him English. "My dad didn't have any aptitude for languages," said Carmel. "And he's very impatient when he feels insecure. It would have been a tough slog. So my sister and I both teach English as a second language now. To honor Auntie Pat."

Who the fuck did Tony honor? Who the fuck did Tony help out? He didn't even give back to the sport that had given him so much joy. Mimi had been at him for ages to coach a local team of kids. "You might even enjoy it," she said. Why had he been so against the idea? Now he couldn't think of anything more wonderful than standing on a field in the sunlight teaching kids to see the music and poetry of football.

He met the frightened eyes of the woman whose hand he still held. She was as nutty as a fruitcake, talked too much, had clearly never seen an AFL game in her life. She wrote romance books for a living. Tony hadn't read a novel since high school. They had nothing in common.

He didn't want to die.

He wanted to take her out for a drink.

69

Frances

The nine guests huddled in the farthest corner of the yoga and meditation studio, wet towels draped over their heads and shoulders, while Tranquillum House burned to the ground.

Frances listened to the sound of the hungry flames and wondered if the crash she'd just heard was that beautiful staircase. She remembered how Yao had said on that first day, "We won't sink, Frances!" and imagined ripples of fire consuming that beautiful wood.

"Our Father, who art in heaven, hallowed be thy name," murmured Jessica into her knees, over and over. "Our Father, who art in heaven, hallowed be thy name."

Frances wouldn't have picked Jessica as a believer, but maybe she wasn't, because she couldn't seem to get any further than "hallowed be thy name."

Frances, who had been brought up Anglican but lost religion sometime back in the late eighties, thought it might not be good manners to pray for deliverance right now, when she hadn't even said thank you for so long. God might have appreciated a thank you card over the years.

Thank you for that long hot sex-filled summer in Europe with Sol.

Thank you for that first year of my marriage to Henry which, to be honest, God, was one of the happiest of my life.

Thank you for a career that has given me virtually nothing but pleasure and I'm sorry for all that fuss about the review. I'm sure that reviewer is one of God's children too.

Thank you for my health, you've been quite generous in that regard, and it was rude of me to make such a fuss over a bad cold.

Thank you for friends who are more like family.

Thank you for my dad, even though you took him a little early.

Thank you for Bellinis and all champagne cocktails.

Sorry for complaining about a paper cut while others suffered atrocities. Although, to be frank, that's why I gave up believing in you—that whole paper cuts for some versus atrocities for others thing.

Carmel cried into her wet towel and jumped at the sound of yet another crash.

Frances imagined the balcony of her room hanging at an angle and then smashing to the ground in a shower of embers.

She imagined billows of black smoke illuminated by fiery light against a summer night's sky.

"The smoke in here isn't getting any worse," she said

to Carmel, to be comforting. "Napoleon and Heather did a good job with the towels."

She could still smell and taste smoke, but it was true, it wasn't getting any worse.

"We might be fine," said Frances tentatively.

"We will be fine," said Napoleon. He sat between his wife and daughter, holding their hands. "It's all going to be fine."

He spoke with such assurance and Frances wished she hadn't caught sight of his face as he readjusted the wet towel, because it was filled with despair.

It's coming for us, she thought. *It's coming for us and there is nowhere to hide.*

She remembered Masha saying, "I wonder, do you feel that you've ever been truly *tested* in your life?"

Jessica lifted her head from her knees and spoke in a muffled voice through her towel. "She never even heard all our presentations."

It was cute the way she still wanted to see logic in Masha's actions. She would have been the kid who couldn't stand it when the teacher forgot to give the quiz that had been promised.

"Do you think Yao is still alive?" asked Zoe.

70

Yao

Yao dreamed of Finn.

Finn was very keen that Yao wake up.

"Wake up," he said insistently. He banged together a pair of cymbals. He blasted a horn in Yao's ear. "Mate, you really need to wake up to yourself."

Yao returned to consciousness while Finn receded. He felt the imprint of something soft and scratchy against his cheek. He lifted his head. There was a cushion on Masha's desk. He remembered the feeling of the needle in his neck. The surprise of it, because that was not a decision he could respect.

He heard the sound of something burning. He smelled smoke.

He lifted his head, turned around, and saw her, smoking a cigarette, looking out the window.

She turned to face him and smiled. She looked sad and emotional, but resigned, like his fiancée when she broke off their engagement.

Masha said, "Hello, Yao."

Yao knew it was over, and he knew he'd never love anyone ever again quite the way he loved this strange woman.

His voice rasped in his throat. "What have you done?"

71

Frances

Still it went on. The burning. The crashing.

Frances's fear peaked and then plateaued. Her heart rate slowed. A great tiredness swept over her.

She had always wondered how she would feel if her life was in mortal danger. What would she do if her plane began to plummet toward earth? If a crazed gunman put the barrel to her head? If she was ever truly tested? Now she knew: she wouldn't believe it. She would keep thinking right until the last word that her story would never stop, because there could be no story without her. Things would keep happening to her. It was impossible to truly believe that there would be a final page.

Another crash. Carmel startled again.

"Wait a moment," said Lars sharply. "That sound— it's the *same* sound as before. It's exactly the same."

Frances looked at him. She didn't understand.

Napoleon sat up straighter. He removed the towel from his face.

Jessica said, "There's a pattern, isn't there? I *knew*

there was a pattern. Crackle, whoosh, small bang, crackle, crackle, crackle, huge scary bang."

Frances said, "I'm sorry, I don't get it."

"It's on a loop," said Tony.

"You mean it's a recording?" said Ben. "We're listening to a recording?"

Frances couldn't get her head around it. "There's no fire?" She could *see* the fire clearly in her head.

"But we saw smoke, we smelled smoke," said Heather. "Where there's smoke, there's fire."

"Maybe it's a controlled fire," said Zoe. "She wants us to think we're in danger."

"So this is her way of making us look death in the face," said Tony.

"I *knew* she wouldn't let us die," said Carmel.

Lars threw the wet cloth on the floor and went to stand in front of the screen. "Well done, Masha," he shouted. "You've successfully scared us all half to death and we'll never be the same again. Could we please go back to our rooms now?"

Nothing.

"You can't keep us in here forever, Masha," said Lars. "What's that mantra you keep repeating? Nothing lasts forever." He smiled ruefully and pushed his damp hair back from his forehead. "We feel like we've been down here forever."

Nothing lasts forever, thought Frances. Masha had made a point of saying that so many times. *Nothing lasts forever. Nothing lasts forever.*

She remembered how she'd told Masha there was no code in the doll and Masha answered, "Exactly."

Frances said now, "When was the last time someone tried the door?"

"I honestly think we've tried every possible code combination there could be," said Napoleon.

"I don't mean the code," said Frances. "I mean the door handle. When was the last time someone tried the door handle?"

72

Yao

"Did you sleep well?" asked Masha. She took a drag of her cigarette.

Yao ran a diagnostic eye over her: dilated pupils, sheen of sweat on her forehead, fidgeting.

"Did you have a smoothie?" he asked. He lifted an empty Doritos packet from Masha's desk, shook it, and watched the yellow crumbs fall. If she'd eaten *Doritos*, she had to be in an altered state. The Doritos were more shocking than the cigarette.

"I did." Masha exhaled smoke and smiled at him. "The smoothie was delicious and I have been experiencing many remarkable insights."

He'd never seen her smoke. She made smoking look beautiful. Yao had never smoked and now he wanted to try it. It looked natural and sensual, the smoke curling languidly from her fingers.

He remembered the first time he met her, ten years ago in that big office, and how she'd smelled of cigarette smoke.

Yao looked at the computer screen on her desk. A clip of a burning two-story house. An eave crashed to the ground.

"You sedated me," said Yao. He ran his tongue around his dry mouth. He felt dull-witted with shock. He couldn't quite comprehend that she had done this.

"Yes, I did," said Masha. "I had no choice."

The sky outside the window began to lighten.

"The guests?" asked Yao. "Are they still down there?"

Masha shrugged moodily. "I don't know. I am sick of them. I am sick of this industry." She took another drag of her cigarette and brightened. "I've made a decision! I'm going back to FMCG."

"FMCG?" asked Yao.

"Fast-moving consumer goods," said Masha.

"Like toothpaste?" said Yao.

"Exactly like toothpaste. Would you like to come and work with me?"

"What? *No.*" He stared at her. She was still Masha, she still had that extraordinary body, still wore that extraordinary dress, and yet he could feel her power over him slipping away as he watched her morphing back into the corporate executive she'd once been. How was that possible? He felt as betrayed as if a lover had admitted infidelity. This wasn't just a job for him, it was his life, his home, it was virtually his *religion*, and now she wanted to leave it all behind to go and sell *toothpaste*? Wasn't toothpaste part of the ordinary world they had turned their backs on?

She didn't mean it. It had to be the smoothie talking. This was not an example of a transcendental insight.

With her medical history, she should not have had the smoothie, but now she had, she should be lying down, with her headphones on, and then Yao could *guide* her psychedelic experience away from toothpaste.

But right now he had nine guests to worry about.

He looked away from her and turned off the burning house footage on the computer. He clicked onto the security program that showed the yoga and meditation studio.

There was no one there. Crumpled towels lay all over the floor of the deserted room.

"They're out," said Yao. "How did they escape?"

Masha sniffed. "They finally worked it out. The door has been unlocked for hours."

73

Carmel

All the men insisted on walking ahead of the women up the stairs from the yoga and meditation studio, ready to slay lions or wellness consultants offering smoothies. It was kind and gentlemanly and Carmel appreciated it, and felt glad not to be a man, but it seemed their chivalry was unnecessary. The house was silent and empty.

Carmel still couldn't believe there was no fire. The images in her head had been so real. She had thought she wouldn't see her children again.

"Surely it won't just *open*," Heather had said when they all stood at the door and Napoleon put his hand on the handle, insisting they all *stay back, stay back, stay back* . . .

It opened, as if it had never been locked at all, to reveal a steel rubbish bin sitting directly outside the door.

Napoleon tilted it forward and showed them the contents. There were burnt fragments of newspaper at the bottom and a pile of melted misshapen plastic water bottles on top. There were still a few glowing red embers left, but that was all that remained of the towering inferno they had all imagined.

They wandered as a group into the empty dining room and looked at the long table where they'd shared their silent meals. Gray morning light filled the room. Magpies warbled and a kookaburra laughed its liquid laugh. The dawn chorus had never sounded so lyrical. Life felt exquisitely ordinary.

"We should find a phone," said Heather. "Call the police."

"We should just leave," said Ben. "Find our cars and get the hell out of here."

Nobody did anything.

Carmel pulled out a chair and sat down, her elbows on the table. She felt the same shocked sense of ecstatic relief as she had just after giving birth. All that shouting of instructions. All that fear. All that fuss. Over and out.

"Do you think anyone is here in the house at all?"

"Wait. Someone is coming," said Lars.

Footsteps approached down the hallway.

"Good *morning*!" It was Yao. He carried a huge platter of tropical fruit. He looked tired, but otherwise in perfect health. "Please take your seats. We have a delicious breakfast prepared for you!" He placed the platter on the table.

Wow, thought Carmel. *He's going to pretend everything is normal.*

Zoe burst into tears. "We thought you were dead!"

Yao's smile wavered. "Dead? Why would you think I was dead?"

"You looked pretty out of it, mate," said Tony.

"We had to play a game called 'Death Row,'" Frances told him, from an armchair by the door. She looked just like one of Carmel's daughters telling tales about her sibling. "It was a horrible game . . ." Her voice trailed off.

Yao straightened a bunch of purple grapes that was slipping off the side of the platter. He frowned.

Carmel took up the slack. "We had to pretend to be lawyers." She remembered that exhilarating moment when she'd spouted all that meaningless jargon that was nevertheless so meaningful to Masha. It had been terrifying but also wonderful. Like an amusement park ride that had flipped her upside down and then round and round. "We had to argue for a stay of execution. I defended . . . Zoe."

As she spoke she realized how farcical it sounded. It was so obviously all just a game. Why had they taken it so seriously? If they told the police about it, they would surely just laugh.

"And then she never even let us *complete* the activity," complained Jessica.

"Yes, I was quite looking forward to my turn," said Frances.

"You were not," said Heather.

Carmel took a single grape from the fruit platter, even though she didn't feel especially hungry. She must have gone beyond hunger. She bit straight through the center of the grape. *Oh my God*, she thought, as the juice exploded in her mouth. She shuddered with gratitude. It was like all the cells of her body reacted to this tiny sustenance. She felt like she was close to some amazingly complex yet breathtakingly simple revelation about the true precious beauty of food. Food wasn't the enemy. Food gave her life.

"I know some of last night's activities might have seemed . . . unusual," said Yao. He was a little hoarse but you had to admire him. He was continuing to play his violin as the *Titanic* sank beneath the sea. "But everything that happened was designed for your personal growth."

"Cut the shit, Yao," said Lars. "You must know it's all over. We can't let anyone else go through what we went through last night."

"We have to close you down, mate," said Tony.

"That boss of yours has to go straight to a secure psychiatric ward," said Heather.

"I will not be going to any *ward*," said Masha.

Carmel's heart leaped in her chest.

Masha stood in the doorway of the dining room wearing a Hillary Clinton–style red pantsuit that looked ten years out of date and three sizes too big for her. "I'm going back to work."

"She's still flying high as a kite," said Ben.

"Masha," said Yao despairingly. "I thought you were resting."

"You all look so well!" Masha studied the group. "Much thinner. Much healthier. I'm sure you are all happy with your results!"

Heather made a derisive sound. "We're thrilled, Masha, we're just thrilled with our results. This has been so relaxing."

Masha's nostrils flared. "Don't use that sarcastic tone! You report to me. I have authority to—"

"Not this again," said Heather. "You're my boss, are you? We all work for you? We've all got to do a Power-Point presentation now or what . . . you *execute* us?" She imitated Masha's accent.

"That's not helpful, my love," said Napoleon.

"I know all about you, Heather," said Masha slowly. "I was there last night. I heard your secrets. You told me everything. You tell me I gave drugs to your daughter, I am such a terrible person to do this, even though I did it to help you and your family. Well, you tell me this: *what drugs did you allow your son to take?*"

Masha's fists were clenched. She held something tightly in her right hand. Carmel couldn't see what it was.

"What sort of a mother are you?" Masha asked Heather. There was a strange, powerful animosity between these two women that Carmel didn't understand.

"That's enough," said Napoleon.

Yao moved across the room toward Masha, as Heather responded to her comment with a peal of scornful laughter. She said, "I'm a better mother than you would ever be."

Masha roared like an animal. She leaped at Heather, a silver dagger held high, ready to plunge into her neck.

Napoleon jumped in front of his wife and Yao jumped in front of Masha at the exact moment Frances stood from her chair, grabbed the candelabra from the sideboard, and swung it wildly at Masha's head.

Masha fell instantly. She lay at Frances's feet without moving.

"Oh God," said Frances. The candelabra hung in her hand. She looked up at everyone, her face filled with horror. "Have I killed her?"

74

Frances

Afterward Frances would try to work through her decision-making process, but she never could. It was like her brain short-circuited.

She saw the two-hundred-year-old letter opener in Masha's hand.

Careful. That letter opener is as sharp as a dagger. You could murder someone with that, Frances.

She saw Masha lunge for Heather.

She felt the unexpected heaviness of the candelabra in her hand.

And next thing Masha was lying at her feet, and Frances had her hands in the air like a criminal because a large policeman was pointing a gun directly at her and saying, "Don't move, please!"

The well-mannered cop was Gus, Jan the massage therapist's boyfriend, and he was just as lovely as Frances had imagined him to be, especially once he put his gun away. Gus did not charge Frances with the murder of Masha, because Masha was not dead. After just a few terrifying moments, she sat up, a hand to the back of her head, and told Frances she was fired, effective immediately.

Jan, wearing a summer dress, was with Gus, looking flushed and excited at the events that had transpired at her workplace. Apparently, she and Gus had been chatting (in the middle of the night; from their glances, Frances deduced it was a post-coital chat) and Gus mentioned that at the end of his shift he'd pulled over a girl driving a yellow Lamborghini for speeding. It was immediately obvious to Jan from Gus's description that this girl could only be Delilah, and as it seemed unlikely that there could be two yellow Lamborghinis in the area, and it therefore looked like Delilah might have stolen a guest's car, and as Jan was already suspicious about the fact that nearly all the Tranquillum House staff had been asked to leave during the middle of a retreat (which the chef told her had never happened before), she had convinced Gus to drive straight to the house with her to check things out.

"She's probably concussed," said Yao, after examining his boss. "Or it might be that she's still tripping."

Gus said that he wouldn't be charging Frances with assault because there were multiple witnesses who all confirmed that her quick actions had most likely saved Heather's life, although Frances knew that Heather might have been Masha's target but the only ones in danger were Napoleon, who had pushed Heather aside, and Yao, who had placed himself directly in front of Masha.

Heather said, "Thank you, Frances." She put a hand

to the side of her neck and considered the potential murder weapon. "That could have been quite nasty."

Heather refused to acknowledge Masha at all, right up until when the ambulance arrived and took Masha to the local hospital. "Thank you for visiting! Please remember to rate your stay with us on TripAdvisor!" she cried out merrily, as the two blue-uniformed paramedics led her away.

More local police officers turned up, and then, once Gus and his friends discovered the large quantities of illegal drugs on the premises, a second group arrived, and these ones had harder eyes and shinier shoes, and they weren't quite as interested in the extraneous details as Gus was.

Yao was taken away in a police car to make a statement.

Before he left, he turned to them all and said simply, "I'm very sorry."

He looked sad and defeated and ashamed, like a teenage boy who has had a party get out of control while his parents are away.

Ben's Lamborghini was found in the car park of the regional airport two hours' drive away. It was supposedly not damaged, although Ben would see about that. Delilah had not yet been located.

There was a lot of tedious paperwork. Everyone had to give long separate statements to the police about the events that had transpired over the last week.

It was hard sometimes to give a logical account of what had happened. Frances could sense their skepticism.

"So you thought you were locked up?"

"We *were* locked up."

"But then you just opened the door and left?"

"Well, you see, we'd stopped trying the handle," said Frances. "I think that was the point Masha was trying to make: that sometimes the answer is right there in front of you."

"I see," said the police officer. You could tell from his face that he didn't see at all and that he knew *he* sure as hell wouldn't have got himself locked in that room. "And you thought there was a fire."

"There was smoke," said Frances, her mouth full of mango, the golden flesh as fresh and sweet as a summer morning. "And the sounds of a fire."

"Which in reality was a YouTube clip of a house burning down played over an intercom," said the cop without inflection.

"It was very convincing," said Frances unconvincingly.

"I'm sure it was," said the cop. You could see it was taking all his willpower not to roll his eyes. "You have . . ." He pointed at her face.

Frances wiped her sticky chin. "Thanks. Don't you just love summer fruit?"

"Not really a fan."

"Not a fan of *fruit*?"

Lars, the only member of the group with any legal expertise, tried to ensure everyone stayed on message.

"We were tricked. We had no idea there were drugs on the premises," he said loud enough for everyone to hear as he was led off for his interview. "We were not told what those smoothies contained."

"I had no idea there were drugs on the premises," said Frances again. "I was tricked. I was not told what those smoothies contained."

"Yeah, I know," said the policeman. He gave up trying and rolled his eyes. "None of you did." He closed his notebook. "I'll let you get back to your mango."

One of the local cops recognized Tony and drove back home to get a Carlton shirt for him to sign, and got quite teary about it.

Finally, as the long day began to draw to a close, and the drugs were removed as evidence, they were all told that they were free to leave, as long as they made themselves available for any future questioning.

"We're free to leave, but are we free to *stay*?" Frances asked Gus, the last police officer there. It was too late in the day to drive six hours back home.

Gus said he didn't see why not, as it was no longer an active crime scene. No one had died and the drugs were gone and they were technically still paying guests. He seemed to be working through the legalities in his mind, reassuring himself of his decision. Jan gave everyone a ten-minute mini massage to release tension. She said they might want to get themselves checked out at the local hospital but no one felt inclined to do so, especially as that was where Masha had been taken. Tony said his shoulder was perfectly fine.

"Is this what you meant when you said don't do anything you're not comfortable with?" Frances asked Jan when it was her turn for a massage.

Poor Jan was horrified. "I meant don't do burpees or jumping lunges!" she said as her practiced fingers performed their magic on Frances's shoulders. "Burpees are terrible for anyone with back issues and you've got to have really stable knees before you do a jumping lunge." She shook her head. "If I'd suspected anything like this I would have informed the police immediately." She looked adoringly at Gus. "I would have informed Gus."

"Does he whistle?" asked Frances, following her gaze.

Apparently he didn't whistle or whittle, but was still just about perfect.

Once Gus and Jan had left, the nine of them went into the kitchen to prepare something for their dinner. They were euphoric with freedom as they flung open cupboards, and there was a moment of awed silence as they all stood in front of the massive stainless steel refrigerator and saw the abundance of food it contained: steak, chicken, fish, vegetables, eggs.

"Today is my twenty-first birthday," announced Zoe.

They all turned to look at her.

"It's also Zach's birthday." She took a deep shaky breath. "It's *our* birthday today."

Her parents moved to stand on either side of her.

"I think we might need a little glass of wine with our dinner," said Frances.

"We need music," said Ben.

"We need a cake," said Carmel. She rolled up her sleeves. "I'm a master baker of birthday cakes."

"I can make pizza," said Tony. "If there's flour, I can make pizza dough."

"*Can* you?" said Frances.

"I can," he said, and he smiled.

Zoe retrieved the bottle of wine she'd smuggled in from her bedroom, and Frances searched the house until she found a gold mine of presumably uncollected contraband brought in by previous guests, including six bottles of wine, some of which looked quite good, from a small room behind the reception desk. Ben found their mobile phones, and they reconnected with the world, and discovered not all that much had happened in the last week: a sporting scandal that only Tony and Napoleon found scandalous, the breakup of a Kardashian marriage that only Jessica and Zoe found relevant, and a natural disaster where the only fatalities involved those who flagrantly ignored warnings, so, you know. Ben used his phone to play music and took on the responsibility of DJ, accepting requests across generations and genres.

Everyone got drunk on wine and food. Jessica grilled perfect medium-rare steaks. Tony twirled pizza dough. Frances acted as sous chef to whoever needed her. Carmel made an incredible cake and became flushed and beautiful at all the praise that was heaped upon her. A surprising number of people danced and a surprising number of people cried.

Lars could *not* dance. At all. It was delightful to watch.

"Are you doing it on *purpose*?" asked Frances.

"Why do people always ask that?" said Lars.

Tony could dance. Very well. He told them that back in the day he and some other players had done ballet classes as part of their training. "Helped build up my hamstrings," he explained as Frances and Carmel clutched each other and giggled helplessly at the thought of Tony in a tutu. He responded by executing a perfect pirouette.

Frances had never been in a relationship with a man who could pirouette or make pizza dough. That was just something interesting to note and not a reason to let Tony kiss her. She knew he wanted to kiss her. The feeling of being at a party with a man who wanted to kiss her, but had not yet done so, was exactly as good as the first time she experienced it, at the age of fifteen, at Natalie's sixteenth birthday party. It heightened everything. Just like a hallucinogenic drug.

They toasted Zoe and Zach.

"I didn't want twins," said Heather, holding up her glass of red wine. "When the doctor told me it was twins, I'm not going to lie, I said a four-letter word."

"Well, that's a great start, Mum," said Zoe.

"I'm a midwife," said Heather, ignoring her. "I knew the risks of a twin pregnancy. But it turned out the pregnancy didn't give me any trouble at all. I had a natural birth. Of course, they gave me a lot of trouble once they were out in the world!"

She looked at Napoleon. He took her hand.

"Those first few months were hard, but then, I don't know, I think we got them into a routine when they were about six months old, and I remember, after I finally got a good night's sleep, I woke up and looked at them and thought, Well, you two are pretty special.

"They always took it in turn to do things first. Zach

was born first but Zoe walked first. Zach ran first." Her words faded a little. She went to take a sip of wine and then remembered she hadn't finished her toast. "Zoe got her driver's license first, which, as you can imagine, made Zach crazy."

She stopped again. "The fights! You would not believe the fights they had! They'd be wanting to kill each other and I'd put them in separate rooms, but within five minutes they'd be back together again, playing and giggling."

Frances realized that Heather was giving the exact speech she would have given if Zach hadn't died: an ordinary proud-mum speech in a backyard, with the younger generations rolling their eyes and the older generation brushing away tears.

She held up her glass. "To Zoe and Zach: the smartest, funniest, most beautiful kids in the world. Your dad and I love you."

Everyone held up their glasses and said after her, "To Zoe and Zach."

Napoleon and Zoe didn't do a toast.

Instead, Napoleon lit the candles on Carmel's cake, and they all sang "Happy Birthday" and Zoe blew out the candles and no one said, "Make a wish," because every single person in that room was wishing the same thing. Frances could see him so clearly, the boy who should have been there, sitting shoulder to shoulder with Zoe, jostling with her to blow out the candles, their lives ahead of them.

After plates were handed around with the (excellent) cake, Zoe demanded that Ben play a song that Frances didn't recognize, and Ben played it, and he and Jessica and Zoe danced together.

There were promises to keep in touch. People friended and followed each other. Jessica set up a Whats-App group on their phones and joined them all.

Carmel was the first one to succumb to exhaustion and say, "Goodnight." Everyone was leaving for home the next morning. Those who were from interstate had changed their flights and transfers to the next day. Carmel was from Adelaide, and the Marconi family and Tony were from Melbourne. Tony was the only interstate guest who had hired a rental car, and he was going to drive Ben and Jessica to pick up their car from where it had been abandoned by Delilah. Lars and Frances, the only guests from Sydney, had declared their intentions to sleep late and have a lazy breakfast before heading off.

Frances somehow already knew that everything was going to feel different in the morning.

They would all feel the tug of their old lives. She'd been on group package holidays and cruises before. She knew the process. The farther away they got from Tranquillum House, the more they would think, "Wait, what was that all about? I have nothing in common with those people!" It would all begin to feel like a dream. "Did I really do a Hawaiian dance by the pool?" "Did I really attempt to do a charade of the Kama Sutra just so my team would win?" "Did I really take illegal drugs and get locked up with strangers?"

At last there was just Frances and Tony, alone at the long table, drinking a final glass of wine.

Tony held up the bottle. "Refill?"

Frances looked at her glass, considered. "No, thank you."

He went to refill his own glass, changed his mind, and put the bottle back down.

"I must be transformed," said Frances. "Normally I'd say yes."

"Me too," said Tony.

He got that decisive, focused, *I'm going in* look men got on their faces when they'd decided it was time to kiss you.

Frances thought of that first kiss at Natalie's sixteenth birthday party, how incredible and glorious it was, and how that was the boy who ended up telling her that he preferred smaller breasts. She thought of Gillian telling her to stop acting like the heroine of one of her own novels. Tony lived in Melbourne and was no doubt very settled in his life there. She thought of how often she'd moved for a man, how she'd been prepared to pack up her life and move to America for a man who didn't even exist.

She thought of Masha asking, "Do you want to be a different person when you leave here?"

She said to Tony, "Normally I'd say yes."

75

One week later

"So, I'm not pregnant," said Jessica. "Never was pregnant. It was all in my head."

Ben looked up from the couch. He picked up the remote and turned off *Top Gear*.

"Okay," he said.

She came and sat down next to him and put her hand on his knee and for a moment they sat in silence and didn't say a word, but somehow they both knew what it meant.

If she'd been pregnant, they would have stayed together. There was enough love left to stay together for a baby.

But she wasn't pregnant, and there wasn't enough love left to try again, or for anything else, except an inevitable, amicable divorce.

Two weeks later

The house smelled of gingerbread and caramel and butter. Carmel had cooked all her daughters' favorite foods for their homecoming.

She heard the sound of the car pulling into the driveway and went to the door.

The car doors flew open and out tumbled her four little girls. They knocked her to her knees with their embraces. She buried her nose in their hair, the crooks of their arms. They burrowed into her, and instantly began to fight over her like she was a favorite stuffed toy.

Lizzie got elbowed in the eye by one of her sisters and wailed. Lulu screamed at Allie, "Let me have a turn hugging Mummy! You're taking *all* of her!" Sadie grabbed at Carmel's hair and tugged, bringing tears of pain to her eyes.

"Let your mother stand up!" snapped Joel. He never did well on long-haul flights. "For Christ's sake."

Carmel managed to stagger to her feet.

Lulu said fiercely, "I am never ever leaving you again, Mummy."

Joel snapped, "Lulu! Don't be so ungrateful. You just had the holiday of a lifetime."

"No need to get cross with her," said Sonia. "We're all tired."

Watching her ex-husband's new girlfriend criticize him reminded Carmel of the euphoria she'd experienced after drinking that drug-laced smoothie.

"Go inside, girls," said Carmel. "There are treats."

The girls ran.

"You look *great*," said Sonia, who looked gray-faced and jet-lagged.

"Thanks," said Carmel. "I've had a really nice break."

"Have you lost *weight*?" asked Sonia.

"I don't know," said Carmel. She honestly didn't know. It no longer seemed important.

"Well, I don't know what it is, but you just look transformed, you really do," said Sonia warmly. "Your skin looks great, your hair . . . everything."

Carmel thought, *Damn it, I'm going to become your friend, aren't I?*

She realized that Joel wouldn't even notice any difference in her. You never changed your appearance for men, you changed it for other women, because they were the ones carefully tracking each other's weight and skin tone along with their own; they were the ones trapped with you on the ridiculous appearance-obsession merry-go-round that they couldn't or wouldn't get off. Even if she'd been a perfectly toned and manicured gym junkie, Joel would still have left her. His "lack of attraction" had nothing to do with her. He hadn't left her for something better, but for something new.

Joel said, "We got seated right near the toilets on the flight home. Bang, bang, bang, went the door all night. I never slept at all."

"Unacceptable," said Carmel.

"I know," said Joel. "I tried to get us upgraded on points but no luck."

Carmel registered the upward lift of Sonia's eyes. Yes, definitely friends.

"So, I've been thinking it might be good if you could help with some of the chauffeuring around to after-school activities this year," said Carmel to Joel. "I wore myself out trying to do everything on my own last year and I want to keep up this new exercise routine I've got going."

"Of course," said Sonia. "We're co-parents!"

"My mouth feels disgusting," muttered Joel. "I think it's the dehydration."

"Send me their schedules," said Sonia. "We'll get it all worked out. Or, if you want, we could have a coffee together, talk it through?" She looked nervous, as if she'd overstepped.

"That sounds good," said Carmel.

"I set my own hours, so I can be really flexible," said Sonia. The enthusiasm bubbled up in her voice. "I'd *love* to help out with their ballet, any time. I always dreamed of having a little girl and doing her hair for ballet and, well, as you know, I can't have children of my own, so I'm never—"

"You can't have children?" interrupted Carmel.

"I'm sorry, I thought you knew that," said Sonia, with a sideways glance at Joel, who was busy running his finger around the inside of his mouth.

"I didn't know that," said Carmel. "I'm sorry."

"Oh, it's fine, I've fully accepted it," said Sonia, with a second glance at Joel that told Carmel it was *not* fine for Sonia, but it was just great for Joel. "But that's why I'd love to help with ballet. Unless you want to keep that for yourself, of course."

"You're very welcome to ballet," said Carmel, who

was *not* a ballet mum and could never manage those sleek ballet buns to the satisfaction of her daughters or their teacher, Miss Amber.

"Really?" Sonia clasped her hands as if she'd been given the most precious gift, and the joyous gratitude in her eyes made Carmel want to cry with gratitude too. The girls weren't going to have to be confused by the arrival of a half sibling and Carmel was going to get out of all things ballet. Miss Amber would love Sonia. Sonia would *volunteer* to help out doing hair and makeup at the recitals. Carmel was permanently off the hook.

Later today Carmel would tell Lulu to never *ever* correct anyone who said how much she looked like her mummy when she was out with Sonia.

"I'll research the best calendar-sharing apps." Sonia took out her phone from her handbag and tapped herself a note.

Carmel experienced another burst of euphoria. She might have lost a husband, but she'd got herself a *wife*. An efficient, energetic young wife. What a bargain. What an upgrade.

She'd be there for poor Sonia when, in ten years or so, Joel decided he was due for *his* next upgrade.

"Can we talk about ballet another time?" said Joel. "Because right now, I really need to get home for a shower." He made a movement toward his car.

"We need to say goodbye to the girls!" said Sonia.

"Of course," sighed Joel. It seemed like it had been a long holiday.

"Was it paleo?" Sonia whispered to Carmel, as they headed inside the house. "Five: two? Eighteen: six?"

"Health resort," said Carmel. "Very trippy place. It changed my life."

Three weeks later

"You're panting," said Jo to Frances.

"I've been doing push-ups," said Frances, facedown on her living room floor, the phone to her ear. "Push-ups work every muscle in your body."

"You have not been doing push-ups," scoffed Jo. "Oh my God, I haven't interrupted you *in flagrante delicto*?"

Only Frances's former editor could both pronounce and *spell* "in flagrante delicto."

"I guess I should be flattered that you think I'm more likely to be having sex at eleven in the morning than doing push-ups." Frances sat up into a cross-legged position.

She'd lost three kilos at Tranquillum House and put them straight back on once she was home, but she was trying to incorporate a little more exercise, a little less chocolate, a little more mindful breathing, and a little less wine into her lifestyle. She was feeling pretty good. The whites of her eyes were most definitely whiter, according to her friend Ellen, who had been shocked to hear about Frances's experiences.

"When I said their approach was unconventional, I meant the personalized meals!" she cried. "I didn't mean LSD!" She thought about it, and then said wistfully, "I would have loved to try LSD."

"How's retirement?" Frances asked Jo.

"I'm going back to work," said Jo. "Work is easier. Everyone thinks I have nothing to do all day. My siblings think I should take full responsibility for our elderly parents. My children think I should take care of their children. I love my grandchildren, but day care was invented for a reason."

"I knew you were too young to retire," said Frances as she tried to touch her nose to her knee. Stretching was so important.

"I'm starting my own imprint," said Jo.

"*Are* you?" said Frances. She sat up straight. A tiny burst of hope. "Congratulations."

"Naturally I've read the new novel, and naturally I love it," said Jo. "Before I think about making an offer, I just wondered how you'd feel about incorporating a little bloodshed? Potentially even a murder. Just the one."

"Murder!" said Frances. "I don't know if I've got it in me."

"Oh, Frances," said Jo. "You've got plenty of murderous impulses lurking away in that romantic old heart of yours."

"Have I?" said Frances. She narrowed her eyes. Maybe she did.

Four weeks later

Lars didn't know he was going to say it until he said it.

Since he'd been back home the dirty-faced little dark-haired boy with Ray's hazel eyes kept materializing just as he drifted off to sleep, and suddenly, irritatingly, he'd be wide awake with the exact same thought in his head, like a brand-new revelation every time: the kid didn't want to show him something terrible from his past. *He wanted to show him something wonderful in his future.*

What a load of nonsense, he kept telling himself. I'm not a different person. That was just drugs. I've taken drugs before. That was a hallucination, not a goddamn epiphany.

But now Ray stood at the pantry putting away groceries, all those protein shakes, and Lars heard the words coming out of his mouth: "I've been thinking about the baby idea."

He saw Ray's hand stop. A can of tinned tomatoes poised midair. He didn't say a word. He didn't move or turn around.

"Maybe we could give it a shot," Lars said. "*Maybe.*" He felt sick. If Ray turned around right now, if he threw his arms around him, if he looked at him with all that love and happiness and need in his eyes, Lars would vomit, he would definitely vomit.

But Ray knew him too well.

He didn't turn around. He slowly put the can of tomatoes down. "Okay," he said, as if it was neither here nor there to him.

"We'll talk about it later," said Lars, with a firm knuckle rap on the granite countertop, which kind of hurt.

"Yep," said Ray.

A little while later, when Lars came back into the house to retrieve his sunglasses after saying he was going out to the shops, he heard the unmistakable sound of a six-foot man jumping up and down on the spot while *shrieking* into the phone to someone who was presumably his sister: "Oh my *God,* oh my *God*, you're never going to believe what just happened!"

Lars stopped for a moment, his sunglasses in his hand, and smiled, before he headed back outside into the sunshine.

Five weeks later

There was a documentary about the history of Australian Rules football on TV. Frances watched the whole thing. It was actually fascinating.

She called Tony. "I just watched a whole hour of television about your sport!"

"Frances?" He sounded like he was puffing.

"I've just been doing push-ups," he said.

"I can do ten in a row now," said Frances. "How many can you do?"

"A hundred," said Tony.

"Show-off," said Frances.

Six weeks later

Napoleon sat in the waiting room of a psychiatrist he'd been referred to by his GP. It had taken him six weeks to get the first available appointment. *That's the mental-health crisis problem right there*, he thought.

Since returning from Tranquillum House, he'd been surviving: teaching, cooking, talking to his wife and daughter, running his support group. It was amazing to him that everyone treated him as if he were just the same. It reminded him of the blocked-ears feeling after a flight, except all his senses, not just his hearing, felt muted. His voice seemed to echo in his ears. The sky was leached of color. He did nothing that he wasn't obliged to do because the effort of existence exhausted him. He slept whenever he could. Getting up each morning was like moving his limbs through thick mud.

"Everything okay?" Heather sometimes said to him.

"All good," said Napoleon.

Heather was different after their time at Tranquillum House. Not happier exactly, but calmer. She had joined a tai chi class in the park down the road. She was the only one under the age of seventy. Heather had never been the sort of woman to have girlfriends, but for some reason she fit right in to this elderly circle.

"They make me laugh," she said. "And they don't demand anything from me."

"What are you talking about?" said Zoe. "They demand lots of you!" It was true that Heather seemed to be spending a lot of time driving her elderly new friends to and from doctors' appointments and picking up prescriptions for them.

Zoe had a new part-time job. She seemed busy and distracted with her university course. Napoleon kept a careful eye on her, but she was good, she was fine. One morning, a week or so after they'd got back from the retreat, he stopped by her bathroom door and overheard a beautiful sound he hadn't heard in three years: his daughter singing off-key in the shower.

"Mr. Marconi?" said a short blond woman who reminded him a little of Frances Welty. "I'm Allison."

She ushered him into her office and motioned to a chair on the opposite side of a coffee table with a book about English gardens and a box of aloe vera–scented tissues.

Napoleon didn't wait for the niceties. He had no time to lose.

He told her about Zach. He told her about the drugs he was given at Tranquillum House and how, ever since then, he'd been struggling with what he believed to be depression. He told her that his GP had offered him antidepressants, and he probably did need antidepressants, but he knew sometimes it was hard to get the dosage right, it wasn't an exact science, he understood and appreciated this, he had done the research, he knew all the brand names, all the side effects, he'd put together his own spreadsheet if she was interested in taking a look, and he knew that sometimes, during that initial period, patients didn't get better, they got worse, they suffered suicidal thoughts, and he knew this because he knew people who had lost family members in that way, and he also knew that he overreacted to drugs, he knew this about himself, and maybe his son had had the same sensitivity, he didn't know, and he was sure that those people at that health resort meant well, and maybe this depression was going to happen anyway, but he felt that he was possibly the one person in that room who should never, ever have been given that smoothie.

And then, limp with exhaustion, he said, "Allison, I am terrified that I will . . ."

She didn't ask him to finish the sentence.

She reached across the coffee table and put her hand on his arm. "We're a team now, Napoleon. You and me, we're a team, and we're going to work out a strategy and we are going to beat this, okay?"

She looked at him with all the passion and intensity of his old football coach. "We're going to beat it. We're going to win."

Two months later

Frances and Tony were taking a walk, nine hundred kilometers apart, in different states.

They'd got into the habit of keeping each other company as they went for walks around their respective neighborhoods.

At first they'd walked with their mobile phones pressed to their ears, but then Tony's daughter, Mimi, had said they should use headphones, and now their ears no longer ached when they finished and they could walk for even longer.

"Are you on your steep bit yet?" asked Tony.

"I am," said Frances. "But listen to my breathing! I'm not puffing at all."

"You're an elite athlete," said Tony. "Have you murdered anyone yet?"

"Yep," said Frances. "Did it yesterday. Murdered my first character ever. He totally deserved it."

"Did you enjoy it? Hello, Bear."

Bear was a chocolate Labrador that Tony often passed

on his walks. Tony didn't know Bear's owner's name, but he always said hello to Bear.

Tony told her about his upcoming trip to Holland to see his son and grandchildren.

"I've never been to Holland," said Frances.

"Haven't you?" said Tony. "I've only been once. I'm hoping it's not going to be as cold as last time I went."

"I've never been to Holland," said Frances again.

There was a long pause. Frances stopped on the side of the street and smiled at a lady wearing a straw hat, watering her garden.

Tony said, "Would you like to come to Holland with me, Frances?"

"Yes," said Frances. "Yes, I would."

Their first kiss was in the Qantas lounge.

Three months later

Heather sat on the end of her bed and rubbed lotion into her dry legs, as Napoleon set the alarm on his phone for the next day.

He'd been seeing a psychiatrist, and he seemed to be doing well, but he didn't talk much about what went on in those sessions.

She watched as he put the phone on the bedside table.

"I think that you need to shout at me," she said.

"What?" He looked up at her, startled. "No, I don't."

"After the retreat, we've never properly talked about it again—the asthma medication."

"I wrote all those letters. It's on the record." Of course, Napoleon had done the right thing. He'd found the right contacts through Dr. Chang. He'd documented it all. There was never any intent to sue but he needed to make sure that what happened was on the public record. He'd written to the authorities, to the pharmaceutical company: *My son, Zachary Marconi, took his own life after being prescribed* . . .

"I know," said Heather. "But you never said anything about . . . what I did."

"You are not to blame for Zach's suicide," said Napoleon.

"I don't want you to *blame* me," said Heather. "But I just feel like you're allowed to be angry with me. You're allowed to be angry with Zoe, too, but you're not going to shout at Zoe—"

"*No*, I do not want to shout at Zoe." He looked horrified at the thought.

"But you can shout at me. If you like?" She looked up at him, where he stood by the side of the bed, his brow furrowed in pain as if he'd just that instant stubbed his toe.

"Absolutely not," he said, in his pompous schoolteacher voice. "That's ridiculous. That achieves nothing. You lost your son."

"Maybe I need you to be angry with me."

"You do not," said Napoleon. "That's . . . sick." He turned away from her. "Stop this."

"Please." She got up on her knees on the bed so she could look him in the eyes. "Napoleon?" she said.

She thought about the home she grew up in, where

nobody ever yelled or laughed or cried or screamed or expressed a single feeling, except for a mild desire for a cup of tea.

"Please?"

"Stop this nonsense," he said through clenched teeth. "Stop it."

"Shout at me."

"No," he said. "I will not. What next? Should I hit you too?"

"You'd never hit me in a million years. But I'm your wife, Napoleon, you're allowed to be angry with me."

It was like she saw the anger shoot through him, from his feet to the top of his head. It flooded his face. It made his whole body tremble.

"You should have checked on the fucking side effects, Heather! Is that what you want to hear?" His voice rose on an ascending scale until he was shouting as loud as she'd ever heard him shout, louder even than when Zach, at nine years old, old enough to know better, nearly ran in front of a car to chase a ball, a ball he'd been told to leave behind, and Napoleon shouted "*STOP!*" so loudly that every single person in that car park stopped.

Heather's heart raced as Napoleon held his hands on either side of her shoulders and shook them violently, as if he were shaking her hard enough to make her teeth rattle, except he didn't touch her.

"Does that make you happy? Is that what you wanted to hear? Yes, I am angry because when I asked you about side effects for a medication you were giving my child *you should have checked*!"

"I should have checked," she said quietly.

He grabbed his phone from the bedside table. "And I shouldn't have pressed snooze on this fucking piece-of-shit phone!"

He threw it against the wall.

Heather saw tiny shards of glass fly.

For a long beat neither of them said anything. She watched his chest rise and fall. She watched the anger leave him.

He sank onto the bed, facing away from her, put his face into his hands, and spoke in a hoarse, heart-broken voice with only pain and regret left, so softly it was barely above a whisper, "And our daughter should have told us there was something wrong with her brother."

"She should have told us," agreed Heather, and she laid her cheek against his back and waited for both their hearts to resume their normal pace.

He said something else but she didn't catch it. "What?"

He said it again. "And that's all we'll ever know."

"Yes," said Heather.

"And it will never, ever be enough," said Napoleon.

"No," said Heather. "No, it won't be."

That night Heather slept deeply and dreamlessly for seven hours straight, something she hadn't done since Zach died, and when she woke she found her-self moving across the invisible, uncrossable expanse that had separated them for the last three years, as if it had never been there in the first place. She had made some bad decisions in her life, but saying yes to a freakishly tall, nerdy boy's polite invitation to see a "well-reviewed film called *Dances with Wolves*" was not one of them.

You're not meant to think of your children when you make love. Sexuality between married parents is for behind closed doors. And yet, that morning, as Napoleon took her so tenderly into his arms, she thought of her family of four, of both her children, of the baby boy who would never become a man, and the baby girl who was a woman now, and the powerful currents of love that would always run between them: husband and wife, father and son, mother and son, father and daughter, mother and daughter, brother and sister. So much love that came about because she said "yes" to a movie invitation.

And then she thought of nothing at all, because that nerdy boy still had the moves.

One year later

Ben and his mother had imagined it so many times that he thought they would surely be prepared when it finally happened, but they weren't.

Lucy died of an overdose during one of her good periods, which is often the way, just when everyone thought that maybe this time she was going to make it. Lucy had started an interior design course. She was driving her kids to school. She'd been to a *parent–teacher night* for her eldest son, which was unprecedented. She had her eyes on the future.

Ben's mother found her. She said she looked strangely peaceful, like a little girl having a nap, or a thirty-year-old who gave up battling the monster that just refused to let her be.

Ben thought first about ringing Jessica. They were on very good terms, although he still squirmed with embarrassment when he thought about the post she'd put on Instagram "announcing" their split, as if they were a celebrity couple who owed it to their public to let them know the true story before the media began hounding them. She wrote: *We'll always be best friends but we've decided the time has come to lovingly separate.*

Right now, Jessica was in the middle of auditioning for the next season of *The Bachelor.* She said it wasn't so much that she wanted to find love, and she doubted she would, but it would be great for her "profile" and it would guarantee her so many thousand more Instagram followers. He couldn't laugh too much because she was an "ambassador" for multiple charities and her Instagram account was filled with photos of glamorous lunches and balls and breakfasts that she and a new group of society friends were so "honored" to have organized.

Ben was back working with Pete. The guys gave him a hard time in the beginning—"You short of a buck, mate?"—but eventually they gave up and forgot he was rich. Ben still had the car, and a nice house, but he'd put a lot of his money into a foundation run by his mother to help support families of addicts.

Lars helped them split their assets without vitriol

and without going to court. That was one thing they'd gained from their retreat at Tranquillum House: meeting a great family lawyer.

Ben didn't ring Jessica to tell her about Lucy straightaway. He couldn't bear to hear the lack of surprise in her voice. Instead, he dialed Zoe's number. They'd become online friends and occasional texters since the retreat but they'd never actually talked on the phone.

"Hello, Ben," she said cheerfully. "How are you?"

"I'm calling—" He found he couldn't speak. He tried to remember to exhale.

Her tone changed. "Is it your sister?" she said. "Is it Lucy?"

She was there at the funeral. His eyes kept seeking her out.

76

Five years later

Yao wouldn't normally have turned on daytime television, but he had just returned home from a stressful time at playgroup where his two-year-old daughter had sunk her teeth into the arm of another child and then thrown back her head and laughed like a vampire. It had been both embarrassing and terrifying.

"Oh yes, you were a biter," his mother told him on the phone. "She gets it from you." She said this with some satisfaction, as if the propensity to bite was a wonderful trait to pass on to your children.

Yao put his daughter down for a nap and pointed a stern finger at her. "Never do that again."

She pointed a sterner finger back up at him. "Never do that again."

Then she lay down, plugged her thumb in her mouth, and closed her eyes. He could still see her dimple, which meant she was just pretending to be asleep, hardly able to suppress her hilarity.

He stood there for a few moments, marveling at her

dimple and the roundness of her baby cheeks, marveling as he so often did that he had been parachuted into another life, a brand-new life as a stay-at-home dad in the suburbs.

He had received a fourteen-month suspended jail sentence after pleading guilty for his role in the events at Tranquillum House. Masha had insisted to police that she must take sole responsibility for the new protocol they'd attempted to introduce and that her employees were nothing more than oblivious, obedient half-wits. She said she was the one who mixed the smoothies, which was true, but Yao had been right there with her, checking and double-checking dosages. Yao's mother said if she'd been the judge, he would have gone to prison. Both his parents had been so angry. They could not comprehend his actions. Most days, Yao could not comprehend them himself. It had all seemed so reasonable at the time. The prestigious researchers! The journal papers!

"That woman had you in a trance," his mother said.

His mother vehemently denied that the incident he'd remembered during his psychedelic therapy ever happened.

"Never," she said. "I would never leave you alone in a kitchen with something boiling on the stove. Do you think I'm stupid? Would you do that with your child? You had better not!"

She said that Yao's fear of mistakes came from no one but himself. "You were *born* like that!" she told him. "We tried so hard to make you understand that mistakes do not matter. We told you again and again that you should not try so hard to be perfect, it did not matter if you made a mistake. Sometimes we purposely made mistakes so you would see that everyone made them. Your father used to deliberately drop things, bump into walls. I said to him, 'That's a bit much.' But he seemed to enjoy it."

Yao wondered then if he'd been misinterpreting his parents his whole life. When they talked about keeping expectations low to avoid disappointment, it wasn't because they didn't believe in dreams. It was because they were trying to protect him. Also, his father was not as clumsy as he had thought.

Delilah did not face court, because no one could ever track her down. Yao thought idly of her at times and wondered where she was; if she was on some remote island, restoring a boat, like the escaped prisoner in his favorite movie, *The Shawshank Redemption*. ("That's every single man in the world's favorite movie," one of the mothers at playgroup had told him once. She knew because she'd tried internet dating.) But Yao suspected that it was more likely Delilah had disappeared into an urban environment and was working again as a PA. Sometimes he still thought of that skirt she'd worn, a thousand years ago, when she worked for Masha.

Yao was disqualified from working as a paramedic or anything in the health industry. After he left Tranquillum House and the charges were settled, he had moved into a one-bedroom apartment in a location virtually equidistant to the locations of his parents' homes, and he ended up getting a job as a translator of

Chinese legal documents. It was dull, laborious work but it paid the bills.

One day he got a call. Afterward, he wondered if a phone call that is going to change your life has a portentous ringtone, because when he heard that ring, as he sat alone, eating his sad dinner for one, he experienced the most remarkable full-body shiver of presentiment.

It was Bernadette, his ex-fiancée, calling to say hi. She'd been thinking about him. She'd been thinking about him a lot.

Sometimes your life changes so slowly and imperceptibly that you don't notice it at all until one day you wake up and think: *How did I get here?* But other times life changes in an instant, with a lightning stroke of good or bad luck, with glorious or tragic consequences. You win the lottery. You step out onto a pedestrian crossing at the wrong time. You get a phone call from a lost love at exactly the right time. And suddenly your life takes a violent swerve in an entirely new direction.

They were married within the year and his wife got pregnant immediately. It made sense for her to go back to work and Yao to stay home with the baby, while he continued doing his translation work, which now seemed interesting and stimulating.

Once he knew his daughter wasn't faking sleep anymore, he went into the living room, sank down on the couch, and turned on the TV. He would treat himself to twenty minutes of rubbish television to soothe himself from the stress of the biting incident, and then he'd get in an hour of work before it was time to think about dinner.

The remote slipped from his hand.

He whispered, "*Masha*."

"*Masha*," said a man on the other side of the same city, a wrench in his hands. He didn't normally watch daytime television either, but he had come over to do a few jobs around his daughter-in-law's house, as his son was good with numbers but not much else.

"Do you know her?" His daughter-in-law lifted the baby girl she'd been breastfeeding while she watched TV onto her shoulder and patted her back.

"She looks like someone I used to know," said the man, carefully not looking at his daughter-in-law because he did not want to see her breasts, and also because he could not tear his eyes from his ex-wife.

Masha looked so beautiful. Her hair was dark brown with bits of blond, shoulder length, and she wore a dress of all different shades of green that made her eyes look like emeralds.

The man sat on the couch next to his daughter-in-law and she glanced at him curiously but didn't say anything else. They watched the interview together.

Masha had written a book. It was about a ten-day personal-development program that incorporated psychedelic drugs, being locked in a room with strangers, and undergoing an innovative kind of therapy that involved facing fears and solving riddles.

"Surely people aren't falling for this," murmured his daughter-in-law.

"Now, obviously, these drugs you mention are illegal," said the interviewer.

"Unfortunately, yes," said Masha. "But that will not be the case forever."

"And I understand you did jail time for supplying illegal drugs while attempting to test out this program."

The man clenched the wrench he still held in his lap. *Jail time?*

"I did," said Masha. "But I will never regret that time. It was very important to me." She lifted her chin. "My time behind bars was a *transformative experience*. I learned so much, and I explain all my experiences in this book, which is available now, in all good bookstores." She picked up the book and held it in front of her face.

The interviewer cleared her throat. "Masha, what do you say about the rumors that people have been attending these courses you offer, held in different secret locations across the country, and that you are, in point of fact, offering LSD and other hallucinogenic drugs to your attendees?"

"That is absolutely untrue," said Masha. "I unequivocally deny it."

"So you are not running these programs in secret locations?"

"I am running very unique, tailored, incredibly effective personal-development programs to small, select groups of people, but there is nothing illegal going on, I can assure you of that."

"I hear there is a waiting list," said the interviewer. "And that people are paying quite hefty fees to attend."

"There is a waiting list," said Masha. "People should visit my website if they would like to go on the list, or call the toll-free number I believe is appearing on the screen right now. There is a special offer for those who call within the next twenty-four hours."

"If there is nothing illegal going on, I wonder why the locations are kept secret and change on a regular basis," said the interviewer. She looked at Masha expectantly.

"Was that a question?" asked Masha, with a seductive smile straight at the camera.

"What a *nutter*," said the man's daughter-in-law. "I bet she's making millions." She stood, and held out the baby to her father-in-law. "Will you hold her? I'll make us some tea."

The man moved the wrench off his lap and took his granddaughter. His daughter-in-law left the room.

Masha was talking about something called "Holotropic Breathwork," which she said was "psychedelic therapy without the psychedelics."

"That's where you breathe fast to get high, right?" said the interviewer, rather rudely and skeptically.

"It is a much more complex, sophisticated process than that," said Masha.

An image appeared on the screen of Masha at some kind of conference center, striding about a stage with a tiny microphone attached to her ear, while an auditorium packed with people looked on with rapt attention.

The man held the baby up and spoke in his native tongue into her ear. "That crazy woman is your grandmother."

He remembered the day their second son was born, only three months after they lost their firstborn so tragically.

"He is yours." Masha refused to look at the baby. Her averted face, her sweat-soaked hair flat against her forehead, could have been carved from marble. "Not mine."

A nurse at the hospital said, "Mum will come around." It was the grief. She was still in shock, probably. Such a terrible thing to go through, losing her son when she was six months pregnant with her second. That nurse did not know his wife's strength. She did not know Masha.

Masha discharged herself from the hospital. She said she was going straight back to work, that very day, and she would send money. She would make enough money in her job so that her husband could take care of the new baby, but she wanted nothing to do with him.

She spoke very calmly, as if this were a business arrangement, and she only lost her temper once, when the man fell to his knees and clutched her and begged her to let them be a family again. Masha screamed into his face, over and over, "I am not a mother! Can you not understand this? I am not a mother!"

So he let her go. What else could he do? She did exactly what she said she would and sent money, more and more each year, as her career became more successful.

He sent her photos. She never acknowledged them. He wondered if she even looked at them and he thought that maybe she did not. She was a woman with the strength to move mountains. She was a woman as weak as a child.

He remarried two years later. His son called his

Australian wife "Mummy" and spoke with an Australian accent, and they had two more sons and lived
an Australian life in this lucky country. They played
cricket on the beach on Christmas Day. They had a
swimming pool in their backyard and his sons caught
the bus home and on hot summer days they ran straight
through the house, tearing off their clothes, and
jumped into the pool in their undies. They had a large
circle of friends, some of whom dropped by their house
without phoning first. His second wife had grown up
in a small country town, and her accent was from "the
bush," broad and thick and slow, her favorite phrase
was "no big deal" and he loved her, but there had been
occasions over the years when he would be standing in
his backyard at the barbecue, turning steaks, a beer in
his hand, cicadas screaming, a kookaburra laughing,
the splash of water, the smell of bug spray, the early
evening sun still hot on his neck, and without warning Masha's face would appear in his mind, her nostrils
flared, her beautiful green eyes blazing with superior-
ity and contempt but also childlike confusion: *These
people! They are so strange!*

For many years he had given up communicating with
Masha. He didn't bother to send photos of their son's
wedding, but five years ago, when their first grand-
child was born and he was awash with the fierce, all-
consuming love of a new grandparent, he had emailed
again, attaching photos of the baby, with the subject
heading: PLEASE READ, MASHA. He wrote that it was
fine that she chose not to be a mother, he understood,

but now, if she wanted, she could be a grandmother and wasn't that wonderful? There was no reply.

He looked now at his granddaughter. He thought he could see something of Masha in the shape of her eyes. He held the baby with one arm and extracted his phone from his pocket with the other, and snapped a photo of her exquisite, sleeping face.

He wouldn't give up. One day Masha would answer. One day she would weaken, or find the strength, and she would answer.

He knew her better than anyone.

One day she would.

77

Reader, she didn't marry him, but he moved to Sydney for her and they lived together, and Tony was there beside her during the resurgence of her career, when Frances's first foray into "romantic suspense" turned out to be a surprise hit. (A surprise to everyone except Jo, who called her up the day after she delivered the revised manuscript and said, in a very un-grandmotherly tone, "You fucking nailed it.")

Frances was also a surprise hit with Tony's grandchildren in Holland, who called her "Grandma Frances," and Tony credited Frances with the family's decision to move back to Sydney, which was entirely unwarranted, as his son Will had gotten a transfer, nothing to do with her. But she was besotted with his grandkids—her grandkids—and all of her friends said that was just so *typical* of Frances, to skip the hard yards and go straight to the good part, where you got to love them and spoil them and hand them back.

But they forgave her.

78

Of course, not everyone gets a happy ending or even the chance of one. Life doesn't work like that. Case in point: Helen Ihnat, the reviewer of Frances's novel *What the Heart Wants*, lost her entire life savings in a mortifying, high-profile cryptocurrency scam and lived in a state of quite profound unhappiness for the rest of her days.

But as she despised neatly tied-up happy endings, she was fine with that.

79

Oh, reader, of course she married him eventually. You've met her. She waited until her sixtieth birthday. She wore turquoise. She had eleven bridesmaids, none of whom was under the age of forty-five, thirteen flower girls, and one page boy, a toddler just learning to walk, who clutched a Matchbox car in each of his tiny fists. His name was Zach.

Every chair at the reception was tied up with a giant white satin bow at the back.

It was the most beautiful, ridiculous wedding you've ever seen.

Acknowledgments

As always there are so many people to thank for their support with this book. Thank you to my talented editors who worked so hard to make *Nine Perfect Strangers* so much better in so many significant ways: Amy Einhorn, Georgia Douglas, Cate Paterson, Maxine Hitchcock, Ali Lavau, and Hilary Reynolds.

Thank you to Elina Reddy for giving so generously of her time to help me develop the character of Masha. Elina is not only a wonderful artist but has the ability to paint such vivid pictures with her words. Maria (Masha) Dmitrichenko was the winning bidder at a Starlight Children's Foundation charity event to have a character in one of my books named after her and I thank her for the use of her name.

Thank you to Dr. Nikki Stamp for answering my questions. She is one of only a handful of female heart surgeons in Australia and the dialogue I gave Masha's heart surgeon came straight from her fascinating book, *Can You Die of a Broken Heart?*

Thank you to Kat Lukash and Praveen Naidoo for help with my Russian and my football, to Lucie Johnson for sharing health-resort stories, and to my brother-in-law Rob Ostric for the expression on his face when I asked how he would feel about driving a Lamborghini down an unpaved road. Thank you to my sister Fiona for instantly answering my texts demanding information. Thank you to my charming fellow guests at the Golden Door health resort for a lovely week where I saw the sun rise, which was very pleasing, although I feel no particular need to see it do so again.

Thank you to my agents: Faye Bender in New York, Fiona Inglis and Ben Stevenson in Sydney, Jonathan Lloyd and Kate Cooper in London, and Jerry Kalajian in L.A. Thank you to my publicists for your patience and for all that you do: Marlena Bittner in New York, Tracey Cheetham in Sydney, and Gaby Young in London. Thank you also to Conor Mintzer, Nancy Trypuc, and Katie Bowden.

Thank you to Adam for helping me create Tranquillum House, for stopping to answer strange random questions at intervals throughout the day, for waking me with coffee, for looking after me, and for always being on my side. Thank you to George and Anna for being beautiful and for helpfully pointing out the swearwords whenever you saw my manuscript open on the screen. Thank you to my mother, Diane Moriarty, for help with proofreading and for being the sort of mother who would thankfully *never* move to the South of France.

Writing can be a lonely job so I want to thank some

of my "colleagues" in the business. Thank you to my sisters and fellow writers Jaclyn Moriarty and Nicola Moriarty, and thank you to my friends and fellow writers Dianne Blacklock, Ber Carroll, Jojo Moyes, and Marian Keyes. Thank you to the talented Caroline Lee for your wonderful narration of my audio books.

Thank you to Nicole Kidman, Per Saari, and Bruna Papandrea for their extraordinary faith in this book before they'd read a single word.

Thank you to my readers. Like Frances, I have the loveliest readers in the world and every day I'm grateful to you.

I've dedicated this book to my sister Kati, and to my father, Bernie Moriarty, because they have always been so strong and brave and funny in the face of adversity and because I suspect even on their bad days they could do more push-ups than Masha.

The following books were useful to me in my research: *No Time to Say Goodbye: Surviving the Suicide of a Loved One* by Carla Fine; *Acid Test: LSD, Ecstasy, and the Power to Heal* by Tom Shroder; *Therapy with Substance: Psycholytic Psychotherapy in the Twenty First Century* by Dr. Friederike Meckel Fischer; and *The Doors of Perception* by Aldous Huxley.

If you or anyone you know is suffering from depression, please call the Substance Abuse and Mental Health Services Administration (SAMHSA) at 1-800-662-4357 or the National Suicide Prevention Lifeline at 1-800-273-8255.